Caledonia

Also by Sherry V. Ostroff

THE LUCKY ONE
A Memoir of Life, Loss & Survival in Eastern Europe

Available at Amazon and Kindle

Caledonia

Sherry V. Ostroff

Bushrod Press

For Arne

**In memory of my parents
Elaine & Herman Vernick.
They taught me to love books.**

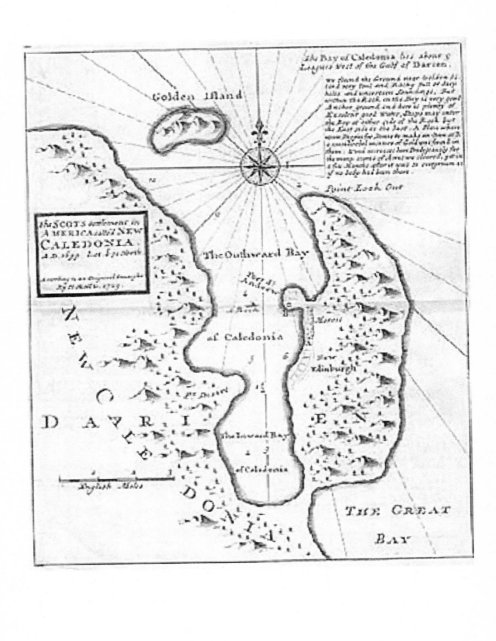

Golden Island

the Bay of Caledonia lies above 5
Leagues West of the Gulf of Darien.

we found the Ground near Golden Island very foul and Rockey full of deep
holes and uncertain Soundings, But
within the Rock, on the Bay is very good
Anchor ground, and here is plenty of
Excelent good Water, Ships may enter
the Bay of either side of the Rock, but
the East side is the best. A Place where
upon Experience seems to make an Open all
a wonderful measure of Gold was found on
there; it was not seen but probly only for
the many signes of America offered, yet in
a few Months after it was to every man as
if no body had been there.

Point Lock Out

The SCOTS settlement in
AMERICA called NEW
CALEDONIA.
A.D. 1699 Lat 9.30 North

according to an Originall draught by
H. Moll 1729.

The Outward Bay

Port St
Andrew

a Rock

of Caledonia

Morris

New
Edinburgh

pt Desert

The Inward Bay

of Caledonia

English Miles

NEW CALEDONIA

DARIEN

THE GREAT
BAY

Part One

One

Cheery Close
Edinburgh, Scotland – 1696

Not many ventured down the close. The dark passageway gave no hint that it led to a large square courtyard surrounded by four- and five-story houses. One of them was mine. The alley was named Cheery Close; probably someone's poor attempt at humor. It was one of many that spread like tree branches off the main trunk, The Royal Mile.

The close, and especially the courtyard, was a sea of heaving mud. Some residents poked fun at Sir Isaac Newton's recent findings that the watery muck reacted to the moon's gravitational pull, like the great oceans. During the summer months, it oozed, reeked, and gobbled up the contents of chamber pots, decaying rodents, and anything foolish enough to step off the wooden planks that served as a walkway. Residents wondered if missing dogs weren't lost forever at the bottom of the Sludge Sea. Mothers warned their children of the danger, if only to keep their shoes free of the filth. Relief came in the winter when the mud froze. Warnings were forgotten. Less waste and smell found its way past our scrubbed stone doorway.

Occasionally, a vendor would brave the close, carrying his bulging bag of goods on his back, singing his wares. Since the marketplace was nearby, a savvy hawker attracted far more customers there, than combing the labyrinth of Edinburgh's closes and wynds. That's why the loud knock on the wooden arched door was unexpected and jarring.

Forbidden from answering the door, I quickly ran up the staircase, hid behind the balustrade, and had a perfect view that would satisfy my curiosity.

Old Simon was entrusted with the comings and goings of the entire household, from overseeing the staff to welcoming guests. Managing the house should have been my mother's responsibility, but she'd died giving birth to me.

Simon had been a part of my world for as long as I could remember. He was as much a part of my family as my father and my brother. He got his name because he looked ancient. I couldn't remember when his three tufts of hair, which stuck out on the top and sides of his head, were anything but snow white. His humped back was a smaller version of Arthur's Seat, a volcanic peak towering near Holyrood Palace. He never looked up, because he couldn't. Instead, when my father spoke to

1

Old Simon, or on the occasion of welcoming a guest, he made the effort by turning his head, looking sideways. The rest of the time, including when he talked to me, he stared at his brown leather mules

From my perch, I watched the visitor enter. Because he had to lower his head, so as not to hit the lintel, I only saw a mass of auburn curls and a brown woolen cloak. But when he'd safely crossed the threshold, the height and breadth of this man was amazing. Perhaps, his height was accentuated by standing next to Simon, who resumed his hunched-over posture.

"Sir, welcome to the home of Salomon ben Isaac. How may I help you?"

"I'm here to see Master Isaac. He's expecting me."

"Your name, sir?"

"Alain MacArthur."

"May I tell him what matter of business?"

The Scot hesitated. Maybe he didn't care to be questioned by a servant. Of course, he didn't know Old Simon was much more than hired help. In my father's absence, Simon handled simple business matters. But Mr. MacArthur answered politely. "I'm here on behalf of my father, Ian MacArthur of Clan MacArthur."

"I will inform the Master of your arrival. May I take your cloak?"

Before the guest responded, I flew down the staircase, thankful my footsteps were silent, and hurried along the back hallway to the library. Because Simon had a pronounced limp, I would get there well before him.

No one knew the truth behind Old Simon's gnarled leg. One story, gossiped among the house staff, claimed a much younger Simon had jumped out of the second story window of a lady's bedroom when her husband had arrived home prematurely. Some told a much less exciting tale. It was simply a matter of his getting kicked by a stubborn garron. Others disagreed. They said it was the result of an altercation with an unruly kitchen boy, caught stealing a freshly baked loaf of bread. One day, I would ask Father.

I entered without making a sound. Father's library was a large area with three floor-to-ceiling windows which flooded the room with long angular rows of light that grew as the day progressed. The other three walls were lined with bookcases bearing the heavy weight of Father's precious tomes. Some believed, a man's wealth was measured by the number of books he owned. If so, my father was the richest man in Scotland. But he did not see it that way. He measured wealth in knowledge and the virtue of a well-seasoned mind.

He often reminded me, "In dangerous times we could lose our home, your mother's jewels, or our silver. But" he'd point his forefinger at his temple — "what's up here cannot be taken from us."

"Why would anyone want to take our things?"

"Ah, my dear, innocent daughter. When war comes, and the world is mad with hate, nothing is sacred. The only object of value we can carry to the ends of the

2

earth is our knowledge." Father usually ended serious discussions with sayings from the ancient scholars. "As the Talmud says, *No one is poor except one who lacks knowledge.*"

My father's extensive library was legendary. In a country where schooling was encouraged for all, his was prized by scholars near and far. Hundreds of books lined the shelves in an order Father created; he could find any text in minutes. His collection included the great philosophers from the Greeks to the modern discourses of Locke and Descartes. Hidden away was the seminal work of Baruch Spinoza. His writing was forbidden since his expulsion from the Jewish community, but Father refused to part with any book. There was also a prized possession of *Don Quixote* written by a fellow countryman, Miguel de Cervantes. Father believed, but dared not to say it publicly, that Cervantes was a *Converso*. His masterful tale was filled with Jewish symbolism.

The sparsely furnished room contained what was necessary. In the center was Father's large wooden desk covered with the tools of a businessman and scholar: quills, a knife for sharpening them, an ink bottle, and an hour candle. The only sound came from the sputtering peat in the fireplace which provided warmth rather than light, so a huge chandelier laden with beeswax candles illuminated the room. The combination of sweet honey, smoky peat, and peppermint tea, for Father's indigestion, made this my favorite room in the house. Immersed in his ledgers, Father did not hear me enter. My shoes were silenced by the thick Turkey carpet.

Normally, I would have thought twice about interrupting. But today I had no time to be polite. "Father. Forgive me. There is an armed stranger to see you. He is in the front hall and says you are expecting him." I had not seen any weaponry on the handsome stranger, but I had assumed he was armed. It was a good excuse to get Father's attention.

He looked up slowly. His long white beard was carefully clipped and combed. On top of his head rested a black skullcap which partially covered a few silvery tufts. His rheumy eyes took a moment to refocus from his near-sighted work. Slowly, he put the quill in its holder and folded his hands.

"Does the stranger have a name?"

"It's Alain MacArthur. He says he's the son of—" I hoped my father would not notice the flush blossom on my face.

"Oh yes. Ian MacArthur's son. I'm expecting him. Nice young man. Tell Simon to send him in."

"Why is he here?"

"Never mind. I will tell you after our business is concluded. Let's not be discourteous and keep our guest waiting. Run along."

It bothered me when I was dismissed like a child. I was fifteen-years old. Old enough to be married and run my own household. Father would often discuss his business with me. He said I had a mind for it and an unusual sense of intuition.

3

Occasionally, I would hear him mutter how he'd wished my brother Nathan shared such a gift or would at least show some interest. So I was surprised I knew nothing of Alain MacArthur.

I turned to leave when Old Simon entered. Alain MacArthur was ushered into the library by an anxious Simon eager to return to his many duties. I was thankful Father pretended it was the first-time hearing about Mr. MacArthur's arrival. Their short conversation provided a fortunate distraction so I could slip behind the Chinese silk screen which hid an indoor privy. I sat down on a wobbly stool next to the chamber pot and leaned forward to adjust my eye to the small slit in the fabric. It was the perfect spot to eavesdrop. But if someone needed the pot, I was in trouble.

With cloak removed, a fair-skinned, slightly freckled Scot, dressed in traditional splendor, was revealed. His full-length kilt swayed with his every movement. Part of his plaid draped over one shoulder, held in place with a silver brooch. The excess, tucked in his black leather belt, created a convenient pocket. His sporran slung off his hips and was centered between his legs. A short grey wool jacket fit snugly over his arms and chest. A basket-hilt broadsword, tied to a leather shoulder strap, hung level with his left hip. The last of his visible weaponry was a dirk, sheathed at his side under his belt. Alain MacArthur, Scottish warrior, with the telltale features of his Viking ancestors, commanded the room.

The difference between my father and his guest was startling. Father was quiet, unimposing, and preferred others to be the center of attention. His unassuming ways mirrored in business as well. Nothing in my father's appearance indicated wealth or country. He did not dress with any distinguishing clan symbols. My family did not belong to a clan. The fine woolens he wore were practical for Scotland's cold weather. As he peered over his spectacles, he looked every inch the scholar.

"Mr. MacArthur. Welcome to my home. How is your father?"

"He is well now. He suffered the flux last winter, and there were times we feared for him."

"I'm pleased to hear he has recovered. When you return, give him my wishes for his continued good health. May I offer you some claret? You must be thirsty after your long trip."

"Aye. Thank you."

My father retrieved two goblets stored in the glass cabinet to the side of his desk. The cut glass sparkled like tiny stars created by the flames of the overhead candles. The stars disappeared once the red wine filled the glass.

"Will you honor my home, sir, and stay for our evening meal?"

"I do not wish to trouble you or your household."

This was polite talk. Food and board were an expected courtesy. Survival in the harsh Scottish climate was dependent on the hospitality of others. While Mr. MacArthur's polite refusal was part of the game, in the end, the visitor would accept.

4

"It is no trouble at all, but the least I could do for the son of an old friend. I will call for my daughter, Anna. She will take care of everything."

At the unexpected mention of my name, I sat back so suddenly, the stool toppled. Not able to stop the momentum, I fell on the porcelain pot, breaking it. And while trying to disentangle my legs from my skirt, I kicked the screen. The framed silk came crashing down, revealing me sprawled unladylike on the floor.

In a moment, my father and the Highlander were by my side. Alain's amused smile animated his scarred cheek. He might have been a warrior, but there was something gentle in his demeanor. He glanced down at the display in front of him. Flat on my back, my skirts twisted just above my knees. My hair, once secured with a pin, had come undone. Alain suppressed his laughter, evident on the edge of his quivering lips. Sitting up, I quickly pulled down my skirts and smoothed them over my knees. He offered a helping hand so I could regain my dignity.

My father was speechless, mortified by the actions of his foolish daughter. But he should not have been surprised to find me in my usual hiding place. He regained his composure as soon as I and my skirts were made proper. As if the entire incident had never happened, he turned to our guest and said, "Mr. MacArthur, may I introduce my daughter, Anna."

TWO
Run Along

My brother was the last person I wanted to see.

"Watch out!" He yelled as we collided head-on. I hadn't seen him coming around the corner where the two hallways met. His eyes became angry slits; lips tightly narrowed against his teeth. His dark brown hair, tied with a leather strip, came undone. Always fastidious in his appearance, it was one more thing to anger him. He grabbed my arm and pushed me out of his way.

Nathan was five years older, a head taller, much broader, and definitely stronger. He lorded over the house and intimidated all who resided or worked there. It was worse when Father was away on business or in his bedchamber ailing from debilitating back pain. Only Old Simon ignored Nathan and got away with it.

He pushed his hair off his face. The scowl and snake-eyes remained. "Don't you ever watch where you're going? You're as graceless as—" He never finished. Something more hurtful took its place. "Who would want to marry someone so clumsy? Must Father increase the size of your dowry just to bribe someone to take you off our hands?" A malicious chuckle emanated from his throat, as if his next thought was more entertaining. "Maybe your husband will beat some refinement into you."

My brother never needed to strike me. His words were like clenched fists wounding my spirit.

There was nothing I could do to change Nathan's hatred for me. He blamed my birth for killing our mother. Everyone was aware of it. But Father pretended the hate didn't exist. He tried to soothe my complaints with excuses by saying Nathan would learn to accept his loss in time. How much time? Occasionally, Father would talk to Nathan and for a brief period, he would be civil, almost kind. But the peaceful interludes wouldn't last long.

I dealt with Nathan the only way I knew. I stayed out of his way.

My days were spent in the library, my sanctuary, while Father tended to his moneylending business. Most of Father's clients preferred their meetings to be private. Except for offers of refreshment, they did not want a lass in the same room. With my father's approval, I hid in the privy. From behind the screen, I noted how customers reacted: a nervous twitch, persistent handwringing, or constant brow-wiping. At first, Father considered my spying unethical, but he came to depend on my observations. He rationalized that the client wasn't being forced to behave in a telltale manner.

Now I found myself the focus of Nathan's anger. I yanked my arm out of his grip and hurried away.

"Where are you going? I'm not done talking to you."

I didn't answer. Nathan hated to be ignored. Besides, I didn't want to tell him about our guest. Let him be embarrassed when he discovered Alain MacArthur sitting at our table.

"Come back here." His voice grew louder. I turned my head, caught one last glance of the monster, and was grateful he chose not to follow.

Nathan was a conundrum. From outward appearances, he looked like a dashing young man dressed in the latest fashion and finest fabrics. To me, he was grotesque.

Safe for the moment, my thoughts returned to our handsome guest and an interesting evening to come. I entered the sunshine-filled kitchen alive with the sounds and smells of cooking and the booming voice of the head cook, Mrs. Gibbons. Her shouted orders to two scullery maids rose above the clanging of copper pots, the stomping boots of workers who trudged in and out of the back door, and the rhythmic clacking of knives on the chopping board. The kitchen was Mrs. Gibbons' realm, and she ruled it like a queen.

"Mrs. Gibbons, Father's invited a guest for the evening meal."

The corpulent woman threw up her arms in disdain. A blood and grease-splotched apron could not conceal the perpetual sweat stains on her faded woolen dress. A dingy white cap quivered above her brows but did not hide the beads of sweat.

She turned, and folded her massive arms, solid like tree trunks, across her chest. "Aye, I shoulda kent your da would have another mouth tae feed. I kent it as soon as I heard the bangin' on the door. Yere father turns no one away, but it would be nice tae have a wee bit more warnin'."

"I would've told you sooner, but Nathan—"

"How will one wee chick'n feed three grown men, I ask ye?" Throwing her hands in the air again, she yelled, "Fiona, get yere lazy arse out tae the coop and knock off the head o' another."

One problem solved; Mrs. Gibbons moved on.

"Dabby MacCreadie! Where are ye, ye wee beastie." Eyeing Dabby, lurking just outside the kitchen door, she yelled, "Ye'll be the death o' this auld woman. I told ye tae fill the water buckets."

At the mention of his name, Dabby jerked his head and quickly shoved something into his mouth. His weasel-like eyes peered back to see if anyone had noticed. The waif-like kitchen boy had stolen one of the freshly made apple tarts cooling on the window ledge. Both Dabby and the ever-present flies had been drawn to the aroma of baked apples, cinnamon, and burnt sugar. Shooing them away did nothing to discourage the hungry brutes.

Dabby wiped his mouth and runny nose with the back of a dirty sleeve. He slunk into the kitchen to retrieve the buckets. Mrs. Gibbons reached for one of his ears, but Dabby was too quick. He ran out of the kitchen, the empty buckets knocking against his legs.

With the entertainment over, everyone returned to their chores. One helper basted the single chicken roasting in a hearth large enough to accommodate an entire steer. It would soon be joined by another, once it was de-feathered and gutted. A second worker sliced carrots and kale at one of two tables in the center of the room. The second table was for chopping meat but never pork. Cheese and butter were prepared in another area of the kitchen. The separating of meat from dairy was done purposefully.

"Where's Sally?" I asked. I didn't see her anywhere.

Sally, a chambermaid, was my friend and Mrs. Gibbon's daughter. She was sixteen, pretty, smart, and round in all the right places. Whenever we went to market, she was always the object of unwelcome leers and comments from the older town boys. To discourage them, she pretended to be dim-witted. When we were alone, Sally would ask, "Anna, ye want tae see my simple look?" I giggled as I watched the light go out of her eyes, replaced by an empty stare. Coming back to life, she exclaimed, "Who would want a woman like that?" I didn't say so, but there were plenty who didn't care what was behind the dull eyes. They only considered what was under her skirts.

Her mother scratched her head. "I thought she was tendin' tae the bedchambers an hour ago. She shoulda been done by now. I have other chores for her. Run along, and if ye see her, tell her tae get...down...here."

This was my day to be told to "run along." I did so, gladly. I couldn't wait to tell Sally about Alain MacArthur. I ran up the stairs, searched my room, but she was nowhere; however, I knew she'd been here. The bedcovers had been smoothed and the drapes had been opened, inviting sunshine to flood the space. My new blue shawl, left hanging on a chair, was now in its proper place.

I returned to the hallway, but when I heard footsteps, I feared it was Nathan. I hid in an alcove behind a drape, lining one side of a window. Instead, I watched Sally come out of my brother's room. She closed the door silently, stopped to straighten her bodice, and tie her strings. Her hair askew, and lips red and swollen, Sally looked up and down the landing to see if anyone saw her shame. She tiptoed down the stairs, quickening her pace. The clicking of her shoes grew fainter as she neared the protection of the kitchen and her mother.

Now I knew why my brother had lashed out when I careened into him earlier. It was the same reason Sally was delayed in returning to the kitchen. I stepped from behind the curtain, and before I could get to the top tread of the staircase, Nathan grabbed my shoulder. "What are you doing here?"

I shrugged out of his reach, turned, and stared into his eyes. I hoped Nathan didn't think I was frightened although every inch of my body rebelled against his touch. In the strongest voice I could muster, I asked, "What did you do to Sally?"

"What the girl wanted. She's been begging for months, and I finally gave her, her due."

"That's not true. Not even if Sally was begging in the streets, would she take your coin."

"You keep talking, and you'll see what happens to your friend...and her mother."

"Her mother? I'll tell father. He would never allow you—"

"He won't believe a word you say. All I have to do is tell our beloved father how Sally has opened her legs for all the town lads. You know he'll be shocked. And since his impeccable reputation is everything to him, he would never allow a slattern and her mother to live under our roof." Nathan chuckled. "Father will have them out on the streets before nightfall. And all because you couldn't keep your mouth shut."

Everything Nathan said was true. Father would believe my brother because he went to market regularly. He would know what the town lads were saying. There was nothing much I could do but console Sally and be her friend. Except, I was the sister of the man who'd raped her.

As I turned to go, Nathan grabbed my wrist. His voice became softer but still mocking.

"Anna, I think you should know Father is thinking of finding a husband for you. But he's so busy with his customers, he asked me to help in the search for a proper groom. Father said I needed a useful task, so he gave me some names to consider. I am in the process of deciding which one will suit you best."

As if Nathan had punched me as hard as he could in my stomach, I lost my breath. I bent over and thought I was going to retch. Nathan bent lower. "You can be

10

sure, Anna, I will give it my full attention. What kind of attention, depends on what you believe you just saw."

When he put an arm around my waist to give feigned support, I tried to pull away. "I know you'll see it my way." He chuckled before he went on. "I'm giving your marriage a lot of consideration. I have narrowed down your bridegroom choices to two. Let's see, um, one is a fat old man who will be sure to drool all over you on your wedding night. The other, well, let's just say he's younger, and leave it at that."

I yanked away from his grip and pushed with both hands. Startled, he crashed against the wall as I flew down the stairs. Nathan's laughter followed me like the tenth plague.

When I entered the kitchen, Mrs. Gibbons was yelling at her daughter. Sally huddled in a corner; defensive arms covered her tear-stained cheeks.

"I sent ye tae clean a while ago. What has taken so long? Do ye expect me tae do everythin'?"

My heart cried out for my friend. Cruelly attacked by my brother, now her mother blamed her for what was not her fault.

"Jesus, Mary, and Bride," Mrs. Gibbons yelled out. "Get over here, girl." The older woman pinched Sally's ear and forced her head up. "What in the name o' heaven is that on yere neck? Suck marks? Who is it? Or are ye goin' tae tell me yere whorin' with the devil?"

Mrs. Gibbons grabbed her daughter and shook her until her head wobbled back and forth. Then she smacked Sally across the face. A red handprint blossomed. "So, that's what ye were doin' when yere supposed tae be cleanin'. Ye want tae shame yere poor auld mother and have us thrown out o' this house? Then, what'll we do? Answer me!"

Sally collapsed in a pile of skirts, moans, and tears. She cried so hard she could barely catch her breath. Her mother stood with her arms akimbo, glared at her daughter, and walked away in a huff.

I ran over, hugged Sally, and helped her to her feet while straightening her apron and cap. She wiped her tears with the handkerchief I had in my sleeve. I told her it would be all right, that I would protect her. In reality, there was little I could do.

Sally took a deep breath. "I will never be safe with your brother around."

Not knowing what to say, I lied. "That's not true, Sally. Father will believe me after I tell him everything."

Sally shook her head violently; her tears flew off her cheeks. "No, Anna. Ye can't say anythin'. Yere brother told me he would put me out on the streets if I didn't do as he wished. And ye aren't safe either. He torments me with tales o' the bridegrooms he's considerin'."

"My father would never marry me off to a man I didn't want."

11

"Your father is old. He's not well. He won't always be around tae protect ye." Sally took my hands in hers. Her tear-rimmed eyes were intent. "Ye must get out o' this house. Ye must save yourself."

For a brief moment, I agreed, but where would I go? I'd lived a sheltered life and knew little of the world beyond Cheery Close. "If I go, you're coming with me. We'll leave together."

"No. There's nothin' ye can do for me. I'm already soiled."

"I'm not leaving without you," I repeated.

Before Sally could answer, we heard my father's voice coming closer to the large dining area where our evening meal would be served. Mr. MacArthur was with him, and they were laughing.

A third voice, my brother's, interrupted. "Father, I need to speak to you on an urgent matter about—"

"Ah, Nathan, my boy. Let me introduce you to Mr. Alain MacArthur." After quick pleasantries were exchanged, Father said, "Nathan, go find your sister. Tell her to join us for the meal. We could all do with some diverting female conversation. Run along."

THREE
El Cid & Chimène

The next morning, I found Nathan outside the door of my bedchamber. He smelled of sleep, sweat, and unwashed hair. His breath already reeked of wine.

To bar my way, he placed a threatening hand on the door frame. A mocking smile revealed uneven teeth. His voice faltered, impeded by slurring his words, "Why didn't…didn't you tell me we…we had a guest last night? Were you out to make a fool…of me?"

Confrontation was inevitable. Escape impossible.

I wondered how long Nathan had been standing there. Had he heard any part of my conversation with Sally? She had arrived earlier to wake up the ashes in the fireplace, empty the chamber pot, set out my clothes for the day, and talk about the events of the night before.

"Yere da had a verra handsome visitor last night. So tall and gallant, a lovely smile. And those eyes. They could get a lass in trouble if she's not careful." She waited a moment to allow me to get the sleep out of my eyes. "Should I be worried about ye?"

"Yes. I mean no. He was charming though." I threw my legs over the bed, my feet dangling below my linen shift, and as I stretched my arms, I stifled a yawn. "Sally, were you spying on me last night?" I chuckled while wiggling my toes. "You don't have to answer. I know you were."

We laughed together, but Sally stopped short. "Charmin', my foot. Anyone can fake charmin'. Yere brother's a master at it. No, I mean the Highlander was handsome. Really bonny. There's nae fakin' that. As my mother would say, he could put his boots under her bed anytime."

I almost laughed again but considering what had happened to Sally the day before, I held back. She handed me my brush. I raked it through the tangles that always came from sleep. "He was indeed handsome. But when I say charming, I mean he was kind. You could see it in his eyes."

"Aye, I noticed his soft brown eyes, and he talked tae ye more than a wee bit."

"That he did, as much as he dared without appearing impolite to Father... and Nathan."

Sally took the brush and continued with the worst snarls. "Anna, did yere brother notice?"

"Nathan kept giving me evil glares, tried to interrupt, and at one point suggested that I run along. But as soon as Mr. MacArthur ended a conversation with Nathan or Father, he turned his attention back to me."

Sally stopped mid-stroke and bent over. "Sounds like an intelligent man. Did yere brother get angry?"

"He was furious. At one point, he brazenly suggested to Alain that conversation might be more interesting with the men of the house rather than with a frivolous maid."

"What did Mr. MacArthur say to that?"

"He ignored Nathan, and when Nathan said it again, Alain turned to my brother and told him what a rare intelligence I had. That he was delighted to be in my company."

"Really? He said that tae yere brother? I've got tae admit, the man's got baws." Sally talked while gesticulating the brush.

"Then, Alain turned his back and ignored my brother like he was a fly on the wall." I chuckled, remembering the astonished look on Nathan's face.

The brushing completed, I pulled my fingers through my smoothed hair and braided it while I finished the tale. "It was like that story I told you about. You know the one where the gallant knight comes to his lady's defense? I've never had anyone stand up for me against my brother."

Sally let out a big sigh. "My favorite story. So romantic."

"Nathan's going to make me pay for this. You know how he likes to be the center of attention."

"Aye." She touched one of the crimson bite marks choking her neck. Her voice turned cautious. "Take care. Stay in the library, near yere father, as much as ye can."

"Alain is returning in a couple of days to complete his business. That's good news. Don't you think?"

She never answered my question. Sally's thoughts must have been elsewhere.

Facing the brute, I decided to do what he least expected. In a cheerful voice and a big smile, I said, "Good morning, Dear Brother. I hope you slept well. If not,

14

you should tell Simon to have one of the maids refresh your bedding. Or better yet, maybe Dabby should do it. We wouldn't want an innocent housemaid anywhere near your bedchamber."

He yanked me through the doorframe and slammed the door. "What was that little act you put on last night?"

I didn't pull back. My face was inches from his. I chose a stinging retort and didn't care about the repercussions. "If you weren't hidden away in your room forcing yourself on Sally, you might have had a notion of what was going on in our home or with Father's business."

Nathan raised his hand but stopped mid-swing. His momentary hesitation provided enough distraction so I could duck under his arm and run down the staircase. I thought about Sally left alone up there. I hoped she remembered the hidden backstairs.

Scurrying along the hallway, I lunged into the library. I hoped my breathlessness wouldn't cause Father to ask questions. But he had already been immersed in his books for many hours. The candles on the chandelier had long icicles.

"Ah, Anna. There you are. A lovely sight for these old eyes."

I tried to remove the fear in my voice. "Father, didn't you get any sleep last night?"

He answered by removing his spectacles and massaging his closed eyes. "Why are you here so early? Is something wrong?"

I normally didn't arrive until later in the day, but I didn't want to tell him about Nathan. I changed the subject. "Father, why are you sitting in that awful chair? You're always complaining about your back. Let me at least add a pillow." I gazed around the library but saw none.

"Don't fuss so. Is that why you came early, to bedevil me? If I have a soft chair, I will fall asleep rather than get to my correspondence and update my ledgers."

"Father, please." I wanted to scold him and tell him he wished to be a martyr. But I would get nowhere. Besides, how could I ever get angry with him?

Now it was his turn to force our conversation in another direction "Did you come for your book?" He bent over to a lower shelf near his desk and tugged on one bound in brown leather with a gilded edge. "Ah, here it is. *Le Cid?*" He handed the book to me. "This will help improve your French. You should strive for fluency, Anna. French is an international language. You never know when you will need it."

I was tutored in French when I was younger, and not being gifted in languages, we both realized my limited fluency would have to be acceptable. Now, all of a sudden, it wasn't. Strange. I sat down and held the book on my lap, looking forward to losing myself in the tragic romance of the dashing El Cid and the beautiful Chimène.

15

"Anna, I'm glad you're here. I have two important matters to discuss with you." He returned his spectacles to their proper perch. Our business had begun.

"So, what did you think of Mr. MacArthur? The two of you appeared to be having a lively time last night. I couldn't hear much of your talk." He took a sip of his peppermint tea. The sharp tang stung my throat. "Ah, the vestiges of old age. Along with poor digestion, my hearing is not what it used to be."

I didn't know what to think about Father's hearing. At times, he could hear whispered conversations across a room, a squeaky door on the other side of the house, or the bark of a feral dog announcing a visitor entering the close. At other times, he couldn't hear someone sitting next to him. I wondered if this was a game he played. Perhaps, by asking for a request repeated, it allowed him time to think of an answer. It afforded him another opportunity to observe telltale facial expressions, anxiety, and tone of voice. My father was astute when it came to reading his customers, his business partners, and his daughter.

"Well...Alain...I mean Mr. MacArthur was pleasant."

"What does that mean? Pleasant. I'm considering a business proposal with his clan. You're usually more direct with your observations. What kind of man is he?"

I knew what my father was asking, but I was so enamored with Alain, I'd forgotten to scrutinize his demeanor and the risk he posed as a potential business partner. I wrung my sweaty palms together, and for the first time in my life, I lied to my father.

"I think Mr. MacArthur is trustworthy. I have a good feeling about him."

My father's eyes widened. It felt like they bore right through me. "That is not what Nathan said. He thought our guest was rude and a bit too bold with you."

"On the contrary. He was a perfect gentleman."

I needed to get my father onto another topic before I was caught in my lie. "Father, what is Mr. MacArthur's business venture?"

"Did he tell you about the Scots Company?"

"No. We talked about the cold summer we are experiencing and the latest gossip about the Thomas Aikenhead trial, and... this and—"

"It's a business venture proposed by Mr. William Paterson. He's the Scot who established the Bank of England. Three years ago, he proposed an Act to form a Scottish trading company to found a colony. Its purpose is to improve Scotland's bottom line which has suffered from famine and poor harvests."

Father walked over to a large globe near his desk. He rotated it until he found the place he was looking for. "It is rumored that Mr. Paterson is proposing a small parcel of land between the two Americas for colonization. It is the perfect location for trade between the Atlantic and Pacific Oceans. If his plan is successful, it will move Scotland into the forefront of world trade. Those who buy shares in the trading company will be well compensated."

"That's ingenious, but it will need massive funding."

16

"Exactly. But England will try to abort the plan. William doesn't want to anger his cousin, the King of Spain, so the Scots must come up with all of the capital. The MacArthur clan fully supports this new undertaking. They've asked for my financial backing."

"Will you?"

"It requires a lot of capital, and I would have to call on my contacts in banking houses in Europe to satisfy the clan's demands. But I'm not sure the plan is well thought out. No one has bothered to ask the Spaniards what they think about a Scottish colony operating a lucrative trade route right under their nose. And there's scant information about the land. Is it good for farming? What about fresh water and supplies? Who will be their trading partners, and what goods are needed?"

Father seemed more thorough than Mr. Paterson and the MacArthur Clan. "Does this mean you won't do business with the MacArthur's?" The thought of my father turning Alain down meant I might never see him again.

"I don't know. This is a big decision. I could lose everything, including my reputation if this endeavor goes under. If I decline to fund it, and the proposal fails, I will be blamed twice. First, for not being a loyal Scot, and second, for maintaining my wealth while others lose theirs. We will be reminded we are Jews, foreigners, hoarding our money."

I knew why my father believed this. I had heard the stories. Once the Inquisition began, our ancestors had been forcibly expelled from Spain, after living there for centuries. We were always thought of as strangers, never Spanish enough. Although Scotland had been a haven for my wandering family, Father hadn't forgotten the lessons handed down to him.

I didn't know what to say. I put my arms around his neck and rested my head on his chest. He patted my hands and shook his head. "Well, enough about business. As it's written in the Talmud: *Don't worry about tomorrow. Who knows what will happen to you today.*"

"Father, I know your decision will be wise and just. I'm sorry I didn't watch Mr. MacArthur carefully. I will pay more attention when he comes again."

We returned to our seats. There was still something else Father wanted to discuss, but instead he put his hand on his stomach and moaned.

"Father, what is it? Are you ill?"

"It's my indigestion. The doctors tell me to drink peppermint tea or add some ginger to my diet. But what do they know? They are fools. I think it's my heart."

When the pain subsided, he regained his composure, clasped his hands together, and took a deep breath. "Daughter, listen to your father. It can never be."

"What, Father?"

His voice became firmer. "My daughter can never consider a man like Alain MacArthur. His clan would never accept a Jewess nor would the church sanction your marriage. I could never give you my blessing."

"Father—"

"I know you were charmed by Mr. MacArthur last night. Young women tend to have foolish thoughts when a few kind words are spoken to them by a polite young man." He got up from his desk, came closer to my chair, and shook his finger. "Nothing, nothing will come of this. That is my will, and in this house, you will obey me."

My father had never spoken to me so harshly, but what he said next was intolerable.

"I have asked your brother to help find a husband for you. I gave him several choices and he has been looking for the best match. The man he will most likely choose, and one I heartily approve of, comes from a family with connections to ours since our days in Iberia. I have done business with your prospective groom for many years. He is an honest man who will be a good husband and provider. One of our own. It is a match to make two families proud."

"Father, I can't." Then, I offered the only excuse I could think of. "I'm too young to get married."

"Your mother married at the age you are now. You're quite capable of running a household. Your husband will be lucky to get such a competent and intelligent woman. And a beauty, too." His eyes teared and I barely heard him say, "I will miss you."

"What do you mean…miss me?"

"Your groom is a Frenchman. He lives in Lyon. That was the other issue I wanted to talk to you about. Maurice will be coming on the next ship from Calais. You need to work on your French, so you can impress him and be a proper wife."

"But Father—"

Father hobbled around his desk and placed his hands on the edge of his chair to steady himself. At that moment I knew the discussion was over, arguing was futile. My father firmly believed his ancestors had charged him with a set of beliefs, and it was his sacred duty to ensure they were passed on to the next generation.

The only sound I uttered was the sob that caught in my throat. Not caring if Nathan was waiting for me outside the library, I thrust back my chair, causing it to crash against the floor. I picked up my skirts and ran out of my former sanctuary. I slammed the door, abandoning the lovers El Cid and Chimène.

18

FOUR
Hindsight
New York, 2005

It was time. All of my dad's affairs were taken care of except for one last thing, a safe deposit box at a large bank in lower Manhattan. I put off emptying the contents because it was the final act of a tragic play with no encores. I feared if I wrapped up this last bit of business, I had accepted his death.

That's how I found myself in a dank subterranean vault. I gathered up the contents of the box, balanced them in my hands, and walked out of the small room made available for the customer's privacy. Wiping away a tear and sniffling quietly into a tissue, I handed back the nondescript key to the gray-haired bank clerk.

She eyed me sympathetically over her half-rimmed glasses attached to a chain around her neck, as I fumbled my possessions. "Miss Duncan," she said, "maybe this will help." She held out a plastic grocery bag. I guess she'd seen many come unprepared.

"Thank you," I mumbled through my tears hoping she heard me.

I just wanted out of there. I ran up the steps and exited into the blinding sunshine, flipped on my sunglasses, and worked my way to mid-town and Penn Station.

My grandparents let me know beforehand what the box contained. There were no surprises, nothing of consequence: three $100 EE United States savings bonds, a copy of a title for a car sold years ago, a Boy Scout badge, a locket with my baby picture and a few strands of hair, and an envelope.

I held the plastic bag close and boarded the train that plied the northeast corridor of the New Jersey Transit. It would take over an hour and sixteen stops to reach the end of the line in Trenton. The train was full of people returning home after a day of working, shopping, or sight-seeing. A short elderly woman, who reminded me of my grandmother, sat next to me.

She smiled and complained at the same time, "My feet. These shoes are killing me." She kicked them off and leaned back in her seat.

I nodded. I wasn't in the mood for talking. Not today.

Unfortunately, older people talk to almost anyone. The woman tried once more. "Hi, I'm Rose. Wasn't today beautiful? If I had comfortable shoes, I would've done more shopping."

I didn't want to be rude, but all I could manage was a weak, "Hanna. Yes, today was nice." What I wanted was to be left alone, lost in my thoughts remembering my dad and another perfect summer day that seemed to mock a national tragedy. On that day there hadn't been a cloud in the sky to block out the sun or diminish the sky's brilliant blue. For me, it was the coldest and dreariest day of my life. The day my dad was murdered.

The woman gave up, pulled out a book from her bag, and began to read.

After a few minutes, the train jerked forward. I settled in for the long ride home and tried to make myself comfortable even though there was never enough room for my long legs. Late arrivals scurried from car to car hoping to find a seat, only to be grateful to lean against a wall or a door. Some passengers were immersed in their phones or newspapers. Others stared blankly out the window. But the car filled with chatter as passengers discussed the latest gossip or the events of their day.

As the train lumbered toward its first stop in Secaucus, I clipped back my unruly hair, leaned my head against the cool glass, and gazed at the New York skyline. I would never get used to the missing twin towers. Their absence was like a gaping hole in a mouth full of teeth. No matter how you tried to cover it up, the smile was never the same.

A conductor collecting fares interrupted my thoughts. The snapping sound of his punch announced him, and quickly he was gone. The train continued southward to Newark, Elizabeth, and Linden while my thoughts returned to New York.

For twenty years my dad had worked at the World Trade Center as a senior accountant for one of the top firms on the east coast. He was well-liked and respected; he loved his job. He looked forward to going to work. Whether I was awake or not, his morning routine included a kiss on my forehead, a readjustment of my blanket, and a whispered, "Good morning, Sunshine," before he slipped quietly from the house. He always arrived at his desk before anyone else, with a box of glazed doughnuts and fresh coffee to share with the overnight cleaning crew finishing their shift. His routine ended on September 11, 2001.

No one saw it coming, totally out of the blue, like the sky that morning. Everyone was in a state of shock. For me, it was the worst pain I had ever felt in my life. Although four years have gone by, I've still not accepted it. The gut-wrenching part — my dad wasn't even supposed to go to work that day.

As the train arrived in Princeton, a taped voice on the train's intercom continually reminded departing passengers, mostly college students, to "watch the gap." They jostled their way to the exits and quickly disembarked. The elderly lady, my co-traveler, left without a word taking her lemon scent with her. After the first few stops the crowd thinned, and I had the luxury of the entire row to myself.

The next stations were Hamilton, then Trenton. From there it was only a half-hour on the Trenton Line to Philadelphia. If I had a few minutes to spare, I'd call my grandparents. They were anxious about my trip to New York.

Dad's parents were my only remaining family. My mother's parents died before I was born, and I lost my mother when I was very young. My grandparents became my guardians for a few months after my father was killed. They were good to me but were a bit overwhelmed with the shock of losing their only son and assuming a parental role once again. I vowed that as soon as college was completed, I would go out on my own but live nearby, so we could visit often.

I exited the train, mindful of the gap, and tucked the plastic bag under my arm. Fortunately, the Philadelphia train was waiting at the platform. I entered, quickly grabbed a seat, and continued to think how different my life would be today if events had been altered.

Dad had helped me move in the weekend before the start of classes. By the time we were halfway down I-95, I realized I forgot my new cell phone. He offered to return in two days with the errant phone. It was a great opportunity to spend the day together before I got too busy with classes, papers, and friends. He checked his schedule to confirm the day.

"Hanna, Tuesday works for me. My new assistant, Carly, can manage the workload. I want to give her some space without always being there to get her out of a jam. She's got to learn and gain confidence."

"Great. Let's go where you and Mom used to hang out when you went to school here. Show me some of the highlights of downtown Philly and the best place to eat in Chinatown."

"Yeah, sure. I'd like that, Hanna. It will be our day, just the two of us."

Just the two of us. I didn't want to tell my dad I was homesick. But then, maybe he already knew. I looked forward to our day together.

I was so disappointed when Dad had to cancel. He was expecting some important client, and Carly wasn't experienced enough to handle it alone. The parents of my roommate Jess lived near Dad and were coming down to replace a broken monitor. They offered to bring my phone and save my dad the four-hour, round-trip drive. Yeah, saved my dad the trouble, but it hadn't saved him.

Thinking about the what-ifs really gets me down. What if there had been just one minor fluctuation in the order of events leading up to 9/11? What if Jess's parents couldn't make the drive, or if Carly had more experience? My father used to tell me that *hindsight is twenty-twenty*. In this case, exploring all the possibilities was especially painful. There are no satisfying answers to the what-ifs. There are no do-overs — period.

21

After arriving home, I emptied the contents from the bag on the kitchen counter. I don't know why I didn't just dump it all at once. I felt like a game show host where I'd build up the audience's anticipation, so they would go wild before Door Number Two was revealed.

The white, padded envelope caught my eye. It was nothing special. The edges were yellowed, and the flap was partially unsealed. I felt something hard inside, wood or metal. I opened it to find a key that looked like a skeleton key, the kind you see in old scary movies. It was three inches long, and the beautifully wrought handle had leaves surrounding a flower. The edges were tinged with sprouting rust. This was no modern-day key.

I looked back into the envelope. It contained nothing in the way of an explanation: no addressee, no mysterious note written in illegible scribble. I wondered if my dad knew anything about this. He had to. It was in his safe deposit box.

I looked closer at the key and noticed some interesting etching along one side. Crudely done, it appeared as if someone, other than the craftsman, took a nail, or the pointy end of a knife, and scratched something. I held the key up against the only window that still captured the last rays of sunlight. My eyesight was not the greatest, so my finger continued the search. The raised lines formed three distinct marks. I wasn't positive, but I squinted again. Then I saw the letters: B…O…S. There might have been a fourth letter. My finger signaled, once again, something more.

There was no ambiguity about the many questions exploding in my mind like fireworks. Why did my dad have this peculiar key? What did it open? What did the letters mean? And most importantly, how would I ever find out?

FIVE
Two Heads

The clock on my phone confirmed the early morning hour. I couldn't sleep. My brain was consumed by the key, and unanswered questions gave birth to new ones. I considered getting up and looking at the key again, but I knew that would answer nothing and sleep would remain elusive.

Instead, I thought about my dad. When faced with a problem like this, he would always advise *Two heads are better than one.* He called these corny sayings kernels of wisdom. To me they were embarrassing when said in front of my friends. But now, I missed his one-liners and his advice.

I decided to put this particular idiom to the test and enlist a second 'head.' Later that morning, I called my best friend.

"Hey Jess. Are you busy after work? Want to come over?"

"No, I mean yes…. I can now."

"What does that mean?"

"You know the cute guy, the one who works in the cash room? He asked me to go out for some drinks after work. Well, he dumped me. He got a better offer…from his father."

"Really? What could be better than you?" I could tell from Jess's voice that she was only mildly irritated. True she lost out on a date, but not to another woman.

"A Phillies doubleheader. He'd prefer to see a bunch of crotch-scratching, tobacco-spitting guys play a little boy's game than spend an evening staring into my baby-blues. Oh well, I'd rather spend time with you anyway." Her tone became serious. "What's going on?"

"We need to talk. Something unusual has come up. I'd rather tell you in person."

"As soon as I'm finished work, I'll come by. But now I'm curious." In her little-girl voice she pleaded. "Are you sure you won't give me a hint?"

"Okay. It involves a key."

"That's a terrible clue."

"That's all you're getting. See ya later."

I knew the day would drag. I tried tackling some unfinished chores, but I lacked the enthusiasm and became distracted by the usual racket outside my center-

23

city apartment. The number twelve bus rumbled by every fifteen minutes, emergency vehicles screamed their way to local hospitals, and teenagers filled the air with their chatter on the way to and from school.

It was late afternoon when the doorbell rang. As usual, Jess looked impeccable even after a day at the bank. Her hair, a new deep-roast coffee color, perfectly coiffed around her face, showed off her apple cheeks, cherry-colored lips, and peachy skin. I often joked that she was a freaking fruit basket. She wore an animal print eternity scarf that flowed generously over a beautiful black top. Below she had on slacks, and black patent heels. Jess's guy-friend was crazy to pass up a date with her.

Before she crossed the threshold, Jess blurted out, "Hanna, your neighborhood needs fumigating. It smells awful."

In this part of the city, distinctive aromas were the norm. A mixture of car exhaust, fried onions, and urine. Exhaust was understandable. The fried onions came from nearby cheesesteak shops. The reek of urine was another story.

"The owner of the red brick house down the street, an elderly lady, had twenty-three cats," I explained. "She died in her sleep, and her body wasn't discovered for five stinking days."

Jess wrinkled her cute little nose.

"The litter boxes overflowed. The house became one big toilet. The stronger cats fed on the weaker ones and the old lady. The house had to be decontaminated, and as you discovered, the stench is still pungent days later."

I stopped when Jess turned an odd shade of green and didn't remind her that the smell had little chance of dissipating. Courtesy of the local derelicts, the same odor permeated the neighborhood when the subway was used as a urinal.

When Jess recovered, she made herself at home. She scanned my studio apartment and offered her assessment in her usual dramatic way, hands waving through the air. "I love this place. It's perfect — the size, the location. But I don't know what the landlord was thinking when he chose the Dollar Store decor."

I agreed. The rectangular living space had floor-to-ceiling windows; the morning sunshine bathed the room in shades of saffron and gold. They were the room's best feature; the purple thistle wallpaper and parquet flooring were not. An unmade bed and dresser filled the far right-hand corner of the room separated by a small folding screen, and in the opposite corner were the dollhouse-sized appliances. Center stage, a plaid sofa battled with the tasteless wallpaper. The flat screen TV, the only new object, was a graduation gift from my grandparents.

With our normal meet-and-greet over, I said, "Hey, Jess, the other day something ...something peculiar happened."

"Did you meet someone? Find the 'key' to someone's heart? Is that what you meant?"

I rolled my eyes. Did Jess ever think of anything but guys? "Don't be silly. The key has nothing to do with a man. Yesterday, I went to New York and closed out my dad's safe deposit box. I sort of knew what it contained. My grandparents had told me. But they didn't tell me all of it. I found a key."

"I was wondering why you asked me to come over on a weeknight. Honestly, I thought this was about some gorgeous guy who had marriage potential. I was prepared to give you the, 'you're-too-young-to-get-married' speech or 'you've-got-to-know-who-you-are-first' lecture."

Jess always made me laugh. It's what made her endearing. "No really, I found an old skeleton-like key." I pulled out the envelope and turned it over. The key fell out, clanged as it hit the table, and then the floor.

I picked it up and thrust it in her face for closer inspection. "It looks like an antique. Look at the shape and design on the handle. Have you ever seen anything like it? I bet a master craftsman created this for someone who wanted a one-of-a-kind key for a special purpose."

Jess picked it up, carefully, as if it was priceless. She turned the key over, closed one eye, and then squinted with both.

"Yeah, it looks old, and it's solid and heavy." She flipped the key, and then pushed her hair behind her ears. "There's something etched on its side. Letters?" She pointed at the same place I'd scrutinized yesterday.

I told her about my discovery.

Jess narrowed her eyes, running her fingers over the etching. "Did your father write anything on the envelope? Did he leave a note?"

"The envelope was blank. Nothing inside."

"Did your grandparents say anything?"

"I'm not sure they even know about the key. Maybe they knew at one time and forgot. Old people forget things." There was another possibility. My dad had a deep dark secret that even his parents knew nothing about.

Jess continued the examination, putting on glasses which she only wore in dire circumstances. "Wait. There's another letter. It's hard to see, but I can feel it. It's in front...of the...B. It looks like another B. No, it's an R. Yes...it's RBOS."

Jess laid the key on the table, clasped her hands together, and took a deep breath. "I think I know what the letters mean, but I may be wrong...I've seen those initials before. A lender at work, who smells like her lunch — tuna fish on rye — is working on a commercial credit account with a bank in Scotland. The...Royal...Bank...of...Scotland." She said each word gesticulating like an orchestra conductor.

"How could that be? My dad isn't Scottish; he's never gone to Scotland. The closest he's ever been to anything Scottish was when he got caught up with all those bagpipers at the Tartan Day Parade in New York five years ago."

25

Jess chuckled, clicked on her phone, and typed RBOS. Sure enough, all of the sites for the Royal Bank of Scotland popped up. She scrolled down to see what else the letters could mean. Nothing!

"Hmm… that's what it is, all right. I recognized the initials except now only RBS is used. There's an International Department right down the hall from my cubicle. Sometimes I hear conversations about banks from all over the world. My co-workers make up funny names for overseas banks. It's just easier to remember them. The Bank of China is B-O-K, so they call it BOK Choi; the Bank of Montreal is BMO or BaMO; Scotiabank, we've shortened to SB. Well, you know what that stands for."

"Okay, the Royal Bank of Scotland is RBOS. Now what?"

"Didn't you graduate from college with honors? The key has something to do with a bank in Scotland. Why don't you go there and find out what this is all about?"

"Why do I have to go to the U.K.? There's a branch in New York."

"No, Hanna. This is an old key. The branches in the United States are recent additions. You need to go to the source. The original. The one that's been around for centuries. It's not like you have anything else going on in your life, like a job. You have the cash."

She was right. There weren't many job prospects with an undergrad degree in archaeology. And money wasn't an issue. I received a substantial amount, based on a formula, from the 9/11 Survivor's Fund.

Jess continued to provide additional reasons just in case I needed more convincing. "Don't you want to be in a country with all those good-looking guys with their sexy Scottish brogues wearing cute little kilts? Besides, if the bank and key don't amount to anything, there are always those romantic castle ruins to get lost in with one of those hunks."

I knew she was getting obsessed over kilted guys. But her idea of going to Scotland wasn't crazy. What was keeping me from going? I needed to find out about the key and what secrets it would unlock. What could be so important that my dad hid it for so many years? The more I thought about it, the more questions percolated in my mind. I knew I wouldn't be satisfied until I went to the source and got some answers.

The sooner, the better.

SIX
Welcome to Scotland

I boarded a non-stop red eye to Scotland out of Newark, New Jersey. Having never flown overseas, I dreaded the thought of jetlag. Before I left, Jess offered helpful advice for overnight travel.

"Take two Tylenol PM. The first one, thirty minutes before you board the plane. The second, thirty minutes after take-off."

"Where did you earn your medical degree? Quack University?"

"So, don't take my advice. Who's the travel virgin? It really works. You'll get a couple of hours of shut-eye and be ready to go when you land."

"Okay, okay. Thanks…I think."

With my carry-on in tow, I looked for my seat number, hoping it wouldn't be near a whiney toddler or an obese traveler who'd spill into my space. Instead, my assigned seat was next to an attractive guy. Two thoughts came to mind. Why were the airline seat gods so benevolent, and how did I miss him in the waiting area? The answer was simple. My mind was on my grandparents.

I had gone to see them before taking off on this wild adventure — although it felt more like a wild goose chase. I had no itinerary, no return date, and I knew nothing about Scotland.

The purpose of my visit was to get answers. Did my grandparents know about the key? What did it unlock? What was the connection between my dad and Scotland? Or, as my dad would say, was I barking up the wrong tree? I intended to broach these questions casually. If I sounded concerned it might upset them, and I would be exactly where I was now: clueless. The other fear was that my grandparents were not as sharp as they used to be. Age and the loss of their only child had taken its sorry toll.

My visit began with hugs, kisses, and questions.

To my surprise, Gramps, usually quiet, started his own interrogation. "So, Hanna, what are you going to do now that college is over?"

27

"I may look for a part-time job at a museum, but most likely, I'll go back to school for my Ph.D."

My grandmother winced. To her, returning to school was just delaying the realities of life: a full-time job with benefits, marriage, purchasing a house, and raising a family. In that order. But then a smile grew. "Well, maybe you'll meet a nice young man in graduate school. A doctor? A lawyer? Who knows?"

And just like that, returning to college had definite possibilities for her.

"You could buy a home. The new development near the shopping center has some beautiful two-stories. We would be closer."

"Grams, Philadelphia's not far away. Lots of people joke that New Jersey is a suburb of Philly."

With the inquisition over, our talk continued onto easier topics as we moved into the kitchen for the evening. Grams refused offers of help and ordered me to sit at the vinyl-covered table with my grandfather. She dashed around the kitchen in her uniform, a flowered cobbler apron with kangaroo pockets filled with recipes and assorted pens. The apron went on at breakfast, and she remained in costume until late at night. I rarely saw her without it.

My grandmother was a wonderful cook but always made too much food. Her style was to prepare enough so no one walked away hungry, and there were ample leftovers to do it all over again. Maybe she longed for a large table surrounded with family. Now, there were only three of us.

When dinner was over, Gramps excused himself to watch the nightly news leaving Grams and me alone to talk. It was his way of giving us 'girl-time.' He wasn't much of a conversationalist anyway.

Rather than ask the dreaded questions, I took the coward's way out and inquired about their health. Seniors talk a lot about their doctors, the rising cost of medication, and the inevitability of cataract surgery. And then, there were other topics.

"Your grandfather had to visit Dr. Lazuli the other day." Grams lowered her voice. "He was having a problem in the bathroom."

Okay, here it comes. The other topic that always seems to come up: dysfunctional bathroom issues.

"When he went to flush, he noticed some of his sh…I mean poop, floated. He was afraid of cancer, so he made an appointment."

Did she just switch from shit to poop? Was I five years old? I bit the inside of my cheek to keep from giggling. It didn't work. I covered my mouth, pretended to cough, but I didn't fool her.

"Hanna, this is important. You should know just in case it happens to you."

I recovered. "So, is Gramps okay?"

"Sure, he's fine. I could have told him that. I looked up floating turds on the internet. It's no big deal."

"What did the doctor say?"

"You mean, what did she say? Your grandfather was mortified to be seen by a woman. He said he's never going back."

"So, what did she say?" I wasn't relying on a diagnosis from WebMD.

"No big deal, nothing to worry about."

Relieved that Gramps was okay, I was thankful when the talk segued into my upcoming trip. Grams had no qualms about my traveling alone to Scotland. Her benign tone led me to believe she knew nothing about the envelope or its contents.

Then I blurted out, "Did dad have any connection with Scotland?"

Gram's trembling blue-veined hands pressed against the bodice of her apron, ironing imaginary creases. "As far as I know, Hanna, I don't think your father ever went there."

What a peculiar response. Wouldn't she know if her only child had gone to a foreign country? Perhaps it was the fading memory of an eighty-four-year-old, but then she corrected herself. "Your father spent a semester in...London. Maybe he had visited Scotland. I don't remember, but then a twenty-year-old boy doesn't always share everything with his mother."

Her eyes misted over. Was she remembering the little boy, all grown up, moving irrevocably beyond her reach? She sighed deeply, and then without any direction from me, she diverted the conversation to a related topic while gathering phantom strands of her silver hair into her bun.

"When I was a little girl my grandmother Hannie told me about some distant relations from Scotland. It was a long time ago. She must have heard of this Scottish connection from her grandparents. I suspect they heard it from theirs.

"We lived in New York City in the same apartment building as my grandmother Hannie. In those days families lived near each other." Was this another hint that I should live closer? I couldn't blame her. Growing old is a lonely business. She searched for a handkerchief and like a newborn joey it appeared from her kangaroo pocket.

"A middle-aged couple lived on the third-floor walk-up. I remember the wife quite well. She was attractive and flamboyant for her age. A flaming redhead with streaks of gray, she cursed like a drunken sailor. Well, she and her husband, a quiet man, were going to Scotland to bring back her aging mother. The woman had fallen on hard times, what with losing her home in the Clearances, and then her son, her sole means of support during the war."

"What were the Clearances?"

"My grandmother told me that was when the owners of the big estates forced the small tenant farmers off their land. The rich guys wanted to raise sheep instead. It was more profitable. So, the land was cleared, leaving the farmers destitute."

Grams sighed and went on with her story. "Ocean travel was a big deal in those days. It was a circus-like atmosphere when the couple paraded down the street carrying their packed valises. That's when I remember my grandmother telling all the neighbors our family had a 'wee' drop of Scottish blood too. Maybe she thought that by making this fact known, we would share the limelight with the redhead."

Slowly, one side of Gram's mouth evolved into a mischievous smile. She chuckled. "What Hannie didn't reveal was somewhere, way back in our family, there was another relation, a Jew. That was something you kept quiet about in those days."

Like the weather, her expression now changed to a flurry of despondency. "I wish I paid more attention to those old stories. I was young and thought they were boring. I didn't have time for the past." She sighed again and placed her tightly folded hands in her lap. "Now, it's all I think of. My grandmother died a few months after the redhead left. It was too late for most of her stories. I know a few, and I must share them with you. I couldn't ask my mother either. She contracted polio after I was born and spent the rest of her life in an asylum. I rarely saw her."

Grams stopped talking, closed her eyes, and remained silent. For a moment I thought she had fallen asleep, but when she dabbed her eyes with the rolled-up tissue in her hand, I knew she was finished. We walked into the living room and found my grandfather asleep. The susurrus of his snoring blended with the creaks and groans of an aging house.

I bent over to give my grandmother a final hug. She whispered in my ear, "When you return, I want to tell you those stories. And I have something that belonged to my grandmother. It's yours now." Did she whisper so as not to wake Gramps, or was this a secret just between us? Her final words were not said quietly. "Always remember, I love you Hanna."

Although I still had some unanswered questions, I walked away with new family information about a long-forgotten Scottish relative and a possible member of the Chosen People hanging out on a limb of my family tree.

My handsome co-traveler was seated along the aisle. I was by the window. When he stepped out of the row, so I wouldn't have to climb over him, his height was the first thing I noticed. His head came to the top of the overhead bin.

His name was Alec, and his Scottish accent was charming. I had no trouble understanding him, and we joked that my Philadelphia accent wasn't a problem.

I had once worried about someone spilling into my seat, but I didn't mind that Alec's broad shoulders touched mine. His dark brown, almost black locks, tied into a ponytail, matched his scruffy day-old beard. He was rugged and outdoorsy, like those guys who rough it on the PBS wilderness shows. I don't watch those programs to learn survival skills in Denali. I watch it for guys like Alec. He wasn't wearing a kilt, thank goodness, because then I would have proof Jess was clairvoyant. But, his tight jeans, boots, and black V-neck t-shirt made up for it. He was a fetching diversion. I forgot about jetlag and the key.

Alec and I talked during the flight, and I learned my seatmate was slightly older and an associate history professor at the University of St. Andrews. He was on summer break but would return to teaching for the fall semester. No wedding band or ring tan line suggested he was unattached. Besides, it was too soon to ask the single or married question, so I went with the evidence.

When we landed, Alec and I separated going through the customs line. Thankfully, we met up again near the exit. I planned to take a taxi, and Alec was heading to his apartment in St. Andrews. Would I ever see him again? I tried to think of something catchy and memorable to improve my chances.

Want to share a cab? But I had no idea where and how far away St. Andrews was.

Hey, do you want to meet up for a drink on The Mile? No, that was too cliché.

Maybe I should be up front and tell Alec I wanted him to be the father of my children.

I didn't have to come up with anything beguiling because Alec obliged. "Can I have your mobile number? Scotland's not a big country. If you are staying in Edinburgh, I could show you around a bit."

"I'd really like that."

"There are a lot of great sites: the castle, Holyrood House, and the Royal Mile. If you're up for it, we could take a drive. I'd like to show off my beautiful country to a beautiful lass."

Castle ruins! Scottish Hunk! Jess was psychic! "That would be great. I'd love to." I said that for so many reasons. I was overwhelmed being in a foreign country even though I spoke the language. I knew no one in Scotland. And I really wanted to see Alec again.

Before departing he gave me a quick hug and whispered in my ear, "See you soon, Lass." For a moment I could feel the solidity of his chest and arms and the roughness of those scruffy day-old whiskers.

Welcome to Scotland.

SEVEN

A Joyful Bride
Edinburgh, 1696

I muffled my sobs to listen for telltale footfalls. Except for the pounding of blood in my head, all I heard was blessed silence. Blinded by tears, my hand groped for the wooden bannister at the bottom of the staircase. A chance to catch my breath and consider what had just occurred.

The library was no longer a safe harbor and Father offered no protection. I was broken-hearted that he willingly sacrificed his daughter to placate an errant son and placed a priority on upholding the wishes of long dead relatives, ancient beliefs, and a strict religious code. I felt betrayed.

I didn't dare allow anyone to find me in my present condition. I stumbled up the smooth wooden treads until I reached the door of my bedchamber. The metal latch barely made a sound. With the world closed off behind me, I felt safe for the moment.

My abrupt entrance interrupted the perpetual nap of my grey-striped cat. She had been curled up in the end of my shawl that hung haphazardly from a chair to the floor. As I neared, she stretched and meowed and before she could scamper away, I scooped her in my arms and nuzzled my damp face in her soft fur. Together we sunk into the bed, my face buried in a warm purring pillow.

I awakened late in the afternoon. The cat was gone. All that remained were a few gray hairs and a tuft of white down. I made my way to the window where pale sunshine still cast long shadows. A mirror was nearby, but I ignored it. I had no desire to make myself presentable. It didn't matter. Nothing mattered.

I wondered how many young women had been forced to accept loveless futures to satisfy the whims of others. Was I to be regarded like the thistle that invaded our kitchen gardens? Beautiful but unwanted? I had often heard Mrs. Gibbons complain about the invasive weed.

"Dabby, get out tae the gard'n and lop off the thistle blooms. I canna have it takin' over my potato patch. Watch out for the thorns. I dinna have time tae sit around and pull out the prickles from yere feet o' anywhere else for that matter."

To my brother, I was the thistle, a pest to be rid of, to lop off my flower, just as I bloomed. I feared God had abandoned me. Would He hear my silent pleas as I

33

stood under the wedding canopy? Would He help me when my innocence was being offered on the altar of the wedding bed? Would He intervene when my husband lacked gentleness and used a heavy hand to assuage his frustration and impatience?

I could make no sense of it. My father often talked about the great love he and my mother had shared. Didn't he want the same for me? Perhaps Father lived a lie. Maybe my mother had been forced into a loveless union, and God deserted her as well.

Why must I, a Jewess, an accident of birth, be forced to carry the burden of my faith? Was I Esther? Was the survival of my people dependent on me?

Except for the glow of the last remaining ashes in the fireplace, my room was dark. A knock came from the door that led to the back staircase. I didn't care what anyone wanted because I planned to refuse all nourishment. Perhaps when I was close to death Father would be ashamed. The knocking continued and grew louder. Could it be Mrs. Gibbons bringing trays of food, my favorites, to cajole me into submission? Or my father's physician bringing a cure. None of his tonics, herbs, and bloodletting would remedy a broken heart. The knocking became more frantic. A voice called my name over and over. But it wasn't Father or Mrs. Gibbons. It was Sally.

"Anna! It's me. Open up."

I worked through the haze and pushed myself off the bed. My cat, who had once again snuggled next to me, let out a disappointed meow as I fought to open the door.

There stood Sally. I put my arms around my last remaining friend and sobbed. She made no attempt to encourage me to hush.

"Anna. Dear Anna."

Sally bent over, as a mother does with a small child. She shook her head. My dress was crumpled, and one stocking gathered around my ankle. "I'm here. I wilna leave ye."

"Sally, my father…my father has decided I'm to be married…leave Scotland forever and live in France."

"Hush. I ken. Yere brother ordered Old Simon tae prepare for a special guest. He made sure the old man understood this visitor would soon be part o' the family. Simon informed my mother so she could start workin' on menus and stockin' up on provisions. I never saw Old Simon in such a wretched state. No one, not even Dabby, has smiled since."

"What am I going to do? I have to run away…leave you." Sally patted my head as I returned to her arms. "There's no way out of this."

"Anna, I came tae tell you somethin' important."

I pushed back all the hair wisps that had worked their way out of my braid and had stuck to my damp face.

"Mr. MacArthur is returnin'. He'll be stayin' at an inn near the market. But I'm sure he'll have some meals here."

"Alain is coming back? So soon?" I moved away from her, straightened my bodice, and without thinking smoothed out the wrinkles in my dress. Suddenly, I could think again. "And when is the…Frenchman coming?" I would never call him my future husband.

Old Simon said it depends on the weather and if the winds are favorable for a Channel crossing.

"Let's hope that Alain comes in time."

Sally stared at me and tilted her head like the cat when she was trying to figure out what I was saying. "What do ye mean, comes in time?" Then Sally's eyes widened." Are ye going to ask Mr. MacArthur to help ye? Ye hardly ken the Highlander. Ye canna go with a man who isn't yere husband."

"Keep your voice down, and don't ask so many questions. I don't have the answers yet. But I'll think of something. I only know I can't marry this Frenchman. I'd rather die."

"Ye've only kent Mr. MacArthur a few hours. Ye canna love him so soon."

"I don't love him. But he was kind to me. I'm sure when I tell him about my predicament he will help."

I thought of a lot of other possibilities, but the one that bothered me the most was why would Alain do this for me? He was hoping to conclude a business deal with my father. Did I really expect Father to offer his financial backing after Alain had kidnapped his daughter? But I knew my father had no intention of saying yes to the MacArthur clan. The business venture was too risky.

"It's clear to me now. I know what I'll do."

"And what's that?" Sally voice quivered as if she was afraid of the answer.

"I'm going to accept this marriage to the Frenchman." I could feel a growing smile spread across my face and the strength of a new resolve flowing through my arms and legs.

Sally's eyes lit up. Her mouth broke into a knowing smile. "Oh, I ken what yere doin'."

"I won't give Father or Nathan any reason to doubt my desire to be married to the man of their choosing. I will be a most joyful bride. Then I can put my plan into action." The shock I imagined on their faces, at my unexpected turn-around, made me chuckle. It felt good to regain control of my future.

"Sally, you aren't to tell anyone. Do you understand?"

"O' course. Not a word, I swear." She raised her right hand. "But what happens if Mr. MacArthur comes after you are wed and on yere way tae France?"

I turned to look at my friend. "If that's the case, my new husband can use my dowry to purchase some mourners, a burial plot, and a headstone. And my father can rend his clothes and lament the passing of his Precious Anna."

EIGHT
Deception

When Sally arrived in my bedchamber every morning, usually we chatted about the latest gossip heard at market or the rumors swirling around the philandering husband who lived on the other side of Cheery Close. Today, our talk was different. As she helped me get dressed, I repeated what I planned to do and the need for discretion.

For the first time in twenty-four hours, Sally pulled a brush through my tangled hair until it gleamed. Rouge, applied to cheeks and lips, erased any hint of my recent misery. When finished, she offered her approval and positioned me in front of the mirror.

"Ye need earrin's. Yere mother's gold ones make yere eyes sparkle." She held one tear-drop filigree bauble close to my ear. "If you're heading in tae the lion's den," she glanced toward the door of my bedchamber, "ye'll need all the help ye can get." She fastened one at a time. "Yere father might soft'n a wee bit when he sees ye wearin' them."

It would take a miracle to change Father's mind, and miracles only happened in Bible stories.

But looking at my reflection, I whispered, "Perfect." Mother's earrings filled me with confidence. I grabbed my shawl and tied it around my shoulders. I was ready to face my future head-on.

Keeping to my routine was important, so as we did every morning Sally and I sat at a long wooden slab near the kitchen hearth for breakfast. The heat helped to keep the morning chill away, although it couldn't stop my trembling.

We ate warm bannocks spread with fresh butter and raspberry jam and filled our bowls with thick hot porridge topped with cream. Sally and I whispered and tittered as usual. One outburst attracted the attention of Sally's mother.

"What's with the tae o' you?" The sight of her meaty hands, white with flour, propped on her enormous hips only made us explode with covered giggles. When we didn't reply, she shook her head, and threw her hands up. White splotches appeared on either side of her skirt, and a floury cloud floated in the air. She tried to dissipate

37

it only to create another. "Well, if ye both have nothin' better tae do then sit here blatherin' and usin' up my workin' space, then off ye go. Sally get out tae the garden and bring back a basketful o' kale. And don't forget the carrots need harvestin too."

As Mrs. Gibbons called out the chores, she continued to raise her voice. "Now Sally, mind me, and dinna come back into this kitchen with mud all over yere shoes o' I'll have ye scrubbin' the floors till it's clean enough to eat on. And don't think I've forgotten you havna polished the silver like I asked ye tae do two days ago. Are ye listenin' tae me, Daughter?"

How could we not? Her voice echoed throughout the kitchen. The glassware seemed to be singing in concert.

"This house is going tae have a lot o' visitors and everythin' needs tae be spotless for the wed...." She stopped mid-sentence, stared at me, and for a moment her eyes softened.

The opening act of my plan began with Mrs. Gibbons.

"The wedding? I was shocked when Nathan had found a husband for me. What bride wouldn't be? But I've had a day to think it over, and I've decided that it's a good...a wonderful idea. I'm old enough, so it's about time. Don't you think?"

With a tilt of her head, Mrs. Gibbons continued to stare at me as if a ghost had taken over poor Anna's body, awakened in the same house, and had breakfast with her daughter?

"I must visit the dressmaker and finish my trousseau. Would you mind if I helped plan the menu for the wedding meal? How exciting to live in France, the lady of my own household, and the center of society with my new husband. But I'll miss you, Mrs. Gibbons." I found it easier if I kept talking.

I planted a kiss on the surprised woman's cheek. Then reached for a bannock and bit off a large piece. If I could no longer fill my mouth with lies, food would have to do. It gave me time to think.

Mrs. Gibbons scrunched her face into a hundred wrinkles. "Well, ye don't...I...." Her head shook back and forth forcing her cap to fall over her eyes. She shoved it back and mumbled something under her breath. Before disappearing into the pantry, she yelled, "Sally, dinna forget the turnips. If they aren't picked soon, they'll get lost in the damn thistle."

Sally and I escaped into the garden. "Did I sound convincing?"

"I...I think so. I believed ye, but I'm sure my mother...." Sally's voice became a whisper and then trembled. She pushed her hair out of her eyes and smoothed the front of her apron with nervous hands. Her eyes went downward. "I have tae get the kale b'fore the rabbits do." She tightened her grip on her basket and left me standing there wondering what was wrong.

"Convincing about what?" The gruff voice came from behind. I turned. Nathan stood in the kitchen doorway, leaning against the jamb, slicing an apple with his knife. After he popped each crescent-shaped slice into his mouth he wiped the juice that dripped from the corners of his lips with his shirt sleeve.

I took a deep breath and forced a smile. "Good morning. I was telling Sally...no one needs to...convince me that Father is doing what's best for my future." Thankfully, my smile didn't fade.

Nathan walked toward me. About to wipe the knife on his pants, he stopped directly in front, blocking the path.

"I must be off. Father is expecting me." I gathered my skirts, walked around him, and stepped into the soft soil, flattening carrot greens and stems. Quickening my pace, I headed for the kitchen.

"Stop."

I froze.

"You never expressed proper gratitude for my finding your intended. Perhaps, you'd like to know more about him?"

My obligatory smile resumed. "My apologies. I'm in your debt. Father told me about my groom. No need to trouble yourself." Unwisely I couldn't help a rejoinder. "Brother, to show my gratitude, I promise to beg my husband to forgo the ancient custom of naming our firstborn after his paternal great-grandparent in favor of his maternal uncle."

Nathan lunged and grabbed my wrist, the same one injured two days earlier. "You don't fool me with your pretense. Nothing you say or do is going to change your future. I watched you shamelessly flaunt your charms in front of your Highlander. Do you think he will want you once he hears about your impending nuptials? You can be assured Father will inform Mr. MacArthur. He'll soon find better prospects elsewhere."

"Mr. MacArthur? I barely know the man."

Nathan snorted. "You can play this game with Father, but it's not working with me. Run along to the library then. At this very moment Father is inspecting the wedding contract."

"That's not true."

"You remember Maurice St Martin, Father's business partner? He visited two years ago. He kept ogling you and couldn't keep his hands to himself. You were only a maid of thirteen. He reeked so foul you had to leave the room."

My lips trembled, not from fear but from anger.

He leaned closer, the muscles in his neck tightened like thin rope. "Old Maurice is thrilled with this marriage. He wants a young lass who will tend to his needs. As soon as your groom arrives you will be wedded and bedded, and Mr. MacArthur will find solace in the arms of another bonny lass."

I had to get away. My unencumbered hand lifted my skirt and I kicked Nathan in the knee. It was the last thing he expected and released his grip. I ran through the kitchen tracking mud all the way to the library.

I rubbed my reddened wrist, straightened my skirt, and took a deep breath. The click of the latch didn't disrupt Father. Perhaps, his hearing wasn't good today. I shut the door behind me and tiptoed to a chair furthest from his desk. While waiting for acknowledgement, I pushed back my hair and exposed my mother's earrings. I needed her help.

"Ah, Anna. I was afraid you would not return after the other day. I know you were upset. Most young people are when they hear a spouse has been found." He paused and sighed. His words sounded rehearsed. He rubbed his eyes with his fingers. They looked bloodshot.

"Father, didn't you once tell me, from the Talmud, *whoever marries for money will have unworthy children*? Is that how it happened with you and Mother? Did she marry for money? Are my brother and I unworthy?"

"Anna, I need to get you situated before I die. My health is not good. My affairs, including my beloved daughter, must be settled."

I could argue with my father, but this dangerous conversation needed to end. "Father, I will obey. I will stand under the wedding canopy with Monsieur St. Martin." I lowered my eyes and fingered the thistles embroidered on my skirt. They were a reminder to remain strong, with thorns ready to defend against anyone intending to lop off my blossom.

Father rose with great difficulty and walked toward me. His movement caused the candle flames on his desk and the chandelier to flare and bend in his direction. The smell of honey filled the room. He stopped and placed his hand on his stomach.

"Father, can I get you your peppermint tea?"

He raised his hand and waved my questions away. He sat again and sighed heavily when the pain had passed.

"Maurice's ship sails in a week, Two at the most."

For events to unfold this quickly, my father and brother must have been planning for months. They kept my future a secret, but I couldn't let my rising anger get in the way of my plan. Not wanting him to see the resentment in my face, I walked over to the fireplace where the kettle was filled with hot water. I poured some over peppermint leaves and allowed the tea to steep. After honey was added, I stirred, filling the air with the steamy fragrance.

Then unexpectedly, Father said, "A messenger came this morning. Mr. MacArthur is returning in a week."

I breathed a sigh of relief. Information about Alain's return was the only reason I'd come to the library.

"Should I let Old Simon and Mrs. Gibbons know they can expect another guest?"

He ignored my question. "If his arrival coincides with your wedding, I will invite him to join in the festivities. Would you mind?"

I had to grab the back of a chair to keep from spilling the tea on my skirt.

"Of course not, Father." I put the cup down. My hand went to my face.

"Anna, are you well? Now the patient was tending the nurse "Sit, sit."

"I'm fine. Just a minor dizziness from all the excitement." I couldn't let our conversation end without getting the answer I needed. "Will he stay here?"

"No, there won't be room with all the wedding guests. I've made arrangements at an inn on Lawnmarket."

"Have you decided about the business venture with the MacArthur clan? Are you going to support them?"

While Father reiterated his many reasons for refusing the MacArthur clan, my mind focused on how I would find Alain and beg for his help. Would he listen? Would he care? I dreaded the possibility that his past attentions had been mere polite conversation or a young man's trifling with the heart of a foolish girl. I was reminded of a saying. *Hope for a miracle, but don't rely on it.*

NINE
Traditions
Edinburgh, 2005

Before I even unpacked my bags at the B&B, my cellphone buzzed. I fumbled to snatch it and squinted at the screen. *Alec.* That was fast. I thought he would call in a day or two.

I touched the green button, ignoring the hammering pulse in my throat. "Hello?"

"Hey, Hanna. I meant to ask you, how about a tour of the Royal Mile tomorrow?"

I didn't need a mirror to know I was smiling. "I'd love to, but I don't know any tour guides," I teased. "I'm not sure my travel budget could afford—"

"Uh...Hanna...I was—"

"Private guides don't work for free, you know, and I'd rather not go alone. That'd be awkward."

"Hanna, Wait. Let me start again." He took a deep breath. "I'll provide the tour." He must have caught onto my ruse, "I'm pretty cheap."

I muffled my laughter and felt a twinge of guilt for teasing him. Spending the day with Alec would delay my purpose for coming to Scotland. But the key had remained a mystery for many years. One more day wasn't going to make a difference.

The next morning, after a traditional Scottish breakfast of hot porridge with cream and drizzled honey, I headed toward The Royal Mile. The air was crisp and cool although it was the middle of summer.

I easily found our agreed-upon meeting place at the esplanade in front of the gatehouse of Edinburgh Castle. The former home of Scottish royalty had intimidating gray stone walls, and it was situated on the crest of a volcanic plug at the head of the Royal Mile. The fortress looked down on a cobblestoned thoroughfare flanked on either side by tartan and souvenir shops. The droning of a kilted bagpipe player caught my attention as he greeted visitors who waited in line to take a snapshot. Those who were patient received a memento that would jog their memory years from now.

Alec was easy to find. He towered above most. I watched as he weaved in and out of a throng of tourists. When our eyes locked, his smile broadened, and he quickened his pace. His warm embrace awakened a shiver down my spine.

Alec began the tour with a lesson on the ever-changing Scottish weather. "By the time you put on your mac, the sun will be out, and as soon as you stow your brolly...umbrella...it's time to retrieve it again. It's possible to experience four seasons in one day. Most people are surprised to learn that some parts of Scotland are almost as far north as Anchorage, Alaska."

I eyed Alec's open shirt and reacted by burrowing my chin in my woolen cowl. "You don't seem to mind the cold."

"Aye, but I come from hardy stock. No true Highlander would ever complain about frigid temperatures or a blinding blizzard. I would see it as an opportunity to invite you to a picnic."

I chuckled while conjuring up a vision of Alec spreading out a blanket and a picnic basket over newly fallen snow while I shivered to death.

My tour included views of the Firth of Forth, the Forth Bridge, and dramatic vistas of Old Town. I stood close to Alec and soaked in the warmth of his body through his layered clothing. The combined odors of spicy cologne, worn leather, and morning coffee lingered about him.

We explored the interior of the castle and entered a room filled with the symbols of royalty: a jeweled encrusted crown, a sword, and a scabbard. Oddly, the exhibition included a two by four-foot block of red sandstone, with a cross engraving and an iron ring at each end.

"What's the purpose of the rock?"

"It's not just any rock. It's the Coronation Stone. Always a part of the crowning ceremony for the kings and queens of Scotland and later England. The newly anointed monarch would sit on the rock, literally a seat of power. In 1296, Edward I stole it from Scotland, and it stayed in England until fifty-five years ago when some university students snuck into Westminster Abbey and took it back. To the Scots, it's an important symbol of our sovereignty and freedom from the yoke of English rule."

I was puzzled. "But why this rock?"

"Some believe it was Jacob's Pillow, from the Old Testament."

I was at a loss. My family didn't go to church and my religious education was nonexistent because Dad blamed religion for most of the evil in the world. He said that the Bible was a bunch of fairy tales meant to glorify murderers, liars, and child abusers. We would often debate the pros and cons of religion.

"What about the arts? The paintings, the architecture, and music inspired by faith."

"Sorry, Hanna. The Sistine Chapel and Handel's Messiah can't make up for the millions murdered because they worshipped differently."

Therefore, what I knew came from Cecil B. DeMille, my classes in world religions, and Jess. Her mom was Catholic, her dad Jewish, and a Protestant aunt or uncle was sprinkled in for good measure. She celebrated everything.

"How did a rock become a pillow?"

"Some believe it served as a head rest for the biblical Jacob when he dreamt about a ladder that ascended to heaven."

"Do you mean the father in *Joseph and the Amazing Technicolor Dream Coat*? I love that musical."

"That's the one." Alec chuckled.

We entered a small, mostly wood paneled room with an ornate ceiling. "This is where Mary, Queen of Scots, gave birth to James VI of Scotland who eventually became James I of England."

"Didn't she lose her head or was that the Mary named for the drink?" I asked.

"She did lose her head. However, you're mixing up your Marys. Bloody Mary was a Tudor, an English Queen, who was Mary Stuart's cousin. It was the Scottish Mary whose progeny would bring on the Jacobite uprisings and the battle at Culloden that would change Highland culture forever."

"The number of Marys and James can be confusing."

"Well, you Colonists have numerous Johns, James and Georges. At least we number ours."

After a couple of hours exploring, it was time for the firing of the one o'clock gun from the north face of the castle. Standing in the open, with no walls for protection, we were buffeted by the cold wind. I tried to control my hair as it whipped around my face. Alec offered to help. His fingers spread wide, combing their way through the strands, securing all the riotous curls, and penned then securely with a clip I procured from my bag.

A man dressed as a soldier greeted the crowd. "The firing of the gun served as a daily reminder for all city residents to set their clocks. More importantly, it alerted ship captains in Leith, two miles away, to set their ship's chronometer. The accuracy of the time pieces was essential so they could find longitude."

"But how could that be exact?" I whispered. "It would take time for the sound to travel the two miles, and when it reached the ears of the ships' captains, it would already be inaccurate."

45

As if the soldier heard my question, he said. "Depending on temperature and humidity it would take about ten seconds for the sound to travel the two miles. It was impossible to be completely accurate, but the Scots were smart. They created a map, and based on location, they indicated how many seconds, after one o'clock, the sound would take to travel. Today, the firing of the gun is no longer necessary. But it's a nice convention and encourages tourists to unload sixteen pounds to get into the castle."

The crowd chortled but quieted quickly as we anticipated the firing of the cannon.

The blast was louder than I expected. I shrieked and reflexively grabbed Alec's arm. I apologized with a quick, "Sorry."

"Not necessary, Hanna." As one eyebrow perked up, he added, "Why do you think I brought you here?"

We left the castle and went back through the esplanade to The Mile. Alec pointed out some of the small alleyways hidden between the shops. Each alley or close had a distinctive name engraved on a metal sign placed above the entrance. Some were rather unusual: Fleshmarket, Skinner, and Bailie Fife.

"Don't tell me. Fleshmarket Close is where the brothels were located." I said.

"No, that's where meat was butchered and sold."

"Sort of the same thing, don't you think?"

"Aye." Alec displayed a playful smirk. "And after the butchering, the hides went to Skinner Close to be cured and tanned. There are eighty closes, and each bore the name of the owner, a former resident, or a trade."

The Mile was like a carnival. A myriad of street entertainers vied for the attention of tourists by offering a lively show and hoped they would be generous with their tips. The first we came across was a pair of jugglers who balanced ten pins simultaneously. Then a frozen knight came to life once coins were deposited in his wooden bucket. On the other side of the street was a fortune-teller. The woman was dressed in a flared red skirt, topped with a not-so-white blouse, and a purple shawl that hung off one bronzed shoulder. Gaudy trinkets covered her wrists and ears which jingled as she moved. A purple and orange scarf held her graying hair in place. I bet the more you paid her, the better your prospects.

"Come closer, dearie. Let Grizelda, the gypsy fortune-teller interpret what fate has in store for you. Is it love, a vast fortune, or long life?"

She was so corny; I couldn't help but roll my eyes. One didn't have to be clairvoyant to predict the love part. After all, I was in the company of a great looking guy.

We walked on until we stood in front of a close with the delightful name, Lady Stairs. I followed Alec single file through a narrow-arched walkway lined with damp grey stones. Anyone who wished to enter on the other end had to wait until we'd passed through.

We emerged onto a courtyard surrounded by tall narrow buildings. The windows at ground level were covered with iron bars. In the center was a lamppost surrounded by a tour group. On the other side was a beautiful five story building: The Writer's Museum.

"What a lovely courtyard. If it weren't for you, I would never have known this place existed."

"At your service, mistress." Alec touched his hand to an imaginary hat, removed it, and bowed.

"Mistress? You mean like a concubine or a prostitute?"

"No, it was common courtesy in the seventeenth century to address a woman as mistress if she owned servants or had a skill. Now, if you prefer to be addressed as a woman of ill-repute—"

"No, that's quite alright. 'Hanna' will be just fine. I hope you don't introduce me to your family…and friends as Mistress Hanna. I don't want to make a bad…first impression."

Alec turned to look at me. One eyebrow shot up. That appeared to be his hallmark response to my frequent slip-ups.

"Sorry, I didn't mean to be so forward."

"It's okay. I'd like for you to meet my friends. As for my family, I'd need to prepare you first."

The museum was constructed from stone that was stained from centuries of soot and smoke. Above the entrance hung a metal sign which bore the silhouette of a writer at his desk. This rested below a beautifully curved Juliet balcony. The building was topped with a domed roof and a spire which made it appear taller.

"This museum celebrates the work of three renowned Scottish writers: Scott, Burns, and Stevenson. It was built in 1622 and was originally the home of Sir William Gray and his wife, Gelda. Their initials are carved over the lintel."

But along with the initials, I also saw the menacing words *Feare the Lord and Depart From Evill*.

After a short stay at the museum we continued down The Mile and entered The World's End Pub for an early dinner. It took a moment to adjust to the darkened bar area. The first thing that caught my eye was the wall that hung over the bar. It was papered with money from all over the world; each signed and dated by its donor. Beyond the bar were cozy intimate spaces, perfect for private conversation. We found a small table in a section with the fewest diners.

Alec offered to order. "Let's start with black pudding. Very Scottish. I think you'll like it."

"Pudding? Black? Sounds awful."

"It's a traditional dish like burgers on the Fourth of July. It's sausage."

"So's a hot dog, but what's in it?"

Alec chuckled. "A little bit of everything. Pork fat, blood, onion, oatmeal."

For a moment, my head started to spin. I swallowed hard, two or three times. "I'm sorry. Can we get something else? I don't mean to be difficult. I'm sure it's very good, but I don't eat pork."

"You don't? Ever?"

I nodded. It was safer than speaking.

Alec's eyes went wide in amazement. I wasn't surprised. This was the usual response I got when new friends discovered my peculiar eating habit. I never announced my aversion to pork in advance, but it didn't take long to figure out.

I knew Alec didn't get it when he asked, "Not even bacon?"

"Nope. No pork chops, no ham sandwich, no pepperoni pizza." The look on his face told me I needed to add, "Really."

"Are you a vegetarian? Or is it your religion?" He appeared genuinely intrigued, like how could anyone get through twenty-two years of life without consuming some part of a pig.

"No, I love steak, and my family is not religious. It's just something we've always done. It's sort of a tradition." That sounded ridiculous especially for a family that believed in nothing.

"Okay. Let's try something else. The Cullen Skink soup."

"Skunk? I can't eat that either." Just the thought of it made me want to heave. Skunk reminded me when Dad and I would go for rides in the country. He would tell me to breathe in the clean country air. Sometimes the air was too fresh, compliments of the recent roadkill.

Alec chuckled. "No, it's Skink. Smoked haddock and potato chowder. Is fish okay?"

"Sure...sounds delicious."

After a dinner of soup, beef and ale pie, and a local beer, I told Alec my reason for coming to Scotland and continued with the rest of the sad family details. "My mother was killed in a freak car accident when I was three. The cause, the police said, was a slick highway. Not even a seatbelt would've saved her. The impact into a line of trees was too great." I hesitated and then added almost as a whisper. "She died alone. No one to hold her hand. No one to say last things to."

Alec grasped my hands in his. They were solid and strong, but with a soothing gentleness. He lowered his face close to mine. I could feel his warm breath against my cheek. "I'm sorry you have had to bear the loss of your loved ones, Hanna. To lose a parent at any age is difficult, but to be so young, must be unbearable."

Over the years many people have said similar comforting words to me, but Alec's felt different. The sincerity behind each, coupled with the way he touched me, meant so much more.

I told Alec about my life in Philadelphia, my apartment, and Jess. "She was my college roommate and a great friend. She's really cool and the reason why I'm here."

"I'd like to meet this Jess."

"Really?"

"If it hadn't been for her, my flight would have been quite dull."

The next morning my eyes popped open as the first rays of sunlight crept across my bedroom. I rolled over and read the bright green numbers on the clock. Four a.m. Ugh! The heavy-lined window drapes now made sense. I plumped up the pillows, pulled the covers to my chin, willed myself to sleep, but got nowhere. Too early to get up, I remained in bed thinking of the previous day. Lovely thoughts of Alec made me feel warm all over.

I must have dozed off again because my phone jarred me awake. Still groggy I checked my caller ID and saw it was Alec. I sputtered. "Hey."

Alec must have slept just fine. His voice boomed like an early morning radio host who always sounds chipper for the benefit of sleepy commuters. "Good morning, Mistress Hanna. I will come by at noon if you like."

I mumbled something that resembled, "Sure."

"If you need more time, I can come later."

"No, I'll be okay. Noon is fine." Finding my voice, I added, "After the bank maybe we could go to The Portrait Gallery or Holyrood House."

My life had taken a turn in the last forty-eight hours. Before I boarded the plane, I'd been focused on my mission: go to the bank, solve the mystery, and return home. Now, the key was a speed bump. Another of my dad's sayings came to mind – *two's company, three's a crowd*. The key was the crowd.

"Hold on, mistress. That depends a lot on you and only if you're up for it. You were very tired last night. Must be jetlag. I don't want to lose you to the faeries."

"Huh?" I was still in a fog, but then his meaning became clear, and so was the fact he wasn't going to stop calling me 'mistress.'

Still tired, I thought it best not to rush my morning routine. I leaned against the headboard and scanned my large room located below street level of a large Georgian-style home. Across from the bed was a floor-to-ceiling oak wardrobe that

49

made up for the lack of a closet. It held all my clothes and within the folds of a black turtleneck, I hid the key.

Eventually, I shuffled my way across the room, and for fun, I opened the wardrobe door and touched the back wall to ensure there was no Narnia. All I got was a whiff of camphor and lemon furniture polish.

After a long hot shower, I towel-dried my hair and shook out the curls. I wondered if Alec found them attractive.

Later, we met at the top of the concave marble stairs that led from my room to the pavement above. Rain probably made the steps slippery, but not today. Sunny and dry, at least for the moment, I bounded up those steps, two at a time.

We walked to St. Andrew Square and entered the flagship branch of the Royal Bank of Scotland. Originally a residence, the three-story, sandstone building hid behind an iron fence fronted by a circular drive. Just inside, two burly security guards stood near a chest-high desk. Dressed in identical dark jackets, their name tags suggested this was the place to get information. The gatekeepers directed us to walk through the lobby to the assistant bank manager's desk.

The exterior of the bank offered no clue to the architectural splendor inside. The two-story lobby looked like it was meant for royalty. My eyes were drawn upwards to the grandeur of the coffered-barrel ceiling which glinted with gold leaf. A plaster border, incorporating an intricate floral pattern, circled the room.

"Alec, do you see the design on the wall? Look up there, just above the doorway. What kind of flower that is?"

"It's thistle, the national flower of Scotland. You see it everywhere: sports team jerseys, business logos, police uniforms—"

"That's the same design on my key...the handle. When I first found the key, I just thought, whoever made it, tried to make the handle...pretty. Holy crap, I never realized the design had a purpose."

"There's an old legend how the thistle saved a band of sleeping Scots from being slaughtered by Norsemen. When the bare-footed invaders tried to sneak up on the Scots, the warriors stepped on the thorns and their howls saved the Scots."

As Alec told his story I could feel goosebumps come alive on my arms, and the hairs on the back of my neck stood at attention. This is the place, I thought. My key has come home.

From the lobby, we walked through white marble columns until we came to a grand rectangular space.

"May I help you?"

In front of us appeared a heavy-set older woman with the most peculiar pair of bright purple cats-eyeglasses. The vivid color reflected off her gray hair giving it a lavender hue. She said her name was Maggie and she was a volunteer greeter.

"This place is beautiful. It's hard to imagine it's a bank," I said.

"Yes, it's one of the most beautiful banks in the world. I'd be happy to show you around."

"We haven't much time. Sorry." I looked at my watch, and realized I'd never reset it for a new time zone.

"Well, I'll be quick. I'll just tell you about this room."

Before I could answer, Maggie started. Alec, of course, looked delighted.

"This telling space was created in 1857 by two famous local architects, Peddie and Kinnear. You are standing on Mintori tiles. Soaring over our heads, three stories high, the rotunda is framed in gilded semicircular arches with figures representing commerce, agriculture, navigation, and the arts. The blue domed roof represents the sky. The dome has five concentric tiers of 120 six-pointed glazed stars circling an oculus, representing the sun. The design allowed for enough natural light to filter in, so the 19th century bank clerks could total their receipts properly."

She stopped; she needed to breathe.

"Why look at that." Maggie pointed to the oculus. In the center of the 'sun' was a bird, and from its outdoor perch it watched us and the goings-on in the bank.

"Maybe the bird wants to make a deposit," she said.

We all laughed, and Maggie seemed pleased at her successful attempt at making potential customers happy. We thanked her for the tour and made our way toward the rear of the teller stations where there was an over-sized wooden desk. The brass nameplate indicated we had found the bank official.

The bespectacled assistant branch manager looked like he belonged in a by-gone era. His grey pinstriped suit and white starched shirt matched the pallor of his skin. I couldn't see his shoes. I was betting they were polished oxfords with double-knotted shoelaces.

We stood in front of his desk waiting for some acknowledgement, but he continued concentrating on the manual in front of him. He lips moved silently as he scribbled something.

Alec cleared his throat rather loudly. "Good afternoon, sir. Could you help my girlfriend with her key?"

The man behind the desk looked up. He straightened his already perfect bowtie with neatly manicured hands that probably never did anything more than push papers. He introduced himself, and then said, "I will be happy to help you.

51

What do you want to know about your key? Does it belong to my bank? The Royal Bank of Scotland, I mean."

"I inherited a key from my father. I believe it may open a safe deposit box here."

"I see. Well, I'm sure I can help. First, I need to know if the young lady has proof she's the executrix of her father's will."

I bit my lip to restrain a sharp comeback. That was the only way I got past the 'young lady' part and his talking about me as if I weren't present. I handed over the necessary documentation.

He flipped some pages, and then asked to see my passport. "It all seems in order. Do you have the key?"

I produced the key from the envelope, and I thought I heard him gasp. His wide-opened eyes told me my ears had been correct. He took the key and held it with both hands as if it were a Fabergé egg. Turning it over, he inspected the etched initials. For a moment, I held my breath hoping the letters had not somehow disappeared.

The manager straightened his glasses and bowtie once again. "We don't get a key like this very often, young lady. It may take some due diligence to identify which box it belongs to."

"Well, how do you do that? Most safe deposit keys have numbers on them. This one doesn't." After a brief pause, I added, "And it's Miss Duncan." He should have known my name from my passport.

"We have our ways." He made it sound as if the identification of an old safe deposit key was a lost art known only to him, and like Merlin, he would conjure up the answer. "Please come with me. I cannot take the key out of your sight." He took out his bar-coded badge from the desk drawer, pushed back his chair, and pulled down on his suit jacket. "Come this way. Your…um…boyfriend can come too…if you like."

Like school children we followed our teacher single-file. Rather than my mind focusing on the key and its imminent discovery, it was exploding with other possibilities. Yes, my boyfriend could come too.

TEN
The Dungeon

The banker led the way down the stone staircase. My hand glided along the wooden railing. Its smooth surface suggested decades of use as many others had followed this same path to unearth their valuables. Were they as anxious and hopeful? Is that what caused me to forget the banker's name even though we'd been introduced moments ago?

The dungeon-like bowels of the bank smelled of damp stone walls and the banker's lavender aftershave. Doorways on either side of the first long hallway had unwelcoming signs: No Admittance, Security, or Authorized Personnel Only. We turned into the second hallway and stopped when we got to the Documentation and Archives room. The bank manager swiped his barcoded ID badge. The door opened with a resounding click.

The room looked like the set of an old detective TV show. A rectangular wooden table and three metal chairs barely filled the space. In the center of the table was a small flip calendar and a metal cylinder filled with pens sporting the bank's logo. All it lacked was a two-way mirror.

We were invited to take a seat. The metal-legged chairs screeched on the stone floor like fingernails scraping a chalkboard. I cringed.

After placing the key on the table, our host cleared his throat. "This is an unusual key, Miss Duncan. I hope you can appreciate that."

I wasn't sure what to think but nodded to be polite.

His forehead furrowed. His trembling fingers went to his bowtie. "What I'm about to say may sound a bit complicated." He spoke slowly, raising his voice as some do when speaking to a child. "The Royal Bank of Scotland was founded in 1727. At the time, there were no safe deposit boxes. Except for some prosperous merchants who did well in the tobacco trade, most Scots didn't have valuables, or much money for that matter. That was especially true after the Darien debacle in the late seventeenth century, compounded by poor harvests and the Jacobite Risings of 1715 and 1745."

I understood him until he began spewing several decades of Scottish history as if it were a past we shared. Puzzled, I looked at Alec. He squeezed my hand. His smile signaled to remain calm; I returned the squeeze in silent acknowledgment.

53

The banker continued. "Wealthy merchants wanted to protect their fortunes, and the Royal Bank of Scotland offered such a service. For a fee, valuables were placed in a wooden box, and the bank offered to safeguard it for as long as the owner wished. Originally, twelve containers existed, and each was paired with a different key."

"Are the other keys like mine?"

"Not exactly. What differentiates them is the design on the handle. No two were alike. This key and eleven others were given to their owners sometime between 1727 and 1749. The boxes were kept in our vaults over the centuries. Once we began offering more modern safe deposit boxes, these old containers were locked away. Each was placed in a separate stall with an additional key needed to open the compartment."

The banker took a handkerchief from his jacket pocket and wiped his brow. I wondered how anyone could be warm in this chilly, subterranean mausoleum. Perhaps the key was causing more stress than I realized.

"After 1750, the bank changed the key design. The thistle was no longer used. So we are certain your key predates the mid-18th century. Over the years, ten of those original keys have been returned to the bank by their owners or their executors. Two remain outstanding. Now there is only one."

A pause in his explanation resulted in an awkward silence, but it gave me time to process the information. That led to more questions which made my head spin. If the key was over 250 years old, did my Scottish ancestor, the one Grams mentioned, have anything to do with it? How had the key traveled from 18th century Scotland to a 21st century bank in Manhattan? What about the Jewish ancestor? Jews were known to be moneylenders and merchants centuries ago.

"Mr....um...forgive me."

"It's Scott."

How could I forget a name like that? "Yes, Mr. Scott, if there are two keys remaining, how do you know which key will open the right box? And do you even have the box anymore?"

The banker fiddled with the key again. I wanted him to stop. My annoyance must have been telegraphed because he placed it on the table and clasped his hands together as if that would prevent him from touching it again.

"Miss Duncan, we have exact methods of identifying a client's property. For centuries, customers have relied on the Royal Bank to be discreet as well as keep their valuables safe. Millions of customers know they can trust us to carry out their wishes. As you can see, we have done just that for your family. You have the key. We still have the box."

"But how do you know which box it goes to?"

"Miss Duncan, let me repeat. I have told you and...er...Mr. MacGregor...each key was individually made. Again—"

54

"It's Mr. Grant, My name is…Alec…Grant."

I waited for Alec to say, *my name is like yours. Simple. Five letters: G – R – A – N – T*. I was thankful he didn't, because maintaining a straight face would have been impossible. Instead he said, "You've already told us about the handle. Now, will you answer Miss Duncan's questions?"

Alec's firmness resulted in Mr. Scott continuing in a more contrite manner. "Before each key was given to its owner a wax mold was made and stored away in our vaults. My assistant is getting the two remaining molds. They are numbered. Whichever one the key fits will tell us which box it will open."

Alec asked, "What do you do with the wax mold after the owner has come forward?"

"We melt it down, of course, they are never considered again. That's why we know there are only two keys remaining…excuse me…now, most likely one left in circulation."

I had another question which I wanted to get out before the assistant arrived. "Would the contents still be in the box after all these years?"

I thought I saw the beginning of an eye roll.

"Of course. A box can remain here, undisturbed in perpetuity, until an owner comes forward. Other banks impose a time limit. If there is no activity, and the owner cannot be found by placing an ad in the newspaper, the contents are forfeited to the government. That doesn't happen at the Royal Bank of Scotland. Our charter is the second oldest in Scotland. We have extremely high standards."

Alec and I sat back in our chairs. He winked and added a reassuring smile. It was comforting to know he had my back. Mr. Scott wiped his brow and quietly blew his nose in a handkerchief before returning it to his inside jacket pocket.

A soft knock at the door announced the arrival of Mr. Scott's assistant. A young woman entered wearing a conservative blue suit and comfortable but unfashionable flats. I bet she had a pair of killer heels hidden in her desk drawer ready to transform at the end of the day from Plain Jane to *Femme Fatale*. In her gloved hands, she carried a tray laden with two wooden blocks and another pair of latex gloves. She placed the tray in front of us.

Mr. Scott made quite a showing of putting on the gloves. The latex squeaked as he flexed his fingers and then snapped the material at his wrists. He gingerly opened one of the blocks revealing a five-inch square of solid yellow beeswax. In the center was an imprint of a key. The banker explained that if my key did not fit this first imprint, then we would try the next mold. I thought of a third scenario. What if my key fit neither?

Mr. Scott lifted my key and placed it into the mold. We held our collective breaths. He looked at the key, and then at us. "We have a…match. The design of the handle fits the mold precisely." We all exhaled at the same time.

"Miss Duncan, let me check what information I have." He fumbled for a card from a manila envelope that came along with the mold. "Umm, our records indicate that the owner received this key in 1730...three years after the founding of the bank." He turned the envelope over and out came the modern safe deposit key.

"Is the name of the original owner on the card?"

Mr. Scott looked at the card again. "No, it isn't. But that's not unusual. Many of the original owners preferred anonymity and under the dictates of a peculiar agreement between the client and the bank, we were, and still are, duty bound to follow the owner's wishes. The key's handle serves as its only identifier. Perhaps the contents of the box will help you identify the owner."

No information was disappointing. Then again, I thought, how would the name serve me? The owner was long dead. I probably wouldn't even recognize the name.

"The bank is getting out of the safe deposit business. We are in the process of requiring living owners to empty theirs. That is not possible with these ancient boxes, so the bank must wait for the owners to present themselves. We are pleased you came in today."

Alec reached over and congratulated me with a hug.

Mr. Scott cleared his throat. "Let me be the first...the second...to congratulate you, Miss Duncan." The banker stood, straightened his jacket, fixed his bowtie for what must have been the tenth time, and reached over to shake my hand. "Do you want the contents of the box right now?"

"Oh, yes. Can I have it now...I mean right now?"

"Of course. We don't keep our clients waiting. These are your possessions. But you will have to come with me." Like a recording he repeated, "The key must remain in your sight at all times."

We went through another dimly lit hallway to a room with a thick door which had a circular handle shaped like a steering wheel. The wall of the vault were lined with row upon row of latched doors of different sizes, all numbered and keyed. Some were small, a few square inches, and others close to the floor were much larger. Mr. Scott bent down and inserted the safe deposit key into one of the lower doors. We held our breaths again until we heard the gratifying click and the entry creaked open.

Still gloved, Mr. Scott pulled out a dark wooden box like a medical examiner hauling out a corpse stored in a morgue. We followed him as he carried the box to an adjacent room and handed me the key. "I will now leave you to uncover the contents in private. Please, take all the time you wish. If you like, you may keep the box. The bank has no further use for it. You may also keep the key. It is worthless once we melt the mold."

With the same bravura as before, Mr. Scott removed his gloves. He straightened his suit, pushed his glasses up on his nose, and retrieved the same used

56

handkerchief to wipe the perspiration on his upper lip. "Is there anything else I can do for you before I go, Miss Duncan?"

Anxious to explore whatever was in the box, I assured him we were fine.

"Wonderful. Please let my assistant know when you have concluded your business today." Without a goodbye or a thank you for being a long-time customer of the Royal Bank, Mr. Scott turned to go. I couldn't wait to hear the door click. But just before he walked out, I glanced at the floor, and the last thing I saw were his double-knotted, polished black oxfords.

ELEVEN

Pas de Deux

1696

Learning French was useless. I was never going to marry Maurice St. Martin or leave Scotland. But it was part of the scheme, and my deceit was necessary.

Father sat at his desk poring over recent customer transactions. I sat nearby. My grammar book opened to the same page all morning, a list of monotony: conjugated verbs. Desperate for any diversion, I watched my foolish cat emerge from behind the privy screen. Each paw extended slowly cornering her prey, a dry leaf. Her stealthy advance was interrupted by the squeaky hinges of the library door. She scurried back to her hiding place colliding with the chamber pot. At the door stood Old Simon and Alain. After the Highlander was announced, the door closed, but not before the cat dashed between Simon's legs and disappeared.

Ten days ago, Father had predicted Alain's return. At times, it seemed he would never arrive. Now, he stood several feet away. A blossoming heat rose from my chest and radiated until every hair on my head tingled. Had Alain noticed? I prayed Father had not.

Alain nodded my way. His lips curved upward. I almost forgot to breathe. Then he turned his attention to my father who removed his spectacles and extended a hand as he hobbled around his desk.

"Mr. MacArthur. I trust you had an easy journey?"

"It was an uneventful trip despite the cold."

"Ah. Some of the coldest weather we've had in a long time," said Father. "1696 will be remembered as the year of no summer."

While the two exchanged pleasantries, I fidgeted from one foot to the other; the heels of my shoes thumped the stone floor tiles. I cleared my throat and stared at Father.

"Mr. MacArthur, you remember my daughter, Anna."

Alain came closer and took my hand. "Of course." While bending over to kiss my hand, his eyes never left mine. "How could I forget the fine dinner at your table, Mistress Anna? The lively conversation was most memorable. I trust you're well?"

"Thank you, sir. My father and I are pleased you've returned safely."

"And your brother Nathan, I trust he's well. I remember we were an interesting threesome." Alain offered a wink meant only for me.

To my great disappointment he let go of my hand and turned toward Father to accept a glass of wine. Both men toasted their future good health and friendship.

Like an opening act, the discussion between the men was cordial. They began with the promising recuperation of Alain's father, the latest about the trial of Thomas Aikenhead, and as they sipped wine, the attributes of a fine French claret. Then, they delved into the realm of business: declining crop production, the newly created Bank of Scotland, and trade with the colonies. They expressed their desire to join whenever their interests coincided. Like a *pas de deux,* they began together, and then danced alone. The real business negotiations wouldn't occur until the final act.

"Mr. MacArthur, I do not think you realize you have made my daughter Anna happy indeed."

At the mention of my name my head jerked up.

"And how could I be the cause of such bliss?" Alain's smile widened, and again, a hint of a wink animated the scar on his face.

A sense of dread washed over me. My throat dried up at the same time my hands became clammy. Nathan had warned me.

"My daughter is about to become a bride."

Alain's smile faded.

With one hand, my father touched his skull cap to ensure its proper place. "It is our tradition that we must do everything in our power to make the bride joyful. Your safe return has added to her happiness."

Alain's words stumbled, but he quickly regained control. "A bride...I...I didn't know." He hesitated before lifting his half-filled goblet. "Clan MacArthur wishes you and your family hearty felicitations." He gulped the rest of his wine and wiped the remnants from his lips with a handkerchief taken from his breast pocket. "Who is the lucky man?"

My father reached for the decanter to refill Alain's glass. "He is a business partner and an old friend. A Frenchman. This union has been hoped-for since Anna's birth."

Alain gazed in my direction, our eyes met, and then I lowered mine staring at my wringing hands. Did he understand this wedding was not what I wanted?

"Will Anna move to France?"

"Yes. A day or two after the marriage takes place. Whenever her husband decides." Father walked over, took my hands in his, and patted them affectionately. "My daughter is overjoyed at her prospects, working on her French every day, planning the wedding dinner." He put his finger under my chin and lifted my face to meet his. "She has made her father a happy man."

I responded in a choked voice, *"Oui, Père. Je apprend. Mon François n'est pas bon."*

Alain responded, *"Je vous comprends tout a fait."*

I hoped, by telling Alain my French wasn't improving, he would recognize my despair. His response, of understanding me completely, gave me hope.

Ignoring our *tete-a-tete,* my father shook his head. "Out of so much joy, I must endure the sorrow of losing my precious Anna."

"Mr. MacArthur, I trust your accommodations are to your liking?" I asked.

"Your father made an excellent choice. My accommodations at Malcolm's Inn are quite satisfactory."

"How long will you be in Edinburgh?"

"Until our meetings are concluded. I have some other clan business to finish as well. It should take at least a week."

"Mr. MacArthur," said Father, "If you find yourself in Edinburgh longer than expected, please come to the wedding. I received word today the groom arrives in one week. I'm sure Anna would be delighted to have you witness her happy day."

Alain mumbled his thanks, but said he hoped to be on his way back home before that.

The thought of Alain standing in the same room while we discussed my nuptials was unbearable. But I had the information I needed, and there were only a few days before Alain departed and the groom arrived.

"Sally, are you here?" Where had she gone? I looked in the kitchen, the pantry, and the dining hall. My search took me to the gardens which were surrounded by a wooden fence that needed repair. I found Sally harvesting the last of the vegetables. She shook off the clumps of soil from the roots before placing them in her basket and then brushed off her apron and adjusted her cap. When she saw me, a smile brightened her face.

I told her about Mr. MacArthur. "I'm going to ask him to help me. I only have a few days."

"How are ye goin' tae do that?"

"I'll tell Father I must go to market tomorrow. Uh, I'll say I need some new ribbons for my hair for my wedding…no, my wedding night."

"You can't go unescorted."

"That's why I need you."

The smile vanished. She looked over her shoulders to see if anyone was around.

"I can't go to market alone. You must come with me." I grabbed her hand and some of the carrots fell out of her basket. As she bent to get them, I whispered in her ear. "Please come with me tomorrow. I'll tell your mother I need you. She won't say no to me. Besides, everyone wants the bride to be joyful."

The following day Sally and I hurried past the area of The Mile called The Tron. This was where the official weighing stations were located to ensure fair business transactions. The most imposing feature was the Tron kirk. The gray stone church loomed over the Royal Mile.

Cold winds tossed our skirts. Wet cobblestones created dark hemlines and plastered leaves to the bottom of our shoes making the slick surface treacherous. We gathered our cloaks tightly around us and pulled on our hoods so only our eyes were visible.

The weather did not lesson the throngs of people. Rich and poor, tradesman or shopkeeper, they all mingled and lingered to catch the latest gossip. Others dawdled to watch lawbreakers get their due. The front of the kirk served as the town pillory. If the crowds were lucky, and they often were, they could watch tongues bored, ears nailed, or worse.

"Why are there so many people out today? Is there something about?"

"Sh! Come here." Sally grabbed my cloak and pulled me off to the side where we wouldn't be overheard. We nestled into a corner of a building with an overhang that provided some shelter. "These nosy-bodies are here tae learn about the fate o' Thomas Aikenhead."

"Alain and my father spoke about the man."

"Aye, he's hardly a man. Only eighteen years old."

"What did he do?"

Sally didn't answer. Instead, she stepped out from under the eaves, put her hands on her hips and admonished two young men closing in on us. "What're ye gawkin' at? Can't two women stand here without the likes o' you disruptin'our peace? Get along b'fore I call the magistrate. My friend here's his niece. Be away, o' you'll spend a night in Tollbooth."

Hearing about my supposed illustrious connections, the men tipped their hats and were off, probably in search of some young women without influence.

Sally returned to our shelter and lowered her voice to almost a whisper. As she continued her story, I understood why.

"Tom Aikenhead foolishly told some school friends, on a verra cold night, he'd wish't he was in hell tae warm hi'self. Then, he mock't the Resurrection, the Ole Testament, and claimed Jesus and his miracles were myths."

It was shocking that someone would make such a bold statement in public. Even I, who subscribed to none of it, knew to keep my mouth shut. Thomas Aikenhead was a fool.

"How did the Lord Advocate find out?"

"A former friend o' Thomas turned him in. Now the boy sits in prison. It's his first offense, but it won't make one bit o' difference. The Lord Advocate is out tae make an example o' him. The word is Thomas will soon be wearin' a rope round his neck b'fore he's nineteen."

The rain had ended, and the sun made a brief appearance which lightened my spirit after such a terrifying story. Malcolm's Inn was just a bit further down the street. I grabbed Sally's arm and put mine through hers. We said nothing more, but I was grateful for her company.

Alain MacArthur had no idea I was coming to see him. But it didn't matter. He wasn't there.

Sally and I started to retrace our steps, back towards the Tron, when I nearly collided with him outside of Cleriheugh's Tavern.

"Good day Anna. I never expected to see you here."

"I thought you were staying at Malcolm's." I eyed the tavern sign above my head. "Sally and I were...I needed ribbons."

Alain looked at my empty basket.

"Oh, I haven't purchased any yet. I...I mean...we thought we would come by and visit before you left Edinburgh."

Alain smiled at my preposterous excuse. Single women didn't enter an inn to seek out a male companion, unless it was to conduct business of another sort.

Sally turned her back. Perhaps, she wanted to give us whatever privacy there could be had on a crowded street.

"Alain, I don't have much time. I lied about the ribbons. I can't marry the Frenchman...please help me..." Either it was my incoherent speech or the flood welling up in my eyes, Alain grabbed my hand and pulled me aside.

At that moment, Sally spun around. Her eyes were round with fright and she grabbed my sleeve. "He's here. I just knew he would be. I could feel it."

"Who's here?" asked Alain.

"Nathan. He's on the other side o' the street. He's seen me, but I don't think he kens Anna's here."

"We have to go," I said. "I can't stay. I'm sorry Alain. I must talk to you, but my brother..."

"What about your brother?"

63

"If he sees me here with you, he'll lock me away until the wedding. I can't let that happen. Please, I'll try to come back another day."

Just then, Sally straightened her bodice and threw back her cloak. "Alain take Anna to Malcom's." When she saw me hesitate, her voice became urgent. "I'll take care o' your brother."

I knew what Sally meant. "No. This is my problem, not yours."

Sally turned, opened her cloak even wider. She walked away from us in the direction of my brother. The last thing I saw was her hand behind her back motioning us away.

Alain and I hurried down the street toward Malcolm's. Inside, he led me toward the rickety staircase, and I followed him to a room at the end of a dark hall. He fumbled for the latch, and we entered a small room he shared with two other men. Fortunately, they were elsewhere, but the smell of whisky and unwashed bedding lingered.

"What's going on?" Alain asked. "I sensed something was wrong in your father's library. You're shaking. Come closer to the fire." He hung up my damp cloak and drew a lavender scented handkerchief from inside his sleeve. I wiped my eyes and damp cheeks. A decanter of wine sat on a desk. He grabbed a goblet and filled it halfway.

Grateful, I accepted the wine and welcomed its warmth. I told Alain about my forced marriage, my vindictive brother, and what he had done to Sally.

"Now, she has offered herself to that brute."

"What can I do to help?"

"I must leave my home. Either with you, or…Maurice is coming in six days. I'll be wed a day or two later. Will you help me escape? If you can't, I'll find another way."

Tears cascaded down my cheeks. Before I had a chance to dab them away, Alain wiped each with his finger. His cool touch soothed my hot skin.

"Of course. I'll help you."

I breathed a sigh of relief and told him what I knew. "My father is never going to lend your clan the money. He made his decision the day you first requested his help."

My disclosure raised Alain's eyebrows.

"You must delay your final meeting when Father will give you his decision. That way, you'll have no excuse to leave Edinburgh early. I'll come back as soon as I can."

"How will you get away?"

"I don't know. Nathan watches me closely. I'm not sure he suspects anything, but after today, if he saw me, if Sally wasn't able…"

Speaking her name reminded me how much danger she was in. "I have to go. Please, don't leave Edinburgh without me."

Alain gripped my arms, his eyes inches from mine. "I'll wait, but if you can't come, even if it's the day of your wedding, I will get you. As long as I'm here, you'll not marry against your will."

I pushed Alain's handkerchief into my pocket, grabbed my damp cloak, and rushed down the stairs. My noisy shoes, clicking on the staircase, caught the attention of some of the men on the first floor. One of them chuckled. Without making eye contact, I skirted them and left.

Sally was leaning against the wall outside the door. Her cloak askew, there were beads of mist on the top of her hood.

"I'm sorry I took so long. What happened?"

"Did ye talk to Alain? Will he help ye?"

"Yes, but Sally…"

She said nothing more. As she adjusted her hood, water droplets ran off her shoulders. Sniffling, she pulled the cloak tightly around her. Before she enveloped herself completely, I saw her loosened laces and a new bite mark above her breast.

TWELVE
The Bridegroom

Old Simon took my cloak. "Your father has been asking for you. He's in his bedchamber."

"Is he not feeling well?" Father never stayed in his room this late in the day.

"Vertigo, Mistress, shortly after you left. Mrs. Gibbons is with him now, trying to coax your father with some ginger tea. He's a stubborn man."

"I'll see what I can do." I hesitated. "Is Nathan home?"

Simon glanced at me in his sideways manner, a scowl on his face. "Aye. You'll find him in the library, but he was adamant about not being disturbed."

"I'll see to Father then."

Simon's face softened. "Aye, Mistress."

I lifted my skirts and continued up the stairs.

Father burrowed under the waves of a dark coverlet. His position was known by his white sleeping cap. It served as a beacon.

Mrs. Gibbons stood over her patient holding a mug of tea. Her loud sigh indicated Father's refusal to take his medicine. "Now, ye know it's for the best. It'll take care o' the dizziness and everythin' else that ails ye."

"Not now, Mrs. Gibbons. I'll retch on your nice clean floors."

"Yere bein' stubborn as usual. Always shooin' the doctors away, thinkin' they ken nothin'. Everyone kens ginger tea works. My mother made it for me, and my grandmother made it for her, and—"

Like Old Simon, Mrs. Gibbons had worked for Father for many years. Only the two of them could talk to their employer this way. But we all knew that once my father's mind was decided, all attempts were futile. But it didn't stop her.

"Nothing but time will cure my lightheadedness—"

"Lightheadedness, ye call it. Let me tell ye—"

Mrs. Gibbons didn't realize I was in the room until I plucked the mug from her hands. "Thank you, Mrs. Gibbons. I'll tend to Father now."

Her mouth hung open, as if she didn't know who to argue with, me or Father. After the door shut behind her, Father told me what had happened. When he had awakened, he could barely raise his head without the room spinning out of control. This was not a new malady. He was familiar with the symptoms and the cure.

"If I add more honey, will you drink it? It can't hurt."

"Yes, but first get a couple of pillows. I cannot afford to lie here all day."

In less than an hour he was propped up to almost a sitting position. He was impatient to get on with his business and little did I know that involved me.

"I have something for you. On my desk. Bring the box to me."

The box looked more like a treasure chest. I placed it on the bed.

He surprised me when he said, "Open it."

The lid creaked. A soft blue fabric hid the contents. After a nod from my father. I pushed it aside and gasped. Two silver candlesticks sparkled.

"Father, they're lovely. But—"

"My wedding gift…to you." He squeezed his eyes shut as if that would stop the tears. Then, he placed a gnarled hand on my head, found his voice, and blessed me. "May you be like Sarah, Rebecca, Rachel, and Leah. May God bless and guard you. May God be gracious to you, show you kindness, and grant you peace."

There was silence between us until I felt the lump in my throat disappear. Just two days ago, I'd been furious with him. Now, I melted.

"It is your religious obligation to light Sabbath candles in your new home just as you have done from the time you became a woman. It has given me great joy to hear you say the prayer and watch the flames dance in your eyes."

"I will cherish them always." I kissed my father's ancient brow and thought about his words. Would the years of my marriage be happy ones? If not, I hoped there wouldn't be many. I prayed there would be none.

I left Father after he promised to finish the tea. Lost in thought, I didn't see Nathan.

"What were you and Sally doing in town? The ribbon vendor is in the opposite direction you were heading."

"Sally wanted to show me…um…to introduce me to a friend. How could I say no?"

"By saying 'No.' Or, was there another reason?"

"What are you accusing me of? I'm Sally's friend and—"

"Sally wasn't with you the entire time. If you went to see your Highlander, I can assure you that—"

"I would never…my reputation—"

His eyes shifted to the box under my arm. "What's in the box?"

"A wedding gift. From Father."

"Let me see." He tried to yank it out of my arms, but in the attempt, Alain's lavender-scented handkerchief came out of my sleeve and floated to the floor.

Nathan grabbed the handkerchief and brought it to his nose, sniffed and chortled. "Surely, you don't use lavender, a man's fragrance."

"I...I don't know where it came from. Perhaps it's yours?"

He put his face so close to mine I could smell his anger. "You and I know exactly who gave you this." He waved Alain's handkerchief and the scent grew stronger. "I won't tell Father. It will kill him. Besides, if word gets out about your careless behavior, your groom will no longer want you. And I don't want you either."

The next day when I arrived to the library, Father was at his desk and Nathan was sitting in my usual place. He looked up, closing *Le Cid* with his thumb to hold his place. "Ah, Sister. You look lovely this morning. I trust you're feeling better and not sniffling any longer."

What game was he playing?

"I found your handkerchief." He pulled the white cloth out of his sleeve and waved it in the air as if he were feigning surrender only to viciously attack the victim.

At that moment, I wished for a knight. Or better yet, his sword.

Without looking up, he said, "I'll return the handkerchief once it's laundered. It has a strange scent, sort of masculine, not something you would use." His eyes slowly looked over the edge of the book; a smirk grew. "I hope you don't mind?"

I answered haltingly. "No, I don't mind."

"Oh, how rude of me. I'm sitting in your chair reading your book. Lovely idea to improve your French. You want to impress Maurice." And then in a whisper, "So you can tell him to...uh... keep his hands to himself." He resumed with a louder voice. "This book, *Le Cid,* a mere fairy tale. No one ever comes to rescue the damsel in distress. Trust me."

I ignored Nathan and turned to Father. "Are you feeling well enough to be away from your bed?"

"The vertigo has worsened my hearing. I'm still dizzy every now and then, but the tea is helping. Mr. MacArthur will be here any moment. He is expecting my final decision."

Father was right. He never heard Nathan torture me with the handkerchief or the knock on the door. Old Simon entered followed by Alain.

69

"Mr. MacArthur, welcome. My son, Nathan, has decided to join us."

As they exchanged awkward pleasantries, the wary eyes of the two young men didn't leave each other until Nathan began to cough. "Something has caught in my throat." He retrieved Alain's handkerchief from his sleeve, covered his mouth.

Alain and I exchanged furtive glances while Nathan continued his charade.

"Anna, I forgot this is yours. Now I've soiled it. Forgive me." He sniffed the cloth and pretended an exaggerated face. "Ugh! The fragrance is nauseating. The smell must be eradicated."

"Don't trouble yourself, Brother. I have more."

Like a tortoise retreating to his shell, Nathan's antics ended when Father spoke. "Mr. MacArthur, I will get right to the point. I'm sorry but I cannot provide my financial backing. There are too many risky unknowns with the proposal. I don't believe this endeavor will be profitable for your clan, for me, or for Scotland. In fact, my experience tells me it will be a disaster. If your clan follows my advice, you will be thanking me instead of bankrupting yourselves."

Father sat back in his chair, put his hands in his lap, and closed his eyes.

"Father?" I asked.

"Unfortunately, closing my eyes doesn't make the room stop spinning." He returned to his client. "Mr. MacArthur, I hope you will convey my concerns and apologies to your father. He is a good friend. This is the first time I have refused him."

There was nothing more to be said. The finality of Father's decision was like an invitation for Alain to leave.

But Father had another surprise.

"Mr. MacArthur, would you care to join us for our evening meal?"

My heart hoped for yes, but it would have been uncomfortable to eat at the same table with a man who refused to do business with you.

"Sir, I appreciate your continued hospitality, but I mentioned I have clan business. The sooner I can conclude that, the sooner I can be on my way home." He stood and wished my father well, acknowledged my brother, and then turned to me.

Our eyes met for what I hoped wasn't the last time.

There was a knock at the door. Old Simon entered. "Sir, I have received news from the port. Mr. St. Martin's ship has docked in Leith. Shall I send a carriage?"

"Yes. As quickly as possible."

The reaction of each in the room was different. Nathan smirked with great satisfaction. Alain's hand tightened around the hilt of his sword. I willed myself not to cry. Father smiled for the first time in days. The vertigo was forgotten.

70

Father, Nathan, Old Simon, Mrs. Gibbons, and I waited in the entryway to greet our guest. Father's eyes turned to the door every time it squeaked or rattled. He looked forward to reuniting with his old friend, soon to be his son-in-law. Nathan paced back and forth, impatient to get the formalities over so he could be off to market with his friends. Old Simon fidgeted and Mrs. Gibbons wrung her hands. Standing next to each other, they traded worried glances. They had much to do to prepare for the wedding.

I was terrified. I had hoped Maurice's ship had floundered. Since that was no longer a possibility, I prayed his carriage toppled or his trip interrupted by greedy highwaymen who'd do more than rob a rich man of his possessions.

Distracted by footsteps behind me, I turned in time to see Dabby disappear behind the wide balustrades on the staircase. He had the best view and waited for the entertainment to begin.

Trying not to think of Maurice, the wedding and what would come after, I forced my mind to focus elsewhere. But I couldn't help thinking about yesterday's dreadful meeting in the library.

After Father's refusal to support the MacArthur clan and hearing of Maurice's imminent arrival, Alain thanked my father for his hospitality and turned his back to Nathan.

Then he looked at me and a faint smile accentuated his scarred cheek. He came closer, extending his hand. He held mine longer than was proper, but not as long as I wished. "Mistress Anna. The members of Clan MacArthur have a special prayer for a bride and groom. I hope you won't mind my saying it now." He placed his fisted hand over his heart. "May you be healthy all your days. May you be blessed with long life and peace. May you grow old with goodness, and with riches."

He said no more. The thud of the closing door precipitated a feeling of despair like I'd never known before.

We all heard the commotion. Our heads turned simultaneously toward the doorway. Old Simon straightened his woolen waistcoat and shuffled to the entrance. Mrs. Gibbons followed.

With a flurry of excitement, our guest and his manservant entered. Nathan had taunted me enough about my bridegroom that I knew exactly which man was Maurice. He was old, fat, and short and jabbered a lot of *oius, nons,* and *mercis* in an odd high-pitched voice. But that was not what was most noticeable. His mud-caked stockings and shoes were.

I was surprised at my embarrassment for Maurice. He had fallen into the Sludge Sea. After a few days of unexpected thaw, the muck had been waiting to swallow the first unsuspecting pedestrian who veered from the wooden walkway. His appearance was wretched, but in a way, comical. I forced myself not to turn when I heard Dabby's muffled titters floating down from the staircase.

Standing next to the Frenchman was Bernard, his servant. The middle-aged man was tall and gangly with stringy hair, a hooked nose, and squinty eyes. His long arms and legs sticking out of his ill-fitting jacket and breeks were also covered in mud.

Maurice slogged into the foyer. His shoes made a sucking sound with each step.

More chortles from the stairs.

Each of Maurice's footfalls became an effort, until his right shoe surrendered. His shoeless foot slipped on the muddied stone tiles, and he went down with a thunderous splat.

Howls erupted.

I covered my mouth, gulped down giggles, and hid my impoliteness.

Bernard dropped the heavy wooden trunk with a thud. He hurried over to help his employer regain his balance and dignity. Once up-righted, Bernard straightened his master's attire and swiped at the many offending stains. Father took a few steps forward to greet his friend but stopped short before his foot reached the worst of the mud-splattered floor.

"Maurice, *mon ami*, I am delighted you are here. My home is yours. I trust your journey went smoothly...at least...um...."

"Ah, Salomon, *merci, merci*. I am delighted to return to you. It's been too long since I've seen my dear friend and his delightful family. *Pardonne moi*, I'm afraid I've fouled your home."

At the mention of the stink and dirty floor, Mrs. Gibbons grunted when she saw her white apron speckled with mud. She put her hands on her hips, shook her head, and made no secret she disapproved of our guest.

I desperately searched for some redeeming qualities in Maurice just in case my plan failed. I was gratified to see the genuine warmth and friendship between two old friends. Maurice's smile and polite temperament were reassuring.

It did not last.

"Bernard, don't just stand there, *Imbècile*. Wipe yourself off. What must these fine people think of us?"

Maurice pasted a smile back on his face. "When I slipped in the courtyard, Bernard dropped everything to come to my rescue. Strong as an ox and dotes over me like a mama with her new-born babe. What would I do without him? *Oh chèr, oh chèr*. What an inauspicious way to begin."

Bernard wiped the mud from his jacket. A few minutes ago, I'd been feeling sorry for Maurice. Now that sentiment was transferred to Bernard. He should have been rewarded for rescuing his clumsy, rude employer.

72

Suddenly Maurice noticed me. Like a man of science who had just made a momentous discovery, he remembered why he had come to Edinburgh. With one foot still shoeless, he limped closer. His grin widened, exposing a mouth lined with yellowed teeth, and several gaps here and there. I took a few steps in retreat.

"Ah, *Mademoiselle*, what a way for a groom to meet *la mariée.*"

I must have looked puzzled.

"You don't know this word? Let me be your teacher and instruct you in your soon-to-be adopted tongue. It means bride. But I am mistaken, *ma chèr.* You are *une belle mariée.* A most beautiful bride. And I am the most fortunate of men."

Once again, I changed my opinion. Perhaps his outburst with Bernard was a result of a long arduous journey. He extended his hand to take mine to kiss. But when I noticed the spittle forming in the corners of his mouth, I kept my hands tightly clasped at my waist. Instead, I responded with a *"Merci, Monsieur St. Martin"* and a quick curtsey.

Maurice chuckled and turned to the others, "Well, well, well. Wait until I'm cleaned up, and then we can meet properly." He winked. "Eh, *ma Chèrie.* What do you say to that?"

My father interrupted the awkwardness. "Yes, by all means. Simon will show you to your room. Mrs. Gibbons will make ready a hot bath and see to your soiled clothes."

"You are too kind, *mon ami.* But we can dispense with the bath. I only need a change of clothes." Then he turned to me. "I don't want to delay getting to know this exquisite woman for one more minute."

"As you wish, Old Friend. We will talk more at the evening meal. Anna has selected a wonderful menu for your first evening with us. Mrs. Gibbons has been preparing all day."

Like a hungry dog, Maurice lifted his nose and sniffed the combination of roasted beef and mud. Then, he limped up the staircase followed closely by Bernard's sucking footsteps. They disappeared behind closed doors, leaving a trail of muck.

The dining table was set with as much splendor as Father could afford and Mrs. Gibbons could muster. It was covered with white linen embellished with embroidered thistles in each corner. The crystal goblets and decanters sparkled. Silver candelabras were placed on either side of a square silver bowl, filled with alternating layers of fresh pears and apples. While not a rarity in Scotland, the fruit was a grand display of wealth due to a famine that wreaked havoc on local produce.

We were seated in our usual places when we had visitors for dinner. But this time, instead of Alain, I faced Maurice.

I hoped dinner would provide another opportunity to uncover some favorable traits in my betrothed. Perhaps he would prove to be an ardent conversationalist with perfect manners. The evening started out promising with benign chitchat. Maurice described his friends, his home, and business in Lyon and was particularly attentive to those areas of his life which would intersect with mine. He portrayed Lyon as *une belle ville,* with a moderate temperature and pleasing vistas as opposed to cold and dreary Scotland.

We continued from one course to the next interrupted only by Maurice's delicate stomach. He made an effort to muffle his problem, but with each gastronomic episode, he pressed his hand to his stomach, just inside his velvet waistcoat. I pretended not to notice what I heard and smelled. But when Fiona offered the tray of sliced beef, she took one whiff and backed away quickly.

I didn't know which was worse, Maurice's stomach issues or when the episode passed. For that was when he spoke incessantly and impolitely.

"*Mademoiselle,* you're to be commended on such fine food. The beef is tender like a baby's bottom, but *ma chèr*, I'm afraid no one is equal to a French chef. It could use a bit more salt and less time on the spit. When you live in France my chef will instruct you on the proper methods of cooking meat."

The stewed apples weren't much to his liking either. "In my youth, I could tolerate rich desserts. You will soon realize I have a delicate stomach." He turned and covered his mouth while he clutched his stomach and belched. Strangely, he didn't seem embarrassed. But his critiques humiliated me.

When one episode of pain passed, Maurice raised his wine glass. "*L' chaim.* I am truly blessed to have such a bride. My friends will be insanely jealous." He turned his gaze in my direction. "I may have to entreat you, my dear, to cook for them as well." Then he turned back to the men at the table. "To my bride."

"Mr. St. Martin. I only suggested the menu. Mrs. Gibbons and Fiona should be the ones complimented." Fiona looked my way when she heard her name. She didn't look pleased.

"Please call me Maurice. After all, we are to be as one. No? But, *ma chèrie*...when we—"

"Thank you, Mr. St. Martin." I had no idea why I was thanking him, but it silenced him. Turning to Father, I changed the subject. "Have you heard the latest about the Thomas Aikenhead trial?"

Father's voice competed with Maurice's lip-smacking as he bit into a roll. "Yes. It's not going well. Mr. Aikenhead has recanted his blasphemy, but it seems the Lord Advocate is not convinced. A trial has been called for. There will probably be appeals, but I don't think it will alter the outcome."

"The trial is good for business," said Nathan. "It will bring customers and gossipmongers to the marketplace. I suspect the town leaders will want to satisfy the crowds with cheap entertainment."

Nathan stopped, and then looked my way. "Anna, you were at market the other day." He hesitated long enough for his words to sink in around the table. "Now, why were you there? Oh yes, to purchase some colorful ribbons for your wedding night? Or, was it to meet with someone at—"

Maurice stopped chewing.

I pushed back my chair. "I'm not feeling well. You'll forgive me, Father. Mr. St. Martin. I've a raging headache." I put my other hand to my temple and closed my eyes to exaggerate the pain.

I didn't wait for farewells or wishes for good health. I picked up my skirts and ran from the room. But not fast enough to hear Nathan say loudly. "The ribbons are to add to her charms. Anna wants to be the perfect wife...in every way."

"Anna! Wait! Come, come into the library. Please." Father shut the door. "Sit." He pulled a chair over for himself and then took my hands in his. They were blue veined, frail, and the skin appeared paper thin.

"You have a fool for a father. I have not seen Maurice in many years. We correspond often, but....now, when I see the two of you together, I am afraid this match is not what I thought." He sighed deeply; his weary eyes equaled his tired voice. "But, I have signed the wedding contract. If I renege, my name and yours will be sullied. You will never marry, and I will be ruined. I cannot have a questionable reputation when my business is all about trust." He lowered his head, nodded a few times, and gazed at the floor.

I was confused. He worried about the importance of trust with others, when I trusted him to make the right decision for me.

"My past defines me. I cannot deny the cry of my forefathers and the stories I have never told you."

Many times before, he disclosed how our family had lived in Spain until the Inquisition. They'd fled and made their way to Scotland. Those were the bookend facts. I thought that was all there was to the tale. I found out I was wrong.

Father settled back in his chair; his hands clasped. "My three times great-grandfather was well known throughout Iberia. He and his family, including five living children, dwelled in Valencia. They lived in a gracious home with many servants. As a financier, he had contacts all over Europe. When his services were needed, the high and mighty, including the ruling house of Spain, called on him. He was one of the most respected lenders throughout the peninsula. Then, it changed.

"The Inquisition in Spain did not target Jews at first. Everyone's faith was suspect. The government believed religious unity would result in political unity. But, greed guided the Inquisitors who earned a fee for confiscated property. The rest went into the government coffers.

"My grandfather chose baptism. He thought it would save him. You understand, our family did what they had to do to survive. But all was not as it seemed. Some families only pretended to be devout Catholics. They were crypto-Jews, practicing their faith in secret. In public, the hidden-Jews, removed their skull caps, memorized the catechism, and attended church regularly. They consumed forbidden foods. But in their homes, they continued to welcome the Sabbath. Crucifixes were covered and images of Jesus Christ were turned away. Prayers were whispered, candles were lit, and then quickly snuffed. For decades, the Jews of Spain did their best to keep their faith alive.

"Our family was reported to the church authorities in 1588. A jealous neighbor claimed she saw candles being lit on a Friday night. My great-grandparents were arrested, taken before the tribunal, and were found guilty. Tortured, my great-grandmother confessed. She was strangled before she was burned. My great-grandsire did not. He was burned alive.

"A few of my uncles were forced to be galley slaves. The rest of the family fled, but they wouldn't have made it without the help of Maurice's ancestors. His family hid mine in a wine cellar. When it was safe, they escaped to Portugal, but the Inquisition followed. Some went to Amsterdam, but my father went first to England, and then headed north.

"Maurice may not be dashing, or young, or a great soldier, but he comes from a good family. One I trust. He will make a good home for you and your children. You will want for nothing. What more can a father wish for his beloved daughter?"

"I understand Father, but—"

"There is one more thing." He leaned forward and took my hands again.

"It is our family's tradition to present betrothed daughters with Sabbath candlesticks. Honoring God's commandment was what your ancestors felt compelled to do, even when it carried a death sentence."

My intellect could see both sides of the argument. My family became martyrs because of who they were. Nevertheless, I couldn't help rationalizing that we were safe now. In Scotland. Why did I have to sacrifice myself?

"You might think the Inquisition is no more, but five years ago, thirty-seven *Conversos* were burned at the stake in Majorca. The Bonfire of the Jews, it was called. Three were burned alive."

A heavy silence smothered us. Father's head drooped to his chest. A candle flickered and died, leaving a long fragrant tendril that ascended to heaven. When I balanced my father's words with what was in my heart, I knew there was only one decision.

"Father?" I gently placed my hand on his arm. "I'm sorry I behaved like a child. I know the importance of keeping our traditions and the memories of those who sacrificed so much." I brought my father's hand to my lips. "I'll do as you wish. I will marry Maurice." Then with a heavy sigh, I continued my lies. "You gave your word, and I will honor it."

THIRTEEN

Boxes

2005

The lid of the wooden box was propped open, held in place by two rusty hinges. The triangular-shaped padlock, its shank askew, lay on the table next to the key.

I sat in stunned silence. I never believed the key would lead to anything but a grand hoax. An occupational hazard due to my training. There were many stories about archaeologists who believed they were onto some Tutankhamen-like discovery, only to be disappointed. I hadn't dared to allow myself to believe otherwise.

We leaned further to get a better view. A leather-bound book filled most of the space.

"Look at the design on the cover. It must have been beautiful when new."

Decorative stitching snaked along its outer edge. The same design was repeated in the center surrounding an embossed thistle with curled leaves. The edge of the cover had dried and separated in several places, but an additional layer of leather protected the book's spine. Two thin, brittle leather strips, used to secure the book, grew out of the spine. They were tied in a bow as if someone had cared enough before consigning the book away for the ages.

Alec tilted his head. "The owner must have been rich to commission a craftsman to create such a book. It might have been for someone dear or to commemorate a special occasion."

"Mr. Scott said the wealthy owned the original boxes? They were the only ones who had something valuable to protect. Or maybe something to hide."

As I reached for the book, Alec stopped me. "It looks fragile. Maybe we should ask Mr. Scott for gloves."

"They aren't necessary. In one of my classes at Penn, my professor had invited a guest speaker who was a bookbinder from one of the living museums like Williamsburg or Jamestown. He told us that books made three centuries ago are in better condition than those made three decades ago. The bookbinding process was slower and a work of art. But the leather needs to be handled. The oil from our fingers keeps it supple and prevents the leather from drying. Just like humans, the books need to be touched - to maintain a healthy appearance."

Alec took my hands and held them for a moment before bringing them to his lips. "Do you mean like this? Or like this?" He leaned over, closed his eyes, and lightly brushed my lips with his. They were soft, warm, and inviting.

"Um…exactly…like that."

Alec kissed me again. Harder and longer until we mutually parted. He continued to hold my hands and brought them to his lips again. We sat in silence preserving our brief interlude as long as possible until our eyes met. I wondered if mine were as ravenous. But it didn't matter. The staccato of someone's heels outside our room returned us to reality.

Alec sat up and cleared his throat, and I squirmed in my chair.

"We should…go on." I reached into the chest, the leather felt cool and smooth. I held my breath and lifted the book being careful of the leather straps that looked like they were about to break off. The book was lighter than I expected, slightly larger than the size of my hand. I brought it close to my nose. It had a strange musty odor.

I placed it on the table. It was time to move on to the next object.

At the bottom of the box were two small bundles. They seemed to be similar in size, and each was wrapped in faded brown cloth that appeared ready to disintegrate. To help decide which to uncover first, I did a silent eeny-meeny-miney-mo. When my fingers touched the winner, several entombed bugs tumbled out of the folds.

I was rewarded handsomely. I discovered a woman's ring. The gold band sparkled when the overhead lights made contact. A purple stone was fixed in the center of what looked like a cluster of tiny leaves. Again, I confronted the national flower of Scotland.

"Many Scottish wedding rings are flat bands designed with the thistle," said Alec. "But this one, because of the raised amethyst, was worn by someone wealthy."

"You know that by looking at it?"

"A woman who had washed clothes and scrubbed floors wouldn't wear a ring like this. Her husband's, or her father's wealth, would have paid for household help."

"Hmm, you have a point." I picked up the ring again and tried it on my third finger, left hand. It wouldn't go over the knuckle.

"Hanna, if this is a wedding ring, most Scots, back then, wore them on their right hand. The left was always considered the dirty or dishonest hand. Think about it. When you make a pledge or swear on the Bible, it's always with your right, the 'good' hand."

I placed it on the pinky of my right hand. It fit. I turned my hand, so the gold glistened against the clear purple stone and dared to think about the woman who once owned it. Had she loved the ring, and the person who gave it to her? "Of course, you're right about the wealth of the owner. I mean it all fits with the box and its contents."

In the next bundle, a disintegrating green ribbon held a four-inch lock of dark-brown hair.

"Seems like the owner tied everything in bows," I said. "I wonder if she ever gave any thought as to who would untie them. I'm sure she could never have imagined a possible descendant from the 21st century."

I carefully lifted the hair, mindful of the fragile ribbon, and placed the delicate curled tendril on the table. At the same time, I touched my hair. It felt the same. I pulled at the ancient curl, and it returned to its original shape. The years hadn't altered the curl.

"There's a lot of information to be found in hair…sex, age, race and maybe cause of death. Get this hair tested for DNA, and then test your own. That might tell you if this is truly your ancestor's."

He leaned over the table and peered into the box. "But before you get too involved with the intricacies of DNA testing, I think you better look inside again."

There, once hidden by the bundle containing the hair was another key.

"Holy crap! It looks like the same key. But it can't be. It has to be different…Mr. Scott said…."

I snatched the first key off the table, and gently picked up the new one. I held them side by side. "The banker was right." The leafy design was the same, and the thistle was present in each, but in the first, the thistle's bloom was still half enclosed by the sepal and in the second key, the flower was completely opened. It was subtle and ingenious. I wondered if each key had the thistle in various stages of bloom. It would have been something to see all twelve at once.

The excitement of finding the last key was taking some time to sink in. What could it all mean? What could possibly be in the twelfth box?

Just then my muted phone vibrated. I noticed three missed phone calls from my grandmother. And voice mail. I tapped the screen and waited for the message.

Gram's voice trembled. "Hanna, you need to come home right away. Something terrible has happened."

As the plane decreased speed and altitude for the final approach into Newark, I pushed up the shade. Rain splattered the window blurring the New York City skyline.

The usual announcements came over the intercom. *Turn off all electronic devices, return your seat to an upright position, and fasten your seatbelts.* The bald guy on my left never closed his laptop. The lady in front decided it was time to hit the bathroom. And the obnoxious teen on the other side of the aisle was still plugged into his phone, banging his two forefingers on the open tray table. I had nothing to turn off as I never connected. I had enough to think about. My mind replayed my frantic conversation with Grams.

When I came up to the first floor of the bank, I quickly clicked the call-back button on my phone. Noting the time difference, I knew it would be mid-day, nap time. But Gram's cryptic message required ignoring time zones.

The phone rang several times. Grams walked slowly, and if she had been asleep….

A familiar frail voice answered.

"Grams!" Silence. "Grams?" Continued silence. Then I heard a nose blowing. "It's me, Grams. I got your message."

"Oh, Hanna, dear. I was worried when you didn't call back right away. Is everything okay?"

That was typical. My grandmother was in trouble, but she worried about me. "Grams, I'm fine." It was easier to answer simply than to explain cell towers, satellite availability, and stone basements. "I got your message. What's wrong?"

"I didn't want to leave terrible news on your machine." It was funny that she called my phone a machine. Sometimes Gramps called a car a machine. I heard her take a deep breath. "I guess this is the best we can do. Oh Hanna, I'm so sorry to tell you, your grandfather is dead."

My brain failed to comprehend the shocking news. I considered asking her to repeat what she'd just said. Instead, my throat tightened. I mouthed "Holy Crap."

Looking around for somewhere to sit, the volunteer guide, Maggie, noticed my dilemma. She ran over and silently directed me to a chair behind an empty desk. I nodded my thanks.

"It was an accident, dear. He was crossing the street near the run-down shopping center. You know the one near us with that rude grocery store manager." She hesitated as if she'd forgotten the important part of her story. "Um, oh my, your grandfather walked right in front of a bus. His hearing hasn't been so good lately. He probably didn't hear it coming. Witnesses said he didn't look right or left." Her voice trailed off followed by a sob and another muffled nose blowing.

"Grams. I'm coming home. I'll be there as quick as I can."

"The driver said he hit his horn…twice. Do you think it could have been his hearing? You don't think — I don't even want to consider — but maybe he just wanted to end it all. He'd been complaining lately about getting older, that the golden years aren't so golden. I didn't take it seriously because a lot of our friends say that." The nose blowing resumed, followed by silence on both ends.

I couldn't believe Grams was suggesting suicide. I knew Gramps hadn't been feeling well lately, and he'd seemed withdrawn. I could hardly blame him. Many of his friends were dying off. But still....

"Hanna, we...I can't bury him until you're here."

"I need to get a flight." I tried my best to silence my sniffling. "I have to make arrangements, and then I'll be home. Okay?"

"Yes, darling. Don't worry about me."

I was 3,000 miles and five time zones away. Asking me not to worry was like asking me to forget to breathe.

"Mrs. Shasta, you know the neighbor across the street, Estelle, the widow with the short grey hair and the snappy dog? What a saint. She hasn't left my side since I got the call from the police."

No, I didn't know her. Short grey hair was hardly a distinctive identifier. Many of the widows who lived near Grams had dogs for companionship. They yapped at everything: the mail carrier, the lawn boy, the air.

After a difficult good-bye, I dialed Alistair for a next-day flight out of Edinburgh. My next stop was Mr. Scott to retain the safe deposit box for a while longer. I explained the situation, and surprisingly he was concerned and helpful. His assistant issued a new box and key to store the items back in the bank vault.

I stepped from the curb, hailed a cab, and before I knew it I was sitting on the plastic covered couch in my grandmother's living room. The ever-present and steadfast Mrs. Shasta joined us for a rehash of the gruesome details. I'm sure she'd heard the sequence of events before, but maybe she was waiting for one new detail Grams had forgotten.

"I had to identify the body. Didn't even look like my Harry." She wrung her hands and dropped them into her lap. "Hanna, if you could've seen your grandfather when he was young. So handsome, so dashing in his suit, bowtie, and bowler, smelling of aftershave and cigar smoke. He cut quite a figure. All the girls in the neighborhood were jealous he was my beau. I felt so proud to be walking next to him. And when he took my hand in his...." She smiled slightly, fell silent, and buried her face in age-spotted hands. I put my arm around Grams and motioned to Mrs. Shasta that she should go. I hoped my eyes said thank you.

The funeral took place the next day. Few showed up: a couple of elderly neighbors, my grandmother, and me. Mrs. Shasta took charge and showed everyone to their seat. Then she sat next to me, leaned over, patted my hand, and whispered, "Hanna dear, more would have come. But they're dead." She nodded her head and clicked her tongue a few times. I bit my cheek to keep from smiling.

Mrs. Shasta's comment reminded me of the harsh reality of aging. I also thought maybe she'd stockpiled funeral-appropriate comments that helped release the pressure. If that was the case, it worked.

After the funeral, the last to leave my grandmother's home was Estelle. She promised to look in later in the day and every day after that.

It was good to be alone with Grams. I knew we needed to talk about her future. We couldn't depend on the good graces of Mrs. Shasta forever. Besides, the woman probably needed help herself. She was seven years older than Grams

The next morning, I found Grams in the kitchen dressed in her flowered cobbler apron. The smell of breakfast filled the room.

"Grams, you didn't have to do this. I would have cooked for you."

She ignored my offer. "Sit down and eat. We have things to talk about. And there's not much time. My life needs to get back to normal as soon as possible. Then, maybe Estelle, will stay home. I've had enough fawning over and being felt sorry for. Her dog is driving me crazy."

I looked at my grandmother. The red-rimmed eyes were gone, replaced by clear, steely blue ones. She reached into her apron pocket and pulled out a piece of folded paper.

"I've decided what I'm going to do now that your grandfather's gone. I'm a single woman again, and I know what's best for me. I've made a list. I need your help, but I don't want to be a burden to you. So, the sooner we complete it, the quicker you're back in Scotland."

When I came into the kitchen, I'd fully expected to find Grams still in the midst of grief, unable to go on with her life. Who could blame her? But instead, I found the total opposite. With a half-eaten piece of buttered and jammed toast in my hand, I said, "Okay, Grams. Let's look at your list."

She didn't hand it to me, but held it in front of her, looked over her glasses, and read. "Number one. I'm moving."

I almost choked on the toast. I quickly wash it down with pulpy orange juice, which didn't help. Grams waited until I finished gagging, and then went on. Her voice, determined as ever.

"I've been trying to get your grandfather to sell this big old house. I wanted to move to one of those assisted-living places years ago. He wouldn't do it. Said it was for old people. Well, I'm old. It's time for me to go. Maybe if I move, Estelle will too. She can be a pest at times, but she has a good heart, and I wouldn't mind our being together. It would feel like I'm taking some of the old neighborhood with me. Besides, her house is too big for her, too."

My shock continued.

"Number two. I need your help to clear this place out. If there's anything you want, it's yours. The rest is going to the second-hand shop or the dumpster. I don't want too many reminders.

"Number three. There are some things I need to tell you. Because one never knows when they'll drop dead or get hit by a bus.

"Number four. After I am settled in my new place, and we've had our little talk, you are to resume your life." Her eyes watered; she breathed deeply and finished her list. "Come and visit when you can. But make it a priority to fall madly in love with some wonderful guy, get married sooner rather than later, and have lots of babies."

Number one was easy. Grams told me the community she wanted to live in, and she'd already placed a call to the director. We visited the facility, picked out her room, and put down a deposit.

Number two didn't take as long as I'd thought. After I took some picture albums and the jewelry my grandmother wanted me to have, I called Sam, The Junkman. Sam was a colorful fellow, more flamboyant than his grey jumpsuit with the name of his business plastered in large black letters on his back. He told me he had been in the business for many years and had cleaned out at least a thousand homes.

"You wouldn't believe the things I find hidden in furniture," Sam declared. "Old people, especially those raised during The Depression, never trusted the banks. They'd stash their money, and when dementia hit, they'd forget where the cash was hidden." As he carted away my grandfather's chifforobe, I wondered if anything valuable was squirreled away.

The "For Sale" sign didn't stay up long. Just as quickly a "Sold" sign appeared on Mrs. Shasta's front lawn, too. Both women remained neighbors at the Paradise Gardens Assisted Living Center and Senior Care Facility.

A week later, safely tucked away in her one-bedroom apartment, I sat with Grams; her wrinkled hands in mine, trying to memorize every detail. It could be our last time together.

"Hanna, I have something to give you. I didn't throw everything in the dump, and this is a cherished family heirloom."

She reached for an old wooden box sitting on her dresser. "Go on. You can open it. It's always been yours. I just needed the right time to give it to you."

Removing the lid, I heard a whoosh, and I thought I caught a whiff of my grandmother's old kitchen. Inside was a blue velvet bag. When I loosened the drawstring, I found one silver candlestick.

"Grams, this is the candlestick you always put out on Friday nights when Dad and I came for dinner. Why are you giving it to me? It was always mine? I don't understand."

I took the candlestick and held it up. I'd seen it many times in my life, but now I really examined it. It was heavy, and definitely not the cheap silver plate sold in stores today. It had been polished recently, and the stem reflected the light on the end table. I turned it over and fingered the engraved letters and funny symbols on the base.

"Hanna, it was given to me by my grandmother, and she got it from her mother. It has been handed down in our family for many years. Centuries, maybe. I don't know when this tradition began or who started it. All I can tell you is what my grandmother told me. I was expected to light a candle on Friday evenings, and someday hand it down to a daughter or granddaughter. Always to a female relative."

"Did Dad know about this? That someday I would get this candlestick?"

"Yes, your father knew. He left it to me to tell you." She stopped. We were both frozen momentarily by the memory of my father. "There's more."

I continued to hold on to the candlestick, cradling it in my arms. It wasn't lost on me that lately I'd been uncovering old family heirlooms stored in boxes.

"I have no idea why the candlestick was to be used only on Friday evenings. I guess over the years, the family considered it a nice little tradition, sort of like getting together after a week of school and work. I don't know why we had a moment of silence after lighting the candle. That was a mystery as well; but I think it's nice to stop talking once in a while.

"But there's one thing I never understood. I told you about my grandmother Hannie, the one who thought there was Scottish blood in our veins. One time, when I was a little girl, we were at her house for our Friday night dinner. She was wearing a beautiful crucifix. I loved that necklace. It was shiny and large. I would often play with it when I sat on her lap. One Friday night, as she was getting ready to light the candle, my grandfather reminded her to take the necklace off. And she did so. No questions asked. Hmm…I always wondered what happened to that crucifix, but when she passed on, no one ever found it. I would have liked to have had it, as a reminder. I loved that old woman, and now I'm…."

I put the candlestick back in the box and replaced the lid. "Grams, I will always cherish this gift, and I promise to give it to my daughter or granddaughter someday."

Grams nodded. Her nodding was usually a sign that she wanted to take a nap.

"Maybe I should go now. You seem sleepy, and there's mahjong at four. "

"Hanna, your dad had no idea. Your father never knew about the key…the one that took you to Scotland."

My eyes must have been the size of saucers. So she knew all along. When I came to visit her and Gramps, and I was trying my hardest to get information out of her. She knew all along.

"I put the key in your father's safe deposit box shortly after he died. Like the silver candlestick, it has been handed down in our family. It's another part of your inheritance. I know nothing more about it."

Questions exploded in my mind. Why hadn't she just handed the key to me? Why was it kept a secret from my father?

She patted my hands. "Now I'm all settled here. I have Estelle by my side. I will be fine. The food here is not so great, the staff doesn't come so quick when you need them, and I'm not crazy about mahjong. But I'll survive. You need to return to Scotland, and this young man you've been telling me about, and find out what's the deal with the key."

FOURTEEN
Without You
1696

The next three days were cold and bleak. Darkness descended by mid-afternoon. With sixteen hours until dawn, Edinburgh settled in for a long icy night. The courtyard of Cheery Close froze once again making access easier. The clip-clop of horse's hooves brought me to my bedchamber window. A shadowy figure on horseback held the reins of another. The horses' warm breath became puffs of white clouds against the black courtyard. What errand could be important enough for one to be out in a night like this?

I chose to remain in my bedchamber since the conversation with my father. This kept Maurice away and Nathan from suspecting my every move. Going to market to find Alain was out of the question. I feared he had returned home. My scheme shattered.

I begged my family's forgiveness. I feigned a debilitating headache, bouts of insomnia, and lightheadedness. From the gossip I had often overheard from Fiona and Mrs. Gibbons, I knew women used these excuses to avoid embarrassing situations or the unwanted attentions of a husband or suitor. Now, I did the same. My only contact with the world was Sally. She brought me food, the latest news, and earlier this afternoon, my wedding dress.

The click of her heels on the back stairs announced her return from the seamstress. Breathless, Sally plopped onto the bed, along with a large brown wool sack by her side. She pushed back her hood and opened her cloak. Despite the frigid temperature, tiny beads of sweat settled on her upper lip. The wispy curls that usually hung down her neck were plastered over her ears and cheeks.

Sally put one hand on her chest; the other gesticulated wildly in the air. "I've somethin'… somethin' important tae tell ye. I talked tae Mr. MacArthur."

"What?"

"I went tae Malcolm's on my way tae the seamstress. The crowds were thick because o' the trial. They kept me hidden in case your brother followed me."

"Did you see Nathan?" I was afraid of the answer.

"No. I dinna think so. But I needed tae hurry so my mother wouldna wonder why I was takin' so long."

"What happened?"

"When I got tae Malcolm's, Mr. MacArthur...he was comin' out the door. We bumped into each other. He apologized over and over again bein' he's such a gentleman."

I wanted to shake Sally to get the words out of her faster. "What happened then?"

"He said he was leavin'. Leavin' Edinburgh."

"Oh, no! When?"

"Anna. Stop interruptin'. Let me tell ye what happened. He's leavin', but he said, not without ye."

"What?"

"He kens the weddin's tomorrow. He's comin' tae get ye."

I sat there unbelieving. At this late hour, I might be saved.

"Are you hearin' me? Ye wilna have tae marry the old fart."

A million questions crossed my mind. Alain couldn't just walk in the front door and tell Simon: *Please get Mistress Anna, I'm kidnapping her.* Or could he? What was to stop a warrior, strong, determined, and studded with weapons? Who would stand in his way? Father? Nathan? Maurice? Furthermore, I was a willing victim.

"Did he say when or where I should meet him?"

"Mr. MacArthur dinna say, all I can tell ye is tae be ready. That's what he said. Tell Mistress Anna tae be ready."

"Yes. I'll sleep in my clothes and have a satchel packed. Can you get me some food? Just tell your mother I'm feeling slightly better, and I'm hungry." I grabbed Sally's hands and brought them to my chest. "How can I ever repay you? You have saved my life. Again."

Then I realized, and maybe Sally did too, this could be our final night under the same roof. We hugged until our arms ached, until Sally pulled back.

"While ye prepare, I'll get what bannocks are left and whatever else I can find."

It didn't take long to get ready. I wore my blue woolen dress over several layers of heavy petticoats. My thick grey stockings would help guard against the cold. Next, I gathered a pair of gloves, another petticoat and stockings, and a shawl. I wrapped one candlestick in the petticoat and the other in the shawl and put it all in my satchel. All I needed was my cape and food.

While I waited for Sally's return, I was curious about the dress. Once I'd dreaded it. Now I longed to see what I would never wear.

I removed the wrapper revealing a golden silk dress. The flared skirt was decorated with thistle blossoms made from flattened silver wire coiled around silk thread. The metal captured the light from the candles so that the dress sparkled. I ran my finger over the intertwining leaves with their imagined, sharp, prickly edges. It was a shame that such beautiful workmanship would never be seen. But I happily returned it to its shroud, and entombed it in my wardrobe,

Sally arrived with bannocks, dried meat, and apples wrapped in a cloth. From under her arm, she produced a small jug of ale. "This will keep ye warm and fill your belly when the food runs out."

Before she turned to go, our eyes locked one last time.

"Godspeed, Anna."

My throat tightened; my voice was lost. I mouthed the words, "And you, my friend."

Sally slipped noiselessly from my room. I blew out the candles and climbed into bed, fully clothed with my shoes still on. And waited.

I was awakened by the sound of footsteps on the ancient floorboards. My first thought was the cat, until I felt her soft warm body nestled next to mine. I turned. The noise ceased in response. But the feeling someone was in the room intensified.

Then I saw a tiny flame. A candle held by someone in white confirmed my suspicion. Was it Alain?

I was about to call out when suddenly, the candle was extinguished, the room flooded darkly. A hand pressed firmly over my mouth. I squirmed and kicked the covers, fighting for air. My attacker doubled his efforts.

"Now *ma chèrie*, don't fight so. It only hurts the first time. You'll thank me later."

Maurice, dressed in his nightshirt and cap and nothing else, removed his hand from my mouth, replacing it with his bruising lips, and searching tongue. His sour breath, suffocating. He hoisted his heavy body on top, pinning me. While one hand was free to snag my hair and hold me back, the other groped. The cat awakened, hissed and growled. Maurice struck with the back of his hand. She cowered and ran for cover.

Was this the same Maurice? The frail older man? The one in my bed was surprisingly powerful, like someone much younger.

Maurice looked down hoping for a glimpse of what he came for. "What's this? You sleep in your clothes and shoes? That will hardly do."

I attempted to kick him, anywhere that would hurt, but my skirt impeded any defense. I tried to scream, but barely emitted a squeak when his hand returned to my

91

mouth. He tightened his grip, and I quickly learned the harder I squirmed, the more it excited him. His thin nightshirt concealed nothing.

"We will be married shortly. Why should a few hours matter?" He chuckled viciously.

I bit his hand and gagged at the metallic taste of his blood. Gasping for air, I sputtered, "Get off me."

"Don't toy with me, Anna. I know you've been begging for this."

"You thought I wanted you? I detest you."

My words enraged him. He stood up quickly. He leaned forward and made ready his fist. I covered my head with my unrestrained arm.

But it wasn't necessary.

Another hand appeared. My ears heard the sickening crunch of bones. Maurice whimpered and fell to the floor cradling his injury. Alain grabbed Maurice's uninjured wrist which frightened the man enough to make him grovel for clemency. Alain tied Maurice's wrist to the bedpost. "I wonder what your host will say when he finds you at his daughter's bed?"

Alain turned to me. "You will not marry a man you do not want." Glancing at Maurice, "Nor one who treats a woman so cowardly.

I grabbed my cloak and satchel, Alain and I rushed toward the back stairs. The steps led straight into the kitchen which was dark and empty. The only light came from the smoldering wood ash in the great fireplace.

In a low voice, Alain said, "My horse is outside. He can carry both of us until we meet up with my tacksman. Filib is waiting for us with another horse."

Already my satchel was heavy and cumbersome. I shifted it in my arms.

"Must you bring that?"

"Yes, I'm afraid so."

He opened the back door. The squeaky hinges were thunderous. We stepped into the cold night air, our warm breath giving away our location.

An angry voice split the stillness. Alain and I turned quickly. Nathan. Not in his night clothes, but in breeks and a waistcoat like he was expecting us.

"Let my sister go. Just walk out of the close, be on your way, and I'll forget this ever happened."

Alain chuckled. "And what will you do after I'm gone? Tie Anna up? Torture her? Force her to marry her rapist?"

"Whatever I do, is none of your business." Nathan brandished the metal blade of his dirk which reflected the light from the newly risen moon.

Alain motioned for me to stand behind him, while never taking his eyes off Nathan. Silently, Alain unsheathed his dirk. Both men, equal in height, breadth, and weaponry, glared at each other.

Nathan made the first move. Lunging at his opponent's chest, Alain backed away so Nathan's momentum threw him off balance. As he went down, he grabbed

Alain's arm and they both slid across the icy courtyard. The two men toppled over one another, each taking turns, having the advantage, with the dirks inches away from their necks. Then, before Nathan forced the dirk out of Alain's hand he slashed at his chest. The knife cut through Alain's jacket and shirt like butter, piercing the skin. Blood blossomed on the white cloth. Alain's bare hands stopped another deadly swipe.

"Nathan, stop. I'll stay. I'll do what you want."

He was deaf to my pleas.

"Please don't harm him." It appeared my brother wouldn't stop until Alain was dead.

"Nathan, put down your knife." The stern voice came from Father. He stood outside the kitchen door. The light from the moon created an aura around him.

"Tell him to stop. I'll marry Maurice. Please." But Nathan fought like a wild beast. A baser instinct had taken over his soul.

I fumbled with the satchel, and once opened, I groped for cold metal. Tightening my fingers around the candlestick's stem, I revealed my weapon. It was hard and lethal. I ran over and hit Nathan on the back of his head. The force caused me to drop the candlestick and it skidded across the ice. Nathan stopped and toppled beside Alain. Blood poured from the gash in his head mixing with that of his enemy.

Alain pulled away and slowly righted himself. He clutched his chest, grabbed his knife, and returned it to its home. I placed the lighter satchel over my shoulder and put my arm around his chest as we limped through the close.

Nathan screamed. "Whore. I'll follow you to the ends of the earth."

We quickened our pace as much as Alain could withstand.

"Stop, Nathan! Enough!" Then Father lowered his voice to one of defeat, but acceptance. "Let her go. Let Anna go."

Like Lot's wife, I turned to take one last look at my home and my father. The moon reflected off the candlestick now in his hand. He raised it for a moment, as if waving farewell. I turned away and cradled the one remaining candlestick still safely concealed in my satchel.

Part Two

I squirmed in the uncomfortable plastic chair staring at the linoleum floor. The buzzing fluorescent lights were no match for the woman moaning nearby. The lingering smell of unwashed bodies and antiseptic cleaner was typical for an emergency room. It was the middle of the night.

A pair of shiny black shoes entered my field of vision. Through layers of polish, they reflected the lights.

"I'm Detective McMurty. Are you a friend of the victim?"

My eyes followed the knife-edged crease on the front of his black pants which led to a white shirt, loosened black tie, and a jowly face. The detective flipped through his notepad with a moistened finger and stopped when he found the page he was looking for.

"Miss Jessica Fishman. Correct?" His voice and demeanor implied authority.

"No. I'm Hanna Duncan. I'm Miss Fishman's friend." My voice sounded tired because I was. It had been a long day.

He glared over half-rimmed glasses sitting perilously close to the edge of his bulbous nose. "Tell me what happened to you and your friend this evening."

I knew he meant last evening, yesterday. "I told the police officer. I...I...forgot his name." I strained to remember although I was sure he told me. "The arresting officer wrote everything. Maybe his name was O'Hearn. Or O'Hara."

McMurty tapped his pen noisily against his notepad. Like a volcano about to erupt, the officer blew out the side of his mouth. I suspect his impatience was mounting when I side-stepped his question. It didn't help matters when I listed stereotypical Irish surnames for the mystery officer.

"Yeah, but I'd like to hear it for myself. I don't rely on secondhand information. If you don't mind, Miss Duncan?" It wasn't a request, but a demand. "Start from the beginning. And just the facts." He sounded like Detective Sergeant Joe Friday, the character in my dad's favorite rerun, "Dragnet." Maybe McMurty watched it too.

I stood, forcing the large man to take a step back. "Detective, I have to see Jess first. I need to know if she's okay. It's my fault she's in the hospital."

McMurty blinked first. A man in a white lab coat caught the detective's attention. "Hey, Doc? Can this young lady see your patient?" He nodded in my direction. "This is her friend."

The young doctor turned and smiled. "Yeah, sure. Not too long, just for a few minutes."

Grateful to get away from McMurty, I followed the lab coat down the hall. Jess was entombed in a white sterile room with her arm in a sling. Most people look terrible in the hospital. There's something about the bright lights that makes them look pale and weak. But that wasn't the case with Jess. Her dark hair splayed on the white pillow like a luxurious halo highlighting her flawless complexion. She looked beautiful and fragile like Sleeping Beauty waiting for a kiss from her prince.

She acknowledged my presence. A half-smile appeared, and her eyes brightened. They followed the doctor who was checking her chart and her vitals on the noisy lighted machines. It was at that moment that I realized her renewed interest might have been more for the handsome doctor than for me. And I wondered how often he checked her chart.

"Looking good, Miss Fishman. Just call the nurse if you need anything. And, Miss Duncan, not too long now. While the patient looks wonderful, she doesn't realize how much this has taken out of her."

I nodded. Once the door closed behind him, Jess blurted out, "Hanna, are you okay?"

"I should be asking you that. You're the one who got hurt playing Super Woman."

She smiled contentedly, and then grimaced when she leaned back. "I dislocated my shoulder when I tried to prevent our petty thief from taking off with your candlestick. I'm surprised we both didn't end up with out-of-whack shoulders."

"I guess he didn't care for the load of mace you sprayed in his face. Do you always carry that stuff with you?"

"Pepper spray," Jess corrected. "It's more effective. Mace doesn't work if the guy is drunk or high. And yes, I always carry it. You never know when some pervert doesn't understand the meaning of 'no'." She stopped, patting her arm gently. "Yeah, I guess he didn't care for a direct shot." She smiled and then chuckled. "He squealed like a pig going to slaughter. Kept screaming he was blind and couldn't breathe. Served him right."

"Well, there's a Detective McMurty now on the case, and he's asking questions. I just had to know you were okay first."

"I'm fine. Did you call my mother? The handsome doctor says I'll be discharged later today, and I'll need someone to help me. This," she nodded toward her encased arm, "needs to remain immobile for a few days. How will I ever take a shower, wash my hair, or even pull on my jeans?" Her eyes grew wider as she remembered the usefulness of two arms. "How will I go to the bathroom?"

"Your mother is coming as soon as she can, but it'll take her a day or two. I told her I would stay with you until then."

"Hanna, you have a flight to Scotland today. Or is it tomorrow? I lost track of time."

"It's today, but I canceled it. I'm not leaving you until she comes."

"What about Alec?"

"I called him. He understands. He's concerned about you."

"Me? We don't even know each other."

"He credits you with our finding each other. If you hadn't encouraged me to go to Scotland...."

Alec and I talked constantly since I'd come back to the States. The time difference didn't matter. My favorite conversations were those that occurred in the middle of the night. I would lay in bed, covered, cocoon-like, my phone giving off a moonlike glow. It was just the two of us, talking about anything and everything.

Jess's voice brought me back. "Oh, funny. But I'll take the credit. I'm a matchmaker." She hesitated for a moment. "Can you do something for me?"

"Sure. You want some water, another pillow? How about a bed pan?"

"What? No seriously. Go find Dr. Good-Looking for me? Ask him to come back to my room. Tell him I have some questions about my injury or, better yet, if that doesn't work, tell him I'm having heart palpitations. Just make up a good excuse."

"He said to call for the nurse."

"No way. A nurse isn't in my future. The handsome doctor is."

In a small, suffocating room, a perspiring McMurty sat uncomfortably close. "Detective, it all happened so fast."

"Let's start at the beginning. Tell me what you and your girlfriend were doing before the attack."

His line of questioning caused me to reflexively finger the torn sleeve on my left arm and rub my shoulder. It was throbbing again, a result of the thief attempting to grab my satchel.

"I had just come back to Philly after visiting my grandmother in Cherry Hill. I wanted to see Jess before I left town, so we had made arrangements to meet for dinner in Chinatown. Then I asked her to come with me to Jeweler's Row."

"Which restaurant did you go to?"

What did that have to do with anything? But I answered politely because I needed to find the good cop in him. "A new place. Wait. I still have the fortune cookie in my pocket." I pulled out the clear cellophane wrapper that incased a folded cookie. "It's from...Tommy Chou's Peking Duck."

McMurty fumbled with his notebook as if looking for the next question. Then, he let his guard down. "Tommy's has great Szechuan orange roughy. The soup with the fish heads isn't bad either."

Good cop found.

"My wife is partial to the sizzling short ribs and pork rice." He smacked his lips and I wondered if he was imagining the aroma of ginger, sesame oil, and coriander. He paused and cleared his throat.

"So, where were we? After dinner, then what?"

Bad cop returned.

"Jess and I headed to Jeweler's Row. My grandmother had given me a silver candlestick, and there were some marks on the bottom of the base. I wanted to find someone who'd know what they meant. Jeweler's Row seemed like the obvious place to get answers. Don't you think, Detective?"

McMurty squirmed. He was a big man and the chair looked uncomfortable. "Which shop?"

"AAA Silver and Gold."

"How long were you there?"

"About thirty minutes, near closing time. I noticed other shops were turning out their lights, so I figured we should leave. I could've stayed longer because the shopkeeper gave me lots of interesting information."

"Then what happened?"

"We started walking south toward my apartment at Third and Delancey. About a block from the jeweler's, this guy jumps out of nowhere, and demands our cash and my satchel."

"Satchel?"

"That's where I kept the candlestick. I wasn't going to let him have it. It's an heirloom. Been in the family for decades."

"Is that your satchel, with the bloodstain?"

He pointed to my cloth bag. It was the kind you wear either as a backpack or hanging from your shoulder. I wore it over my arm so the candlestick wouldn't hit my back with each step.

"I swung at the thief and hit him before Jess pepper-sprayed him."

"No, Miss Duncan. That's not how your friend tells it. You hit him after Miss Fishman sprayed him."

"It all happened so fast. What does it matter if I hit him before or after?"

"Well, if he dies, it matters." He stopped and let that thought linger between us. "Maybe you didn't need to hit him after he went down. Could be manslaughter you're facing."

Was he trying to put the blame on me? Whatever happened to self-defense?

100

"Lucky for you, the guy's just banged up. You really walloped him. Broke his nose. That's where all the blood came from."

"Detective, let's not forget Jess and I are the victims here. We didn't go after this guy. He came for us. Besides, I'd no idea what the effects of pepper-spray or mace would be." I couldn't tell if I got through to him, and then I realized an awful scenario. Did McMurty think we were a bunch of hookers, and we'd just robbed our John instead of providing paid-for services?

"Listen, the thief you're painting as Mother Teresa hurt Jess. I defended her with my satchel. It worked, and I would do it all over again. So, if you want to read me my rights, go ahead. This was self-defense, and you know it. If you aren't going to arrest me, then I'm going back to Jess, and we're going home."

I walked from the room, slamming the door so hard it echoed down the hall. I nearly bumped into Jess's doctor as he came out of her room.

"Your friend will be discharged shortly." He stared at me. "Are you okay?"

I made up a story about hospital smells making me nauseous. Without saying goodbye, I entered Jess's room to find her pulling out her clothes from a hospital-provided plastic bag with her one good arm. She was in great spirits.

"Can you help me?"

Still angry with McMurty, I snapped. "Why didn't you ask your doctor friend to help you?"

Jess took a step back, startled by my response. I apologized and told her about McMurty's accusations.

"Don't worry Hanna. Sam, I mean, Dr. Goldblatt, said the robber admitted what he did, and it corroborates our story. I don't know why McMurty gave you a hard time. Maybe, he's just practicing for his next case."

"Sam? Jess, did you ask him for a date?"

"Sort of. If you call meeting for a cup of coffee a date." She gave me a sly smile. "More importantly, we exchanged numbers."

"So, you caught him?"

"Hook, line and sinker." She smiled. "Now, don't look at me like that, you with your Scottish hunk tied around your finger. Were you expecting me to let the good doctor get away? If I walked out of this hospital, who knows if I'd ever see him again. I'm not leaving anything to Fate or a fortune cookie."

With the mention of food, my stomach rumbled. I hadn't eaten anything since last night. I retrieved Tommy Chou's cookie from my pocket. Tearing open the cellophane wrapper, I gently pulled the thin slip of paper still curled around the broken cookie. I unfurled it, and on one side it read the Chinese word for 'Bon Voyage' - *yāt louh seuhn fūng*. Turning the paper over, I squinted.

A great discovery awaits you.

SIXTEEN
Hallmarks

Exiting the arrival's gate, I shielded my eyes against the sun's glare and searched for Alec. I spotted him leaning against a wall, one leg bent for balance, checking his phone; his sunglasses perched on top of his head. I shouted and waved; his face lit up with a broadening smile. Meeting halfway, I melted into his opened leather jacket. Strong arms wrapped around me, pressing me to his chest. His scruffy beard tickled as our lips met. How good it felt to be back.

He whispered into my ear. "I missed you, Lass. I didn't realize how much, until you were gone. Now, I'm not letting you out of my sight." He pulled back and put his finger under my chin. "Do you hear me, Mistress Hanna?"

"Yes," I answered, a little overwhelmed but pleased with his effusiveness. "I missed you too." I readjusted the satchel strap on my shoulder and put on my sunglasses. "I accept your offer." I playfully grabbed his arm. "The part about never letting me out of your sight. Promise?"

"Aye." He smiled and kissed the tip of my nose. "How was your flight?"

"It was long. No dashing Highlander to make the flight interesting."

"Are you sure about that?" He looked at me with his characteristic raised eyebrow.

"Positive."

He grabbed my carry-on with one hand and held my hand in the other. We walked to his car without saying another word although I was bursting with news.

We stopped for breakfast at a little out-of-the-way place with the unusual name, "Squat and Gobble." With the breakfast crowd mostly gone, we had no trouble finding a vinyl-covered table flanked by two rickety chairs.

My stomach growled by the time the traditional Scottish breakfast of tatties, eggs, meat, and two scones arrived. I offered Alec the thinly sliced ham the Scots called bacon and the extra scone. He laughed when I pronounced it with a long 'o.'

"Ach, a scone, you mean. It rhymes with gone."

In my best Eliza Doolittle impression, I asked, "Would you like my 'scaaawn'?"

He snorted and snatched it from my plate, slathering it with butter and strawberry jam.

Now that my brief lesson in Scottish dialect ended, our conversation moved to my experience with Detective McMurty, Jess, and Dr. Sam.

"The guy who attacked you and Jess, did he confess?"

"Yes, there won't be a trial. The judge will sentence him, and since he's a repeat offender, he'll get some additional jail time. Jess is relieved. She was afraid he might stalk her."

"Maybe her doctor-friend will make her feel safe."

"Doctor friend? She's way beyond that by now. Jess's probably ordered a subscription to *Bride* magazine and checking out the latest styles in engagement rings."

"Your friend works quickly."

"Let's just say she doesn't let an opportunity slip through her fingers." I smiled and lowered my eyes. I hoped Alec didn't think my mentioning rings and brides suggested how I thought about our relationship. I preferred going slow and savoring every minute of getting to know Alec.

I stuffed the last bit of scone in my mouth and washed it down with coffee that had too much sugar and cream. "Do you want to see my grandmother's candlestick?" I reached for the satchel, untied the flap, pulled out a rectangular box, and placed it on the table, "Open it."

When Alec tugged at the lid, I heard the familiar whoosh. He loosened the blue velvet bag and pulled it out, I heard him catch his breath. "This is a beauty. No wonder you fought for it." He held the seven-inch stem, turning it around and over.

"The stem is designed to look like a Corinthian column with an elaborate capital holding a fixed sconce." I pointed to the top of the candlestick. "This edging around the sconce is called fluting. But what makes it special is the unweighted eight-sided base with two more tiers of fluting in the same swirled design."

"You sound like an expert on candlesticks."

"I took notes."

"I don't know much about the art of silver-making, but the workmanship looks superb."

I smiled as if the compliment was for something I had created. "That's what the jeweler said. This could only have been created by a master craftsman, and it had to be commissioned by someone with great wealth."

Alec handed the candlestick back. Its familiar mass fit snugly into my palm as if it belonged there.

"I know what I'm about to say may sound bizarre, but every time I hold it, I have a sense of connection, a familiarity. It's as if it knows me, like we're old

104

friends...or something. I can't explain it but even my telling you this makes me feel weird." I shook my head. "Just forget what I said. It's crazy."

"No, it's not surprising you feel that way. It's a family heirloom. From what you've told me, it's been handed down for decades. Perhaps, you have a heightened sense of sentimentality toward it, knowing where it came from."

"I think it's more likely my brain's playing tricks." I chuckled. "I don't know...but, what I do know is when the attacker tried to take it, I would have killed him for it. Or died in the attempt."

I placed the candlestick on the table, and my fingers kissed the metal. "I've never felt such a strong connection to an object before."

"Did you get any more information from the jeweler?"

"Yes. That's the most interesting part. This candlestick was made in Edinburgh around the end of the 17th century — 1696 to be exact. There's a lot of information from the hallmarks. They're stamped on the base."

Alec turned the candlestick over. There were three small designs, and each was in excellent condition. The first was a lower-case q, the second was a capital P inside the shape of a heart, and the third had three castle turrets.

"Each has their own meaning. The letter q is for the year 1696. The P indicates this was made by Master Craftsman James Penman and the castle represents Edinburgh."

Alec looked puzzled. "The castle signifying Edinburgh and the mark for the craftsman makes sense, but I don't get the letter q for 1696."

"The q was the assayer's mark. Each letter of the alphabet designated a different year, different assayer. It was important that the precious metal be exactly what it was purported. To be considered sterling silver, it had to contain 92.5% silver and the remaining metals were usually copper or something else. If at any time the proportion of silver wasn't correct, the authorities could easily identify the assayer, and he was punished. The weight of the precious metal had to be trusted. A pound of silver had to be accurate."

Alec took another sip. "That's where we get the term for the sterling pound, or the British or Scottish pound."

"Yes. But this is what I don't understand, and I didn't think to ask the jeweler. There are twenty-six letters in the alphabet. That would only cover 26 years of assayers' marks. So —"

"They probably used different typographic styles — or fonts. If you look at writing styles, whether it was chiseled in stone by Roman masons or in the Gutenberg Bible, they are vastly different. Fonts varied from century to century and from one country to another. So, even by 1696, there were many choices. Every twenty-six years they could change to a different font"

I returned my attention to the candlestick. "The jeweler said that except for some minor blemishes, which is expected in something this old, this one is in remarkably good condition. If it were meant to be part of a pair, and I had the mate, which of course I don't, it would be worth almost $20,000."

"Did your grandmother ever hint about another?"

"No. In fact, she never talked about the candlestick until I was ready to leave. The jeweler estimated that for a single candlestick, I could expect $6,000."

"That's still impressive. Do you think your grandmother knew the value?"

"I doubt it. But I suspect, even if she did, she would never have sold it. And neither will I."

Alec reached over and put his mug-warmed hand on mine. "I haven't said this to you yet, but I'm so glad you weren't hurt in the attack. When you called that morning, and told me what happened, I felt powerless. My first thought was to take the next flight to the States. I was angry with myself because I wasn't there to...." He stopped. I knew the words he wanted to say.

A comforting silence engulfed us. We continued to hold on to each other until the waitress offered to refresh our coffees.

When we returned to St. Andrew Square the skies darkened, the wind whipped the hair around my face, and huge raindrops splattered on the sidewalk. It was true Scottish weather. The sudden chill reminded me to pull my cowl tighter around my neck. Until now, my fleece gloves had been tucked away in my jacket pocket. We ran the last few yards, entered the bank, and shook off the rain to the dismay of the two security guards.

We found Mr. Scott engaged with an older couple, so we sat in the waiting area, and I looked up at the oculus. No bird perched there today. Too windy and cold. The banker raised his head and silently nodded acknowledgement. He directed a series of additional unspoken cues toward Maggie who came over right away.

While straightening her purple glasses, Maggie asked, "May I help you? She stared at Alec, then at me. An all-knowing smile broadened on her almost-purple lips. "Oh, I remember both of you." Then she patted my hands. "I'm sorry to hear about your loss. Are you okay, dear?"

Except for the purple glasses, Maggie reminded me a little of Mrs. Shasta. Perhaps, it was the gray hair, her calling me "dear," and her hand patting.

"Yes, I'm fine. Thank you. I'd like to open my safe deposit box. May I speak to Mr. Scott?"

"Of course. But as you can see, he's currently with customers. I can call his assistant to help you." She reached for a phone at the same time she pointed towards the staircase. "Head downstairs, and Miss Buchanan will meet you."

On our way, I whispered to Alec, "So that's the assistant's name. I'd forgotten it. I'm terrible with names."

"If you lived in Glasgow you would have had no trouble remembering. Buchanan Street is a major thoroughfare, named for a rich merchant who made a fortune in the tobacco trade with the American colonies."

"Do you think she's a descendant?"

"Probably not. Otherwise, she'd own the bank."

I chuckled as we started down the staircase. After Miss Buchanan brought us the box, I explained to her that we needed to see Mr. Scott, and we were willing to wait until he was finished with his customers. Sooner than I thought, he arrived.

"Miss Duncan and Mr. Grant. What can I do for you today? Are you ready to remove the items from your box?"

"Not just yet. We found this in the box." With two fingers I held up the most recent ancient key.

"Yes, I know you have the key."

"No, this is a different one. Another one. This is the twelfth key. It's different. The thistle bud is fully open."

Of all the things I could have said, this had to be the last he expected. His eyes were glued to the key. His hand trembled as he reached for the back of a chair for support. After a moment he straightened his bowtie and pulled down on his jacket.

"I found it in the box we opened with the first key a couple of weeks ago. If you remember I had to leave quickly, but now I've taken care of…issues at home, and I'd like to open the twelfth box."

"Yes…of course. I am sorry for your loss…we must go through the same procedure. Even though it's the last key it still has to fit the wax mold."

I wouldn't have expected less from Mr. Scott. I appreciated his attention to detail. In fact, my opinion of the banker changed since our last visit. He was helpful, polite, and his elitist demeanor, although still evident, was a throw-back to an earlier era.

It didn't take long for Alec and me to find ourselves sitting alone in the same room near the vault. Like a treasure chest, the twelfth box sat in front of us, demanding its contents uncovered.

With a raised eyebrow Alec said, "I know what you won't find in this box."

"And what would that be?"

"Another key."

I laughed and, with it, some of the suspense was diffused. "Okay, let's see what other surprises my ancestors left me. Wouldn't it be nice if it included a letter that simply read:

Dear Hanna,

107

Thanks for coming to Scotland and opening the boxes we left just for you. Here's what all of this means. You are now the heiress to a castle, a title, and a chest full of gold.

Love and kisses,
Your ancient relatives

I lifted the lid. Inside was something wrapped in a brown woolen cloth. It looked like the same cloth we found in the first box. Where the fabric was folded or creased its fibers fell apart in my hand.

I took a deep breath and carefully pulled on the shroud. I couldn't believe my eyes.

"Holy Crap."

Although the partially covered object wasn't the key to a castle or clues to a great fortune, it was one I never expected. I had exhumed the exact duplicate of the candlestick given to me by my grandmother.

SEVENTEEN
The Hanging
1697

January 8 was no colder or windier than the day before or the one after. It was winter, after all. But it would be remembered as an unfortunate day for Thomas Aikenhead. On a road somewhere between Edinburgh and Leith, the accused was hanged for his crime of blasphemy. His head lolled grotesquely, his ashen face swelled, and sightless eyes gaped at those who came to witness his execution.

The crowd swirling in front of the scaffold knew a good hanging when they saw one and praised the efficiency of the hangman. Moments before, the executioner placed the rope with a simple slip knot on one side of the neck behind the ear. The jerk from the drop broke the boy's neck, making the end quick and painless. If not done correctly, he would've died of strangulation or decapitation. Today, the master executioner earned his coin.

It was six days since Alain and I had left Cheery Close. We'd never intended to witness the execution but were caught up in a wave of enthusiastic and curious onlookers. Alain thought it best not to go against the tide. If we drew notice to ourselves, some might question our religious convictions. Or they may think us sympathetic to the victim which was just as dangerous.

I was no stranger to the saga of Thomas Aikenhead. For two months, the arrest, the trial, and the appeal process, to William III himself, had been a topic of conversation in my father's home. I thought it a strange coincidence that Thomas was leaving this world at the same time I was leaving mine.

Alain and I found ourselves tightly wedged in the middle of a seething crowd. The reek of unwashed bodies and foulness beneath our feet sat heavily in the back of my throat. Our senses were on alert for petty thievery. I kept one hand on my pocket and the other secured in Alain's arm as the mob shouted their approval for the macabre event.

"Serves him right. He got what's comin'," screamed an old man standing much too close.

"Should've happened sooner, if ye ask me," said his companion who shook his broad fist in agreement.

"Did you see? He wanted to repent. Repent, my arse," said a toothless woman straightening her cap which failed to conceal her stringy gray hair. She cleared her throat. Her spittle dripped down the back of the man in front of her.

"Aye. He'll burn for his wickedness," said another who wrapped a tattered shawl around her swollen belly.

Pulling my cloak tighter, I gathered the hood over my head, not only to block the biting wind that played with my hair and stung my ears, but to shield me from the awfulness of humanity.

The taunts from the crowd did not drown out the ominous caws of circling crows. My eyes followed them until they'd found a perch on a nearby tree where they waited patiently for a grisly morsel.

When the accused stopped dangling, he was unceremoniously cut down. Near the scaffold waited a farm wagon which served as a hearse. A crude wooden box, part of which hung over the edge, sat in the wagon bed. When the body was thrown into the coffin, it toppled, spilling the contents into the mud. Another man helped the gravedigger stuff the body back inside, tossed the box on the wagon, and nailed the lid shut.

The gravedigger scurried up behind the horses, and without warning, the wagon lurched forward disappearing down the road. He would be paid once his task was competed.

The mob began to disperse and return to their tedious lives. I tightened my grip on Alain's arm. Together we forged a path through the remnants of the crowd. We hurried to leave this place and put all the events of the last few days where it belonged, in the past. Ready to resume our journey to the safety of the Highlands, we were mindful of the possibility of being followed.

Shortly after leaving Edinburgh, I learned the details of my escape which included a bit of luck named Filib.

Filib was Alain's cousin, although the two men shared no resemblance. While many Highlanders are tall, a result of Viking blood comingling with the Scots, Filib was short. But he made up for it in girth and surprising strength. His barrel chest and muscular arms and legs were solid like tree trunks. His raisin-black eyes, set deep, twinkled on the rare occasion when he forced a smile. Most Scots are great storytellers, but Filib rarely spoke, and when he did, he used as few words as possible. He was honest and a true friend, never hesitating when Alain asked for his help. I liked him almost immediately.

Alain and Filib had been together for as long as they could remember. They had shared a nursery and a wet nurse when Filib's mother died in childbirth. Their fathers were inseparable as well. Although the elder MacArthur was the laird and Filib's father, his tacksman, title didn't get in the way. Both were from clan MacArthur and each a landowner.

Alain was fortunate that the wound he'd received from Nathan wasn't serious. Nevertheless, the exertion and the loss of blood had taken its toll. With my support, we'd been able to walk quickly out of the close, distancing ourselves from Nathan's screams. Nearing The Mile, Alain had stumbled. We'd stopped momentarily so he could readjust his arm around my shoulder. Out of nowhere, Filib and the horses had come to rescue us. Silently, the Little Scot lifted and pushed Alain onto his black Percheron. Filib hauled himself up behind, and holding onto his weakened friend, the two rode as one. I had followed on the little Garron.

In the middle of the night we made our way to Leith Walk, a pedestrian walkway that connected Edinburgh with Leith. The ground was gravel-covered, which under normal circumstances would crackle with every step and announce our location to whoever chose to follow. Tonight, it didn't matter. Towering oaks, on either side of the road, offered no leafy canopy to shield the roadbed from a persistent snowfall which muffled the horses' hooves and erased our trail. Like statues, our heads and shoulders turned white. Every so often, we remembered we were alive and dusted ourselves off.

Our destination was somewhere between the city and the port of Leith. After we had gone a safe distance, Filib pulled on the reins. The horses snorted. The mist from their hot breath mingled with ours.

"We'll stop here. The animals must rest." Filib nodded toward Alain. "He must sleep."

Alain slid off the horse. He wrapped his plaid under and around to keep out the cold and then sat against a large oak. I quickly rummaged through my satchel and offered stale bannocks and ale. Alain shook his head and closed his eyes.

Filib had left to water the horses and hobbled them. He returned with an arm full of wood and quickly made a fire. Although a grove of gorse and alder was between us and the road, I wondered if the fire served as a beacon for Nathan's hounds. The flames dancing off Filib's broadsword lessened my concern.

Filib chewed hungrily on the bannocks, gulped down the ale, and headed to the stream. I put on a second pair of gray woolen stockings, hoping the extra layer would keep out the damp chill.

Alain began to shiver. I touched his hand and brushed the back of my fingers on his cheek, his skin felt hot. Fever. I wrapped his plaid and my cloak around both of us and held him tightly to share my warmth and calm the tremors.

When Filib returned he huddled on the other side of the fire. His weaponry, sword and dirk, were unsheathed and placed by his side. He would not sleep. The little Scot was on watch.

111

I lay awake wondering what Nathan would do next. He wouldn't forget, and although he was in no great rush to get his sister back, I knew pride would force him to seek revenge. For a few pieces of silver, a tracker could be hired; someone who would be swift, experienced, and ruthless.

Feeling a bit guilty that these two men had endured so much on my behalf, I tried to keep Filib company on his watch. I started by offering a meek, "Thank you." He grunted in return and continued to scan the darkness.

After a gulf of silence, he said, "I came because Alain asked it of me. Nothing more."

At the mention of Alain's name, I looked down at his face. His eyes were shut, brow furrowed. The only sound was a soft gurgling snore. He was sleeping like the dead. Any talk between Filib and I was not going to awaken him.

"Tell me what happened...when you and Alain came tonight."

"The back door was unlatched."

What Filib said made no sense. "The kitchen door wasn't bolted? Mrs. Gibbons always locked it before retiring. And Simon checked it as well."

"The kitchen maid...she let him in."

"Fiona?" It couldn't be. Fiona wasn't brave enough to do such a thing. And even if she wanted to, she always slept too soundly. Most mornings Mrs. Gibbons had to shake her roughly. I was puzzled because Filib described the accomplice as a kitchen maid.

"Don't ken one from the other."

Then I realized. Sally. It had to be. Sally must have shown Alain the back stairs. That's how Maurice hadn't seen him. Now it all made sense. She knew Alain was coming.

"How did you know to return just when we needed you? When Alain was wounded."

Filib didn't answer right away. He shifted to find a more comfortable position. His plaid slipped, unnoticed, off his shoulder. While I was fending off the cold, Filib was enjoying it.

"A lad came."

"A boy? Hm. Was he small, thin...runny nose?"

"Aye. A weasel."

"Dabby," I whispered. Sally would have had to bribe him to go out on a cold winter night. Perhaps the promise of a generous helping of apple tarts and fresh hot rolls in the morning. But Dabby had been the right choice. He would've been quicker than Sally. And sneakier. Nathan would never have seen him.

"Dabby might squeal. He's only quiet when his mouth is full."

"I paid him well."

"I'm grateful, Filib."

He replied with a grunt, rolled over, and pulled his plaid tightly around his shoulders. He was finished talking for the night. The fire crackled, catapulting cinders into the darkness.

Filib was a strange little man but certainly not complicated. My father spoke about men like him. They lived by a code of honor; allegiance gave them purpose. Gratitude was not expected nor required. Men like Filib were a rare breed.

The crackling snap of a twig. A thump of wet snow falling from a limb. Something crunching. I lifted my head slightly, opened one eye and peered over the edge of my hood. The fire glowed dully. A few coals came to life briefly. Did the fire stir from a light wind or from the movement of an animal nearby?

I sat up. The snow beneath was gone, melted from the heat of our bodies.

"It's nothing," Filib said. He shook off the snow and grabbed his dirk. "I'm going to take a piss."

A short time later I awoke to soft whinnying and clinking of a harness. I watched Filib prepare the horses for the day's journey. The soft gray of daybreak was outlined by the black bare limbs of the oaks. The ground had been repainted with fresh snowfall. I brushed the snow away and pulled on Alain's plaid to reveal his face. The rush of cold air ended his hibernation. His eyes opened. They were clear, not fever glazed. The skin felt cooler.

"Good morning."

Alain silent acknowledgement was a weak smile. Grabbing the remaining bannocks from my satchel, I tore a small piece. "Here, you must eat."

Filib came over with a flask of whisky and a cup of water.

I lifted my skirt and began tearing one of my petticoats into long strips. Together, we wrapped Alain's chest. While the oozing had stopped, it was too soon for a proper scab to have formed. The wrap would help keep dirt off the wound and provide a layer of protection from the irritation caused by his blood-dried shirt.

While I finished with my patient, Filib gathered his weapons and sheathed them again,

"Did you hear footsteps last night?" I asked.

"Nay. You were dreaming."

"It wasn't a dream. The sound awakened me, and you told me it was nothing."

"Aye. That it was."

Filib turned away before I could see the look on his face. His tone was abrupt, and he dismissed my concerns too quickly. He returned to readying the horses, a chore I thought he had already completed.

With the increasing daylight I noticed many footprints in and around our camp. Some were older, partially filled in with snow, others fresh. I wish I had taken notice last night. Perhaps it was my imagination, or Filib had to relieve himself many times during the night.

When all was ready, he helped hoist Alain onto the horse. Again, the two men rode together while I followed. The snow stopped; the damp chill that came with it disappeared. Now, it was just cold that found its way through my layers of clothes to my bones.

We continued toward Leith until we reached the home of Goodman Patrick Pettcarne. A squeaky sign swung over the entrance. The name "Pettcarne" was inscribed above a crude picture of a pillow and a tankard. The sign made it simple for those who couldn't read. For a price, the Goodman opened his home to travelers who needed a place for the night. There was no guarantee of a bedchamber or even a bed, and when the inn was full, travelers were offered either a straw mattress in the corner of the kitchen or in the barn loft above the horse stalls. For warmth, the kitchen was preferred.

Pettcarne was a former worker for the MacArthur's. Out of deference for Alain and Filib, they got to sleep in the owner's bed with the down mattress. Mistress Pettcarne was none too happy about losing the one comfort in her life and the privacy a latched door afforded. Sleeping on the floor didn't help her disposition or her back especially after bending over a double-oven pot all day long. She took revenge by publicly scolding her husband, swatting her children like flies, and if a customer requested a second mug of ale, she made them wait until she was good and ready.

I shared the upstairs loft with the Pettcarne's three small daughters. The girls slept on the same stained mattress, the youngest in the middle. The loft smelled of stale urine and a shite-filled nappie. I choose to sleep on the floor; my rolled-up cloak served as a pillow. On our first morning, I awakened to find I was covered with Alain's plaid.

We stayed at the Pettcarne lodging house for five days until Alain had recovered the strength to travel. By then, Filib had returned from a bit of scouting. He had made inquiries to see if anyone was searching for me. He'd doubled back on our trail to ensure we hadn't been followed. I wondered if Filib shared my trepidation.

When we announced our imminent departure, Mistress Pettcarne's mood brightened. Her scolding ceased, and her back pain was suddenly cured. She hummed an out-of-tune ditty while she plopped an extra helping of thick porridge into each of our wooden bowls, and then filled a basket with bannocks freshly blackened by being too near the coals. Her unfamiliar generosity knew no bounds. Her good nature continued as she advised us where to get food for our journey. I wondered why she didn't offer any of her own for sale.

"Just down the road a wee bit. You'll see the carts. The apple farmer has the biggest, juiciest apples. He'll treat ye fairly. Your nose will lead ye to the pastry vendor. Ye may get a good bargain taeday. Especially the apples. Not many will be buyin'. Most'll be gawkin'."

"And why is that?" I asked, genuinely curious.

"'Tis the hangin' o course. Thomas Aikenhead. The fool's goin' tae get what he deserves."

I looked over at Alain. "We'd best be going. Thank you for your hospitality and your bed."

Glancing at the ladder to the loft, her three daughters sat on a different step. I felt sorry for them. This was all they would ever know.

While Filib made sure the horses were watered, saddled and packed, Alain and I set out in search of food. We walked in the direction of Mistress Pettcarns's pointed finger and found many going in the same direction. Men and women walked alongside us toward the center of the market area. I would never have guessed they were heading to a hanging. From their good-natured banter, punctuated by giggles and laughter, I'd have expected a festival.

As we approached the looming scaffold, I noticed a tall man standing where the ground was slightly elevated. He was dressed in black except for the large white feather stuck to the side of his hat. His beard was matted and dirty and a fresh scar spanned the bridge of his nose to his ear just under a cloudy eye. He walked toward me and tried to block my way. He must not have seen Alain, because when confronted, the man in black acted like he had accidentally bumped into me. He tipped his feathered hat and hissed, "Forgive me."

Alain must have sensed my alarm. He gave the intruder a threatening glance, pulled me to his other side, and put his hand on the hilt of his sword. The man turned and disappeared in the mob.

The crowd was like a tidal wave thrusting us forward toward the scaffold. We had no choice but to watch the spectacle. Thomas Aikenhead stumbled up the steps to the hangman's noose. As was the custom, he made a brief statement. His wavering voice was barely heard over the jeers of the audience. At first, he cursed his accuser, but then forgave him and all who were involved with the trial.

I scanned over the heads of the people squeezed around us. The scaffold, splintered, and weathered, mocked the living trees around it. Beneath one crooked limb stood the man in black, his hat tipped to one side covering his milky eye. Rather than watching the hanging, his head was turned in the direction of a woman by his side. They were deep in conversation.

Without warning, Thomas Aikenhead dropped. His neck snapped. The crowd gasped and then cheered. But my attention was still on the man under the tree. For a moment he saw me. Quickly, I turned away but couldn't help taking a second glance. He placed something into the woman's hand. She smiled as she inspected whatever it was. He refocused his attention on the execution while biting into an apple.

Mistress Pettcarne put her hand into her pocket, pulled her shawl closer around her shoulders, and turned to go.

EIGHTEEN
Skirts

Alain and I hurried to meet up with Filib and be on our way.

"Did you see Mistress Pettcarne by the apple cart?" I asked. "She was with the man who bumped into me. She was so particular about sending us to the apple vendor."

"Bumped? He looked like he had more sinister ideas in mind. Are you sure it was the same person?"

"I could never forget him, the scar, the white feather." I looked back, expecting the man with the milky eye to be right behind me.

Alain stopped and turned to me. "I believe you, Lass. My father always said to never question a woman's intuition. Your sex can interpret signs and warnings like no man. Let's see if we can purchase food from Goodman Pettcarne and get away from this place."

On the first part of our journey we backtracked on Leith Walk. As we neared Edinburgh the number of pedestrians increased. Mothers held onto their youngest children and scolded the older ones to behave. Men struggled with bulging packs filled with goods for sale, and ragged beggars pleaded with outstretched palms. Soon we veered off the main road and headed northwest along the Firth of Forth toward Stirling and then the Highlands. Our destination was Alain's home near Loch Lomond. Filib estimated it would take three to four days as long as we didn't encounter much snowfall.

Now that Alain had regained his strength, we rode together on the larger horse. Swaying with the rhythm of the slow plodding hooves the air was filled with scent of the pines, fresh snow and horse. We rode mostly in silence. As our distance from Leith increased, I felt childish for raising the alarm about the man in black and Mistress Pettcarne. The innkeeper's wife probably knew many people, and she was privy to gossip and the comings and goings of locals and strangers.

The road widened a bit so we could ride side by side. Alain spoke loud enough so that Filib could hear over the horses. "Anna, you're not to go anywhere without Filib or me. When we settle down for the night, one of us will always be on watch and you'll sleep between us. It could all be a coincidence, or that man could be Nathan's hired thug. We should know shortly. If he's going to try anything, he will probably do so before we get too far into the Highlands. The odds are in his favor while it's just two of us to he has to overcome."

That was true, but there was another consideration. If attacked, either Filib or Alain would feel compelled to defend me. That lessened their advantage. I thought about mentioning it, but I didn't want to remind them of my weakness.

Filib responded with his usual, "Mumph," and allowed his horse to fall behind us once again.

Unlike most winter days in Scotland, this one was a rare sunny one. The dappled sunshine played in and out of the thin grove of trees. At times, the shade became as dark as night, but the next moment my eyes were blinded by the glare reflected off the snow.

The only sound that punctuated the silence was the crunch of the horses' hooves and the occasional explosion of feathers from a covey of grouse. At other stretches, our voices echoed through the stillness. Long bouts of travel became opportunities for Alain and me to get to know each other.

"Let me introduce you to Caesar." Alain leaned forward and patted the thick muscular neck of the enormous black stallion. His broad face and large eyes were characteristic of a Percheron. "His French grandsires carried an armored knight onto the battlefield. Now, he spends his days pulling heavy loads or mating with the local mares. He thinks he's the laird of the stable. If another stallion arrives on the farm, they quickly learn who is king."

"Have you told him what happened to his namesake? The Ides of March are but two months away. Maybe Filib's horse is plotting right now."

Alain chuckled. "That would surprise Caesar. Phineas is a gelding, a gentle old soul."

Caesar picked up his gait and then abruptly stopped dead in his tracks. I thought hearing his name he was trying to show off. But when he backed up a few steps, tossed his head up and down, snorted loudly, and tried to turn, Alain quickly dismounted. He stood in front of Caesar and grabbed the reins.

"Whoa, Caesar. Whoa, Laddie."

Filib got off his horse, and I slid down from Caesar.

"Must be an animal nearby or something that didn't smell right," Alain said.

Once Caesar calmed down, we continued our journey, but now we walked. At midday we stopped. The horses were watered and hobbled and chomped on grass shoots poking through the snow.

Then it was our turn to eat. Filib unwrapped two scrawny roasted hens and a few blackened bannocks from the Pettcarne's hearth. He handed my portion to me, and then walked off toward some trees and disappeared.

"Is he hunting for something?"

"In a way." Alain scoffed. "Let's hope he's downwind."

When Filib returned he took a swig of whisky from his flask. He wiped his sleeve across his mouth and passed the drink to me. "It'll keep you warm. Fill your belly."

The whisky burned, but the warmth percolated to the top of my head. Unfortunately, the drink created another problem. Before I could think of a way to resolve it, Alain said, "I'll check on the horses. I'll be back shortly."

The men had taken care of their needs, and the very thought made my mine greater. Crossing my legs didn't help nor did biting my lip. Desperate, I willed myself to ignore the little stream that gurgled nearby.

When Alain returned, I blurted out, "I need...a bush or a tree."

The beginning of a smile formed. "Of course, Anna, Forgive me."

Each man looked at the other.

"Oh no. I'm going alone," I said.

Not knowing which was worse, maintaining my pride or holding my water, I pointed in the direction I intended to go. "I promise to scream if I see anything...or anyone...threatening." I picked up my skirts and ran toward a large yellow elm.

Alain called out. "I'll come halfway. You won't even know I'm nearby."

I didn't argue because I knew I couldn't convince him otherwise. True to his word, he stopped before the elm and allowed me blessed privacy as I released my suffering. When I emerged, we walked toward the creek so I could wash up. Although the water was icy, it felt good on my hands and face.

As we continued on our journey, dark gray clouds crowded the sky. Snow threatened. Luckily, we came across an abandoned croft with a partial thatched roof which was home to many birds. They immediately flew off as we neared. The croft door was wide open, and several pieces of broken furniture were tossed about inside and out. In the hearth sat a cracked pot stained with a blackened residue on the bottom and one side. The remains of a straw mattress leaned against a wall. Its contents scattered, as if someone were searching for treasure. In the loft hung a dry soiled nappie. There was no way to know how long the house had been abandoned, but since we were only staying for the night, it didn't matter. We were thankful for a partial roof and the broken furniture made a warm fire.

Filib headed to the creek to fish, and Alain and I tended to the horses. We brought them into what was left of the barn, and I found some oats abandoned in a wooden bucket.

When Filib returned he proudly showed off a half dozen small brown trout he had caught. And something else. At his heels was a skinny rat with gray tattered fur and a big black nose. It was a malnourished puppy who decided he'd rather sit than take another step. Filib gave the dog's rump a push, and the pup slinked over and rubbed against my skirts. I leaned down to scratch behind his ears, and he rolled over on his back begging for more. His tail wagged so hard his entire body went with it. When I stopped, he whimpered and brushed against my skirts again.

"Poor puppy," I said. You must love my skirts.

"Fleas."

I backed away.

Filib put the fish he caught on the mantle and gestured to both of us. "Come. Have a look."

The pup yipped at our heels as we followed Filib in the direction of the stream. The little Scot was a man of few words, but none were needed when he pointed to the remains of an adult dog. All that was left was fur, bits of flesh, teeth, and bones. A spear had pinned the animal through the ribcage to the ground. The crows had done their job and now the maggots were taking over.

The pup crept to the carcass, sniffed, and whined. He then lay beside the body, his tiny paws outstretched with his head between them. This must have been the pup's mother.

"I found the pup here."

"Whoever did this to a dog…I'd hate to think what they might have done to the family who lived in the croft." Alain took my hand. We were both in need of human touch after the inhuman display in front of us.

As we turned for the house, the pup didn't budge. I waited and called, "Come on. There's nothing here for you anymore." He whined, looked at his dead mother, and back at me. "Come on boy." Then I thought, "Skirts. Come on, Skirts."

As if he recognized his new name, the pup came running into my skirts. I scratched behind his ears. "Good boy Skirts."

"Skirts?" said Filib scratching his beard. "For a laddie? Mumph."

The next morning, after we ate the last of the trout, we were on our way. The ground, covered with a layer of fresh snow, was not enough to slow down the horses.

120

As the day grew warmer, the snow mixed with mud and created a brown slush which squished under each step.

Skirts followed us, running in and around the horses' hooves. His barks sounded more like squeaks. I didn't know if he followed us because of the promise of food, the feel of my skirts, or both. But I was glad for his company. Filib promised that when we stopped for the night, he would rid the dog of his fleas.

Our old pattern of traveling resumed. Silence taking its turn with conversation.

"Tell me why your father refused to back my family." Alain's question assumed I knew about my father's business decisions. "Hiding behind the screen in his library, you must have heard a lot."

I burst out laughing and tried to turn around to look at him. I could just imagine his smirk. "You knew?"

"Aye," he teased. "It wasn't hard to figure out. Your impromptu entrance allowed us to meet, and if you remember, I held your hand for the first time."

"I do remember. And yes, I know why my father refused. He believed the entire scheme was based on unreliable information with too many risks. The Spanish and the English would never accept competition from Scotland."

"I've read reports about the proposed colony. It was written by a surgeon and he described the land as a Garden of Eden."

"If it's the man my father told me about, he's a pirate, someone not to trust."

"Was there another reason?" he asked.

"Turning down the loan had nothing to do with your family. It had everything to do with mine. My father is careful with his investments. He learned that if a transaction doesn't go well, the Jew will be blamed. If he makes a profit, the Jew will be called greedy. My father believes there are certain investments it is best to decline." I hesitated before going on. "But there was another reason." How to say the words that might hurt the man who had been willing to risk everything on my behalf?

"After that first dinner, my father accused me of having feelings for you. He forbade me to consider you anything more than the son of his business partner. Generations ago, my family had to run for their lives because of their religion."

"But I would never harm you. Haven't I proven that?"

"Yes. Over and over again. But Father doesn't see it that way. He would never accept a gentile into our family, and he said your family would never consent to a Jewess."

"And you, do you feel the same...as your father?"

"I don't know...what to think. I mean, I have never experienced the kind of hatred my father speaks of."

There was an unanswered question between us. One that I had laid at Alain's feet. He took a deep breath. "Is your father right? Do you have feelings for me?"

I didn't hesitate. "Yes, I do."

Alain answered quickly. "And I you."

Nothing more was said, nor needed to be.

Darkness came early at this time of the year. We set up camp and for the first time I slept soundly between my two dear sentinels.

The next morning, Skirts came bounding over and buried himself in my lap. A leafy ring hung around his neck.

"Pennyroyal," Filib explained. "The pup will soon be free of the buggers."

The collar exuded a strong smell of mint. I grabbed Skirts by the scruff of his neck and held him high. His little legs kicked in all directions and his tail wagged furiously.

"Silly Skirts."

Filib went to saddle up the horses, Alain began packing up the camp, and I announced the need for a bush or a tree. Alain offered to accompany me, but I pointed out my destination, a nearby clump of pine bushes. We laughed when Skirts followed, offering his protection. He yapped at my heels, running in front and then attacking my skirts from behind.

When I emerged from my privy, I headed for the stream below. I longed to wipe the grime off my face and arms and quench my thirst. Something whisky couldn't do. I held onto some branches to balance myself to get down the slippery embankment.

Leafless trees from the top of the embankment towered above. Clumps of melting snow bombs fell from overhead limbs exploding when they hit the earth. Every time one came thudding down it sounded like a giant's footfalls. Skirts, the intrepid hunter, pretended the clumps were prey and he yapped at each one.

I laughed at his antics while I hiked my skirts to my knees and stepped onto a flat rock in the stream. Bending over I soaked my handkerchief and dragged it slowly across my face and around my neck. A few droplets followed the nobs of my spine. Patches of my dress flowered into a darker shade of blue.

Another thud of snow. I turned and spied a red squirrel scampering up a tall tree. A wide-eyed buck stood motionless. We stared at each other until it ran off, disappearing among the trees.

The pup started to back off and whine.

"Come here Skirts. What kind of hunter are you?" I reached out to get him, but he backed away even further. "Well, then. You'll just have to follow when you're good and ready." I turned to go and bumped into a solid living wall that reeked of whisky.

It was the man in black.

I tried to scream, but a grimy hand covered my mouth. I bit into a finger, and he responded by hitting me hard on the back of my head. He wrapped his other hand in my hair and pulled me roughly to his horse.

Struggling to get free, my captor bent over, and whispered in my ear. "There'll be no more o' that."

I remembered nothing more.

My head throbbed. Turning from one side to the other, a large tender lump reminded me of the frightening events at the stream. I had no recollection how long ago I'd been kidnapped.

Slowly, I opened my eyes and blackness dominated my vision until the stars crept into view. They flickered between the lacy limbs of a mighty tree that towered above but gave no hint to the hour. Was this late evening or the middle of the night?

That's when I realized a sour stench came from a rag that covered my mouth. Was I gagged because I screamed? Would Alain or Filib have heard me? Then my heart sank. The stream, where I was abducted, was in a ravine and the rushing water would have drowned out my cries for help

The frozen ground was hard. My woolen cloak, layered skirts, and stockings provided little protection from the cold and discomfort.

My wrists were loosely bound. It took little effort to free them. I slid the rope in my pocket and pulled the rag down from my mouth so it hung like a noose. Then, I returned my hands behind my back pretending they were still tied, but my relief at being able to breathe in fresh air did not last long. I was repulsed by a strong male odor. The broad back of my abductor was inches away. His loud snoring reassured me he was asleep.

I needed a weapon. I scanned the ground for an unguarded dirk or sword. Nothing. The enemy was careful. A fallen branch was within easy reach, but it was too heavy to heave over my head and strike before my abductor realized what had hit him. The element of surprise was essential

Then, partially hidden under dried leaves, but outlined by a thin layer of snow, was a rock the size of my palm. I inched closer until my left hand grasped the cold deadly object. It was the perfect weight, and one side had a jagged edge, good enough to inflict serious injury. I hid the rock behind me and rehearsed the stages of my attack.

I remembered watching my brother learn how to defend himself. All young men from wealthy homes were instructed in the basics of personal defense.

"Nathan, why strike your opponent's eye first?" The tone of the instructor's voice clearly showed his impatience with his recalcitrant student.

"To blind him, of course. Do you think I'm stupid?" Even as a child my brother thought he was superior to everyone.

"A true strike to the eye will inflict the most pain and leave your adversary disoriented and blind. That will give you the opportunity for a mortal blow, a slash to the neck. And the second choice? If you can't get to the eye?"

My brother remained silent and refused to answer. Instead, he picked at the dirt under his fingernails with his knife.

"Go for the jaw," the man said. "If you hit hard enough, the head will snap back, and your enemy will black out. At which point, you—"

"I know, slit his throat." Nathan gestured with his finger across his own.

"If you miss your opportunity to quickly disable and destroy your enemy, your fumbling will only serve to enrage him, and you will die." The tutor shouted this important final instruction as Nathan walked away.

What advice Nathan had so pathetically disregarded, I treasured. With my new-found weapon I had to strike accurately with sufficient force. It was my only chance.

I shifted the rock in my sweaty palm and waited for the next silent interval between snores. When the slumbering monster inhaled deeply, I rose like a cat ready to spring.

Footsteps. A gruff voice.

"Whacha doin there? Yere not sleepin' the night away, are ye?"

I pulled back my hand, lowered myself, and concealed the rock. I tried desperately to clear the confusion in my brain. When faced with the irrational, the mind tries to create order out of chaos. Was that the slumbering man? Was he talking in his sleep? But the voice sounded like he was awake, and there were footsteps. That was when I realized my greatest fear. There were two of them.

I didn't see the new man, but I recognized the voice. It was my abductor, the man in black.

"Huh? Leave me be." The sleeper next to me also sounded familiar.

The man in black approached his partner and kicked his legs hard enough that I felt the tremor of the thump.

The sleeper sat upright and yelled back. "Give me a minute, Harley. Or would you rather I pissed on you?"

Harley. The man in black had a name. "It's your turn tae be on watch. I'm not doin' all the work. Everythin' is fifty-fifty ye said."

Now I wondered who the sleeper was. His identity would have to wait when he disappeared into the blackness of the forest.

With his partner gone, Harley reached for a log and stirred the ashes until the remaining coals glowed. Then he threw the log on top, sparks flew, and the dry wood caught. Rising flames reflected off of Harley's broadsword and dirk as he placed each by his side in preparation for sleep.

I quickly closed my eyes when he glanced my way. Harley came closer. The hairs on the back of my neck stood up. He bent down and stroked my cheek, and his hand continued down and traced the curve of my breast. As he did so, I could hear his breathing grow heavier.

"Sweets, ye like this?" He talked as I pretended to sleep. "So young and fresh."

He fumbled with my cloak, groping hands made their way inside feeling every curve and indentation. Harley lowered himself on me and began rubbing his clothed body against mine. The heat of his breath, coming quicker now, was directly on my face. The smell of whisky was overpowering. Then with a sense of urgency he quickened his movements. I remembered the rock, but it was useless. His weight pinned me down.

The crunch of dead leaves and small twigs announced the return of his partner. Out of the darkness emerge Harley's partner.

"Hey, what are you doing? Leave her be."

Harley's body froze. He rolled off.

"The Old Fart doesn't want damaged goods, or we won't get paid. You'll find more experienced entertainment in town. The whores will be crawling all over you once they hear the jingle of silver in your pockets."

I recognized the voice. It was Bernard. Maurice's valet.

Harley grunted, rolled up his jacket, and placed it under his head

"I'll wake you and the girl right before sunrise. We need to be in Leith early. The ship is due to sail with the tide. Maurice doesn't like to be kept waiting."

"Aye, I hear ye. Now shut your trap, and let me get tae sleep."

It didn't take long for his snoring to fill the air along with the sounds of the spitting fire and awakening birds.

I must have dozed because the next thing I knew Bernard was shaking me.

"Time to go. Here."

He tossed a dried bannock in my lap.

I ate in silence watching the two men pack the horses. The rock, concealed in my pocket, would have to wait. My original plan was no longer an option. I could possibly injure one man and get away. But two, was impossible.

The only other choice was to delay my being handed over to Maurice.

Harley approached. Remembering a few hours ago, I drew back. "Finish eatin,' Sweets. We need tae be on our way." He tossed his flask next to me, picked up his belongings, and returned to his horse.

I ignored the flask. The thought of putting my lips to something that Harley's mouth had touched made me want to retch. I ate my dry breakfast slowly.

Now it was Bernard's turn. "We need to go. Now! You're riding with Harley."

"Did my brother send you?"

"Nathan? No. Your bridegroom still wants you. He said he got a wee taste, and he's an appetite for more. Don't want to disappoint the rich bastard."

He closed in and reached down to grab my arm, but I was quicker, and pulled back. "I can't. I need to um...I need to visit that tree over there."

"Huh? You aren't going alone. I'm not losing you when I'm so close to getting paid."

I pulled myself up and spoke as forcefully as I could. "Do you think Maurice will approve your witnessing my most private moment? I'm only going behind that big oak. Besides, where am I going to run? I don't know where we are. And frankly, a warm soft bed, even with Maurice in it, is starting to sound inviting."

Bernard snickered. "Your Jew will be happy to hear that. Get to the tree and make it quick. If not, I'm sending Harley to get you. He won't care what Maurice thinks."

I took my time walking to the giant tree. Its girth could easily hide three large men. Instead of lifting my skirts, I peered around and watched my captors.

"Come on, Girl. Pissing doesn't take that long," said Bernard.

Harley chortle in agreement.

I heard a branch snap coming from the opposite direction. My ears followed the noise and in between the vee of a split tree was the Little Scot. He pointed to the brush, and there was Alain. Alain gestured a silent message that I should go back to my kidnappers.

I retrieved the rock from my pocket and showed it proudly. Alain shook his head.

Defiantly, I closed my fingers around the rock, came out from behind the tree, and with the most confidence I'd felt since awakening, I returned to my captors. I had options once again.

126

NINETEEN
Grippin' O' Flies
2005

I'd never seriously considered those little slips of paper found in Chinese fortune cookies. The cute sayings and predictions rarely made sense. That's what I used to think. This time the prophecy was eerily correct. The candlestick was an unexpected discovery.

I placed the candlesticks side by side. They were identical in weight, height, and design. But there was one difference. My grandmother's gleamed, as if it had just been polished for a Friday night dinner. The new arrival was black with tarnish, and scratches, scars, and dents were clearly visible. It looked like it had gone to war and lost.

"I know this sounds foolish and a bit anthropomorphic, but they do look like they belong together. Don't you think? Like twins separated at birth, except one had a very hard life."

"Aye. That they do. I wonder how one is so battered, and has been locked away in a box here in Edinburgh, while the other is in mint condition and turned up in New Jersey?"

"Maybe, we're looking at this wrong. We have no proof they were meant to be a pair. It's easy to come to that conclusion because of the identical design. But what if the silversmith made a few of the same candlesticks and two unrelated customers came into his shop and purchased them."

"Wait. You can't make sense of the seventeenth century by forcing it into the context of our modern times. Craftsmen didn't line their shelves so a customer could browse and someday make a purchase. They couldn't afford to literally pour that much capital into a valuable item. Besides, most people were poor. Only the wealthy could afford such a piece. It was a way to put their silver to good use."

"Let's be pragmatic. Could it just be an accident that a twenty-first century woman inherits two identical three-hundred-year-old candlesticks? Perhaps. Are we one-hundred percent certain? No. But the questions we need answers for, are why were they commissioned, and what were the conditions that caused the separation?"

I picked up the tarnished candlestick. On the underside were the remnants of three hallmarks. One was too scuffed up to read. The second was partially worn away, but we were able to piece together the small q, the assayer's mark. The last stamp, the three turrets, wasn't damaged. We knew for sure conception occurred in Edinburgh in 1696.

Then I turned over my grandmother's candlestick. They were identical except for the half-inch tube-shaped opening. Both were off center, one to the right, and the other to the left. I squinted down the dark narrow opening of each. That's when I noticed the light reflect on something inside the tarnished one.

"There's something inside the stem." I put my forefinger into the opening. It felt like a Chinese finger toy. The deeper I put my finger, the tighter it got. Afraid it would get stuck, I only went as far as the second joint. I wiggled and scraped against an edge. It wasn't hard or sharp, but it had some give. I thought to flick it with my nail, but I didn't want to damage whatever it was.

"If you had to guess, what do you think it is?"

"Paper? It's flexible enough to adapt to the curve of the stem."

"Aye. Let me see what I can do."

"Your fingers are way bigger than mine. Or haven't you noticed?" I wiggled my fingers in front of his face.

Alec took the candlestick and tilted it at different angles so he could get the maximum amount of light from the low wattage bulbs overhead. He tried more than once, stopped abruptly, "It appears there's something rolled up inside."

"I was joking when I said it would be nice to find a 'Dear Hanna' note. Maybe my wish is about to come true."

Alec returned the candlestick to an upright position. Tiny flecks of paper and fragments of a moth's wing fell like snowflakes. For a moment, the wing was whole, but then disintegrated into dust as soon as it hit the table. "It looks like we found our moth, at least a part of her," Alec said. "She or her young must have been munching on their…last supper."

"Pulling the paper out has to be done carefully with the correct tools, or the rest of whatever is in there will come out in fragments."

"I talked to one of the professors at the university. He has done a lot of work in the field of preserving and deciphering centuries-old documents. I already mentioned the journal. I'm sure he'll help us with this, I was going to take you to see him as soon as we finished here."

"Okay, but let's leave the candlesticks in the safe deposit box. Now that I have the pair, their value just tripled. I don't want to take the chance of getting mugged again. We can keep everything else in the box too. Except the journal. I'd like to work on one discovery at a time."

We emerged from the bank and were greeted with a warm breeze. The perfect late-summer weather matched our buoyant spirits.

"Hey, Alec! Hey, wait up!" A burly young man waited for traffic to stop before crossing the busy street. He waved and picked up his pace. Alec turned in the direction of the voice. At first, he smiled, but it soon disappeared.

The man was the same height as Alec, but much broader. His ginger beard surrounded dark fleshy lips, and his wavy hair was stuck out in all directions as if he just got out of bed. Above the beard were soft russet-colored eyes, similar to Alec's. Even without an introduction, there was no question the two were related.

"Iain, what are you doing in town?"

"I could ask the same of you." Iain glanced at the building. "Bank business?" Then he glanced my way and the familiar eyebrow shot up. "Looks like you're a...um...busy."

"You could say that."

The sound of a passing police siren cut the air. Alec waited for the piercing wails to climax and disappear down a nearby street.

"Hanna, this is my little brother. Iain, this is my girl —"

Iain didn't wait for Alec to finish. "I'm meeting up with some old chums at Tiles. You want to join us for a beer?" Alec noted his brother's rudeness and responded by putting his arm around me. Iain failed to make amends, and only made it worse. "Um, you could bring your...a...friend."

Either Iain was oblivious or chose to ignore the obvious.

Alec pulled me closer, his hand tightening around my shoulder like a vise. "No, not today. We have plans."

Iain continued to cajole Alec. "Come on, it'll be fun. For old-time's sake. These are your friends too. Or were." He lowered his voice and leaned toward Alec's ear. "Listen...uh...there's someone coming to the pub. She's been asking for you. You could have a good time." Iain jabbed his brother lightly in the ribs. "Eh, what do you say?"

Alec knew I heard. He looked at me. "No. I mean it. Not interested"

Iain's uncomfortable gaze told me I was an intruder. "I don't mean to steal your boyfriend, Lass." He turned to Alec and patted him on the shoulder. "Well, if you change your mind you know where you can find me."

"Don't wait around."

Alec grabbed my arm and we walked away. I turned to look at Iain standing on the street corner, staring after us.

"You never told me you had a brother."

Still agitated, Alec stopped. "Aye. Remember I mentioned I would like for you to meet my friends, and I don't mean the chumps Iain was referring to. But meeting my family is something I must prepare you for. Didn't you notice? My brother has already had one too many. There's an old saying here in Scotland. *A dram brings truth unco close.*"

No interpretation was necessary.

The next day, we rented a car for our drive to St. Andrews. From Edinburgh we crossed the impressive Forth Bridge over the Firth into the county of Fife. The journal was on the back seat safely stored in Alec's briefcase.

The ninety-minute drive gave Alec the opportunity to lecture about the history of St. Andrews' most famous sites: its golf course and the university. Conversation allowed me to forget he was driving on the left side of the road.

"The Old Course, as its name suggests, is one of the oldest golf courses in the world. At one time the land was used simultaneously for golfing and rabbit farming."

"You're kidding. Rabbit farming?"

"Aye. The rabbits were brought in when the golf course almost went bankrupt. A farmer purchased the land under the condition that golf could still be played, but he also leased the land to rabbit farmers. The rabbits and the golfers didn't get along, so the players took matters into their own hands. One day they decimated the animals by clubbing them to death. Perhaps, that is how the golf…club…got its name?"

The dour Alec from yesterday was gone; the playful one had returned.

"But that's not the end of the story. In the early 1800's a wealthy golfer, with the ironic name of James Cheape, had enough of the rabbits. He purchased the land and declared it to be used only for golf. After he died, the Cheape family sold the land, but maintained the right to have six free tee times every day in perpetuity. Even during professional tournaments, they could bump the great golfers."

"The Cheapes must have loved golf."

"No, they never played. In the early 1990s, they sold their right for almost a quarter million pounds which was close to a million US."

"Sound investment. Great story. But not good for the rabbits."

"I wouldn't worry about them. You can still find their progeny hopping and multiplying on the links."

Alec hesitated for a moment while he waited to turn left into a round-about. Driving on the other side of a straight road was one thing, but I closed my eyes as he fearlessly dashed around the traffic circle. Alec looked over. "I know what you're thinking. It's what everyone says about history professors. We know a little bit about a lot of stuff, and most of it is useless."

"No, that's not what I was thinking." I took a deep breath, glad to be alive.

130

Alec leaned over and shook my leg. "Hey, are you okay? Was my story that bad?"

"Oh no, I really enjoyed it. I was just thinking about…all that's happened since I've come to Scotland. At times it's overwhelming."

"You know, Hanna, I'm here for you. As long as you want me. But if you change your mind, well, then the only thing I have to say is *naething to be done in haste but grippin' o' flies.*"

"What?"

"Never act hastily – unless you're trying to kill flies."

"Okay…if I need an exterminator, I know who to call. Seriously, I'm grateful for all you've done. I've enjoyed our time together."

Alec chuckled.

"Really, I mean it," I said.

"I love being with you as well." Alec had that look like he was about to kiss me.

As we entered another round-about, I gripped the door handle and changed the subject. "Now tell me about the university. Wait…I know. It's very, very old. Everything in Scotland is ancient."

Alec began to tell me about the university while my thoughts remained on the possible kiss. It would have to wait, but I promised myself it wouldn't be forgotten.

St. Andrews was a charming coastal town located on a plateau bordered by the frigid waters of the North Sea. Lining the small streets was an assortment of gray stone buildings sprinkled with modern architecture that seemed out of place. Populated by 16,000 permanent residents, St Andrews mushroomed when 8,000 students and staff crowded the local coffee houses, filled the parking lots, and leased every rental during the fall and spring semesters.

We traveled on Old Scores, a thoroughfare that hugged the rugged coastline. The day had been mostly cloudy and cool, but when the sun made a welcome appearance by midday, it prompted a return of sunglasses and partially opened car windows. My head swiveled back and forth like a bobble doll as Alec grabbed my hand or patted my knee to point out an interesting sight.

Alec pulled over across from a castle ruin. It jutted out on a rocky promontory overlooking a sandy beach. The roof was missing and only a few stone walls remained. A bunch of noisy sightseers, necklaced with cameras, strolled toward what may have once been a drawbridge leading to a gateway. After numerous photo opportunities, they quickly disappeared into the castle-keep.

"Much of Scotland is filled with skeletons of old castles, some thought to be haunted," said Alec. "This one is no different. However, what you see isn't the original. That was built around 1200. The clergy, both Catholic and Protestant, and Scottish and English royalty, all called this fortress home. Not at the same time, of course. Then it became a place of religious persecution, and it's rumored to have had a ghost or two."

"Well, it wouldn't be fun without a ghost running amok to frighten the tourists."

Alec resumed our slow drive on Old Scores. "Aye. St. Andrews boasts a variety of specters. Besides the usual, there have been sightings of dogs and horses pulling carriages. Even the golf course claims a *Bodach-Glas,* a dark grey man, who awaits golfers at the final hole. If the golfer sees the ghost, death is imminent. Of course, some might prefer that if they've had a bad day on the links. "

Alec reduced his speed even more as we approached the parking area. There was barely enough room for one lane of traffic. To our right was a promenade along the sea cliff. On the other side nestled two, three, and four-story stone buildings. Most looked like private residences or University offices. "Maybe we'll get lucky and find a parking spot. This is close to my office."

"So why is St. Andrews a magnet for the supernatural?"

"Historically, the town has had its share of witches and that usually means an ample supply of ignorance and hysteria. Older women were most at risk, particularly those who were widows or wise-women, as healers were once called. Women were considered morally inferior, and thus, easily tempted by the devil."

"Are you scared to be with me?"

"Not yet. You're still young, so I'm safe. My favorite story is that of Cardinal David Beaton, the last prince of the church in Scotland before the Reformation. He suffered from some ailment and sought treatment from a wise woman, Alesoun Piersoun. She cured him, but rather than pay the two shillings for her services, he declared Mistress Piersoun a witch and had her burned at the stake."

"Nice guy. I guess he didn't want to part with his money."

"Aye, But Mistress Piersoun got her revenge. The locals murdered him. But not before he accused a popular reformer, George Wishart, of heresy and had him burned at the stake. To make sure Wishart died in a spectacularly gruesome manner, Beaton placed bags of gun powder around the doomed man's neck. The Cardinal stood in the window of St. Andrews Castle and watched the gruesome spectacle."

He stopped his explanation abruptly when he found a parking spot. "That old building on the right, St. Katherine's Lodge, is where my office is located.

"You have an office in a lodge?"

"At one time it probably was. Today it's where the history department has their offices."

What I thought was going to be a short walk turned out to be something else. Alec took my hand. We crossed the street and stood before a tall stone obelisk called Martyrs' Monument. It was situated overlooking the cliffs. Alec pulled me around to the side of the monument that faced the sea. He put one hand around my waist and pressed me against the stone.

"Oh. The stone is cold."

We quickly traded places.

He pulled me to him. I responded by arching my back, encircling my arms around his neck and tilting my head toward his. His other hand joined its twin at my waist and if it were possible, he drew me even closer. As one of my hands went to cup his face, I felt his lips, warm and soft. They parted ever so slightly as they brushed mine. It was the kiss that was overdue. He pressed his forehead on mine and whispered, "I've wanted to do this ever since this morning."

"Why here? Why not just kiss me in the car?"

"It's a tradition – to kiss a girl at Martyr's Monument."

Alec resumed his hold and his kiss. We remained oblivious to our surroundings when we were startled by nearby snorts and giggles. Turning, we'd found our audience. It was a bunch of teenagers. They were enjoying every minute of our romantic display.

Alec threw back his head and laughed. "Run along now, ye Peeping Toms." Grabbing my hand, he said, "Come on Mistress. There's someone I want you to meet."

"Hanna, I'd like to introduce you to Professor Ira Mason, our preeminent historian on all things late middle ages to the early modern period with a particular fondness for the Golden Age of Spain. When he has nothing else to do he writes volumes of history books, teaches several classes, which are always overflowing, mentors younger professors like me, and deciphers old manuscripts."

"That's enough Alec. You'll either scare Hanna away or she'll wonder how any mere mortal can live up to those credits."

Dr. Mason was a wizened old man who looked out over the top of his half-moon glasses. A few wiry hairs sprouted from his balding head which allowed the sprinkling of age spots to be clearly visible. He extended an equally age-spotted hand. I was taken aback by his firm grasp.

"It's a pleasure to meet you, Dr. Mason. I'm sure every word Alec said is the absolute truth."

133

"Ah, a very intelligent woman. Welcome, my dear. Any friend of Alec's is welcome, and —" Ira stopped. His hand went immediately to the top of his head. His eyes looked up as if his cranium were transparent. "Ah, I've lost it again."

He scanned the carpet, the top of a gray file cabinet, and stopped when he found a black circle on top of a pile of books. "If only I had a lock of hair to attach my *kippah*. Maybe glue would serve me better." He cupped the cap and plopped it on his head. "A *kippah* is my prayer cap. I wear it all the time except when it prefers a different perch."

"I've seen many Jewish men in New York wear them. At the University I attended, one of my philosophy professors was religious. I…wasn't expecting—"

"A Jew in Scotland?" Dr. Mason turned to Alec with a smirk on his face, "You left out the most important part." He returned to finish his own question. "Many of my tribe have found a home in Edinburgh and more so in Glasgow in the early 1900's. But I've heard tales about some showing up in the sixteenth or seventeenth centuries escaping the Inquisition."

He hesitated as if he forgot something. "Ah, my bad manners. A missing kippah is a poor excuse not to welcome a guest properly. How about some tea? I have a wonderful oolong."

From a cupboard he took out a beautiful red and white mug painted on all sides with birds soaring over marshland. He placed tea leaves in a diffuser and poured hot water in the mug. Then he covered it with a matching lid. In a few minutes, the tea was properly steeped.

"Sugar and cream?"

"Sugar, please."

"A good tea is like fine wine," Ira said. "It should be enjoyed slowly, with good friends, and served in a lovely cup."

"Thank you." I took a sip. "It's delicious."

While he prepared his own cup of tea and coffee for Alec, I perused the professor's office. Disorganized order reigned. An ancient roll-top desk was buried under a literary mountain - an overflow of books of different sizes, colors, and thicknesses: hardcover, paperback, and leather bound. Bookcases were filled from floor to ceiling, and the overflow was piled waist-high in the corners of the room. Any space not book-laden was filled with reams of papers and folders. A musty book smell mingled with the oolong.

Dr. Mason must have noticed my taking inventory. "I'm afraid my office is a perpetual mess."

"The professor has quite a reputation among the staff for…um…his unique filing system. We all joke about it," said Alec.

It was clear that a professional respect as well as a friendship existed between the aging teacher and his young protégé. Earlier Alec explained that the professor had been more than just his mentor. Ira was like a beloved uncle and the university had become home.

"At my age I don't see any reason to change. We'll see how you fare when you've been teaching as long as I. Unfortunately, I won't be around. I'll leave it to Hanna to remind you about this conversation."

Dr. Mason pulled on a cardigan that reminded me of Mr. Rodgers. "The administration affords me a larger than normal office; the prerogative of being the most senior historian on staff. Although this room is a bit chilly, I consider the extra space for my books worth it."

"One of my favorite professors had an office like this. He could always find anything in seconds. I bet you can too."

"Ah, a wise woman."

"Professor, I told Hanna what happened to the unfortunate wise women a few centuries ago. She may see your compliment a bit differently."

"Forgive me, my dear. I promise we will not be lighting up the pyre anytime soon." His friendly smile did not cover up a missing molar. "But tell me; are you the young lady who inherited an ancient journal?"

Alec quickly interjected. "I assure you there could be no other."

"Well then. I've uncovered and inherited many a rare book in my time." He walked over to a closet in the far corner of the room. Wood and glass doors covered more book-lined shelves. This must have been where he kept priceless editions because the closet had a key.

The professor reached for a book that was aged but in remarkably good condition. "This is a rare edition of Pierre Corneille's work published in 1682. Have you ever heard of Le Cid...El Cid? I have a copy of almost every edition. It's a particular favorite of mine and it is Corneille's seminal work. This particular copy was given to me by a colleague when I was about Alec's age. He knew I was fond of the play. He found it in Edinburgh – squirreled away in the back of an old bookstore."

Professor Mason placed the book in my hands. My fingertips glided over the smooth leather cover and I put it to my nose to breathe in its age.

"You may open it."

On the title page was a picture of a bride and groom holding hands. They stood before someone in an elevated chair, a king perhaps, and a throng of people. Above the couple, centered, was the word *tragedie*. Carefully turning the pages, I noted it was in French.

"Professor—"

"Please can call me Ira. Here, I'm always Professor or Dr. Mason. It's nice to hear my first name once in a while."

"Okay...Ira. Why don't you mind my touching this old book?"

"It hasn't been buried like your journal which requires great care when opening after so many years. Alec tells me you haven't done that yet. I'm impressed with your patience. Most would have been too curious, and in the process might have destroyed an important artifact."

"I did an internship on a dig in Boston. We came across an eighteenth-century ledger from a glassmaker's shop. The pages were riddled with bug holes, and the ink had destroyed some of the writing. It was a huge disappointment, and I learned a lesson from that experience."

"That's correct. You need the right tools to open an ancient book." The old man pushed aside some books so he could open a narrow closet filled with small boxes and more books. He rummaged through some containers. "Ah, here it is."

He carried a cardboard box to his desk and cleared away some papers and moved a skull to the top shelf of his desk.

Until this moment, I hadn't noticed the skull. "Is that real?"

"You mean Torquemada? Yes, quite real."

Alec cleared his throat loudly. Ira winked as if this was a secret they shared.

"I must make a confession. This is not the skull of the real Tomás de Torquemada. I inherited it from another colleague, who retired five years ago. He told me the skull was to serve as a reminder, that if I didn't retire soon, I would start looking like it."

I couldn't help but laugh. "Why did you give that name to the skull?"

"Why not? Every drawing I've seen of Torquemada shows him with a scowl. This skull has the same look. Don't you think?"

To me it looked like any other skull. I saw no scowl or grin for that matter.

"I like to think that the first Grand Inquisitor got his due, and now his head sits on the desk of a Jew, a descendant of those he tried to destroy. I have no idea whose head it is, but it goes over well with the first-year students when they come to my office."

The first item Ira took out was called a micro spatula. It was about seven inches long and was used to slide between the pages to gently lift them. This, he explained, helped to prevent thin paper from tearing. "In the old days, booksellers would grow a long fingernail on their index finger that served the same purpose." He took out two more objects: a snake and a cradle. The snake was a foot-long piece of cloth folded over a weighted chain. He demonstrated by opening a book and placing the snake along the inside edge. "This will allow the book to stay open without using your fingers. But some books can't be opened flat. That's why you need a cradle. It's to protect a dry and brittle spine from breaking." The last item was a pair of thin white gloves which he tossed into the trashcan. "You don't need them. Gloved fingers can bend and tear pages. You only see them worn in the movies."

I pulled out the journal from Alec's briefcase and presented it to Ira. He gently ran his fingers over the smooth binding tracing the embossed thistle; then turned the journal over and around. "Ah, good. There's no mark."

"What are you looking for Professor?" asked Alec.

"Markings left by the bookbinder. That was done in the fifteenth and sixteenth centuries and then resumed in the nineteenth century. No markings indicate this journal is from the interim centuries and helps to identify its age and authenticity."

Ira continued to inspect the journal's covering. "Vellum binding. Good, fine quality calfskin. You can see where it has dried out some, but no deterioration or red rot. I'm amazed at its flexibility considering how long it's been stored." Ira looked at both of us and smiled. "Ah, sorry I could go on and on. Are you ready Hanna? To open the book?"

"Yes." I looked at Alec and smiled nervously.

"Let me warn you. It's common for a book of this age, to be riddled with bug holes."

"Yes, but we have to open it anyway."

"Then let us begin. Carefully untie the leather straps. Don't rush it. I will assist you. They appear brittle and may break."

Like a surgeon hovering over a patient during delicate surgery, I pulled on the tied straps. My first attempt resulted in one breaking off. Ira's eyes told me to go on. With the fragile broken piece out of the way, the rest of the untying was much easier.

I took a deep breath, picked up the spatula and opened the front cover.

TWENTY
Swiss Cheese

The inside of the journal resembled Swiss cheese. It was riddled with tiny holes made by entombed insect larvae. The width of most cavities was less than the diameter of a pencil eraser; their depth went through several pages. Others were chasms in comparison. One industrious forager burrowed straight down and emerged along the edge of the book. Thankfully, the text remained readable.

"I know the bugs are no longer alive, but it's disgusting." I said. "Wasn't there a method to remove them?"

"Back then, freezing was one way," said Alec. "Today, I've heard microwaving works, but a colleague of mine, who works in the rare manuscripts section of the library, doesn't recommend it."

"Especially if you heat your lunch shortly after you've fried some bugs," I said. "Hardly appetizing."

Our discussion was interrupted by the absent-minded tapping of Ira's spoon as he stirred cream into his third cup of tea. "The material used to create books like this one, cotton, leather, and linen, was like chocolate to the little buggers. Glue made from collagen was also a treat. The bookworms or lice are harmless to humans, but as you can see, they caused quite a bit of damage."

In reaction to our conversation, I scratched my head.

Ira smiled. "This isn't the kind of lice that plants nits on a human hair. In the seventeenth century these bugs thrived because the environment was perfect. People didn't wash, and homes and public places like inns and taverns were infested. It is not surprising that your journal has turned into a coffin for the creepy-crawlies."

While the professor and I bantered about bugs, Alec sat engrossed in the journal. I loved watching him, deep in thought, bent over, inspecting the ancient pages.

"This paper is made from rags," Alec said. "It's thicker than the kind produced in the colonies which means it's English-made. The spatula won't be necessary."

The professor cleared his throat. "Well then, are we ready to investigate what's within the journal?"

"Yes, Professor…Ira, I mean, I'm ready to weave my way around the bug holes."

"It's not that simple. You don't just open up a book this old and read. You have to learn how to decipher the unfamiliar writing. Some of the letters and words will look like they were written yesterday; many will appear foreign. But there's so much we can learn by just turning the pages. Beyond the words, there is a story to be told. Here, let me give you an example."

Ira started at the beginning where we found a few entries by an Alexandra Cora Campbell MacArthur. Then he turned a few pages and found most were signed by Anna Rachael MacArthur. "The fact that this journal was owned by two women, and one wrote just a few entries, could be a story in itself. Maybe we'll learn why."

He turned back to the middle of one of Anna's pages. "See how the ink is fuzzy? It has a penumbra, a shadow. Some of that is a result of the iron gall ink used at the time." Ira pointed to the facing page. "Here the writing is smeared. Based on its slant our author was perhaps left-handed and smeared the ink with the heel of her hand or the sleeve of her dress."

Ira fumbled through several desk drawers until he procured a large white feathered quill. "Try writing with a swan's feather. With your left hand."

Being naturally right-handed it was an awkward exercise, but I could see what Ira was talking about. My left hand dragged along the paper following the imaginary wet ink from the quill. To avoid this, I made a concerted effort to keep my wrist up. It didn't go well.

"I guess someone who was left-handed would be better at this."

"You would've learned to compensate, my dear. You'll notice that most southpaws hook their hand to avoid the ink. Or use a left-handed quill."

"Quills were right-handed or left-handed? I just thought it was a feather."

"Our ancestors were a clever lot. A left-handed quill would have been a flight feather from the right side of the bird. Vice-versa for a right-handed quill. Since most people are right-handed, so were most quills. Anna may have been forced to use one that didn't work for her."

Ira turned to the next few pages checking each carefully. In the crease of one, we found the dried-up fragile remains of a petal. We couldn't tell what kind of flower it was, but the idea that Anna felt compelled to press a petal in her book was another poignant reminder that this was the story of a real person.

On the next page, Ira pointed to a few places where the ink had faded. "Perhaps the book was left open in direct sunlight or an inferior ink was used. But here, where the ink is lighter and then darkens is where the quill needed to be re-inked. Quill pens held enough for a couple of words. The constant re-inking lengthened the time it took to write." Then, he pointed to a place where the nub of the quill had worked itself to a blunt point. Sharper lines resumed after the quill was sharpened.

Further into the book we stopped at a page where there was a faint reddish stain the size of a nickel. It was darker where the drip hit the page, and then created a tail as it flowed across and dried.

"Ira, could this be blood?"

"Or wine." Alec said. "Although blood would be more dramatic."

"We'd have to do some testing to know for sure, but in some cases it's just a matter of reading the words near the spill. Anna may have written some clues." Ira pulled the journal closer and turned on his desk lamp against the darkening room. He pulled out a magnifying glass. "My eyes aren't what they use to be."

I watched him mouthing the words.

"Please, read them aloud."

July 14, 1698

Our ship, the St. Andrew, set sail from Leith in the early morning with the tide & beneficial winds. Our destination is a mystery, except our new home will be called Caledonia, & we are Caledonians. An adventure awaits us. I pray that God keeps us safe & the seas calm. It seems all of Scotland has come out to cheer us on. The banks are crowded with people waving & shouting hurrahs. We stopped briefly in Kirkcaldy to take on Willian & Lydia Paterson. They were scheduled for the Unicorn but insisted on sailing on the St. Andrew. Mr. Paterson has business with Captain Pennecuik. Two stowaways were found this morning. They will replace the sailors who have deserted our cause.

"Now, let's see what she wrote on the next page."

July 22, 1698

We are to sail west. Rumors are rife about our destination at the Bay of Darien in the Americas. There was much excitement until Mr. Paterson forced the captain to inventory our supplies. We only have provisions for six months rather than nine. The beef & bread are already damnified.

We do not care for Captain Pennecuik. He is no gentleman. He is loud & brutish with the sailors. But he keeps order & the men do his bidding. We are handling the ship's movement well. Occasionally, my stomach swirls. Lydia is not so fortunate.

141

"I think we can surmise that the stain is not blood. It's probably wine to soothe a nervous stomach from the ship's heaving and the excitement of going to sea. But there's another clue in her writing. Her pronouns suggest that she is not traveling alone. Nor would I expect a young woman to do so."

"Professor, may I?" Alec turned a few more pages. "Look at the difference between these two pages. Here she writes with a flowing hand, the style matches her previous writing. But here, the handwriting becomes erratic toward the end. And then breaks off. She stops mid-sentence with the quill dragging on the last letter."

"Maybe she was interrupted by a knock at the door," I suggested. "Or she was so seasick she had to run to the nearest bucket."

"She doesn't continue for," Ira turned the page, "five days. For someone who wrote often, something more important halted her hand."

Ira turned more pages. A later entry was dated: *November 5, 1698, New Edinburgh.*

The climate, the tainted food & the brackish water have caused many to fail. Mistress Paterson is unwell. The surgeon is doing what he can, but I have lost hope for her. I fear the worst misery is yet to come vpon us. Two Spanish cruisers have anchored at the mouth of the harbor. Their sails furled. Even from a distance the blue & yellow uniforms of the Spanish soldiers are visible. The Spaniards are playing a game of cat & mouse. We are the vermin. All are fearful they will attack. Remembering Father's words have frightened....

Ira took off his glasses and rubbed his eyes. He stared out the window. The day had grown cloudy again. Raindrops sprinkled the windowpanes looking much like the bug holes splattered in the book.

"Well, we know why our heroine stopped writing so abruptly. For some reason, the presence of the Spanish ships frightened her. And this has something to do with her father. It was common knowledge back then that the Spanish would never accept a Scottish colony right under their nose, but the foolish colonists established it anyway. Still, there's something about our heroine that kept her from writing for several days."

Ira's eyes were slightly bloodshot. Rubbing them didn't help. He touched the top of his head.

"Ira, it's still there."

He nodded, smiled, and patted his head for good measure.

We continued going through the book. Sometimes forward. Other times we flipped back a few pages. We found numerous splotches of dried wax.

"I have a feeling your ancestor did much of her writing at night. She may have wanted to go out on deck during the day to get fresh air. Or she had chores to do, like caring for the ill, including her friend...Mistress Paterson."

142

Alec continued to notice oddities with the entries. "Some are quite long and go on for two pages, while others are just a few lines. And here are more stains. Some look like grease stains. Perhaps she was writing while she ate and had nothing to wipe her hands with. If there was a tablecloth available, she could have used the edge, but unless she was invited to dine in the captain's quarters, I doubt she would've had any refinement like that in her cabin."

Toward the end of the journal we noticed that one page was almost dog-eared, and the writing was again smeared, but this time from some colorless liquid. We wondered if it was water carelessly splashed when she washed her face or hands. Or, I thought, trying to add to the drama, maybe it was tears.

Ira glanced out the window. The daylight was fading. "I mentioned before that I would show you how to read the manuscript. It's not hard. At first you will stumble a bit and have to remind yourself what the different letters are, but once you get used to it, you'll read it like any book."

Turning to a new page, Ira pointed to an example. "Look at the word *distress*. The first and second s's look more like f's without the crosshatch."

"The last s looks normal." I said.

"Correct. The funny looking s's were not f's at all, but were written different due to location in the word or if it was a hard or soft s." He pointed to other examples. "The 'u' in 'upon' is written like a 'v.' 'And' is an ampersand, and some of the spelling is different. There is a silent 'e' at the end of words like *foote* and *newes*, and 'y' is used in place of a long 'i' like in *vyolence*. But context will also help you figure out the words."

"Let me try and read a page. I turned a few pages and chose a passage we had not looked at yet."

August 12, 1698

Many are ill. I am not feeling well. Perhaps it is the ague that has come vpon me. The ship makes no movement & we pray to God to bring the wind. It is hot & rains in torrents & dampness is everywhere. Captain Pennecuik announced we are in the Sargasso Sea. I must eat but cannot. Alain fears my condition. He says nothing. I see it in his eyes. Cook Innes has taken pity on me & has prepared a broth with pork fat & pease. The biscuits are hard. Cook fried them in bacon grease. As hungry as I am, I cannot eat a morsel. Tis against the laws of my father's fathers for my lips to touch swine.

Here the entry ceased. I slowly closed the journal. We sat in almost perfect silence; the ticking of the clock was the only sound. I needed time to absorb what I had learned about Anna. She was ill, but there were people who cared for her. And if she was my ancestor, I found a connection. We both didn't eat pork. Anna knew why. I did not.

Ira broke the quietness by clearing his voice. He removed his glasses and took out a wad of tissues, wiped his eyes, and blew his nose. "It's clear to me what's going on. I wasn't sure before, but I now know why Anna stopped writing so abruptly when the Spanish ships arrived." He swallowed once or twice before going on. "I'm afraid the Inquisition has found our Jewess.

TWENTY-ONE

Only Yours
Scottish Highlands, 1696

"Bon dieu! What's taking so long? A piss isn't that difficult," Bernard's voice intensified in frustration and anger. We met head-on as I came around the tree tripping on a root hidden by the snow.

Bernard grabbed my right arm and dragged me in the direction of the horses. "Come on. You'll be riding with him." Bernard gestured toward Harley who acknowledged his new chore with an evil grin.

My stomach clenched at the thought of Harley pressing against me. I knew that once I was imprisoned in his clutches, it would be more dangerous for Alain and Filib. Getting on that horse was not an option.

The uneven ground made it difficult to keep my balance. I continued to misstep catching my shoe in slippery snow-filled depressions. That unleashed a string of French curse words. It was during this confrontation with Bernard, I realized a way to improve my odds. I fell again on purpose.

"Get up." When Bernard wrenched my arm to force me to move, I went limp so that my dead weight made it harder. He crouched down and shouted in my ear. "Get up, I say, or I'll drag you by your hair!"

Forcing him to bend over was to my advantage, because when he reached for my hair, Bernard forgot to defend himself. I yanked my head out of his reach, wound back my stoned fist, and aimed for his eye. While my hand hit bony socket, the rock struck dead center. Nathan's tutor would have been proud of his unintended student.

Bernard's scream echoed through the forest. He dropped to his knees and lowered his head while both hands covered his face. He rolled onto his back and then returned to his knees in agony; his stringy hair flying in every direction. For an instant, I saw his afflicted eye filled with blood. The eyelid fluttered uncontrollably.

While Bernard was flinging himself, a gold ring rolled out of his pocket and lay partially hidden by the snow. I didn't reach for it. This was the moment I needed to take advantage of my enemy's weakness. A larger rock appeared a few feet away, not close enough to reach,

Harley swaggered my way. I tried to back away, but I went down in the snow. My skirts hindered my escape. All I could see was the dirk in his hand; the sharp blade appeared to be pointed at my chest. Unexpectedly, Harley walked right by me and headed toward Bernard. With one slash he cut his partner's throat. Blood spewed from Bernard's throat. The horses, frightened by the smell, whinnied, pulled on their tethered reins, and ran off.

"Damn it." Harley's quick get-away had disappeared. He turned back to look at his dead partner. "Much obliged, Sweets. I've been meanin' tae take care o' that bugger for some time now. You just made it a wee bit convenient."

Harley bent down and reached for the ring and held it between his thumb and forefinger. "I had to cut off her finger to get this. Wasn't easy. That blasted dog nippin' at my heels. I took care of them. Both bitches." He held up his dirk and turned it in front of his face. The blood dripped down the cold steel over his hand. "My so-called partner was stealin' me blind o' my hard-earned property."

The murderer put the ring in his pocket, and then wiped the blade in the snow leaving a long thin stain. "Let's get goin'. The crows'll finish him off."

"Where are we going?" I didn't care about his answer. My concentration was on the rock, still in my hand, sticky with Bernard's blood. I grasped it tightly.

Before Harley could respond, another voice answered. "The lass is not going anywhere. Drop your weapon." Alain flexed his sword to remind Harley the dirk was no match.

"I don't think so." Harley reached down and grabbed me quickly. He put one arm around my neck so tight I could feel his muscles tighten. Barely able to breathe, I reached up with my hand to search for some space between his arm and my throat. In the process I dropped the rock. Harley chuckled and returned the dirk to my chest. Together we walked and stumbled backward. "The lady's brother wouldn't appreciate it. He's promised me a pretty price tae get her back in tae the lovin' arms o' her family."

For a brief deadly moment, I felt the turn of his head. He must have looked back for the horses, hoping they'd return, when he hissed, "Guess we'll be walkin' after—" The last sound that came out of his mouth was a gurgle. Harley had forgotten an essential element of the tutor's lesson. Never take your eye off your opponent's weapon.

I could feel a shudder go through him. His arm still around me, we went down together. I quickly untangled myself and gasped at his opened eyes. Neither was focused.

Alain's sword had gone through Harley's neck. When he pulled it out blood gushed from the wound.

Alain rushed to my side, got down on his knees, and lightly put his hands on my shoulders. When I leaned in on him, he put his arms firmly around me. At first, I was too overcome to cry, but when the sobs came, I struggled for air.

I don't remember how long I clung to Alain, but I do remember him saying, "It's over Anna. You have nothing more to fear." I nodded, knowing that was true, but held onto him, nonetheless.

Filib rounded up the horses and cleared the camp. Then the little Scot stood near the dead and gestured to Alain who gently walked me over to the grisly sight.

"I know Bernard would not touch you. He worked for Maurice. But did Harley?"

"He tried. Bernard stopped him. He had orders from Maurice to deliver me unmolested. Harley didn't care. His employer was my brother."

Alain nodded and took my hand stained with blood. Whose blood, I couldn't say. I told Alain and Filib all I knew about each man's treachery. "Harley hoped to increase his purse by double-crossing Bernard. He planned to get his share once I was delivered to Maurice. And then he was somehow going to kidnap me again and take me to Nathan."

Filib spoke. "You foiled their plan. You're a clever lass."

Searching in my pocket, I found a cloth and wiped the drying blood off my hand. When that didn't work, Filib reached down and offered a handful of snow. Freed of any bloody remnants, my hands were wet and raw. After I wiped them on my skirt, I turned to face both Scots. "My brother wanted me back, but he didn't care how it was done. He only wanted possession of me to assuage his false pride?" I took a deep breath and tried to swallow the choking feeling in my throat. "I will never return to my father's house. I no longer have a brother. He is dead to me." With both hands I grabbed the right side of the bodice of my dress and pulled until there was a small tear in the seam.

I could feel the eyes of each man. Puzzled, they said nothing, waiting for me to continue.

"Can we go? I want to leave this place."

Alain said. "There's one more thing." He gestured toward Harley's body.

I averted my gaze from the dead man sprawled near the dying fire. "Was it necessary to kill him?"

"Aye. He might have had the strength to kill you if he was only injured. If we had let him live, he might have made it back to Nathan. You would always live in fear, wondering if your brother would send someone else."

"But when Harley doesn't return, won't Nathan wonder what happened?"

"Yes, but by that time you'll be living under the protection of my clan. Harley needed to pay for dishonoring you. He knew that the moment he touched you."

Alain turned me toward the crumpled body. "Look at him, Lass. His death is payment to restore your honor. If you want, I will give you my knife and you can stab him yourself. It is your right."

I wanted nothing more than to turn away from his sightless stare into eternity. "That's not necessary."

147

"He'll never harm you again. You never have to worry if he's following you, waiting to strike. It's important to look at his lifeless body and know that."

I nodded.

Just as we turned to leave, I said, "Wait. There's something I must get." I reached down and searched Harley's pocket until my finger touched a cold metal object. I placed the ring in Alain's outstretched palm. "I believe this belonged to the woman who lived in the abandoned croft. Harley killed her for it, along with Skirts' mother who tried to defend her mistress."

I picked up my skirts, walked toward the horses and looked up. The thick morning clouds had parted, the air no longer smelled of snow. The sun began to lighten the day, the gruesome darkness gone. A new sound replaced the night echoes. On the lower bough of the towering oak, perched a murder of crows. Their raucous caws reminded us they had a job to do.

After many hours of traveling, the horses picked up their pace as we neared the MacArthur home. Caesar and Phineas were anxious for their stalls. The pull of fresh straw and an extra helping of oats in their feedbags were hard to resist. When we arrived at a crest overlooking the snow-covered glen, Alain and Filib held the reins taut to keep the horses from bolting home. In full sun, the virgin whiteness played in and out of the trees despoiled by the track of elk that marked its path from one side of the tree-line to the other.

Alain adjusted his plaid around our shoulders as he surveyed the familiar sight. He sat up on his horse and with obvious pride in his voice he announced, "Thistlestraith."

A large two-story house surrounded by a waist-high stone wall sat in the center of all the whiteness. Puffs of smoke billowed from three chimneys conveying a sense of warmth, and safety. Filib and Alain joked about the fresh baked bread, beef pies, and mugs of ale that would be forced on them by the cook.

Filib clicked at his horse and made his way down the hill leaving us alone. Horse and rider left a trail in the snow which crossed the elk tracks.

"Alain, will your father know who I am?"

"He has done business with your father, but he's never mentioned you."

"No, I mean, will he know that I'm a Jew? I don't want to cause trouble for you."

"You are under my protection now. Nowhere could you be safer."

Alain was naïve. He thought it was a simple matter to keep the haters away. But I'd heard my father's stories. As a Jew, I could travel to the ends of the earth, and I would never be safe.

His voice interrupted my thoughts. "Anna, why did you tear your dress back there in the camp?"

"It's a sign of mourning for my dead brother."

"But he isn't dead."

"To me, he is."

The sun went behind the clouds and a damp chill returned. I pulled the hood over my head and shuddered.

"Come, you're cold."

Caesar picked up the pace as we neared the barn. Like his namesake, he pranced like a conqueror. He snorted and neighed, and one or two mares responded. As soon as we got off, he went straight to his stall. In no time, his burden was forgotten.

A stone path led to the house. It was softly lit by the faint glow of candlelight and the fireplace that emanated through the windows.

"Anna. Wait." Alain touched my arm and pulled me back inside the barn. His eyes were dark and serious, his eyebrows knitted. He took my hands in his. "I said before you are under my protection."

"You have put yourself in harm's way. You and Filib. Now you bring me to your home. I am forever grateful. I will leave as soon as I'm—"

"Anna marry me. As a member of my family, my clan would protect you."

"I cannot ask you to do that. No priest would consecrate a marriage between a Jew and a Catholic. When I asked for your help in saving me from a life with Maurice, I had never meant for you to sacrifice yours."

"There is nothing I wouldn't do for you. From the moment we met, I knew you were to be mine. There's no one I have wanted more."

"But—"

He pressed one finger to my lips. "Shh. Nothing you say will change my mind. If marrying you means I can never walk into my father's home, then I will turn Caesar around, and we will be off. And if a new home won't welcome us, we'll go to the ends of the earth until we find our sanctuary. Only with you can I be at home."

Refuting his argument was useless. This was a man who knew what he wanted. I was glad of it. For I, too, wanted nothing more than to be with Alain for the rest of my days.

He leaned forward and kissed my forehead, my brow, and my cheeks while pushing an erstwhile curl off my face. "Promise me now Anna Isaac, that you will be mine."

"My full name is Anna Rachel bat Salomon Isaac. *Bat* means 'daughter of' in Hebrew. I promise Alain...MacArthur. Is there more? To your name?"

"Alain Alexander Iain MacArthur."

I lowered my eyes and the tears overflowed. Wiping them away with the back of one hand, I quickly took a deep breath so my voice wouldn't be swallowed by sobs.

"Alain...Alexander...Ian...MacArthur. If you will have me, I promise to be yours and only yours. Forever."

TWENTY-TWO
The Laird's Chamber

Nightfall had inundated the world around us. Pale clouds and the threat of snow gave off a soft gray glow that lit up the entrance to the barn. The smoky incense cast off from the house chimneys reached us on the wings of a light breeze that also played with the straw scattered around the stalls.

Alain and I stood close, heads nearly touching. The cold air was no match for our combined heat.

"Handfasting," Alain said. "It's an ancient custom."

"We would be husband and wife? It's that simple?"

"Aye. Almost."

"The Church approves?"

"The priests don't like it. It lessens their authority, but the Highlanders have a special preference for the old ways. With handfasting we would not need to announce banns or get the blessing of our parents. A priest and witnesses are unnecessary."

Caesar whinnied and snorted while his hooves kicked the wooden stall.

Alain looked at his horse and chuckled. "Aye Caesar. You will make a fine witness." He turned and his tone became serious again. "But only if the lady agrees to my proposal."

"I promised I would be yours, but when I asked, just now, if handfasting would make us man and wife, you replied, 'almost.' What did you mean?"

"Handfasting is a betrothal, a promise of a future marriage. It's not legally binding. It lasts for a year and a day, and at the end of that time, if you feel you cannot be my wife, for any reason, you may walk away."

How simple, considerate, and decent compared to the marriage I had been almost forced to enter. Now, I was in control. When I gazed into Alain's soft brown eyes and saw the man I had grown to love and respect. I realized I was willing to relinquish that control. There was no reason to fight back this time. "Then how does our betrothal...or handfasting as you call it...turn into a marriage?"

"We are not husband and wife until we consummate the marriage, when you are ready. Then and only then."

151

Other than the thud of his sword against the barn door we were silent like two souls sitting on the precipice of a lifetime together, contemplating our first act which would bind us forever.

"You probably haven't heard of handfasting in Edinburgh. The kirk has declared it unlawful."

"I am not familiar with any customs outside of my family. I have only attended the marriage of distant cousins. The ceremony was lovely. The heavily veiled bride shared a cup of wine with her groom as they were wed under a canopy. The canopy was held over the heads of the couple and symbolized the tent my forefathers lived in when they wandered the desert."

"Whether it is a marriage between two of the same faith or a Christian and a Jewess, it should be one of mutual consent."

The Anna who lived in her father's house would have lowered her eyelashes, blushed and answered in a faltering voice. But not today. And not with Alain. I clasped his hands tighter. "I will not change my mind. Not in a year or a year and a day. I am ready to welcome you as my husband. When I said I would be yours forever, I meant every word."

Alain's eyes glistened. "I am sorry I can only offer you a barn as our cathedral and a horse as a witness. I wish you were attired in the finest silks."

"I had a beautiful dress. It was embroidered with metallic thread so that it glowed in the candlelight. My father spared no expense for a wedding feast overflowing with exotic foods and hired musicians to entertain the guests. But it meant nothing. The Talmud tells us, *A woman prefers poverty with love to wealth without love.*"

Alain's hand fumbled in his pocket. He retrieved the gold ring and held it between his thumb and forefinger.

"It is customary for the groom to give a gift of value to his future bride. It symbolizes his respect for her and ensures his promise to protect and defend her honor."

"That's the ring Harley stole from the woman he butchered." I shuddered visualizing the last time I saw it in his bloody fingers. "How can I accept it?"

"That poor soul fought to keep her ring. She must have cherished it. How better to honor her than by wearing the ring as a symbol of our life together? She would never have wanted Harley to have it. If she could speak from the grave, she would give you her blessing."

He placed the ring on my third finger, right hand. Instead of feeling cold, the metal was warm from Alain's touch. "I've heard it said that you should wear the ring on your right hand while we are betrothed. And then once we are married you may switch it to your left."

I clenched my fingers into a fist to embrace a new friend.

"There is one more part of the custom - the handfasting. The symbol of binding our lives together." Alain looked on the floor of the barn and then at the front wall. "We need something to bind us together."

"Will this work?" Reaching into my pocket, inside the folds of my dress, I pulled out a rope. "This is what was used to tie my hands."

He took the rope and held it like it was a string of pearls. "Aye, this will do."

"Wait, may I add to the ceremony?" Before he could answer I took the shawl out of my satchel. "Do you have any whisky?"

Alain thought for a moment and then went into the stall across from Caesar where Phineas stood swishing his tail. Alain returned with a flask. He smiled wryly. "I know where Tom, the stable boy, hides his stash. I am sure he won't mind."

Like biblical Rachel, my shawl served as my veil. I pointed to some elms at the edge of a graveyard. "Let's stand under the trees. The branches will serve as our wedding canopy."

Alain made a large enough loop in the rope so our hands could fit through. We held onto each other and let the rope drape on our wrists. He gazed at the sky and waited a few moments before speaking.

"Anna Rachel, I will take you to be my wife."

As if God approved, a light swirl of snowflakes danced in celebration clinging to Alain's eyelashes and my veil.

"Alain Alexander Iain MacArthur, I will take you to be my husband."

With no clergy to tell us what to do next, we did what was natural. Alain lowered his head and pressed his lips to mine. And I accepted his token of love.

He opened the flask, offering me the first sip. It was not a cup of wine, but under the circumstances the burning liquid couldn't have been sweeter.

"Father, I'd like to introduce you to my wife."

'Wife' was a new and strange word to my ears. I glanced at Alain. He stared straight ahead at his sire.

Laird MacArthur was a tall man with a full head of snow-white hair tamed by a leather thong. His height and the intensity of his dark brown eyes were the features he had bequeathed to his son. His large aquiline nose must have been responsible for his deep nasally voice.

"I sent you to Edinburgh to conduct clan business." His shifted his focus on me. "Now I understand why you took so long." Returning his gaze to Alain, "Your clothes are blood-stained, and you've brought the forest in with you." He sniffed and turned up his nose. "Smells like you've been sleeping in the barn, and with no warning you walk in here and present this woman as your wife?"

His rebuffs swirled about our heads; the quiet in the room became unsettling until his scowl disappeared. "You could at least tell me the young woman's name."

For the first time since we'd entered the house, Alain straightened his back so his height matched his father's. "Anna Rachel MacArthur is my wife."

I took a step toward the tall man and was grateful when he extended his large hands, the backs of which were matted with white.

"Welcome to my home, my family, and my clan. I worried about my son. I thought he would never find the right woman. From what I can see, he has done well." He turned to Alain. "She doesn't scare easy." The Laird's grin almost divided his face in two. As he embraced us at the same time, I heard him mumble. "Aye, like a barn."

That's when I noticed the impatient young woman standing behind Alain's father.

"Brother, why didn't you tell Filib to warn us you were bringing home a wife? I would have made sure Cook kept supper warm."

Alain held his arms out and his sister rushed toward him. The two, genuinely glad to see each other, hugged while Alain lifted her petite frame and swung her around. Her long black hair swayed every which way. Davina pulled back and smacked her brother's arms to let her down.

"Father is right." She waved her hand in front of her nose. "I'll get Molly to start heating water for your bath."

"Anna, this is my sister, Davina. She's younger by several years, but feels the need to rule the house, scold her big brother, and pretend to be my mother."

Then Davina turned to me. "Now let me get a look my new sister." She circled me as if inspecting the embroidery on a new dress. "Not bad, Alain. But I have a feeling Anna's too good for you." Davina winked. "Are you sure you want this big brute for your husband? Let me ken if he doesn't treat you right. Our mother is no longer here to set him straight, but I'll take care of him."

How different was Alain's family! Mine was somber and serious; his was playful and not afraid to show affection. And he had a sibling who adored him.

"Come with me. Based on how much Filib ate, you must be famished. Cook is done for the day, but I am sure I can find something." She took my hand and chatted all the way to the kitchen.

The room was warm from the hearth and still smelled like fresh baked bread from the morning. I forgot how ravenous I was until Davina placed a plate of food and a goblet of wine in front of me. Alain's sister asked many questions. I couldn't blame her. One look at my torn bodice and filthy skirts covered with burrs and dried mud would pique anyone's interest. I hardly looked like a bride. I was careful with my replies and kept the details sparse.

I liked Davina immediately, but I was grateful when Alain entered the kitchen before our conversation became awkward and revealed too much.

154

"Davina, we've had a long day. It's time we retired."

"But Anna hasn't eaten yet. I'm afraid that's my doing. I've been talking too much." Davina scooped up the plate and began to cover it with a cloth.

"Leave it. I'll come down for it later." Alain gave his sister a kiss on the forehead.

We said goodnight and I plodded up the stairs. I was pleased with my new family and my home at Thistlestraith.

Alain led the way down the darkened hall with a lit sconce. I glanced over my shoulder and saw we were being followed by our elongated shadows. We stopped before the largest and most intricately carved door.

"The laird's chamber?" I asked.

"My father thought it would be fitting for our wedding night."

The moment we entered I was reminded of Father's library. The beeswax candles filled the air with their sweetness along with that of wintergreen. In front of the fireplace, stood a tub filled with steaming water. The minty scent came from a cake of soap.

On the huge canopied bed were a folded white shirt and a plain cotton shift.

"Your father went to a lot of trouble."

"This is the same room he shared with my mother on their wedding night."

The mention of his absent parent reminded me how little I knew about Alain.

"Let me see if I can get us something to drink. If I don't, I suspect we'll soon hear a knock on the door."

Thankful for this gift of privacy, I quickly shed my dirty clothes. I couldn't resist the warm bath, the fragrant soap, and the sublime luxury of washing my hair.

When Alain returned, I was in my shift toweling my hair. He proudly held up a decanter of wine along with two goblets. As he poured, the light from the fireplace reflected on the ruby waterfall.

"Thank you." I put the cool glass to my lips and didn't stop until it was gone. Alain refilled my glass.

I took my time between each sip, filling the void with questions. "How old are you?"

He chuckled after taking a gulp and stirred the remains in his goblet. "I'm twenty-two."

"Oh." I drank again, and although he didn't ask, I offered, "I'm almost sixteen."

"Sally told me you were fifteen."

"Oh, did she?" I said along with another swallow. It was amazing how much better the second glass tasted. "What else did she tell you?"

"She told me about your brother and what he did to her...and you."

I drained the rest of the glass and looked at the bottom as if somehow, more would magically appear. "If Nathan discovers how she helped me, he will take it out on her...and her mother. I'm not there to protect them, although there was little I could do." My eyes welled up when I thought of my friend's predicament.

"Let your worries rest on my shoulders."

Alain filled my glass a third time. I sighed and willingly accepted his offer. I swirled the wine with my little finger and then stuck it in my mouth to ensure not a drop was wasted. Then with my hand I wiped my wet cheeks.

Alain put his bent forefinger under my chin. "What is it? Is something wrong? Is this not what you expected?"

"I know how to run a household, manage servants, and keep accounts balanced, but I'm afraid I know little about what it takes to be a wife. Maybe if I lived on a farm I'd be better educated. Mrs. Gibbons and Fiona used to gossip about the goings-on between a man and a woman, but they'd always stop talking when I entered the kitchen. My father would never...I'm sorry. You've married a foolish girl with little to offer."

"A foolish lass? Never." He placed my empty glass on a nearby table and cupped my face in his hands moving the damp curls from my face. "By agreeing to be my wife you have made me the happiest of men." One hand went around my back; the other brought my lips to his. The kiss was warm with a promise of more, but he pulled away slightly "Besides, I'm not so experienced myself. Aye, I've seen the horses do it, and some kine too. Most of what I learned is from Filib, Tom, and some of the other men. But to hear them talk, they're a flock of crowing cocks."

I didn't know if it was the vision of cocks or too much wine, but I laughed so hard I fell on the bed. "Do you mean?"

"Aye. All the young lads, at least the ones I know, lie about their experience with the lasses. It's not manly to admit that you haven't lain with a woman so they make up tales that would shame even the most experienced whores."

I laughed. Remembering my empty glass, I asked, "Can I have a wee bit more wine?" I squeezed my thumb and forefinger together to show how much.

"I think you've had enough for now, and I'd best take my bath before the water cools."

Those were the last words I remembered. It must have been close to dawn when I opened my eyes. The leaden sky that winked through the slit of the window covering was the first hint of a new day. Soft breathing, the extension of a leg, and the warmth of the mattress reminded me I wasn't alone.

I turned and met the red curls partially covering Alain's face. I pulled my twisted shift from under me while Alain propped his head up with his hand. "Good morning, my lovely Jewess."

"Shh. No one must hear you say that."

"It will be our first secret."

"Did you take your bath already?"

"Aye. A while ago."

"I must have fallen asleep. I was so tired and the wine...." My hand went to my head and I tried to rub away the pounding.

"There was no waking you, so I let you sleep."

"Thank you. But we were supposed—"

"We have the rest of our lives and—"

I didn't let Alain finish. I leaned in, put my arms around him, and kissed him fervently. His lips responded, lightly, at first. He put his arms around me, pulled me close and pressed hard. My hands wandered along his tight back muscles and meandered up and down the nobs of his spine. With little effort he flipped me on my back, and half of his weight pressed against me. I squirmed and let out a gush of air.

"Did I hurt you? Am I too heavy?"

"Oh no. Not at all."

His hand came up, untied the string of my shift, and cupped my breast. I moved my hand to his chest and found one nipple which perked up the moment I touched it. Alain's breathing became deeper and more desperate. I helped him pull my shift up around my waist while he moved on top. With a sense of urgency, for both of us, I wrapped my legs around him, and he entered me.

Our joining was accompanied by a chorus of moans and squeals. Not from pain, but from the primal pleasure we discovered in each other. Quickly, our movement found a rhythm as we became a single moving force. Too soon, Alain's body went limp. Beaded with sweat, his chest rising and falling with his heavy breathing, he rolled to my side.

For a few minutes we said nothing but stared at the ceiling.

"I cannot say I'm sorry for what we just did. But maybe I should apologize," he said.

"For what?"

"I told you before the handfasting that I wouldn't force myself on you. I would wait until you were ready. But, once we started, I couldn't stop."

"But I didn't want you to stop."

"Then you enjoyed it?"

"Yes. Yes, I did."

I put a hand under my head and turned toward Alain. My finger draw circles on the hairs on his chest.

"I'm ticklish you know."

157

"I have a lot to learn about you."

"And I you."

"Alain, does this mean our betrothal has now become a marriage?"

"Aye. I'm afraid I'm yours - for all eternity."

"No priest will demand our marriage to be sanctified in a church?"

"Well, they'll want it, but it's not necessary."

"So, no one needs to find out who I am? It can be our secret? And Filib's?"

"Yes, Mrs. MacArthur. No one can take you from me now."

"Then there's something I must do." I removed the ring from my right hand and placed it on my left.

The sun's rays were now making their way into our room and skittered across the bed causing Alain's skin to glow. His leg muscles rippled as he jumped out of bed and grabbed his shirt. Pulling it over his head it fell to his knees.

"It's time to head to the kitchen, Mrs. MacArthur. We need to start our marriage off with some proper nourishment. Wine and love are not enough to live on."

TWENTY-THREE
The Rule of Three

My learned father did not always rely on books to guide him. He also used The Rule of Three which should have made no sense to an educated man. Pronounced in Latin, *omne trium perfectum* Father said that events occurring in threes were a sign of perfection, completion, and positive energy in the world. His evidence came from Genesis. On Day One, God created the heaven and earth, but there was nothing else. On Day Two, He separated the opposing forces of heaven and the seas. On Day Three, the seas were set in their place exposing the dry land. Thus, my father explained, after three days of creation, divergent forces harmonized so life could exist.

I became a believer in The Rule of Three after a triad of visitors turned my world upside down.

During the first few months of my marriage, I quickly bonded with Alain's family. Many hours were spent in Davina's company which brought us closer. It didn't take long for a sisterly bond to blossom.

We shared household chores, and some I found disagreeable. She giggled when I must have turned three shades of green while stirring the lard and smelly lye to make soap. I fared far worse with the blood sausage, maybe because I was expected to eat it.

The sausage preparation took up much of the kitchen work area. Pork fat was cut into small chunks on a wooden table, a huge bowl sat nearby for mixing, and water bubbled in a black metal pot. It was a hot smelly task and left me drenched.

Davina handed me a large wooden paddle. "Put the onions into the pork fat and I'll add the barley, oats, cream, and spices."

Whenever I slowed down to arch my back, Davina reminded me, "Don't stop mixing."

"Ugh, it's nauseating."

After adding each ingredient, Davina put her hands on her hips and nodded with satisfaction as she watched the mixture bind. "But it tastes divine." She bit her lip and looked at me curiously. That habit of hers usually meant she was puzzled. "Don't tell me you've never eaten blood sausage?"

159

I swallowed and nodded limply while patting my forehead and cheeks with the edge of my apron.

Davina moved to the wooden bucket half-filled with pig's blood and strained it to remove any clumps. Then she poured the blood into the cereal mixture turning everything into a dark pink mass. I stirred the paddle round and round in rhythm with the room spinning around my head. The mixture thickened until the stirring became too difficult. My back and upper arms ached.

Alain's sister dipped one of her fingers, put it in her mouth, and it emerged clean with her lips making a sucking sound. "Go ahead, try it."

I clamped one hand over my mouth and rushed out to the garden releasing fresh fertilizer onto the tiny shoots. By the time I stumbled back, Davina hummed while funneling the gelatinous mixture into casings. She stopped and was about to bite her lip. "Am I to be an auntie? I figure you must be in your third month. Don't worry. I won't say a word."

I wasn't pregnant but didn't discourage Davina's cheery thoughts. It was easier than having to explain my aversion to eating blood sausage. As Davina massaged the casings so the mixture spread evenly, I gestured the need to return to fresh air. The earthy scent of hay and horses was preferable.

Walking toward the barn, I spied off in the distance, just at the tree-line where the glen opened up, two riders approaching. One was Filib on Phineas. But I couldn't quite make out the other. The little Scot had been away for a fortnight. Clan business explained Alain.

I shielded my eyes and squinted. Filib's riding partner was a woman. Her skirts flounced and her cloak billowed behind like a sail. There was something else moving around the horses, much smaller.

I covered my mouth to muffle cries of joy. It was Sally. And Skirts.

As soon as the horses stopped, Sally slid to the ground and into my arms. Howls and barks harmonized with our cries. Skirts, overjoyed with our reunion, ran in and around our skirts. Sally and I stepped back; we giggled at the sight of our soaked cheeks. I hugged her again to ensure this wasn't a dream. "I thought I'd never see you again."

"Aye. I hated myself for not sayin' goodbye. Thin's happened so fast. Before I kent it, ye were gone. I wept for days. My mother got tired o' my bawlin,' but I kept my mouth shut and didna' tell anyone what I kent."

We were distracted by Skirts nipping at our heels. He was not to be ignored.

"Skirts. I missed you." I scratched behind his ears, and he rolled on his back; his tail wagged furiously. "How did you...? I mean, how is it possible you're both here?"

Sally nodded toward Filib while he walked away with Phineas.

"Filib," I called, "I don't know how you were able to get Sally or find Skirts, but I'm forever grateful. Thank you."

"Mumph. Thank your husband."

I lightly kissed Alain's forehead, his lips, and his closed eyes. His eyelids fluttered, a smile formed, and one lid opened. "Did you sleep well?"

"After last night. And the middle of the night, and then at dawn. I might have been in bed, but I didn't get much sleep."

I snuggled my back against his chest. I could feel the muscles on his legs tighten.

He draped one arm around me, pulling me closer while his other hand went under my shift to caress my thighs, stomach, and breasts. His lips lightly kissed the back of my neck and the edges of my ears as he whispered, "I can't get enough of you. Even when I think you have quenched my thirst, the moment we're apart, I want to lie with you again." His voice faded. "I'm afraid you have me totally under your control...."

The sleepy smell of him mingled with the last of the smoky peat from the fireplace. I pulled the covers over us trapping the heat and nestled in.

"Alain?"

"Mmm."

I tried again but this time he answered with a light snore. Slowly I untangled myself out of his arms, grabbed my shawl, and headed to the kitchen.

As if she'd always lived at Thistlestraith, I found Sally in the kitchen balancing a large wooden bowl on her hip. She scooped dollops of thick porridge into a smaller bowl for Filib. As Sally entertained everyone with her humorous and sometimes bawdy tales, Filib watched her every move.

"Good morning, Sally. Filib." I nodded to the others.

I edged close to Sally and asked in a hushed tone, "Come with me? I have so much to tell you." After Sally's unexpected arrival, we found little time to speak privately.

Except for the kitchen, Mr. MacArthur's study was the warmest room in the house. It faced east, and if it was a sunny morning, the stone walls soaked up the heat and light flooded the room. The only furniture was a large oak desk, covered with journals, books, and papers, and a couple of cushioned chairs flattened by years of use.

"How's Father?" I asked before we even sat down.

"Ach. He took it hard when ye left. Locked himself in his library for many days and wouldna come out even for food. Old Simon begged him, but ye ken your father is stubborn. My mother left food outside the door. At first, he ate nothin', just tea and some broth. Right before I left with Filib, your father seemed to improve, but still spent much o' the day holed up in his library. He hasna spoken tae Nathan since that night."

Sally and I talked for much of the morning. I told her what happened after I left Edinburgh, my encounter with Harley and Bernard, and my unusual marriage to Alain. "Did Nathan or Father find Maurice tied to my bed?"

"No. Bernard found him first. Maurice accused your father o' renegin' on the marriage contract and announced he was leavin' on the next ship bound for France. After Bernard and Maurice left, I followed them tae The Mile. Maurice hired a carriage tae take him tae the port and handed Bernard a heavy purse. Right away Bernard purchased a horse and rode off in a different direction."

"And somehow, his path crossed with Harley's, each hoping to enrich their purses by turning me over to Maurice or Nathan. Or in the Harley's case - both."

"Thankfully, that's over. Ye now have a good life wi' Alain."

"And you. Will you stay here too?"

"Aye, there might be someone who'll catch my fancy."

"Filib?"

"Perhaps," she snorted. "He's a bonny lad. Quiet. I like them that way. Broodin' and mysterious."

"He couldn't keep his eyes off of you this morning."

"Really. I hadna noticed." She rolled her eyes, and we succumbed to girlish laughter.

"Wouldna' it be lovely livin' here, havin' dozens o' bairns and growin' auld together?"

"Yes. It would be." I didn't want to lessen her joy, but I needed to explain the arrival of the local priest, Father Drummond.

As God's representative in the local parish, Father Drummond visited every fortnight. He arrived late in the afternoon so he could conveniently stay for the evening meal. The only mystery was if he planned to stay the night.

The priest was a heavy-set man. Alain maintained it was from all the food the farmers' wives offered. Anxious to show off their culinary skills, they were as generous as they could be even when harvests were meager.

His head was clean-shaven except for two furry dark eyebrows that resembled wooly bear caterpillars in autumn. And like the little critters, his eyebrows wiggled and appeared to crawl across his forehead whenever he became agitated. Except for his clerical collar, he was clad entirely in black and his cassock swayed in rhythm with his gait.

Father Drummond had two irritating habits. In the midst of conversation, he would close his eyes, direct his face heavenward, and interrupt whoever was speaking. Perhaps he felt God had given him the right to force his opinion and pronounce judgement on all issues. The second was he thumped his knuckles to accentuate a point and the crescendo grew along with his ire. This usually occurred when seated at a table; it was best not to disagree with Father Drummond while he ate.

I chose to remain distant until Father Drummond decided this was the time to get to know me better.

"Did I offer my hearty felicitations upon your marriage, Mrs. MacArthur? You've joined a good Christian family, and Alain is a fine man."

"Thank you, Father." I looked away hoping that would end our short conversation. But he would not be put off.

"Curious, I never saw the banns announcing your marriage."

Alain grabbed my hand. "Anna is from Edinburgh and—"

"I don't know how anyone could live in that devilish stink of a town, full of sinners who will burn in eternal fire." He rapped his knuckles; the plates rattled. "No better than Sodom and Gomorrah. Your soul is safe here rather than that godless place." At the end of his short sermon he crossed himself and recited the Trinitarian formula. "In the name of the Father, the Son and the Holy Spirit." Father Drummond glared around the table. The others did so as well. My hesitation was noted.

Alain was not intimidated. "No banns were needed because we were handfasted. Anna is my true wife, and MacArthur is her name and clan. Now we—"

"Handfasted, you say. Tis no marriage. Not in the eyes of the church. Are you planning to force this woman to live in sin and stigmatize your bairns?"

"We were married by the old ways, accepted by my ancestors for—"

"Then do right by this woman, Man. Preserve her honor and marry her in the church. I will perform a proper ceremony as soon as banns are posted."

"We will—"

"And the sooner the better."

Once the evening meal was over Laird MacArthur took out his fiddle. He held the instrument just above his elbow and pulled the bow across as if sawing a tree. His playing was lively and in no time, everyone, except Filib, clapped and stamped their feet. Alain pulled me onto the makeshift dance floor, and we swung each other around. At the conclusion of the lively number, Alain's father chose a rather slow somber song while Davina added the lyrics. It was a perfect opportunity for Alain and me to slip outside unnoticed and move to a more private place by the smokehouse.

"What are we going to do about Father Drummond?" I asked. "He's a stubborn man."

"He can insist all he wants. He'll be gone tomorrow, and then the matter will drop."

"Until he returns. Are we to go through this every two weeks? And when we have children, will he be more insistent?"

Alain put his arms around me. His strength reassuring although a part of me couldn't let go of the Father's words. "I'm afraid he'll continue with his talk of hell and damnation and spread rumors about your family."

Alain turned me around. "Our family," he corrected. "I told you when I married you that you had nothing more to fear. You are my wife, a MacArthur."

I nodded. But instinct told me this wasn't going to end well.

Just as I finished relating my story to Sally, there was a knock at the door, a latch lifted, and in walked Father Drummond.

"Forgive me Mrs. MacArthur…I'm about to leave, I wanted to thank you for your hospitality."

Relieved he was going I stood up, tightened my shawl, and wished him a safe journey.

He turned to Sally. "Would you mind if I had a private word with your mistress?"

"Father, Sally is not the hired help. She is a guest and my friend."

"Ah, forgive me."

Sally walked past, holding her skirts to ensure she didn't brush against the priest; then glanced back. My pleading eyes met hers before she closed the door.

Alone with Father Drummond, I soon realized his thanks was just a pretense to save my soul.

"Why are you hesitant to wed Alain before God? It's most unusual."

I may not have liked his argument, but from his point of view, it was a reasonable request. If I had been raised in the church, why wouldn't I want a church wedding?

I clasped my hands to still their trembling and stared directly into his eyes. "I'm not sure I understand you, Father. You seem to have already accepted my

164

marriage even without God's blessing by addressing me as Mrs. MacArthur, my married name."

"I only addressed you in that manner out of politeness while I am a guest in this venerable home."

"Polite, you say? You accuse me of being a harlot and have damned my unborn children—"

"Your marriage isn't legitimate. Even if Alain has had carnal relations with you, it's still not sanctified in the eyes of the Lord." He glared, the twin caterpillars flagellating on his blood sausage face. "Handfasting is a pagan rite. Perhaps you're an unbeliever. Then your soul will be damned for all time."

His voice became louder and instead of banging his knuckles he fisted one hand into the other. "Your children deserve parents who adhere to the true faith? Why should they bear your guilt?"

"Father Drummond." A stern nasal voice caused the priest to whirl around. Alain's father stood in the doorway. "The horse is saddled so there's no need to walk." When he saw the priest turn back toward me to resume his lecture, the Laird added, "Anna, Davina needs you in the kitchen."

Just as Sally had, moments before, I skirted the priest keeping my distance. Alain met me outside the door and took my hand. We hurried away to our bedchamber. Once we were alone, I fell into his arms. "He's going to figure it out. Your family will not want me, and I'll be forced to leave."

"That won't happen."

"How can you say that? Your family barely knows me."

"Last night I told my father everything."

Father Drummond continued his visits. I dreaded them because now he approached the legitimacy of my marriage with a renewed fervor. He watched my reaction when he brought up religious rites and customs familiar to any Catholic-born Scot. Alain did his best to avert the inquisition and made excuses for our leaving the table early. On one visit I kept to my room claiming an excruciating headache. Our diversionary tactics were successful temporarily. But Father Drummond kept unleashing his hounds.

I stayed in the company of others' so as not to be alone with the priest, but on one occasion it couldn't be helped. Laird MacArthur suffered from a painful sore throat and a persistent cough. Various remedies were tried. Davina mixed up the family recipe of melted mutton suet and beeswax. She spread the yellowed mixture on a cloth, placing it just under her father's nose and covering his mouth and throat from ear to ear. It was to stay in place until the smell became intolerable.

When the cough persisted, I suggested my father's remedy. Tea made from fresh horehound leaves. The herb was starting to flower, so it was the perfect time to take cuttings of the dark veined leaves from the wild patch near the family garden.

That is where Father Drummond found me. Alone.

He made no polite introduction, offered no good wishes for my health or gratitude for the hearty meal to come. The Father ignored civility.

"Mrs. MacArthur, marriage is between the baptized. Are you?"

His booming voice startled me and the nearby birds nesting among the bushes. Like tiny bombs, the birds exploded into the air, flying in every direction.

"Father? I didn't hear your coming. The birds." I was using my father's old tactic, forcing a question to be repeated so I had time to think of an answer.

"Have the holy waters of baptism washed away your original sin? It's a simple question. I know your husband was baptized. I administered the sacrament. But you?"

"How dare you ask me such a question."

"How dare I? I have been appointed by the church and God Almighty. The Christian home is the vessel where your children will receive their introduction to our faith. I must ensure that it's truly a domestic church."

"My children will be brought up properly."

"Mrs. MacArthur, once again you have eluded my questions. About baptism, your home, and your children."

"I'm not avoiding your questions. I am shocked by your effrontery." I took a deep breath and what I said next surprised the priest and myself. "I have been baptized, and my children will be raised as good Catholics"

I picked up my basket, my skirts, and walked away. When I glanced back, I saw the birds circling over Father Drummond's head. His closed eyes were raised toward the heavens while he crossed himself and whispered the Trinity.

For several weeks we heard little from Father Drummond. He had developed a catarrh which kept him in bed and away from me. Instead of making his rounds, baskets of food, along with various tonics, tinctures, and herbal teas were delivered to his door. I hoped that none of them work.

Davina was obliged to pack a basket, and Sally was asked to bring it to him.

"Ugh! I hate goin' near that man, religious o' no."

"I don't care for him either, but you're just delivering his food. Nothing more."

"I wish't it was nothin' more. The last time, he wanted me tae hold his hand. Then he asked me tae sit on the edge o' his bed. Did ye ever notice how close he

166

sits? Whenever he walks by, he rubs his body against mine, and then asks forgiveness. Tis no accident, I tell you. The man's a prick."

"Then there was the time when the Laird played his fiddle, and everyone started dancin'. That crazy priest asked me tae dance. He placed his hands on my waist and pulled me close. Too close. Filib kept glarin'. If the man wasn't wearin' a clerical collar, I think Filib would have knocked some o' his teeth out" She snorted. "Not that he has many left."

I resolved that I would give Sally some other chore to do. Unfortunately, that meant one of the other kitchen maids would be subjected to his advances.

I didn't feel bad for wishing the priest a prolonged illness. And I didn't offer to make any horehound tea.

With Father Drummond out of the way, at least temporarily, a third visitor arrived. On a cold dreary day in June, Mr. William Paterson, his wife, and young son arrived at our home. Although I had never met the gentleman, he was no stranger. My father had often spoken of the founder of the Bank of England. Now he proposed the creation of a trading company which would offer shares to finance the undertaking of a Scottish colony.

Mr. Paterson cut an impressive figure for a forty-year-old man. His wide forehead, topped with a long curly wig, made his straight-edged nose appeared longer. Although he was a man to be taken seriously, he appeared jovial in nature. He loved to laugh and he did even if nothing comical was said. His habit was to place one hand on his stomach while he erupted into boisterous chortles.

Beside him sat a demure woman dressed in somber colors. William Paterson looked like a peacock next to her. She was introduced only as his wife, and she said nothing the entire visit. Her only movements were a slight smile, an occasional nod, and patting her husband's arm.

Their son, Young Wills, looked like his father. He sat quietly between his parents until his mother pulled a small spinning top from her pocket. The boy called it a teetotum. Wills politely asked to be excused and ran outside to play.

"You have honored my family by coming to my home, sir," began Alain's father. "Welcome to Thistlestraith."

"I am pleased to finally meet the great Laird MacArthur. Your support and prior financial backing of the Company is legendary. Scotland needs more patriots like you."

"I hear it won't be long until we set sail."

"Aye, that is true. Ships have been ordered and building should commence shortly. It seems we will have no trouble finding colonists. Hundreds are signing up."

"Splendid. I wish I were twenty years younger."

"You can still do so. My wife and I will be enlisting. Isn't that right, Mrs. Paterson?" His wife nodded and raised her hand to pat his but stopped mid-air.

"I'm afraid that won't be possible," said Laird MacArthur. "The doctor thinks I'm not up for such a strenuous adventure."

"Perhaps your son could go in your place. With the support your family has given to the cause, there's no doubt he would be accepted."

Now it was my turn to reach for my husband's arm.

"I doubt he'd want to leave his bride anytime soon."

"Yes, yes. Newlyweds. I remember." Mrs. Paterson patted her husband's hand. Perhaps she wanted to remind him to be discreet. "There is an easy solution to the problem. Mrs. MacArthur...Anna...can come too. We expect some of the married men will bring their wives, and I'm sure she will be a great companion for Mrs. Paterson." He looked at his wife. "Why the two of you will be like sisters."

I couldn't help but glance over at Davina. I didn't want another sister. "How long would we be away? In the new colony, I mean?"

"Caledonia is forever, madam, like the English colonies to the north. Certainly, you could come back, but with ocean travel being a dangerous affair it would be many years before you could consider such a thing. We mean to establish a base and people it with Scots who will work, marry, give birth, and die there. This is a holy cause. Those who are chosen to be the first Caledonians will shine with God's favor. We anticipate twelve hundred souls to set out. But from the response we have received so far, we could invite twelve thousand and still have more begging."

"You're very persuasive, sir," Alain said. "My wife and I will have to discuss this."

"Perfectly understandable. This is a big decision, but I'm sure you'll make the right one. I'll let the company know to save three berths for you in the hopes that you will say yes."

"Three?"

"Well, just in case Laird MacArthur has a change of heart. I hear the fountain of youth could be nearby." Mr. Paterson grabbed his stomach and roared with laughter. No one else joined in.

During our evening meal I hardly paid attention to the conversation. My mind was on the proposal set forth by Mr. Paterson. Leaving Scotland would solve one problem – it would put an end to Father Drummond and Nathan. But how could I leave all those I loved? I would miss Sally and Davina and the kindly Laird MacArthur.

Alain and I would have to discuss this, weigh our options. But all were overshadowed by the faint flutter I felt inside.

TWENTY-FOUR

Queen Bee

2005

"*I* must go home." Those four words, by themselves, weren't particularly unsettling. They weren't uttered with dread. But the four that followed were. "My father is ill."

"Of course, you must." From recent experience, I knew the tug at the heartstrings could be especially strong when dire family news surfaced.

I wasn't sure Alec felt the same pull. He rarely talked about his family. I knew only the basics. Mother and Father resided on the Isle of Skye. Iain did too, although he traveled a bit. Alec didn't spend much time at home, even for holidays – except for Hogmanay.

Alec's family emergency would postpone, at least for a couple of days, the next step in our discovery of my ancient ancestor. The paper hidden within the candlestick would have to wait, as well as the remaining contents in the safe deposit box.

"You'll come? To Skye?"

"Do you think your mother wants a guest? I don't want to burden her." What I really wanted to say was - wouldn't I be making a bad first impression? Imposing at the worst possible time.

"My mother won't notice."

"That's understandable. She's got a lot on her mind."

"She'll pretend to be all worked up over my father, but in reality, it'll be more about her. My mother likes to be the center of attention."

Still feeling uneasy, I tried again. "I could stay at a nearby hotel. We could meet for coffee, dinner…or whenever you have a free moment."

"I need you, Hanna." This was said with an edge of desperation in his voice. "It'll be easier knowing you're with me. Besides, my mother has hired help, so an additional guest won't be a burden. Perhaps, we can put some of that old-fashioned Scottish hospitality, which my family talks so much about, to the test."

171

We set out toward Alec's family home on the largest island of the Inner Hebrides. Our seven-hour drive began in a rainstorm. Gushing rivulets streamed down the windshield and the rhythmic whooshing of the car's wipers tried to keep up with the ever-increasing downpour. The wind buffeted the car while vehicles going in the opposite direction dumped torrents of rainwater on the side and front windows. Once we veered off the main highway, and headed west, the rain lessened to a drizzle.

The two-lane road passed through many picture-postcard villages. The streets and sidewalks were empty of shoppers and children at play. Only the parked cars and flowerpots set out on window sills and door stoops hinted of recent human activity.

"One thing I've noticed about people who live in northern climes, they appreciate the short growing season. Look at all the flowers." I pointed to one house in particular. The steps leading to the front door had blue and white petunias, the colors of the national flag, draped across each stair and railing.

"I think you'll appreciate my mother's gardens. They're quite something – very elaborate. She has won awards from the local horticultural society. Three years in a row."

This was the first time Alec had said anything positive about his mother. Perhaps gardening was the key to making a connection with her. This encouraging development didn't last.

"I hope you'll have a chance to show me her gardens."

"My mother wouldn't be too happy about that. The garden is her realm. I'm afraid you'll have to wait for an invitation from Her Majesty."

Once the rain ceased only a few errant raindrops were slurped up by the wipers. Alec leaned over, squeezed my hand, and smiled uncomfortably. Like someone who was about to go underwater, he took a deep breath and took the plunge.

"My father is gravely ill. The clinical term is Fibrodysplasia. It's also known as Stone Man's Syndrome. It's rare. Less than a thousand people, worldwide, are afflicted. My father's muscles and tendons are literally turning to bone."

"Can the doctors cut out the bone?"

"No. That just increases the rate of calcification. The diagnosis came a few years ago. Lately, it has gotten worse. He's now confined to a wheelchair. Luckily, we're still able to care for him at home with the help of a nurse."

Not knowing the right words, I tried to console him. "A debilitating illness can be hard on a family. My Great Aunt Beatrice had Alzheimer's. At first, her family noticed some minor forgetfulness. Everyone kidded her about it. Sort of like

172

how people joke when you can't find your keys. But when Aunt Beatrice forgot what keys were, her children took her to a specialist."

"How old was your aunt?"

"Ninety-one."

Alec never took his eyes off the road. "My father is fifty-eight. In the beginning, we thought it was bone cancer. Not even the doctors knew. But then, one day, his right arm literally froze in place. That's when the diagnosis was made."

"Do you wish you were home more? To be with him, I mean?"

"Aye. I offered to take leave from work. My mother turned me down. She's an independent sort with a wide streak of stubbornness. Must be the Highlander in her. I remember thinking how generous it was, her sacrifice for me. I don't think she realized how bad it was going to get. None of us did."

We arrived at one of many roundabouts. Alec stopped talking to negotiate his way in and out of the circle. A tap on the horn alerted a driver in a rental car to yield. Once out on the straightaway he continued the rest of his story.

"Then there was the night I came home. I wanted to surprise my mother and help with Father's care."

His tone was dark. "Did something happen?"

"My mother wasn't home. The nurse gone. I found Father alone in his bed with the side rails locked so he wouldn't roll out. He must have been trapped for hours." Alec lowered his voice to almost a whisper. "I found him moaning like a caged animal. Shortly after, I heard a car in the driveway, the jingle of keys, and hushed voices. When I came into the foyer, there she was…and not alone. When she saw me, she quickly reached into her purse, thrust some cash at this guy, and shoved him out the door."

"If this is hard to talk about, you don't need to tell me."

"No, I want to. I told you I had to prepare you for my family." He took a deep breath. "My mother made excuses. She claimed the nurse was unreliable and had to let her go but hired no replacement. I asked her why she didn't call me or Iain. She explained she didn't want to bother us. She was desperate for relief of an hour or two. She thought my father would be okay."

Alec stopped for a moment and took another deep breath. "I can understand her needing companionship. She's still an attractive woman. But I found out later she lied. She was away for more than a couple of hours, and this relationship had been going on for some time. That was the reason she didn't want me or Iain around and why she fired the nurse."

"How did you find out all the details?"

"I located the nurse."

We turned onto a road that was a single track, enough for one car although traffic went in both directions. On either side of the roadbed, every quarter mile, there was a cut out. This allowed an oncoming car to yield.

There were other obstacles. An errant sheep or *Hellan coo*, as Alec pronounced a Highland cow, would also share the road. One beep from the horn was usually enough to scatter the sheep. The long-haired coo was another matter.

The antics of the roadside creatures provided a brief diversion from Alec's story. But once they were safely out of harm's way, Alec continued. "I might as well tell you everything. It's easier to shake the skeletons out of the closet all at once. My brother Iain can be difficult. And overbearing."

I remembered the confrontation between the two brothers outside the bank.

"Iain is involved with the right-leaning SNP, the Scottish National Party. Like all who share the same belief, Iain dreams of Scotland's past glory. And the only way to achieve that is for Scotland to regain its sovereignty, independent of the UK."

"Haven't the Scots been fighting for this for centuries?"

"Aye. But sometimes that means my brother prefers to look backwards rather than to the future. That's what Mr. Scott was talking about when he mentioned Darien and The Risings of 1715 and 1745. Those events almost bankrupted Scotland of its wealth and soul. Today most Scots are content with the *status quo*, including me. But Iain will argue your ear off if you dare to disagree with him. The minute we're together, we get under each other's skin. Iain is always trying to pull me toward his way of thinking and his right-leaning comrades. At one point, I did. That lasted until I met Ira. He showed me both sides of the argument. Iain couldn't deal with my change of heart."

"Sort of like a civil war. And your parents. To which side do they lean?"

"To the right. That's not unusual. Many on Skye are attracted to the old ways and some still speak the traditional languages: Gaelic and Scots. But my parents aren't firebrands like Iain."

I couldn't help but compare Alec's family to my own. Except for nationality and geography, there really wasn't much difference. My father and grandparents were confirmed liberals and would talk incessantly against the initiatives proposed by American conservatives.

"But it goes much deeper. Iain is a staunch Catholic and nothing but the old-fashioned religion will do."

"Will he have a problem with me?"

"He will barrage you with questions to see where you stand, not with politics, of course, because you aren't Scottish, but with religion. He's not afraid to be in your face about your beliefs. But I don't want you to worry. I won't let him get away with it."

174

"You know I'm not Catholic. I'm not anything. My father didn't believe in organized religion, and now it seems I may have a Jewish ancestor. I guess that won't please your brother no matter how many generations ago that was."

Alec pulled the car into one of the turnouts to let an oncoming car pass. He put it in park and turned to me. "You don't have to please my brother. His political and religious views, which he uses to measure someone, aren't mine. They mean nothing to me. As my guest, and someone who is becoming more and more important to me, I won't allow him to bully or treat you discourteously. I promise you, you've nothing to fear."

We continued our drive, and at last made our way to a scenic lane on a treeless peninsula overlooking Staffin Bay. The sun had returned, and I lowered the car's visor. Reaching into my satchel on the backseat, I felt the box that cradled the candlestick and found what I was looking for. My sunglasses. I put them on, but realized they were bent out of shape. I showed my crooked specs to Alec. It was good to hear him laugh. I threw the mangled glasses in my bag. It didn't matter. There weren't too many sunny days in Scotland.

The public road dead-ended at a gate which Alec unlocked. We continued on a private lane until we faced a large two-story stone home with two massive chimneys. A crude gravel path encircled the house like a cul-de-sac. From each side of the house were panoramic windows. They were ideally placed because the home was situated on a hill, overlooking the bay, surrounded by gorse-covered mountains.

We drove around the back until a barn, a shed, and a parked car came into view.

"Looks like my brother got here first."

Alec parked and turned off the ignition. Immediately, I heard the squeal of unoiled hinges. A heavy back door opened.

"Here comes the welcoming party."

Three people emerged; only one I recognized. I looked at Alec and was startled by his icy stare. His white knuckled hands gripped the steering wheel. "Asshole," he hissed.

"You told me about your parents and your brother. But you didn't mention you had a sister."

"I don't."

Sound travels easily in old homes like Alec's. Worn out area carpets and thin wall hangings couldn't muffle angry voices that bounced off plaster walls and high ceilings. Unless whispered, arguments were heard along with footsteps and creaky bedsprings providing cheap entertainment. That's how I came to hear the late-night argument between Alec and his brother. Their voices floated through walls and along floorboards into the guest bedroom.

"Why is Kate here?" Alec asked.

Kate was the young woman who I mistook as Alec's sister. I learned she was the daughter of old friends of the family and lived in Portree, the main town on the island. As her name suggested, Kate had the look of old Hollywood: shapely, sophisticated, and stunning. Parted on one side, her thick brown hair fell in waves down her back. Exotic, almond-shaped blue eyes and big pouty lips were enough for any man to get lost in. Kate was the red meat Iain tossed to Alec during our brief encounter outside the bank in Edinburgh.

"Sort of a welcome home present. Eh?"

"Not interested. I told you before."

"Come on Alec. I just thought—"

"That's the problem, you didn't think."

"Not too long ago you would've done anything to be with Kate. You guys were inseparable." He chuckled. "You'll thank me someday. You'll have great looking kids."

"What do I have to do to get it through your thick skull?" Alec paused and lowered his voice, just slightly, as if he remembered the thin walls. "Look, I appreciate your…um…thoughtfulness. Kate was fun when we were in college, but it wasn't serious or long term for either of us." He paused again. I envisioned Alec standing before his brother, being thoughtful with each word he chose.

"Kate's not the lass I want for a wife. I want a woman."

"You don't think Kate's enough woman? Man, are you blind or something?" Iain paused followed by an abrupt noise, like a fist pounding a table. "You're an insensitive ass. What the hell were you thinking? Bringing home a stranger when we're dealing with a difficult family matter."

"I'll try and spell it out for you one more time. I'm only interested in one woman. And it's not Kate."

"There's one simple truth about you, Brother. The family isn't a priority. Neither are the old ways and the church. You're a lost soul who feels no obligation to the past."

"That's not true. I love my country and my family, but I will not choose someone based on which God she bows her head to."

"You're wrong." Iain's voice became louder as if that would make Alec understand. "Someday you'll see I'm right. I hope it's not too late when you do. The old ways and your faith are everything, and Kate would see eye to eye on that."

"So why don't you marry Kate and make the family ghosts happy. I'll not ask for your blessing or Mother's. I'll choose my wife with or without it."

The voices were stilled. There was only the sound of footsteps on the stairs, and then, a click of a doorknob. Alec's bedroom was next to mine. I got into bed and huddled between scratchy sheets smothered by a camphor smelling quilt. Tears of joy dampened my pillow.

Thoughts of Alec and my strange surroundings contributed to my not falling asleep. I couldn't help but think about all that had happened since our arrival.

It was late in the afternoon when Alec parked the car behind his house. Walking towards the welcoming party, he put his arm around my shoulder to announce we were a couple. His mother, Mora Grant, was the first and only one to extend a hand.

Mora was what my grandmother would have described as a classic beauty. Classic because her looks didn't whither with time but grew more lovely. Her thick white hair, with a hint of silver, was swept into a chignon at the base of her neck. She was tall, slender, with almost translucent alabaster skin. Her attire was ageless as well. Attention to detail, like her neatly manicured nails and matching antique earrings and brooch, hardly suggested a sick husband.

My reintroduction to Iain was polite but short. He greeted me with a nod, mumbled we'd already met, and retreated into the house. Kate followed after Alec introduced her as a family friend.

Alec showed me to the guest room, and then disappeared into the library to meet with his family to discuss his father's worsening condition. It wasn't until the early evening when we reunited in the formal dining room. Kate had been invited to stay for the evening meal. Scottish hospitality.

Centered in the room was a long table that could have sat a dozen guests and probably more if leaves were added. The heavy oak chairs were placed strategically while the unused ones stood like sentinels against the wall.

Alec's father didn't join us, so Iain and his mother sat on large armed thrones at either end of the table. Alec and I sat next to each other. Kate was directly across from Alec. Like securing the high ground before a battle, she had an unfair advantage and made full use of it. Every time Alec looked up from his plate, he was confronted with Kate's inviting smile and the occasional toss of her hair which reflected the lights from the large chandelier above. I glanced from Iain to his mother and wondered which one I had to thank for the seating arrangement.

But Alec was on to the ruse. He pivoted his chair ever so slightly toward me and unless addressed directly by Kate, he ignored her. Out of the corner of my eye, I thought I saw fumes pouring from more than one funnel.

Dinner provided an opportunity for informal talk, a chance to size up Alec's family. His mother made sure to mention that Kate and Alec had known each other since childhood; the two families always thought that someday they would be united.

177

It was an awkward conversation considering the two childhood lovers and me, the interloper, were sitting within arms' reach.

"Once they ended up as freshman at the same college, they became inseparable," Mora droned on.

If eyes could growl, Alec's did. "That was a long time ago. We were young and we've moved on. I will always consider Kate a good friend, and I'm sure she thinks the same."

I glimpsed at Kate. Friendship wasn't what she had in mind. I forced myself to look at this from her perspective and realized this had to be difficult for her too. She was sitting across the table from a man she obviously still loved. Now he was rejecting her. Publicly. Her lips quivered into a faint smile, I returned in kind, and then changed the subject.

"Alec, did you tell your family why I came to Scotland?"

Alec suggested that I tell the story which I was happy to do; a safe topic, or so I thought.

"Why that's fascinating, Hanna," Mrs. Grant said haughtily. "I'm sure Professor Mason will be quite helpful. You probably won't even need my son. Besides, his classes will start soon. He's so busy with his students and spends all of his time lecturing, grading papers, and whatever else professors do."

Alec turned his head in my direction and discreetly raised one eyebrow. I bit the side of my cheek to keep from laughing. But Alec's mother made it clear. She preferred Kate.

"Have you found much information about your ancestor?" Now it was Iain's turn. He slurred his words. We hadn't even gotten to the main course, and he was on his third or fourth glass of cabernet.

"I've only read a few passages from the journal. Anna…the woman who wrote it, lived in the late seventeenth century. She was one of the colonists who traveled to Darien…Caledonia, in 1698. It seems she was Jewish."

"Really? I never heard of any Jews going to Darien." Iain smirked as he quickly glanced toward his mother and then back at me? "Does that mean…you're Jewish?"

"What does it matter?" Alec cut in.

"Don't get so defensive. I'm just asking the lass a question."

I put my hand lightly on Alec's arm. I could feel the heat radiating through his shirt. "I don't mind answering. No, I'm not. We aren't sure this woman is my ancestor. We'll know better once we've had a chance to get DNA testing done."

"I'd like to hear the results of that one," said Iain.

178

The next morning Kate was gone, and I met Alec's father.

Even in a wheelchair, I could tell that at one time he had been robust. But the ravages of disease and strong medications made him appear frail and old. He was still able to talk, but Alec told me that eventually that would stop when his jaw locked.

At the present, Mr. Grant's right side was partially frozen. No longer flexible, his arm was pressed tightly against his side. The upper chest area was stiff, and his neck had little mobility. The right leg was rigid so the knee couldn't do its work. Instead, the leg stuck out at an awkward angle. Walking even a few steps was no longer an option. The man was becoming a statue.

Alec's father had every right to be depressed and angry, but instead, he displayed a sense of humor and offered droll conversation. The only person he seemed to have a problem with this was his wife.

"Good morning Hanna. It's nice to meet you." He held out his left hand to shake mine. It was warm and firm. "My son has told me much about you. All good, I assure you, but based on his description, I feared meeting you."

"Why's that?" I looked at Alec, but he just shrugged his shoulders.

"I was expecting a goddess." Suddenly, he raised his voice. "Our son has good taste, don't you think, Mora?" He spoke to his wife as if she couldn't hear well. The unhappy look on her face caused Mr. Grant to squeeze his eyes shut and laugh heartily. Then he squinted to see who else laughed along with him.

I liked him immediately.

Alec's mother ignored the question. His father leaned as best he could, held up his hand and pretended to whisper. "The queen bee is not humming today." Then he raised his voice again. "I've heard about your little escapade here in Scotland. I hope you're enjoying the country."

"Yes. Alec has taken me all over Edinburgh. I've seen a bit of St. Andrew and he's promised to show me more of Skye on our way back. From what I've seen, the island is beautiful."

"Aye, it is. Our tradition tells us that Skye is Gaelic for winged, the shape of the land."

"I didn't know that. I thought it was because when you drive along the roads and through the mountains you feel like you have ascended to the clouds."

"Alec, she's okay. More than okay. You can keep her." Again, he broke into laughter which ended in a bout of coughing. His new nurse pounded his back and covered his mouth with a towel. When that didn't relieve his cough, she wheeled him away.

Breakfast resumed, but now it was a quiet affair. Iain gave us furtive glances. His mother picked at her food and rarely looked up except the one time she chose to address me.

"Hanna. Alec told me you would like to see my gardens."

179

I wiped my mouth with the napkin. "Yes, I would. Living in the city I don't have much of a garden except for a few marigolds and petunias."

"Perhaps after church. It's Sunday, you know, and we always go to hear Father Wilson. I wouldn't miss his sermon unless I was on my death bed. Perhaps you'd like to join us?" She looked over at Alec. "My son would probably appreciate it."

"No, we aren't coming," Alec said. "Hanna and I will keep Father company. I want to spend more time with him before we head back to Edinburgh tomorrow."

"You're leaving, so soon? You just got here." Mora looked unhappy; but her scowl wasn't for her son. It was for me.

"Remember. I'm a very busy professor."

"Alec, I've been giving some thought to the rolled-up paper in the candlestick."

"Okay. What's your plan?"

Iain and Mora had left for church a while ago, and Alec's father was napping. We sat on a bench on the back porch overlooking the bay. The water mirrored the coast, so there was two of everything: mountains, roads, and crofts. The air was filled with the earthy smell of arborvitae and the late summer rush to autumn.

Alec put his arm around me, opened his jacket, and pulled me close against his chest.

"Neither of our fingers can get in far enough to grip the paper—"

His other hand went to my knee and then moved northward. He playfully ran his finger from the bridge of my nose to the tip and then brushed the back of his fingers along my cheeks. I pushed back my hair, which invited him to tickle the edges of my ears.

"Are you listening to me?" His touch was giving birth to goosebumps and shivers down my spine.

"Aye."

Teasingly, I asked, "Is that all you can ever say? Aye?"

"Aye. Sh! I'm concentrating." He moved closer and covered my lips gently with his.

I said nothing more because I couldn't. His lips turned hungry, pressing hard. They devoured my words. Then just as quickly he stopped.

"Come." He grabbed my hand and pulled me down a path along the hedge wall on the edge of the garden. I guessed Alec's intentions, but we never made it that far. We stopped in our tracks as soon as we heard footsteps and a throat clearing.

"Ah, there you are." When Alec's mother saw us together, her voice became brittle. "I thought Hanna wanted to see my gardens. But if you're too busy—"

"Oh no. I'd love to."

"Well then, come along." She straightened the wide-brimmed straw hat that shielded her face. Then she pulled on garden gloves and tucked a basket for collecting flowers in the crook of her arm. Maintaining the image of classic beauty took work.

Alec found an excuse to leave the two of us alone. Before he left, he gathered my face in his hands, and planted a kiss. Out of the corner of my eye I saw his mother turn her back.

Alone in the garden with Mora was uncomfortable. The parting kiss didn't help. Did Alec do that purposely? Was this his way of letting his mother know he was serious about me, and there was nothing she could do to prevent it? Like his mother, I, too, was powerless. I could do nothing about the kiss because I wanted more.

On the return trip we meandered through some of the most beautiful landscape in the world. Our first stop was Mealt Falls just south of Alec's home. We followed the path from the parking lot to the end of the cliff and watched the rushing water descend over 180 feet into the Raasay Sound. I took my turn with other tourists to hang precariously over the edge of a protective barrier to take in the breathtaking view.

From there we traveled south of Portree and took the ferry to Mallaig on the mainland. Passing through Fort William we drove sixteen miles to Glencoe. Carved out by the river Coe, the valley was walled-in by mountains dotted with cotton balls of sheep. The village had a post office, church, general store, restaurants, lodges, and B&B's.

"For a place so beautiful it has a tragic history," Alec said. "You might find it has some relevance to Anna's story."

"Really? Do you think she lived here?"

"I doubt it. Besides her journal starts in 1698. The massacre was six years earlier when the MacDonald clan resided here."

"Massacre?"

"Aye. After William III came to the throne, each clan chief was expected to swear an oath of allegiance. The oath had to be taken by January 1, 1692. The laird missed the cut off by three days due to a ruse meant to detain him and because of bad weather. He was told not to worry and gave his oath anyway. Better late than never was his thinking. He returned home, and a few days later, a small army contingent arrived in his village. True to Scottish custom the MacDonald's offered food and a place to stay. But early in the morning of January 13th, the soldiers attacked their sleeping hosts slaughtering seventy-eight men, women, and children. A few escaped to tell the tale."

"Why didn't the soldiers honor the oath?"

"Because they were part of the Campbell clan. There was a feud between the Campbells and the MacDonalds over some cattle rustling. The massacre was revenge."

"But how would that effect Anna? She wasn't a MacDonald or a Campbell."

"Because of the political repercussions. The government investigated the massacre for many years, and it influenced future decisions including Darien. Think about it in today's terms. Watergate happened in 1972. The investigation took several years, and ultimately changed the way your government operates. Forty years later, Americans still compare every political scandal to that one. The planning for Scottish colonization started only three years later. Both the English and Scottish governments were consumed with the investigation and that affected the implementation of Darien."

Alec and I didn't talk much for the rest of the two-and-a-half-hour ride to Edinburgh. Settling back, I clipped my hair so it wouldn't get tangled from the wind and squirmed in my seat trying to find a comfortable position. I was anxious to get home, back to Anna.

TWENTY-FIVE

Thistlestraith

1698

Every level of my home was filled with activity. At dawn, servants scurried in and out of bedchambers. They removed night-soil pots and added clean water to basins. On wash days, a huge cauldron of water was heated over a wood fire. The night before, undergarments were soaked in urine, and then rinsed before sheep fat and ash were used for scouring the worst stains. After rinsing many times, the clothes were wrung out and spread to dry on thorny gorse bushes.

Work in the kitchen was done by the cook, Davina, Sally, and me. It was a never-ending task to prepare food for the day, tend to the gardens, and chickens.

Alain and Filib oversaw the fields, and they helped Laird MacArthur with the tenants and clan business.

I was most content to be a part of this noisy and industrious household.

The one activity I looked most forward to was wool waulking. Women from nearby farms would gather to process the wool. It involved shrinking and thickening the woven fabric so it would protect the wearer from wind and rain. It took all day.

First, the wool was greased with melted oils from the liver of the dogfish. Then it was soaked in stale urine and water to break up the oil and set the colors. To ensure the process was spread evenly over the entire seventy-foot length of fabric, we bared our arms to knead it in a clockwise direction on a door slab called a waulking board. To help distract us from the smell and our aching arms and backs, we sang songs in Gaelic. Since the words were repeated over and over, I quickly did more than just hum along. Davina interpreted the lyrics, and most of the songs were about young lovers, bairns, or the loss of a sweetheart.

When we weren't singing, the air was filled with lively banter. The women were delighted to catch up with neighbors whom they may not have seen since the last wool-waulking. The activity served as a welcome change from the drudgery of unending chores, and the elders in the group were more than happy to entertain us with their sage advice for curing a colicky baby or reining in a wayward husband.

Others enjoyed spreading the newest gossip.

"Did ye hear about the spinster lady, ye ken, the one with the old mother? It's a good thin' she's almost blind and can't see how her daughter's waistline is bloomin'." To emphasize her point, the storyteller's arms hovered over her own paunch to show how far along the spinster was.

Some stories brought tsks and nods. Others, tears of laughter.

"Ach, that's nothing. I saw Sammie MacPherson sweet talkin' the Widow Duncan. I wonder what his wife'll say about that. He's such a scoundrel, but bonny, aye? I'd send my Hamish out the door if Sammie talked tae me like that."

Some tried to outdo their friends with a more scandalous story.

"I ken a tale that'll curl your toes. The other day I smelled somethin' unholy. I followed the stench till I reached Jenny Bird's. I hid behind the gorse and watched what she was doin' all the while holdin' my nose. There she was, stirrin' a pot with a big paddle, while hummin' some devilish song. It scared me so; I started prayin' to the Lord." At this point of the story, the others around the table crossed themselves. "My prayers were answered when I saw Father Drummond comin' by. He walked right up to Jenny, and just like that she stopped singin'. The good father said somethin' to her, and they went inside. I bet he was savin' her soul. Bless him." All the women crossed themselves a second time, whispered a prayer, and ended with a chorus of Amen.

Waulking the wool became a reason to celebrate. Each woman brought her best dish to share, in addition to the bounty provided by the MacArthur kitchen. The task created hearty appetites, so, we, along with the men, enjoyed a substantial meal.

One morning, a few weeks later I walked by the study where Laird MacArthur worked most evenings. The bookcase above his desk held rows of ledgers. Many went back several generations containing the financial history of the farm and the clan. After Alain's father had discovered I had a keen interest in my father's business, the Laird shared the contents of the accounting books. I recognized the familiar neat rows of figures detailing the income and expense sides of his transactions.

Today, the room was unoccupied. I couldn't resist a moment or two of blessed solitude, although the growing life within was a reminder I was never truly alone. Placing a hand on my bulging waistline, I could feel the precious movements which I imagined a tiny arm or leg.

My attention turned to a smaller desk just under the window. For a writer, the placement was perfect. Even on cloudy days, enough light poured in. When inspiration was required, the prospect of the glen, a small grove of elms, and the mist rising over the loch were enough. On the desktop sat a leather-bound journal. My fingers touched the smooth covering and lightly followed the embossed thistle design.

I opened the book and the pages unfolded naturally to an entry near the beginning. The disciplined penmanship, with its uniform slant, was typical of a woman's.

March 7, 1692

I thank God that Alain has arrived safely into the good home of my brother, Angus. I pray the Lord in His mercy will give me the strength to endure his two year absence. As painful as it is, we have done what is best for him. Angus will oversee Alain's education, so his sharp intellect will flourish. Little Davina misses her brother. It breaks my heart to see her tears. I don't let her see mine.

Seven ewes have given birth this week & five more are expected. Next year's shearing should be profitable.

The yearling has arrived. My husband contemplates the prospect of adding to our stables.

I must remind Hamish to repair the thatch over the kitchen. The birds are collecting bits of straw for their nests. The snowfall does not deter them.

I felt like an intruder reading someone's private thoughts. My guilt wasn't strong enough to stop. I turned the page.

March 13, 1692

I spent part of the day administering to Flora & the twins. It was a difficult birth, but God has brought her through the ordeal. I doubt she'll have any more children but maybe it is for the best. Little Agnes, Colin & the babes are enough for a widow. When Flora's well, I will find a place for her in our kitchen. She needs the food for her brood.

Frightening news about the MacDonalds of Glencoe has spread throughout the Highlands. The family was murdered in their sleep & even the youngest was not spared. God rest their souls.

Two pigs were slaughtered. Cook made twelve strings of sausage today. I ordered her to send one to Flora.

Four more ewes were born this week. One died.

I wondered if this Flora was the same who worked in the kitchen. She was a pleasant woman, but her eyes always had a sad look. Her pretty daughter helped when needed, and I never saw the other children. I reminded myself to ask Davina.

Before I turned to the next entry, I could sense the presence of another. I glanced over my shoulder and found Alain's father filling the door frame. Feeling like a trespasser, I gasped in embarrassment, closed the book, and took a step back.

"I'm sorry. I didn't mean to…but the journal is so lovely."

Towering above me, he reached over, brought the journal to his nose, and sighed deeply. "This was my wife's. She placed it here on the last day she found the strength to add another entry. I've left everything the way…it was, the day…she died." He pointed to a spot outside the window. "She's buried under that grove of elms, in the family graveyard."

It was the same location where Alain and I exchanged vows. Perhaps her spirit had been watching over us.

"When she returns, I want her to find everything as she left it."

"When she returns?" I was reminded that the Scots were a superstitious people, especially the Highlanders, and a belief in ghosts was a part of the culture. "And have you seen her?"

"I have felt her presence. Sometimes, in the middle of the night, I hear her skirts swishing on the stairs. At other times, I have felt her cool hand touch mine or her lips against my forehead." He looked at me for a moment and smiled slightly. "After I've had these encounters, a scent of lemon would fill the air. Cora used to drink tea made from lemon verbena. To help her sleep, you know." He hesitated. "I'm not losing my mind; I can assure you."

"I didn't mean to imply…I've never felt the presence of a departed loved one."

"Wait until you're my age and many have gone before you. Then you'll have plenty of ghosts to keep you company in the middle of the night."

I shivered at the thought. At the same moment I felt the baby move. My hand moved automatically to comfort it.

"Are you okay Anna? Should I send for Davina?"

I smiled inwardly as I found his concern charming. Before me stood a fearless Highlander, a warrior in his own right, who had watched his wife experience several pregnancies. But like most men, he still found the connection between a mother and her unborn, fragile and mysterious.

"No, I'm fine. The baby is active this morning. Perhaps he enjoys hearing stories about his grandmother."

He handed me the journal. "I don't mind if you read it. You should know about Alain's mother."

This time I turned back the leather cover and read the first page which I had skipped in my initial hurry to get to the entries. Alain's mother had written her full name: Alexandra Cora Campbell MacArthur. Her birthdate was listed along with her husband's and children's. She'd also added the date of her wedding.

Skipping the first two entries I went to the third.

April 1, 1692

Father Drummond is expected today. He is new to the parish & has quickly visited all the families. I overheard the kitchen maids gossip about his manner. Perhaps, they have mistaken his meaning, but I too, find him odd.

The catarrh that torments my chest has weakened me. Cook's ginger & honey tea has helped somewhat. I do not have the energy to join in the evening meal. I will not be sorry to miss Father's visit & his endless sermonizing.

One of Flora's wee twins died yesterday. She is bearing up as best she can. Father Drummond says it is God's punishment for her sins. I asked Cook to bring Flora a basket of food. The little ones must eat.

"There were many days between entries. Was she ill?"

"Aye. My Cora loved to write. I gave her this as a gift, but God had other plans. I'm not a religious person, but I can't accept any other explanation for why she was taken from me."

I turned to the next page. There wasn't much written, and the handwriting wasn't as neat. It appeared to have taken much effort to write each word.

May 1, 1692

Flora's other babe has died.

Nothing is helping with my affliction. Now blood. The doctors say more rest, cool rags for the fever & honeyed tea.

Alain has been called home. I pray to the Almighty that I will live long enough to see my dear sweet boy.

Nothing more was written. I closed the journal and placed it back on the desk.

"The journal was meant for the wife of the Laird. Alain is my heir, and you will be the Lady of Thistlestraith. I'd like you to have it."

"But perhaps, you may someday...." I didn't intend to be so forward with my father-in-law. But most widowers remarried quickly. Laird MacArthur was still an attractive man and had considerable wealth.

As if he read my mind, he said, "I shall never marry again. I've had plenty of opportunity. Father Drummond constantly harps on the church's view of holy matrimony and has paraded local spinsters my way. But there was no one like my Cora." He let out a sigh and tapped the journal. "It's yours now. And properly so."

"Thank you. I will treasure it, always." I was truly grateful and looked forward to continuing Cora's story.

"Anna, before you go, I have something for you. My finding you here in the study was no accident." From a top shelf on the bookcase he grabbed a rectangular-shaped box. From that he pulled out a folded sheet of paper. "Yesterday, I received this from Edinburgh…from your father. It was addressed to me, but it's meant for you."

Like the lemon verbena that infused Cora's things, I thought I caught a whiff of Father's peppermint tea.

Dear Sir,

I hope this missive finds you in good health. Please forward the contents of this box to Anna.
Your obedient servant,
Salomon Issac

My father once told me he would never bless my marriage to Alain. I believed this note showed he had kept his word. He never wrote 'daughter,' and after being away for eight months, he expressed no concern for my well-being. The fact that the note reached me meant he knew where I lived. And that meant Nathan did as well.

In our bedchamber I showed Alain the journal, the box, and the letter. He sat on the edge of the bed and stared at the box. "You're not opening it?"

"No. I know it's the other candlestick, the one I used to attack Nathan on that awful night."

"Perhaps he's trying to reach out to you? It could be a peace offering."

"He will never accept our marriage. That was made clear after you first arrived in Edinburgh."

That's when I realized now how similar my father was to Father Drummond. Their approaches may have been different, but they were after the same result.

I was awakened by the sound of someone humming. Sally sat in a corner of the room working on her mending. She seemed happier these days, always smiling and singing. Thistlestraith agreed with her.

"That's a pretty little tune. I don't think I've heard that one before. So, Miss Sally Gibbons, what's the reason for all this cheeriness? Could it be someone special has magically turned my friend into a contented woman?"

"Perhaps. But a woman shouldn't divulge personal information, especially affairs o' the heart." She put down her sewing and giggled.

"Yes, but a woman might share with a trusted confidant."

"Yere right. My heart is burstin'. I've been waitin' tae tell ye, but there's rarely a quiet moment in this house. And so little privacy." She blushed. "Filib and I are...handfasted. We're just waitin' for the proper time tae tell his family." She sighed deeply.

"I'm happy for you. Have you and Filib....? Sorry, I didn't mean to...." Now it was my turn to blush.

"Not yet. But we will. Tonight. Before Filib and Alain are off collectin' the rents for the rest o' the week." She snorted, "Now I guess that popish pig will be houndin' me tae get married in the church. But we had no choice. My not bein' Catholic, I mean. My mother would disown me if I became one. No, this was the only way."

She hesitated for a minute. "Anna, what's it like? I mean, what's it like to be with a man?"

I must have looked stunned because she quickly added more to her question. "I know I was forced on by your brother, and other men have tried. I'm so afraid it will be like that. What I want to know is, what's it like to be with a man you want more than anything?"

Sally wasn't the kind of person to cry. So, when I saw the tears well up in her eyes I knew she was hopeful that this time would be different.

I spoke slowly and chose each word with care. "When I'm with Alain, my entire being craves to be ravished by him, carried off, and conquered by his power and strength. But there's this trust between us, so that while I have given up control, I know he will be gentle."

Sally whispered, "Ah. I think Filib will be like that. He's a good man, and I ken he won't hurt me." She thought for a moment. "Remember I said how lovely it would be tae bide here the rest o' our lives and have a dozen bairns."

"Yes, I remember. I can't think of anything more wonderful."

Mr. Paterson came to visit again. This time he was alone. When his eyes found my blooming waistline, he said. "I'm afraid the new colony is no place for someone in your condition."

I blurted out. "Our child will be here well before July when we're expected to sail. The babe will be at least three or four months old."

Mr. Paterson narrowed his eyes to show his displeasure at my being so outspoken. He was used to a more reticent woman. "The long voyage is not for one

189

so fragile. Many of the strongest won't survive. If something should happen to you, Mrs. MacArthur, there will be no one to feed your child. It will take months to establish a foothold on the mainland. And there are no guarantees we can establish a crop for a suitable harvest by October. Sick children will only serve to distract the parents who need to focus on building the colony."

"But you are taking your son." My voice was harsh, my tone accusatory.

Paterson glared. "My wife and I have made the difficult decision to leave our son in the care of Mrs. Paterson's sister. It is too dangerous even for someone well beyond infancy and has a strong constitution."

"Anna," Alain said, "I'll go, and send word when the colony is established, and there is decent shelter and enough food. Then you and the bairn can join me."

Mr. Paterson nodded in agreement. He was more than happy to exclude a harping wife only to gain her strong young husband.

I placed one hand on my swollen belly as if to accentuate my protest. "I'm sorry, Mr. Paterson. If my husband is going, so am I. We won't be separated."

Paterson's eyes pleaded with Alain to control his stubborn wife. Alain took my hand in his. "Mr. Paterson's right. A long voyage and a new colony are no place for a bairn. The stories I hear from the English colonies testify to that. But if you insist on coming, the child must stay in Scotland. Davina will care for him and when he's older and stronger, we will send for him."

"I can't leave my child. You can't ask that of me." Anger welled up inside. I thought I would explode. "How dare you."

Alain's voice became forceful. "It is the only way. My sister will be a good mother."

"You forget yourself. I am the child's mother. No other."

"Do you want our child tossed into the sea or buried in an unmarked grave so far from home? Davina will love him, and keep him safe, and will see to it that he never forget us."

The men in front of me became a blur. I was unable to speak. I knew they were right. By fleeing the room without a word, I offered my silent agreement.

TWENTY-SIX
Let There Be Light
2005

Black iron gates guarded the entrance. The exterior looked like the residence of minor royalty. In fact, it was the Central Library of Edinburgh.

The multi-storied building was located on George IV Bridge, a few yards from the Royal Mile near St. Giles. Most Edinburghers walked by the impressive exterior without a second glance, including the commuters who stood at the bus stop outside the front door. With the looming shadow of Edinburgh Castle nearby, it wasn't surprising.

Tall brass lanterns were perched on stone posts on either side of the front doors. *Let There Be Light* was carved on the lintel.

"That's an interesting play on words."

"Aye. It's in Genesis."

"I might not have had the formal religious background your mother would've preferred, but I do know the basics."

"Sorry. I didn't mean to imply...." He hesitated before he went on. "Did my mother say something on your garden tour? I should never have left you alone with her."

"Your mother grilled me about my family, and where I stood religiously. She implied, rather strongly, that faith was important to your family, that her sons had been raised with strong religious beliefs. She said you'd never change and hinted you might be accepting in the beginning of our relationship, because...how did she say it...*your lust would cloud your reason, but over time you would grow to detest your rash decision.*"

"Why didn't you tell me this?" His voice rose, his face closed in on mine.

"I knew my religion, or lack of it, wasn't a priority...to you. I heard you tell your brother."

One eyebrow lifted.

"When you were arguing about me...in the parlor...on the first night. The walls are thin."

"Did you hear...everything?"

I nodded.

191

A slight smile returned; he took my hands in his. "Then, Mistress Hanna, you know how I feel. About you. I don't care what my mother believes, or my brother."

"Yes. But are you sure—"

"The only faith I know is how I feel when I'm with you." He put my face in his hands and kissed me gently.

When the kiss was over, I stepped back and nodded toward the lanterns. "Perhaps that's the reason the over-sized lamps have been placed so prominently on stone pedestals. They're showing the way…to the light that comes from knowledge."

He held the door open, waited for a mother and child to exit before we took a step inside. "Don't want to keep the professor waiting."

If we were late, it was well worth it.

Ira had suggested the library for a meeting place because he had some family business to attend to in Edinburgh, and it was a convenient location considering my B&B was only a few blocks away. An old friend of his was the head librarian of the Reference Section. Ira was certain we could get a small private room.

Our get-together was my request. I wanted to show Ira the candlesticks and hoped he could help explain their meaning beyond the obvious.

As soon as we entered our eyes were drawn to the high domed ceiling. I held my breath as I tilted my head back and whispered, "Holy Crap." The main room was in the shape of a cruciform. It was flanked by archways with two stories of book-shelving around the perimeter. Rows of wooden desks filled the center of the room, some occupied; most were empty. Patrons were reading or plugged into electronic devices. Even blindfolded, I would have recognized the perfume of musty books.

We spotted Ira emerging from an office behind the reception desk. His battered briefcase dangled from one arm while he shook the hand of a tall bearded fellow. The man leaned over and patted the little professor on the back. This must have been his friend. Together, they looked like the old cartoon characters my dad loved to read: Mutt and Jeff.

After the tall man returned to his office, Ira scanned the room. When he saw us, he waved, and motioned for us to follow him up the staircase.

We entered a small meeting room practical enough for our purposes. A long wooden table surrounded by six sturdy chairs took up most of the space. One wall was all glass with a row of blinds pulled tightly to the top. Untangling the cord, I lowered and shut the slats. After my experience in Philadelphia, I felt safer not having the candlesticks exposed. The room was chilly. I zipped my sweatshirt, and Ira secured the last two buttons on his sweater and pulled the sleeves down. The only one who didn't mind was Alec. His body was always a furnace.

"Hanna, did you know the Scots have American philanthropist, Andrew Carnegie, to thank for this library?" Ira asked. "He donated fifty thousand pounds so Edinburgh could have this fine place."

"No, I didn't. I've heard of Carnegie. I had a friend who went to Carnegie-Mellon, but I didn't know he sent money back to his homeland."

As was his habit, Ira put one hand to his head to ensure his *kippah* was still there. "I hear you have something special to show me."

Ira examined each candlestick like a mother counting her newborn's fingers and toes. He turned them every which way to get a better perspective of the matching hallmarks, the scars of one and perfection of the other. He brought each in turn under the overhead light.

"Let me make sure I understand this. The battered one was kept in a safe deposit box in Scotland. The other was given to you by a relative who lived in New Jersey?"

"Yes, my grandmother."

After a few more moments of silent inspection, the professor whispered, "Incredible." Sniffling, he reached into his pants pocket to fish out a handkerchief. I noticed his eyes were watery and his nose was red.

Placing both candlesticks back on the table, he clasped his hands together. "These are magnificent works of art, created by a master. The buyer must have been wealthy indeed."

"That's exactly what the jeweler in Philadelphia said."

"Well, I'm not surprised you have many questions. I'm afraid my dear, so do I. But ladies first."

"Thanks. What do you think was their purpose other than bringing light into a room?"

That reminded me of, *Let There Be Light.* How ironic my trying to understand the meaning of an ordinary tool whose primary function was to bring light into the darkness. "Why would someone spend so much money for an ordinary item when inexpensive ones would do? I mean, of course the rich would splurge because they could. Is there something else about them that would encourage someone to spend so much? And then go to the trouble to ensure their survival."

"I think we should assume they were commissioned for a special purpose. Especially because they are a pair. Seventeenth century families had many sconces of all sizes and designs. But two identical ones like these, in silver, were for some other reason. Perhaps, they were meant to be displayed for a grand occasion; a wedding would be the most likely reason. The owner was probably accustomed to showing off his wealth. Or it could have been a gift."

Ira pushed his chair back and stood. "Ah, my sciatica is acting up. I need to walk around. Hard seats are not good for my lower back." As he paced, he asked, "Did your grandparents always live in New Jersey?"

193

"No, they were originally from New York. My grandfather came to this country in the 1920's. My grandmother's family, however, had come before the Revolution. About ten years ago my grandparents relocated to New Jersey."

Ira sat again and brought his clasped hands to his forehead where his pointer fingers rubbed his brow. Our conversation was temporarily interrupted by the giggles of children as they walked by the room. The shadows on the blinds followed them. An adult chaperone was heard shushing and reminding the children to use indoor voices. Their sounds soon disappeared, replaced by the hum of the heating system.

"Alec and I agree. The candlesticks are a pair, but we don't know why Anna has them?"

"Based on what we already know about Anna, I assume these were Sabbath candlesticks. In a Jewish home it is the obligation of the woman to light the candles every Friday evening before sundown."

"Why is it that only a woman does the lighting?"

"Ushering in the Sabbath is done at home. The home is a woman's realm. Therefore, she is the one who welcomes the day of rest by literally bringing in a spark of spirituality."

Alec interrupted. "Didn't you tell me that your grandmother always had you and your father over for a Friday evening dinner?"

"Yes, but not to celebrate the Sabbath. We aren't Jewish. It was just a weekly dinner with the family."

"But you had a moment of silence?" Alec asked.

"That can hardly be considered religious or anything to do with the Sabbath."

Ira cut in. "For Jews, it's more than that. Honoring the day of rest is one of the Ten Commandments and a mandate from God. The Sabbath is the holiest of all holidays. No one works, marries, or is buried either. All mourning ceases on the Sabbath. The only ritual that takes precedence is the circumcision of a newborn son. And that's only if his eighth day of life falls on a Saturday."

Ira got out of his seat again, limping at first. This time he opened his briefcase and took out a pill case. Alec offered to get some water and returned with a cone-shaped cup. Ira emptied two pills into his palm and gulped them down. Returning the case, he asked, "Tell me about your Friday night dinner and the moment of silence."

"There really wasn't much to it. My dad and I rarely missed coming, except when I had the chicken pox, the roads were icy, or I was away at overnight camp. When I was a teenager, it was hard to miss outings with my friends. But Grams was adamant. She would always tell me that Friday nights were for family. My friends could see me any other time. When my father was killed, Grams stopped making demands on me. I guess she didn't want to see his empty chair. Instead, I became the one who insisted on continuing the Friday night dinners. I needed my family more than ever."

I closed my eyes for a moment, remembering. "It was always a special dinner: tablecloth, gleaning china, and silverware. And the candlestick. My grandmother had everyone sit in their assigned spots while she lit the one candle. After a minute of silence, she would announce it was time for dinner. That's it."

"Did she cover her head, or put her hands over her eyes? Did she say a prayer?"

"No. Nothing like that."

"Did she ever mention how the candlestick came to her?"

"Yes. She said it was handed down from her Grandmother Hannie. Wait…wait a minute. I do remember something Grams told me just recently. She told me that Hannie had a beautiful crucifix. On Friday evenings, when she lit the candle, my great-great-grandfather would remind her to remove the necklace. When dinner was over she would put it back on. Grams always thought that was strange. Don't you think so?"

"On the surface, especially to someone who doesn't understand the significance of that ritual. Yes."

"Taking off a crucifix is a ritual?"

"Yes. What I mean is there might be a perfectly logical reason for Hannie's actions. She probably didn't understand it herself. Just something the family always did."

"Now I'm really confused."

"I believe we can clear it up. How much do you know about the Spanish Inquisition?"

"The Inquisition lasted for hundreds of years until it was abolished in 1834. Before that, wherever Jews fled, they were hounded by the Spanish. A few escaped with Columbus in 1492. Some speculate Columbus himself was Jewish." Ira chuckled. "Not likely. The person who came up with that idea sold lots of books. The reality was Jews were not safe in the Spanish colonies, so many converted, and disappeared into history."

"Why did you ask me what my family did on Friday nights?"

"I've read articles about Spanish Jews who fled to the New World. Some made it to the American southwest when it belonged to Spain. The refugees tried their best to keep their identity a secret, and therefore they had to alter the way they celebrated the Sabbath."

Ira stopped talking. He seemed to remember something and reached into his briefcase. It was not for pills this time. Instead he pulled out a folder. "Let me show you." He brought out a newspaper clipping. "Here. This article is about a man whose

195

family lived in New Mexico. He always suspected he had Jewish ancestors because his Catholic family acted strangely on Friday evenings. Before lighting candles, a painting of Jesus was turned over. When he questioned this weird practice, his family said it was something they had done as far back as anyone could remember. No prayers were said. But they observed a moment of silence."

Ever since I'd discovered the key and the contents in the safe deposit box, I'd had many moments when a shiver ran down my spine or the hairs on my neck stood up. Ira's story was no different.

Alec noticed my reaction. "Are you okay?"

"Yes. I'm fine. It's just a lot to take in, like connecting the dots, except these are three-hundred-year-old dots."

"I'm just suggesting a theory," said Ira. "Anna knew enough to hide her identity but did what she could to save the remnants of her observance. Pieces of ritual were handed down until what survived was just a shred of the original. It's like children playing whisper down the lane. What you have at the end is hardly how it started out."

"Did the guy in the article ever find out for sure?"

"Yes. He tracked down the graves of his family. Some of his early ancestors clearly had Jewish surnames and Jewish markings on the headstones. He was lucky because he would never have figured it out if it weren't for remembering his family's simple, but unusual practice of turning a picture over."

"Did he convert to Judaism?"

"He remained a Catholic. He said that's who he was and planned to remain so. But his discovery revealed the sad tale of his ancestors."

"Wow. That could be my story? Anna's too?"

"We can't be sure. But it's a start. Although it still doesn't explain how the candlesticks became separated."

"Perhaps, I'll learn that in the journal. One other thing, Professor." I pulled out a small plastic box from my satchel, opened it to reveal a tiny rolled piece of paper about two inches long. "Inside the battered candlestick, I found this."

"How did you get the paper out?" asked Alec.

"I used a pair of padded tweezers which helped to keep from ripping the paper and made for a better grip. I latched onto one end and turned the tweezers, so the paper rolled even tighter. This made the diameter smaller. After several tries, the paper became small enough. It slid out with one tug."

Ira sat down again, the tiny parchment in his hand. The edges were uneven. It looked like tiny teeth had chewed bits and pieces. He gently unrolled it, stopping every so often when it wouldn't give. He played with it some more until he was able to unfurl it halfway.

Professor Mason, descendant of Spanish Jews who fled the Inquisition, silently read the words on the parchment.

"Do you know what it says?" I noticed his eyes were still wet, but perhaps now it wasn't due to his cold.

"Yes. It contains a few sections from the Torah. Jews are commanded to put this scroll, kept in a case called a mezuzah, on their door posts. Perhaps your ancestor was saving this for her home in the New World."

Alec chimed in. "I'm afraid not. This was found in the battered candlestick. We know Anna was headed for the Scottish colony and most likely had the other one."

"Yes," I said. "I forgot that one tiny detail. So many different directions Anna's story could go." I ran my fingers through my hair. Knots made it impossible, so I just put it up with a clip. I reached into my satchel for the journal. "Thank you, Professor. You have given me much to think about. But there's only one way I will find out what happened to Anna, and I need to start from the beginning."

TWENTY-SEVEN

Ghosts
1698

Ten tiny fingers. Soft translucent nails tipped each one. I tickled the middle of Alexandra's palm, and five small fingers encircled my forefinger like an octopus ensnaring its prey. Her milky breath filled the air as I embraced her, willing myself not to forget. I pulled back and stared into the deep pools of her sapphire eyes. I prayed they would remember me.

I turned my right hand and the sunshine reflected off a ring Alain had given me shortly after Alexandra's birth. It was a thistle ring – an amethyst set in gold leaves,

"It was my mother's wedding ring," he had said.

"It's beautiful. But shouldn't it go to Davina?"

"My father wanted you to have it. It was meant for the Mistress of Thistlestraith."

I started to place it on my left hand, but that would mean removing the plain gold band, my wedding ring, that once belonged to the woman murdered by Harley.

"Wear it on your right hand. My father will understand."

I understood as well. This was Laird MacArthur's way of accepting me into his family.

I returned my attention to Alexandra and almost didn't notice the swish of skirts and a presence until a friendly voice spoke.

"Ah, she's bonny. She looks just like ye, Anna, but she's got her da's eyes. It won't be long until the lads will be lining up to have a chance to get lost in them."

Startled. For just a moment I thought it was Sally.

Davina extended her finger and touched Alexandra's forehead following the bony path down to the tip of her nose. This created a toothless smile interrupted by a noisy belch. Alexandra grasped her auntie's finger and they wagged together as if shaking hands. The baby and Davina gurgled.

"She's a strong wee one. My brother brags about it to everyone."

I tried to join in her friendly chatter, but instead I buried my face in Alexandra's warmth. The recent loss was still painful.

199

"Let me help ye with washin' the soiled nappies. Ye need tae regain your strength." Sally spoke firmly. Her hair askew, the sunshine catching the ends sticking out every-which-way from under her cap. She clutched the basket of soiled nappies with her arms, and quickly extended them to hold it as far as possible from her nose. "Ach, these nappies are worse than Auld Reekie." Alexandra responded to Sally's sing-song voice by kicking her little legs as hard as she could, reminding me of Skirts when I scratched his belly.

Sally leaned over the babe's cradle. "Who'd imagine such a bonny little lass makin' such a stink?"

"As soon as Alexandra's fed, I'll come down and take care of the nappies. I'm feeling stronger today. I won't have you waiting on me."

"Tis not you I'm waitin' on. It's your delicious babe." Sally scurried out the door before I could say another word. She clip-clopped down the stairs while humming one of the many tunes she had learned since arriving in the Highlands.

Sally and Filib had been married almost six months. At first handfasted, they had given in to Father Drummond's demands when he hadn't wasted anytime going after the newlyweds. The wedding quickly followed Sally's conversion. On a chilly day, the priest's commanding voice and gesticulating eyebrows united the couple.

Sally looked radiant when Filib placed his mother's gold wedding band on her finger. Having never owned anything so fine, she stretched out her fingers to stare at it. After a few nervous giggles, the priest cleared his throat reminding Sally there was a ceremony to conclude. Father Drummond and the guests were impatient for the food and the barrels of ale. At every opportunity, he glared at me as if to say he had won one victory for God.

At first, they lived with Filib's old father and his new wife. But Sally returned to Thistlestraith to help with Alexandra after a difficult lying-in. Although, as Sally explained it, there was another reason for her staying.

"Filib's step-mother, Maude, is a difficult person with a mean disposition. That's the best I can say about her."

"Davina calls her a saint. Filib's ailing father needs constant nursing."

"A saint, is it?" Sally crossed herself. Now a Catholic, she showed her new-found devotion by making the religious sign every time a holy word was uttered. "Then Davina should live with that she-devil. She'd know what I'm talkin' about. Besides, she's gone a bit daft, if ye ask me. Lately, she's been seein' and hearin' thin's."

That reminded me of Alain's father describing his wife's spirit. At least she was a friendly one. "When did you ever hear a Highlander tell a story that didn't include a ghost or two?"

"Nay, I don't mean what my mother used to call a 'glimmer.' Maude keeps complainin' about some lad comin' around and askin' questions."

"Questions? About what?"

"Ach, I don't know. About me. Filib. When I question Maude, she says she doesn't remember o' maybe she's mistaken. Then in the next breath she'll tell me she sees him pokin' in the barn or just sittin' and starin' at the house."

"Have you told Filib?"

"Aye, of course, but none o' us have seen this 'apparition' o' hers. Includin' Filib's father. So, now I'm stuck livin' with an auld crazy woman who bosses me 'round. It's like I'm livin' with my mother again. Its Sally clean this, and Sally wipe that. Fetch the wood, fill the buckets, wash and mend the clothes, churn the butter. Ahh! There aren't enough hours in the day tae do all she expects. And so particular. I never do anythin' up tae her standards." A slow smile came across her face. "When Filib comes home, she leaves me be. But then I'm too tired tae greet him properly. If you get my meanin'."

"Perhaps she's just lonely and is making up these stories."

"Aye. She's lonely for one reason. She's a miserable woman and no one wants to be around her. Even Filib's father can't stand her and tae think they're newly married. They should be like lovebirds."

"Doesn't she help?"

"Help? The woman sits on her bum the minute Filib walks out the door and his da starts snorin'. Men are blind tae what goes on between women. I know it won't be long, and we'll have our own place. Then I'll have the strength tae get me a bairn."

After nursing Alexandra, I carried her to the back of the house, near the kitchen. This was where we did the laundry. I placed Alexandra in a box and after rocking her gently, she soon fell asleep.

Cleaning the nappies began with separating them. The very soiled ones were scrubbed on a rock and then soaked overnight in a large pot filled with hot water and lye soap. Sally had to make her way down to the stream and haul the heavy buckets back up the steep ravine. The well-worn path was either frozen or muddy from the water that sloshed over the sides of the buckets. Sally wouldn't allow me to do this backbreaking chore until my strength returned. I felt guilty as I watched my friend disappear down the path to the stream.

I did the simpler task of hanging the urine-soaked nappies to dry. These needed no washing. Flora told me that the dried urine offered some sort of protection to the newborn, and since I was an inexperienced mother, I didn't argue. The cloths fluttered in the breeze and the smell of urine filled the air.

"Have you seen Sally?" It was Davina. She had emerged from the kitchen, smelling of yeasty bread, her hands covered in flour. The flour had somehow made it to her dark hair making her appear older.

201

"She went to get more water." I looked at the half-filled pot; Sally had a few more trips to take. Then I glanced at the baby who was still lost in her dream world.

"Filib is looking for her. Maude is feeling poorly. She hoped Sally would come home and help with the evening meal and put Filib's father to bed."

I decided not to hurry the unwelcomed news.

Skirts, no longer the malnourished little rat, lumbered from the direction of the stream. Lately, I hadn't given much attention to the dog now that my life was consumed with Alexandra.

"Here Skirts. Come on boy. Would you like your belly scratched?"

Skirts usually enjoyed a good rubbing, but not today. The dog edged closer and then backed off. When I was finally able to touch him, his fur was matted and wet. His paws were caked in mud. "Were you playing in the stream? You better not go in the kitchen. Flora will give you a scolding and no scraps for you." When I pulled my hand away, my fingers felt sticky. They were red.

"Skirts!" I checked his paws and his belly. Clumps of mud fell on my aproned lap. He shook off the dampness, splotches of red and brown flew in every direction. With this much blood he should have had a deep wound, but instead he backed away and started to howl.

I heard footsteps, turned, and saw Filib and Alain.

"Skirts. He's covered in blood."

Alain's eyes widened when he saw my stained hands. He pulled me to my feet and quickly looked me over assuring himself that I wasn't harmed.

"Where's Sally?" asked Filib.

"I...don't...know." And then I did. "She went to the stream to fill more buckets."

Hearing our loud voices and confusion, Davina reemerged from the kitchen. I picked up my skirts and as I ran toward the ravine I yelled, "Davina, take Alexandra inside." Quickly outpacing me was Filib, followed by Alain.

We could hear the stream before we reached it. Most days, the water tumbling over the rocks babbled incoherently. Today it hissed. The grassy places where Sally had trudged were still depressed. The soft soil at the bottom of the incline along the edge of the stream showed her path. Signs of her slipping were evident along with a strip of ribbon that flapped at us from the thorny blackberry bushes.

Cascading over a trio of large rocks and splashing onto many smaller ones, was a solitary waterfall. At its deepest point, the water was waist-high, but near the shore there was a flat rock where one could stand and dip a bucket easily in the shallows. That was where we found one overturned and another smashed.

I called out my friend's name, but Sally remained silent.

I ran along the edge of the stream, my footprints crisscrossing hers until I noticed a larger pair.

Then I found her.

Splayed out on her back in the ankle-deep water, her eyes stared blankly at the sky. Gathered around her thighs, drenched skirts drifted with the water current. The front of her white shift was soaked in blood leaving her exposed skin waxy and gray. Below her chin a gash grinned gruesomely from ear to ear.

Filib and I ran over to Sally's lifeless body. Alain stopped and turned toward the direction of snapping branches and splashing water. He drew his sword and disappeared into the overgrown brush and alder.

Filib sank next to his wife and held her limp hand. He pressed it to his lips, rocked back and forth, and emitted a primitive sound from the center of his being. It was a cry inherited from ancient ancestors and surfaced in response to the deepest loss imaginable.

Filib and Tom carried Sally's body on the same board used for waulking wool. I followed and was quickly joined by Alain. His shirt was splattered with various shades of brown and dark red. He wiped his dirk in the grass and that's when I realized it was blood that stained his shirt.

He took my arm. "Anna, I must talk to you."

"After I make sure that Sally—"

"We must speak now." He words were firm, his voice determined.

I stayed back and let the pallbearers go on without me. The women of the house would know what to do. It was their turn to take over the grisly task.

Alain and I walked toward the graveyard where his mother slept. Her headstone had a simple inscription: A.C.M. and the year 1692. The top of the gray slab was a thin veil of green moss.

Alain placed one hand on the cold stone like he was seeking spiritual guidance. He took a deep breath. "I killed a man today. It was the man who murdered Sally."

"How...do you know...that?"

"He confessed. It was your brother. Nathan."

I couldn't make sense of his words. His lips moved but the words had no meaning.

"I had no choice. Nathan left me no choice. When you and Filib ran toward Sally, I saw someone darting among the trees. I gave chase and overtook him. Before I realized it was your brother, I saw only his knife. He lunged and missed, and then I stabbed him. It was too late when I realized who attacked me. His knife was covered with Sally's blood.

"Nathan still lived a few moments more although we both knew the wound was fatal. I asked why he murdered Sally? He said he thought it was you. Sally must have fought back to keep him from going after you. He ended up killing her."

When Alain finished his tale, silence engulfed us. I sat next to the gravestone and ran my fingers along the carved initials. The stone felt gritty and tiny flecks came off on my fingers. Alain lowered himself so that our eyes met. His were filled with tears.

"Once again Sally has saved me. I always knew it would come to this."

"Forgive me."

"There's nothing to forgive. You were only doing what any man would do, protect his family."

"But he was your brother."

"No. I told you my brother was dead. I cannot grieve for him. If he was truly a brother he would not have abused me when we lived in the same house, he would not have forced me to marry against my will, nor would he have sent his henchman after me. And now this. He has taken my dearest friend."

We stood and Alain put his arm around me. Together in the growing dusk we turned in the direction of the house and the unbearable sorrow it contained.

"Do you think Sally could be buried in this place?"

"By marriage she's a MacArthur. I'll talk to Filib."

"I would like her to be near your mother. I think they would like each other. Sally needs a friend."

After the body was washed by female friends and relatives, a wake was held at our home for seven days. Sally's body was never left alone. I was told this was so the Devil would not steal her soul. Every so often I noticed the person watching over Sally's body touched her hand. It was as if they were checking to see if she was really dead. I overheard one of the neighbors giving a different reason. It was to keep the mice away.

The door to the house was left ajar so Sally's soul had a chance to flee and all the mirrors throughout the house were covered so her spirit wouldn't see its reflection. I wasn't a stranger to some of these customs as they were like those of my family. We also sat with the deceased as a sign of respect, and mirrors were covered for the same reason.

During the wake, the house overflowed. The seven days of mourning turned merry. The tables groaned with an abundance of food and the whisky loosened the tongues of storytellers. They told about the deceased and the antics of local ghosts.

One old neighbor declared he'd rather attend a Scottish funeral than an English wedding.

Sally would have been awed by the number who paid their respects. It was a reflection of the new life she had created with Filib and her acceptance into the community.

I never got to witness Sally buried near Alain's mother. Women did not attend funerals. I was told Father Drummond extolled Sally's Christian soul which is what she would have been proud of. That and respectability.

July 9, 1698

It has been one month since Sally's death. I still cannot accept it, & expect her at any moment to come walking into my room complaining about Maude. Sometimes I think I hear her footsteps or her voice mingling with the others in the kitchen. Laird MacArthur told me that someday this would happen.

Tomorrow my heart will break once again. Alain & I are leaving in the morning for Leith. In three days, we will board one of the ships headed toward God knows where. Davina will take charge of our darling Alexandra. Davina promises to write often & include a lock of hair once the babe has enough to sacrifice.

Mr. Paterson offered the MacArthur clan three berths. Alain's father is not well enough to join us. Therefore, Filib will. We are grateful for his companionship. It will be good for the little Scot to get away from the reminders of so much pain. Here, he sees Sally everywhere.

I have given Davina some final instructions. She is to make sure that Alexandra inherits the candlestick, the one from her grandfather. I am leaving a lock of my hair tied with Sally's ribbon and Cora's wedding ring. It is only right that this gift, from her Highlander grandmother, stays in Scotland.

The other candlestick is coming with me. Someday, I hope, when Alexandra joins us in the new colony, our candlesticks will be lit together.

No parent should have to give up their child. But today, that's what I'm about to do. Soon, another will feed her, watch her take her first wobbly steps, and soothe her tears. Alexandra will eventually learn to call Davina, Mother. How long will it be until I see my daughter again? Alain said it would be a year. But the unspoken truth, we know it could be longer. Perhaps never.

I have learned it is far easier to accept such an arrangement before I held my living child in my arms. Now that it's time to go, I can't bear the thought.

Alain reached for our daughter. He held the babe while snuggling his face in her chest for the last time. A tiny hand grabbed his nose. Alain chuckled. I suspected it was only to muffle his cry.

The distinct sound of wagon wheels and horses' hooves, crunching over gravel, tugged at my heart. Davina came into the room and Alain gave our daughter to her.

As we walked out the front door, we clutched each other for support.

The wagon lurched forward, jostling our belongings, for the two-day journey to the port. Before we passed the graveyard and the giant elms obstructed the view, I turned back for one last glimpse. I was relieved to see nothing.

Part Three

TWENTY-EIGHT
The Sabbath
2005

Esther Mason covered her head with a cream-colored scarf. After she lit the candles, her hands slowly circled the twin flames three times as if she intended to capture the flickering light and the waxy scent and bring them within. Then she cupped her hands over her eyes and slowly recited a Hebrew prayer. Although not expected, the guests seated around the table bowed their heads as a sign of respect. Everyone, except me. I watched the ritual and admired the quiet beauty of the moment. The room shimmered in shades of ivory and gold.

In the center of the linen-covered table were Anna's gleaming silver candlesticks. Their reunion had been three-hundred years in the making.

The scene reminded me of Friday nights at my grandmother's home. Her tradition wasn't meant to replicate the Jewish observance of the Sabbath. But I couldn't deny the similarities. This was the reason Professor Mason had invited me to his home, so I could experience what my ancestor Anna would have done every Friday at sunset.

Before we arrived, Alec told me that the Masons opened their home one Friday each month and invited students, faculty, family, and neighbors to join their Sabbath celebration. He recounted fond memories of frequent invitations and Esther's gracious hospitality and bountiful table. The home-cooked meals were a wonderful departure from the institutional food served in the university's cafeteria.

Ten were seated around the table. Three of the guests were Ira's graduate students. To my right sat Reverend Prescott Walton, a recent widower and long-time neighbor. At the other end of the table was an old colleague, Charles Smith and his wife, Adele. Dr. Smith taught biology and conducted research in genetic sequencing.

Ira invited everyone to fill their crystal goblets with the heavy sweet wine. When all were ready, he stood and raised his wine glass, closed his eyes, and sang a short prayer thanking God for the fruit of the vine. After an Amen, he proclaimed "*l'chiam*, to life," and it was repeated around the table along with a clinking of glasses and sips of wine.

Alec reciprocated a toast. "*Slainte*, health."

"*Slainte mhor agadi*, great health to you," replied Ira followed by more clinking and more wine. "There's never enough good wishes, no matter what the language and tradition."

Esther placed a large oval plate, covered with an ornate embroidered cloth, close to her husband. She lifted the cover with a flourish and revealed a braided bread. The surface was dark and shiny reflecting the glow from the candles.

Ira picked up the loaf and tore at one of the braids. "Some prefer to slice their challah. My family's tradition is to tear," He passed the bread around for each to do the same. The inside was the opposite of the hardened crust. It was pale yellow, soft, and yeasty. After another short prayer, we all had a taste of the bread. The meal was ready to be served.

One of Ira's students said, "This challah is delicious." She pronounced the beginning of the word with a 'ch' sound as in church.

Ira gently corrected her. "It's pronounced 'chuh' as if you are trying to clear your throat after a nasty cold."

The student giggled and then practiced saying the word. When she got it, everyone applauded her efforts.

"Mrs. Mason did you bake this?" I asked.

"No, but in my younger days, I did. My back and my shoulders cannot take all the kneading required. Besides, there's enough to do with making the soup and all the other traditional food. Lately, I must get the bread delivered from Glasgow or London. There are no kosher bakeries in Edinburgh."

"I've eaten challah before. It makes great French toast." I was careful with my pronunciation to avoid giggles. "Even we non-Jews love it. Although there are fewer kosher bakeries in Philadelphia, I can buy it in a supermarket. But it's not as good."

"Hanna, I have asked Esther to make a special dish for you in honor of your many times great-grandmother. It's called *Alheira*. It's a sausage the Portuguese Jews used to eat."

"I thought Jews were forbidden to eat pork."

"No, no, dear," Esther said. "This sausage is made with veal, olive oil, garlic, paprika and bread. The garlic is how the sausage, *Alheira,* got its name. *Alho* means garlic."

"Was your ancestor Portuguese?" asked Adele.

Before I could answer, Ira said. "Hanna's ancestor was from Spain...but—"

Esther leaned over and patted her husband's hand. "Ira. I know you love to talk history, but we aren't in your classroom right now. Let Hanna tell her story."

Chuckles were heard round the table especially from the students. He looked at his wife, his mouth open in surprise and nodded for me to go on.

"My ancestor's family fled Spain during the Inquisition. I don't know the route they took, except somehow they ended up in Scotland." I told Adele about the

210

journal, how it had come to be in my possession, and how Alec and Ira had been helping me to piece bits of Anna's story together.

Ira was about to speak but checked for his wife's approval. She nodded, pushed back her chair, and announced she would be back with the soup. Alec offered his help, but Esther thanked him, and explained she preferred her guests enjoy the conversation.

Ira cleared his throat. "Believe it or not, the sausage plays a part in the history of the Inquisition. Once the Inquisition arrived in Portugal, Jews were given a choice of expulsion or conversion. Those who converted were forced to prove their devotion to their new religion. That included the Portuguese custom that all housewives hang their freshly stuffed pork sausages in the communal smokehouse. Any who were identified as *Conversos* were scrutinized to make sure they did as well. So they wouldn't go against their religious dietary laws, the hidden Jews secretly stuffed the sausage with duck, chicken, or veal. In this way, they could join in the custom and go undetected.

"Ironically, later the Portuguese Christians liked the Jewish recipe better, and they adopted it. You can now find the sausage in certain areas of Portugal, especially in the city of Mirandela, in the northern part of the country. That's where my family came from."

"I don't think I knew that," said Alec. "I always thought your family came from Spain."

"Maybe they did at some point, but the story goes that they lived in Portugal. When the Sephardim, the Iberian Jews, had to flee, many went to Amsterdam. Others to Morocco and Mexico. My family made their way to France to conduct trade. I'm not sure if it was Marseilles or Lyon."

"I wonder if your ancestors knew Anna's family."

Esther's return was announced by the swinging door that separated the kitchen from the dining room. Wearing a Grams-style apron, Esther placed a heavy white tureen in the center of the table. When she withdrew the lid, all eyes stared at the golden broth flecked with carrots and dill surrounding golf ball-sized dumplings. Esther proudly asked, "Who wants matzoh ball soup?"

Many more courses followed. Besides the *alheira,* dinner included brisket, oven-browned potatoes, steamed broccoli, pearl onions and peas, an apple noodle kugel, and five different desserts. When a guest's plate was partially empty, Esther insisted they have more. The only way to say 'no' was to hold your hand over your plate. The students ate as if it was their last supper, but the mountains of food never seemed to diminish.

211

"You always make too much," said Ira.

"My definition of enough food is when the leftovers could feed you again tomorrow evening. Anyone for seconds, Thirds?"

"My grandmother used to say the same thing."

"I guess that's our generation, dear. We get a lot of pleasure feeding our guests."

Esther got up to clear the dishes and refused my offer of help. "I have a system for clearing the table. Besides, I have a feeling Ira is dying to question you about your journal."

Once his wife disappeared, Ira asked, "So, tell me, what has happened to Anna? What's going on?"

I reviewed the events of Anna's life for those who didn't know her story. "The last entry I read was about Anna and Alain's painful decision to leave their newborn daughter in Scotland while they traveled to the new colony."

"The way you tell it, it sounds like the events happened in the recent past. Not three centuries ago. Where did they leave from and when was this?" asked Adele.

"They sailed from Leith on July 14, 1698. The colonists had no idea where they were headed. The Scots Company kept the location a secret for fear the English would try to stop their efforts. Anna and her husband Alain went blindly to an unknown future to create Caledonia."

The students politely excused themselves after dessert. Esther tried her best to offer them a second helping, but their night was just getting started. The local pubs were awaiting them. It wasn't long ago that I would have eagerly gone with them. Now I stayed with the adults. We convened in the living room where Ira assured us the chairs were more comfortable.

After some chitchat about an upcoming conference, the new science department chair, and what I thought of Scotland, the conversation returned to the Inquisition and religious identification.

"Professor...Ira, you mentioned this evening the importance of the *Conversos* trying to maintain some of their traditions like keeping kosher as best they could. That got me thinking about those Friday nights at my grandparents'. Grams never served pork."

"Maybe your family just didn't care for it," said Adele.

"No, I think it's more than that. I've never eaten so much as a ham sandwich or a slice of bacon. Do you think it's possible, if Anna is my long lost relative that I'm carrying on one of her traditions?"

"I may be able to help you," said Professor Smith. He was a tall man with graying hair and rimless glasses that were always sliding down his nose. He didn't bother to push them back and took the easy way out, peering over them. "I've been told you have a lock of hair that may be from your ancestor. It's possible you could get the DNA from the hair follicle and we could see if it matches yours. I know someone who is an expert at doing this procedure."

I thanked the Professor for his help, and now I understood why he was invited.

Reverend Walton had stayed mostly silent throughout the evening now spoke up. "Have you finished reading the journal?"

"No. In fact, I've just begun."

"I'm surprised. I would imagine you would want to go through it as quickly as possible."

"I don't mind taking my time. First, there is the writing and language to sort through. And then there's the research. I often find that I get to a certain point, and I need to understand what's happening before going on. It's sort of a rabbit hole."

"Ah, I have encouraged Hanna to go slow and savor each entry. What's the rush?" As if the logs in the fireplace agreed with Ira, a charred log split creating a shower of sparks that quickly went up the flue.

"Ira," I asked. "Do you remember the part in the journal where Anna fears the Spanish ships coming into harbor? Why couldn't Anna just pretend to be Catholic? Who would know? I mean, she's not a man."

Alec raised one eyebrow, and a smile crossed his face.

"Well, that's true Hanna. A Jewish man could not hide his religious identity. One look at the family jewels...."

"Ira?"

"It's okay Esther. My students are gone. We're all educated adults here." Turning to the Reverend, "I think our esteemed expert on all things religious may be able to help you."

Reverend Walton sat up from his slouched position in a big wing chair. He brought his hand to his mouth to squelch a burp. "Excuse me. Esther, the dinner was superb. You have outdone yourself."

"Thank you, Reverend. And don't make yourself a stranger."

"Of course, we..." The Reverend stopped. He remembered he was no longer a 'we.' "What Ira means is I was born and raised a Roman Catholic. My family had lived in the Highlands for generations. But when I met my dear wife, I converted to bring about harmony to at least one side of the family. Unfortunately, my own family has had little to do with me since, although I have tried to reach out to them. Religion is still a serious business here in Scotland."

I looked over at Alec. I wondered if it would be the same for us.

"I guess you can say I took my conversion seriously. Here I am an ordained Presbyterian minister. But I haven't forgotten my Catholic roots. So how can I help?"

"Is there some secret code that only Catholics know?"

Reverend Walton looked over at Alec, the only born-and-remaining Catholic in the room. "Well, Alec, is there a secret handshake?" He laughed at his own joke. "I think every group has their secret nuances that only true believers would know. Ira, do Jews have any? Can you tell if someone is pretending to be Jewish?"

"I don't think we have to worry about that," said Esther. "Whoever heard of a Christian pretending to be Jewish? Why would someone want to put himself in harm's way?"

I hadn't noticed Esther had rejoined the group. The apron was gone, and her flustered look from serving dinner was history. She took a seat near Ira. "We have a way of finding out if a stranger is Jewish. My mother used to say a Yiddish word or two in conversation. It would not be a common one, but something only a Jew would know. If the stranger perked up or answered in Yiddish, the riddle was solved."

Alec smirked. "Members of my very Catholic family have some peculiar habits. For example, if someone mentions the word 'Jesus' they will cross themselves or bow their head. If they go by a church, they will do the same." Alec chuckled to himself.

"What so funny?" I asked.

"Religious fervor can get a wee bit dangerous. Once when I was little, my mother, hoping for an extra blessing from the Lord, crossed herself and bowed her head while driving by a church. That momentary distraction almost drove us into a ditch instead. She was so thankful we weren't hurt, that she ordered my brother and me to get out of the car and get down on our knees. I wondered, even as a small child, why God almost killed us after my mother showed such piety."

"My parents did something similar," said the minister. "They would bow their heads when they walked by a church or a graveyard. Walking was a lot safer." The minister looked around the room chuckling and then continued. "So, what does a Catholic do that a Jew would be ignorant of?"

"I know nothing about rosary beads," said Esther. "To me, it's a necklace one says a prayer over. But I know there's more to it. I think they're a mystery to most Jews."

Alec reached over and grasped my hand. "I have a different take on this. What could give away a Jew wasn't their ignorance about Catholicism. Anyone can learn the prayers. The difficulty was undoing what had become second nature, their Jewishness. To forget about eating kosher, dressing a certain way, speaking Ladino, and ignoring holidays had to be impossible. If a housewife cleaned her home, bathed her children, or baked on a Friday afternoon, she was suspect. We joked before about the 'family jewels,' but, Jewish parents faced a grave decision whether to perform

214

one of the most holy dictates of Judaic law, and if they went ahead with the circumcision, they were sentencing their infant and themselves to expulsion or death. What a challenge knowing an ingrained misspoken word or deed would be deadly?"

Esther stifled a yawn, and when the clocked chimed again, I noticed Adele glance at her watch. It was getting late and although we could have gone on for hours, it was time to depart.

Professor Charles retrieved his jacket and tam o'shanter. He reminded me, "Let's talk soon about that DNA testing."

After the others left, Esther gave me the candlesticks which she had wrapped and replaced in their boxes. "Please come again. I want to hear what happens to your ancestor."

Ira patted Alec on the back. "I know where Alec will be Monday morning, but what's next for you, Hanna?"

I looked at Alec and we both smiled. "It all depends on the journal. Everything hinges on where Anna wants to take me."

TWENTY-NINE
Neatness Begets Order

"*Hey* Alec. It's me. Did I miss your call? I'll talk to you when your classes are over." After ending the connection, I rolled over and squinted at the small digital clock on the end table: 9:05. Alec's double-header had just started. He wouldn't be free until noon.

Alec was my alarm clock. He called me during his fifteen-minute walk from his apartment to his classes. He wanted his voice to be the first I heard each day. A real romantic at heart.

Most of his classes were in the morning. The afternoon was spent in his office meeting with students and department meetings. At other times, he was squirreled away in the library immersed in research. But when he was free, he'd call.

We were past the stage in our relationship where I wondered if Alec was still interested. That's why I thought it strange that I hadn't heard from him yet. Perhaps, he was lost in conversation over some historical minutiae with a colleague or student and calling me had completely slipped his mind.

Sitting up in bed, I fluffed the two feather pillows for support and pulled the covers to my chin. With nothing much to do until Alec was free, I thought about catching up with Jess or Grams. I wanted to tell Grams about dinner at the Mason's. Wouldn't she be surprised to learn that her Friday night dinners might have a connection to Anna? I could just hear her now. *Oh Hanna, that's lovely. So kind of the Masons to invite you. And how's your young man? Are you madly in love yet?* I promised myself to call her more often. But that idea was quickly squashed. The shafts of gray light spilling through the edges of the drapes reminded me that morning in Scotland meant the middle of the night on the east coast of the United States.

Jess and I used to talk daily. Now, maybe every other week. I suspected her life was busy with Dr. Sam. It wouldn't be long before Miss Fishman became Mrs. Goldblatt. They were just waiting to see where he would be accepted for his residency.

"If Sam gets an offer in another state, we'll never see each other," I said.

"What are you talking about? You're the one who moved to another continent."

"Moved? I only came to open a safe deposit box." But I had to admit she was right. I'd been in Scotland for four months, since the beginning of the summer, and had no intention of leaving soon. "Okay. But when I come back to see Grams, we must visit."

"When will that be?"

I had no definitive answer. Except for Grams, I had no reason to come back. Besides, Grams nearly shoved me out the door like a mama bird pushing her youngest out of the nest. Hadn't she told me to get started with my life, fall madly in love, and have lots of babies?

"Hey, you got to be my maid of honor," Jess said. "If it weren't for that candlestick, I would never have met Sam."

"And you're the reason I met Alec. So, you have to be there for me too."

Funny how things had worked out. Wait! What was I thinking? Planning my wedding? Tempting the Fates? Holy Crap! I had to stop. But Jess didn't give a hoot about jinxes, fairy godmothers, or fortune cookies.

"I want all my bridesmaids to wear ballet-length dresses in champagne pink with rose satin sashes. You, my maid of honor, will be the loveliest of all, in a floor length deep merlot. Maybe we'll tie the knot at a vineyard in Brandywine."

Jess hesitated. Even on the phone I could tell she was deep in thought. "Hey, why don't we have a double wedding? Twin brides. That would save us a ton of money. We could get a bagpiper for Alec. He could wear his kilt and one of those cute little fanny packs that hang on his hips."

"You mean a sporran?"

"Whatever. And you could dazzle him in one of those pretty tartan wedding dresses. I saw one in a bride magazine. I'm sure my dad will be thrilled to walk us both down the aisle."

A lump lodged in my throat at the thought that someone else, not my dad, would have the honor. Life could be wonderful and cruel at the same time.

The buzz of my cell phone brought me back to the present. Not Alec. I let the unknown number go to voice mail. It was Charles Smith with good news. He had found someone who could help with the extraction of DNA from the lock of hair. I'd get back to Charles later, after I heard from Alec.

At one o'clock there was still no word. I left another message and tried not to sound annoyed. I lightly chided my absent-minded professor and threatened that soon I would have no choice but to call the local hospitals and the city morgue.

Maybe he'd gotten waylaid by a student who wanted to talk about grades or extra credit. Alec told me how some of the freshman still thought they were back in high school and could improve their grade with an additional project. I told him that reminded me of Jess who tried the same tactic. But she quickly learned it was easier to flutter her long eyelashes or stick out her pouty lips at some young gullible professor. Like magic, her grade was raised to the land of the living.

"How did you feel about that?" asked Alec.

"It was difficult. I worked hard to get decent grades."

"Aye. I bet you weren't the kind of student who'd settle for just a passing grade."

Alec said the university had its share of Jesses. But I never worried about the temptations swirling around him. We were committed to each other, and I knew handsome Dr. Grant was mine.

Three p.m. I stared at my phone and willed it to sing, but instead, another logical reason surfaced. Maybe he just forgot. But after last night that was hard to believe.

We didn't leave Ira's until almost midnight. After driving me home to Edinburgh, I felt terribly guilty.

"It's such a long ride back. It's almost 1 a.m. Do you want to stay?"

We had not spent a night together yet, and I wondered how Alec would take my suggestion. I leaned toward him and kissed the tip of his nose. Then I tugged on his lower lip before kissing it. Was I no better than Jess? I shook my head to dislodge her from my mind.

"I'd like nothing better, Mistress."

I opened the door and reached out for his hand.

He hesitated. "I can't. Sorry. I have my Western Civ classes early in the morning. If I stay with you, I won't sleep. I won't want to." His one eyebrow shot up. "But Hanna, I do want very much to be with you." He towered over me and placed one hand on the door frame. "I've been meaning to ask if you would consider moving to St. Andrews?"

"Wouldn't it be difficult to find an apartment now that the semester has started?"

"I wasn't suggesting you get your own place." He put his forefinger under my chin and lifted it so my lips touched his. They were warm and supple.

"My apartment is a wee bit cozy. But it has all we need. One lavvie, a galley kitchen with barely enough room for one cook, I gather we can squeeze in another… and a…bedroom."

It's time. I remembered thinking those same words when I closed out my father's safe deposit box. Like then, this was a watershed moment in my life. A new chapter. "I'd like that very much."

"I'll call you first thing…on my way to class." Alec put his arm around my waist and pulled me closer. "Hopefully, it will be the last time I wake you up with a phone call." He smothered me in his arms. There was no other place I'd rather be.

I heard nothing from Alec the rest of the day. Running out of excuses, I imagined him lying in a ditch somewhere or comatose in a hospital.

I was about to look up Ira's number when my phone buzzed in my hand. "Ira! You must have read my mind. I was just about to call you. Do you know where Alec is?"

My fears were confirmed by his ominous tone. "He didn't show up for his classes today. This is not like him. He never called in nor has anyone seen him on campus. One of his colleagues went by his apartment, and Alec's car is not there. I hoped he was with you."

"No, he's not here. Perhaps I should call the police or the local hospitals." I realized how difficult that would be. In and around the capital, there were at least a dozen hospitals and many more between Edinburgh and St. Andrews. Not all hospitals had emergency rooms or cared for seriously injured patients. I didn't know which to call.

"I'll call you back if I hear anything."

A few minutes later my phone rang. It was Ira. "There's been an accident, and Alec's in Victoria Hospital in Kirkcaldy. His brother called me because he figured someone at the university should know why Alec didn't come to work today. Here's Iain's number."

I jotted it down. "I've got to go to the hospital. I'll rent a car."

"I know you're anxious about Alec, but it will be dark soon. Kirkcaldy is a forty-five-minute drive and that's if there's no traffic. Visiting hours are only until 8 pm. Wait until tomorrow. You'll have the entire day to sort this out."

I wasn't surprised that Iain hadn't called me. After all, I wasn't family, but more importantly, he didn't approve of our relationship. That made me worry all the more. Alec must have been badly hurt, otherwise he would've demanded his brother let me know.

My fingers trembled so that it took three tries to tap out the international code plus Ian's number.

"Yeah?"

"I just heard. Is Alec okay?"

"Nothing for you to worry about." His words were clipped; his voice showed no emotion.

"Can I talk to him?"

"No. He's out cold. A wee bump on the head."

What did that mean? Was Alec in a coma, on life support, or just sleeping?

"I'll rent a car tomorrow and come to the hospital."

"Don't bother. He's only here for observation and will be discharged tomorrow afternoon."

"When he awakens, tell him I called?"

"Yeah." Click. The call ended the way it began.

I didn't care about Iain's rudeness. But I wouldn't be brushed aside. If I were in the hospital, Alec would do everything he could to be with me. Iain could pretend that I didn't matter, but he was going to find out I didn't scare so easily.

Early the next morning, I plugged the postal code into the GPS of the rented car and drove the thirty miles over the Forth Road Bridge to Kirkcaldy.

The hospital campus consisted of several high and low-rise buildings. Locating Alec wasn't difficult. As I approached his room I saw, through the open door, Iain staring out the window. Did he already know I arrived? Mora was seated on the edge of the bed blocking Alec's face.

"Here, let me do that for you," his mother said while she poured water into a cup and adjusted the lid with a straw. Instead of handing it to Alec, she held it for him. Was Alec so incapacitated that he couldn't feed himself? Then I heard his strong voice and his words weren't slurred.

"Thanks. I can do this myself. So, what's the diagnosis?"

"The senior doctor said the impact caused a closed brain injury which bruised the tissue," Mora said. "He suspects you'll be fine in a couple of days. Discharge will happen later today. You're to follow up with the GP as soon as possible."

"You know you're lucky to be alive. Falling asleep at the wheel is—" Iain was brusque and impatient. Did he know why Alec was driving so late at night? Because of me?

"Did you call Hanna?" Alec asked.

"We spoke."

"Is she coming? What did she say?"

Just then Alec's brother looked up, saw me standing in the fluorescent lit hallway and smirked. He avoided Alec's question. "I'll be right back."

Iain stepped out of the room and gestured toward an empty waiting area. He hissed. "What're you doing here?"

"What am I doing here? I was worried about Alec. I'm not leaving without seeing him, and if he doesn't want me here, he'll have to tell me himself."

Iain brought his face so close to mine that the stench of alcohol forced me to turn away. "I don't think so. Forget about my brother. Besides...." His eyes lowered, slowly and deliberately. His uncomfortable gaze undressed me. "You could do a whole lot better. Aye, I could satisfy the needs of a hungry lass." He brought his

221

hand up to my face and touched an errant curl. Repulsed by his touch, I pushed him hard in his chest which put him off-balance and headed toward the safety of the hallway.

Trailing after me, Iain yelled my name. A passing nurse raised her forefinger to her pursed lips.

Alec's mother came out of the room. "What's going on?" Mora looked at Iain and then at me, "When did you get here? Well, it doesn't matter. Alec's been asking for you."

Before I followed her, I turned to glare at Iain, but only saw his back as he walked down the hall.

Although Alec and I had talked about moving in together, we hadn't imagined it would be the result of an accident.

Alec's flat was on the second floor. His description of the place as cozy wasn't an exaggeration. My studio in Philadelphia was a penthouse compared to this. I led him to the loveseat; the two club chairs didn't look sturdy enough for a man of his size. A pole lamp provided the only light and in front of the sofa was a small coffee table loaded down with magazines and mail.

After a second trip to empty the car, I returned with my suitcase and carried it into the bedroom which doubled as a library and office. One wall was covered with bookshelves from floor to ceiling. Each was filled. Along the front wall, under a draped window, was a small metal desk with Alec's computer. On the opposing side was a queen size bed covered with a blue flowered quilt tucked under two pillows. Someone had taught Alec to be neat and tidy. I smiled as I remembered my dad saying, *Neatness begets order.* It was a quote from some ancient poet.

When I returned to the front room, I found Alec fast asleep, so I spent my time unpacking and figuring out where I could put my things. I explored the tiny refrigerator and was delighted to see that milk and beer weren't the only contents.

Based on the doctor's written instructions Alec needed to rest for at least a week. Any suspicious complications like numbness, vomiting, weakness, or severe headaches had to be reported immediately. In addition, for the next couple of days, Alec had to be awakened every four hours. Even through the night.

I covered my snoring patient with a faded crocheted afghan. With nothing to do for the next few hours, I grabbed the journal, curled up in one of the club chairs and floated back in time with Anna and Alain to the start of their journey.

July 13, 1698

After three days, Alain & I arrived in Leith. Although I had never set foot in this port town, the name evoked nightmarish memories of Maurice. My dear husband has reassured me, the Frenchman is across the sea back in Lyon, & I am safe.

Our tiny fleet consists of five vessels. Three will carry supplies & 1200 colonists. Two will transport more provisions.

Our ship, the St. Andrew, is captained by a crude & impertinent man, Robert Pennecuik. He is the Commodore of the fleet & has an ego to match. The captain has no time for any of his passengers & clearly wishes we were cargo: silent & profitable. The sailors on the St. Andrew flinch whenever he barks an order. They curse under their breath & stay out of his way. Not an auspicious way to begin a voyage. The only good I can say about him is that he is an experienced seaman. I should be grateful for that.

The pier bustles with activity. One could easily get run over by the many carts hauling casks & crates. Their drivers add to the din by screaming threats to anyone foolish enough to get in their way. Although stowing provisions in the ships' holds started six months ago, last minute additions of meat, cheese & biscuits, stored in barrels, are everywhere.

Tomorrow we sail for Caledonia as soon as the tide is favorable. It is with great sorrow that I am leaving my child in Scotland while I follow my love to the ends of the earth. God protect us & my lovely babe.

Anna Rachel Isaac MacArthur

"Alec, wake up." I gently nudged his shoulder, and after a scary few seconds he opened his eyes. "Are you okay? Would you like something to drink?"

As if the mention of a drink triggered an autonomic response, Alec licked his lips. "Um…water is fine. And then I want you."

"We both won't fit on the couch."

"I own a bed."

After I helped Alec to his feet, we made our way to the bedroom. I gently placed him on one side and got around to the other. Edging my back against his chest, I felt his arm slip under mine.

"Alec, are you okay?"

"Now I am."

"Does your head hurt?"

I heard him mumble, "No."

"I read some more of the journal…"

"Shh."

"Alec?" I whispered.

The only response was the reassuring sound of his breathing. The journal would have to wait until the morning. Snuggling closer, I too, was soon fast asleep.

THIRTY
Saint Andrew
July 14 - August 2, 1698

We were the pride of Scotland. The entire country wanted to share in our glory. Thus, wave after wave of farmers, shopkeepers, wives, laborers, and craftsmen put aside their tools and swarmed the pier in Leith for the opportunity to wish us Godspeed.

As the sun sailed overhead, the *Saint Andrew,* the *Caledonia,* the *Unicorn,* the *Dolphin,* and the *Endeavor* traveled east through the estuary along the Fife coast. After a brief stop in Kirkcaldy to pick up the Patersons, we passed the small towns of Elie, St. Monans, and Anstruther on our portside. The Isle of May was on our starboard.

It appeared that God was with us. At the moment the tidal current marched back out to sea, strong favorable winds pushed us along with little effort. There was no need to unfurl the main sails and therefore became less demanding for the deckhands. Thus, they were able to turn their attention to the spectacle on shore.

The banks along the firth were flooded with people cheering and waving colorful hankies. Perched on the shoulders of their fathers, small children were given the best view in the hope that this momentous occasion would be emblazoned forever in their memory. Older children wished to retain the excitement for as long as possible. Chased by yapping dogs, they raced along the verge in a futile attempt to keep up with the ships. Rising above the din, the higher pitched voices of women called out their hurrahs while wiping away tears of joy. Men on horseback held on to their hats as their steeds pranced nervously amidst the fanfare. They pulled tightly on the reins to maintain control, and in the process lost their hats anyway. Every so often, a rider would break away from the crowd and race down the road disappearing behind a bend or a grove of trees. His mission was to alert the next town of our approach.

Alain and I stood at the railing. My hair and skirts whipped into a frenzy. The captain's colorful red pennants, flapping on the main mast, were mere playthings in the gust.

Although the crowds had buoyed the spirits of all on board, they left me disconsolate. Every child held in a mother's arms reminded me of Alexandra. I glanced at Alain and wondered if he felt the same. But he too was caught up in the anticipation of a great adventure. His look of wide-eyed excitement told me, that for the moment, his child had escaped his thoughts.

Somewhere between Kirkcaldy and Elie one spectator at the forefront of the crowd, caught my attention. He was somberly dressed in a long white beard overflowing his chest. The elderly man wasn't cheering, just standing at the edge of a hillock. His gaze never left us, and just before he faded into the distance, he raised a hand in farewell. My mind played tricks and tried to convince me that the man was my father. But in reality, Father had no idea I was sailing away from Scotland.

Just as the ship sailed by Largo Bay, I heard the crew talk about a secret meeting in the Captain's quarters below. Pennecuik and the Councilors, who were chosen to oversee the colonial government, opened a sealed packet with instructions from the Company Directors. The orders detailed our route along the eastern coast of Scotland to the Orkney Islands to pick up more provisions. In this way we avoided any English ships waiting in the Channel to detain us. King William did not want the Scots to found a colony. After the Orkneys, Madeira Island was our next stop and where the second set of orders would be unsealed.

At dusk we rounded the point at Crail and continued along the sandy shores of St. Andrews. Entering the North Sea, the changes were dramatic. Waves slammed into the wooden hull and rocked us to and fro, and as we left the estuary, we said goodbye to the smell of rotting fish and sewage. It was replaced by fresh air and sea spray.

If there were any well-wishers on shore, their voices were blurred by distance and the roar of the ocean. One town saluted us with a cannon blast, but we did not respond. The captain was not on deck to issue the order. By nightfall, only a few faint lanterns were visible.

When we could see no more, Alain and I went down the ladder to our new home on the gun deck. It was a wide and lengthy space with cannons situated at the port holes. Under our feet were broad planks edged with wide gaps so that any lanterns below created eerie beams of light. The same fissures were above. I was told that during stormy weather, rainfall would form waterfalls of misery, soaking everything and everyone. In battle, this was the most dangerous part of the ship.

Our quarters were crowded and tight. Passengers slept within inches of each other. The few married couples were cordoned off by a large sheet draped to provide a modicum of privacy. It offered little. We were surrounded by a horde of snoring men who filled every space. Filib placed his hammock between the guns which afforded him fresh air from the portals.

The latrine was in the bow or the head of the ship. It was merely a hole in the deck that opened to the sea. The wind carried away any stench and was kept clean whenever the bow dipped, and a wave washed over. There was no door, no curtain, and no privacy, so the few women stood watch for each other. In stormy weather buckets were provided on the gun deck. The motion of the ship sloshed the contents, tipped the buckets, and fueled the fetid air. The stink permeated our clothes, hair, and skin. On our first night, I realized a frightening fact. This was to be my home for at least six months.

The next day most of the passengers spent their time on deck. The crew scowled and grumbled when we got in their way, and some old-timers were irritated to see women on board. We were considered bad luck.

On the quarterdeck, Mr. Paterson joined Captain Pennecuik. He wasn't so grandly dressed as when I'd seen him last. The wig was gone, his graying hair was tied back with a thong, and his clothes were more suitable for a long journey. Since all of us would be wearing the same clothes for months, comfort and practicality were important.

I scanned the deck for Lydia Paterson. But she was nowhere. She and her husband never retired to the married couple's section. Alain told me that since Mr. Paterson was one of the members of the Council, they enjoyed a small private cabin.

Pennecuik and Paterson were huddled together, deep in conversation. The captain saw us, nodded, and both approached.

"Mr. MacArthur, sir," said Pennecuik. He turned to me, "Mrs. MacArthur." Rather than follow the rules of polite conversation and ask about our health and shipboard accommodations, the captain got right to the point. "Madam, allow us to have a word with your husband in private."

I turned, but Alain grabbed my hand and placed it on his arm. It was my signal to stay. The captain glowered. I concluded he expected all to obey his orders without question. "Captain. Mr. Paterson. What can I do for you gentleman?"

The two looked uneasy. They hesitated before speaking and Paterson shuffled from one foot to the other. The captain spoke first. "Mr. MacArthur, you are aware that we have a Council, assigned by the Directors of the Company, to make the difficult decisions in the best interests of all the souls on this voyage and Scotland?"

"Aye. I am, sir." Alain stared intently at the two men, but his firm grasp on my arm told me he was just as focused on my being by his side.

Mr. Paterson continued. "That same council will continue their good work once we have come to our destination by promoting law and order and provide for the security of our colony. One member on the Council has taken ill and may not survive. The surgeon is attending him now. We must have a full council and we are in need of a replacement. Being that your father is Laird MacArthur, and you represent an old and honorable family, we would like to offer you a seat on the Council." Before Alain could respond, Mr. Paterson added, "That would mean you and your wife would be offered quarters befit your new station. Nothing fancy, mind you. Space is at a premium. Nonetheless, it is important to maintain a sense of decorum for each councilor."

Alain glanced my way; his eyes searched mine for agreement. Was it the position he wanted? The authority? Or the few square feet of privacy? I responded silently with a smile to match his.

"I'd be honored, sir."

"Wonderful," said Mr. Paterson. "Our next meeting will be three days hence on this ship. Then, you will have a chance to meet the others."

The captain's eyes scanned the main deck. They rested on the boatswain, Mr. Duff. He was a middle-aged man with thinning brown hair and was presently supervising several seamen who were repairing sails and rigging. Feeling the captain's gaze, Duff approached. His nose was red, probably from drink, and when he spoke, the gaps between his dark stained teeth forced him to whistle.

"Yes, Captain,"

"The MacArthurs are moving to a cabin near the officers' quarters. Get some of your crew to clean it first and then bring up their trunk. And whatever else the MacArthurs need."

In a whispered hiss the boatswain replied, "Whatever you say, sir." He turned and scowled. Duff appeared none too pleased to be interrupted from his work and temporarily demoted to cabin steward. Turning his attention to two deckhands, he yelled at one and kicked the other. "Off yere lazy arses. Ye heard the captain."

The two men groveled in compliance and sniggered at their superior just as Duff had done to the captain.

In the short time I had been on board, I quickly understood there were two levels of hierarchy on the ship: the officers and the crew. The officers had Norman titles like captain and lieutenant. They lived in better quarters and had more to eat and drink. The crew, boatswain, coxswain, quartermaster, and seamen were words based in the Anglo-Saxon language. More than six hundred years after the Battle of Hastings, the influence of the victors was everywhere.

"Mr. Paterson. I have not seen Lydia...Mrs. Paterson...about this morning."

"Ah, she's a wee bit nauseous." He flicked his hand to emphasize that it wasn't serious. "Once she gets her sea legs, she'll be up and about."

"Please tell her I was asking for her."

"Ah. You may tell her yourself. There she is."

Mr. Paterson ran over to help his wife up the ladder from the deck below. Lydia Paterson, paler than I remembered, put her arm through her husband's and walked over. She smiled weakly.

"Ah, my dear, take deep breaths and allow the breeze to revive you." Lydia did no such thing. Instead she brought the handkerchief to her mouth, held it there, and closed her eyes until the worst of the ill-feeling passed. When Lydia turned her head to wipe her face, her cloak was caught in a gust and separated behind her like a pair of angel's wings. Her blue woolen dress and the partlet she wore for extra warmth were revealed. And something else. Even though her stays were doing their job to hide her secret, I detected the source of her illness. It was not the fault of the sea.

For the next few days, while our husbands were engaged in meetings, Lydia and I spent time walking the deck, keeping each other company, and sharing our lives.

"Anna, you must miss your child. What a sacrifice you have made to leave her behind."

I never told Lydia that it was her husband who had insisted we leave Alexandra.

"I fear for my own child." She put one hand on her expanding waistline revealing her secret to me.

"Wills?"

"No, he's safe in Scotland. But the one to come, it's a dangerous time to bring a young one into the world. So many hardships, and there is mention of ship's fever on board."

I was aware of what she spoke of. The first passenger to become ill was the Councilor my husband replaced. He had come down with a bout of chills, high fever, and severe headaches. He was immediately quarantined to sickbay. Duff and his crew followed the captain's orders. As a preventative, they smoked our cabin and swabbed it with vinegar as a preventative.

On days when Lydia's condition kept her from leaving her cabin, I explored the ship on my own. I especially wanted to seek out the surgeon, Silas Wilson, who had a rudimentary knowledge of caring for the sick. He spent his days in the small, dank, and airless sickbay. Its purpose was not to cure, but to quarantine. Mr. Wilson was easy to locate. His loud snoring led me to a passage near the galley where he was propped up against the bulkhead. Dead drunk.

Picking up my skirts, I quietly stepped over him and entered the galley. I'd heard that the second-best source of medical advice was the ship's cook. If Mr. Innes had any knowledge of herbs, he would also know their cures.

The cook was an older man, short like Filib, so that he never had to duck beneath the low overhead anywhere on the ship. His spectacles were perched on the top of his head, but since he squinted constantly, I doubted he ever wore them. This had created deep tanned furrows on either side of his eyes.

He was an affable sort and a passable cook based on the porridge I'd eaten this morning. It was not lumpy or gummy, but I had a feeling the head would be occupied all day. Mr. Innes was well-liked for his good humor and experience at sea.

"Mrs. MacArthur. What brings ye down tae the netherworld? I have extra biscuits if yere still hungry. But I can't guarantee they aren't rock hard." He reached into a barrel and offered two in his dirt-lined palm.

"No, thank you. I'm still working on that fine porridge you made this morning."

The cook smiled broadly. It wasn't often that he heard compliments for his cooking skills. Most of the time, the crew derided him for the monotonous menu of porridge, salted meat, dried peas, and biscuits. The roll, offered and refused, was tossed back into the barrel after Innes removed something and tossed it into the fire.

"What is it then I can do for ye taeday?"

"I...was wondering if you know a cure for seasickness?"

"Are ye feelin' poorly? Ye look in fine fettle."

"It's not for me. But for a friend."

"Well, the best way round the sickness is tae eat. But if yer friend is already ill, that won't help. Some say a mugful of seawater will do the trick. Cleanses the stomach and the bowels. If yere friend has a pasty complexion, there ain't nothin' that will help."

"Why is that?" I immediately thought of Lydia. Normally, red faced, she was paler due to her condition.

"Dunno. But it's a known fact that people who're darker, like yerself, suffer less." He smiled and winked as if I had proven his theory. "But I tell ye what yere friend can do. They should put their head on a hard surface. A board or book. Close their eyes and think good thoughts."

"Does that work?"

"Aye. It worked for me in my early days at sea till I got used tae the world swayin' under my feet." He stopped for a moment, raised his eyes as if searching his memory. "Perhaps, it was those good thoughts that cured me." He grinned. "Now don't go askin' me about what was goin' on in my brain. Yere a lady, and that means I have tae act more gentleman-like. Besides, tae tell you the truth, most o' the time I fell asleep."

I smiled while imagining Mr. Innes as a young man. He may have been agreeable looking, although he was probably shorter than any woman he was ever interested in. And hopefully cleaner too.

"Thank you. I'll be sure to share your advice with my friend."

"Tis the Paterson woman, I'm guessin'. Her seasickness has nothin' tae do with the sea, mind ye." He gave me an impish grin. Then his demeanor changed. "Mrs. MacArthur? I see your husband is now a man o' some importance. One day

230

yere nothin' and the next...At least ye got some privacy for the trouble that's comin'."

"What trouble is that?"

Ignoring my question, Mr. Innes gave me some unwanted information about his own change of circumstance. "One day I'm swabbin' the deck for that loudmouth Duff, and the next, the Captain orders me tae start makin' the porridge. All because my predecessor got swept overboard while takin' a dump. He had the shits so bad he forgot about the porridge and let it burn. The Captain doesn't like brown bits in his bowl. He was hoppin' mad and didn't regret when a rogue wave swept the shitter overboard. I never thought the Captain was a religious man till that day."

"Mr. Innes. You said the ship is in trouble. What did you hear?"

He leaned closer and spoke almost in a whisper. "Life aboard can be mighty borin'. If there's one thin' seamen are fond o', it's a bit of gossip. I'm just sayin' I've been hearin' thin's. This ship and all t'others are in a heap o' worry. Maybe ye should find out from yer husband. He's in a position tae know o' these matters. It's not my job tae account for the food on board. But don't go tellin' anyone ye heard this from Innes the Cook. I don't need the captain reacquaintin' me with his cat-o-nine tails for speakin' my mind."

I flinched when Mr. Innes raised the back of his shirt to reveal the crisscross scars going in every direction like a mass of small snakes. The skin had healed but the deep welts showed the intensity of the strap.

"Mr. Innes, your secret is safe with me."

"Thank you, Mrs. MacArthur. Yere a real lady."

"And thank you for the advice. I'm sure Mrs. Paterson will be grateful."

While the Councilors' meeting lasted well into the night, it was not until the next day, in the confines of our cabin, that Alain had a chance to relate what had happened. We had plenty of time to talk, because as it turned out, the ship was going nowhere. We were off the coast of Aberdeen and the winds had disappeared, and a dense fog enveloped our tiny fleet.

"The meeting deteriorated into non-stop arguing. It was so contentious at times that several members had to be restrained."

"What could cause the Councilors to come to blows?" I knew it wouldn't take much. Whisky and ale helped to shorten tempers and reduce common sense.

"A shortage of provisions."

"We just started out a few days ago."

231

"Miscalculation by the Directors or the pursers. Nine months of provisions were supposed to be allotted, but we'll be lucky to have enough for six. After less than a week at sea, our butter supply is so low it won't last four months."

"Was the food stolen? Or were we told there was more than there really was?"

"It was a combination of bad luck and not keeping accounts straight. No one considered the food consumed by the crew while still in port. Or did they think to check on those supplies before we left, or we could have taken on more in Kirkcaldy. Mr. Paterson tried to warn the captain that a recount was necessary, but he failed to do so. In addition, here we sit in the fog. Who knows how long before we move again. Every day that we go nowhere, we consume more food. We may not have enough to make it to the colony. The meat wasn't stored correctly and is starting to turn. The bread is infested with bugs."

The image of Cook Innes removing something from the biscuit caused an unwelcome reflex in the back of my throat. "Then we must turn back?"

"Our hope is in the Orkneys. Once we dock, we'll send for food from Leith. That means we will consume more food while we wait, but we have no choice. The Council voted to ration what's left."

Alain took my hands in his and held me close. "What I've just told you must not go beyond this room. If the passengers and crew learn the truth, they will mutiny. Or worse."

I nodded in agreement, but I was reminded of Mr. Innes' words. The rumor had already spread, and we were in trouble.

We never set foot in the Orkneys. Heavy fog draped around us again which made anchoring impossible. We feared running aground, crashing into rocks, or colliding with other ships. Captain Pennecuik had his seaman call out warnings every thirty minutes. At first the other ships replied, but when all went silent, he resorted to firing his pistol, ringing the ship's bell, and beating a drum. When the fog lifted somewhat, and we were able to see land, no one knew if it was the Orkneys, the Shetland Islands, or the Hebrides. We were lost.

Seventeen days after we'd sailed from Leith, we finally escaped the fog completely. With no other ships in sight we thought we were all alone in the Atlantic. Our spirits were buoyed by a school of long-nosed gray seals. They swam briefly around our ship, appeared to beckon us to enter the immensity of the ocean, and then were gone. Miraculously, forty-eight hours later, the *Caledonia* and the *Dolphin* come into view. Believing the *Unicorn* and *Endeavor* were lost, we turned our direction southward to the island of Madeira.

THIRTY-ONE
Lies, Lies and More Lies
August 3 – August 28, 1698

It's the middle of the night. The ship creaks and groans as if it is daring to pull itself apart. The rhythmic thuds of white caps lapping against the hull make sleep difficult. I imagine the ship slicing through the blackened sea. A light breeze sneaks in, mixing the smell of brine with the faint tang of vinegar and male sweat.

I glanced over my shoulder at the two opened portals. Most nights the stars or the moon fill the space with their welcoming luminosity. Tonight, there is nothing but all-encompassing darkness. I could barely see my hand when stretched, and yet, I could sense Alain smiling.

"What are you so cheerful about? At this hour."

"Trouble sleeping?" Alain's voice husky from sleep.

"I asked first."

He chuckled and turned on his side. His warm breath inches from my face. The fingers of his free hand slowly and deliberately traced my hills and valleys stopping at the strings of my shift. The smooth linen fell effortlessly off one shoulder exposing a breast. Alain lowered his head, and I wrapped my arm around his neck and pressed him closer.

Only temporarily sated, he traveled on. His hand found my thighs. He stroked and massaged until he found the cleft between. I lifted his nightshirt to expose and direct him. Our breathing became rhythmic and deepened until we both shuddered with tiny gasps.

Moments passed before he rolled back on his pillow staring at the nothingness of the overhead. Through the window, a morning star winked.

"I often lay awake at night watching you sleep, hoping…you'll open your eyes." He rolled over and looked directly into mine. "I've heard most women don't like to lie with a man. They've been taught it's their duty to please their husbands. But I want you to be satisfied. Are you?"

"How could I not. You're very gentle…and loving." I didn't have the experience of a courtesan. However, common sense told me that tenderness, patience, and passion were the hallmarks of a great lover.

234

He sighed deeply. "I'm a very contented man."

"Well...um...I'm even more pleased you're a man."

He tossed back his head and laughed so hard our bed shook.

"Sh. The walls are thin. That awful captain will be sure to make fun of us...me...in the morning."

"Ah, he's just a jealous old coot and perhaps a wee bit sex-starved, as is most of the crew."

"Sometimes, when you aren't around, he goes out of his way to get my attention, and when he does, he smirks while rubbing his groin. Perhaps he's got the itch, but he finds great entertainment in my embarrassment."

Alain's tone became serious. "He's a crude man. None respect him. The crew wouldn't object if he suddenly found himself keeping company with the fishes. You can see it in their eyes, hear the curses under their breath, and watch the vulgar gestures behind his back. Perhaps you should stay in our cabin when I'm not with you. Or keep company with Lydia."

When I nuzzled closer, I could almost feel his fists clench. I covered his face with kisses and felt his tension ease. Laying my hand on his chest, I played with the curly hair.

"Now it's your turn to answer my question." Alain said.

"At times I wake in the middle of the night. Scared. I'm not sure what the fear is: this ship, our future, the uncertainty all around us. I keep it to myself. Why should the two of us lose sleep?"

"I don't want you to face your fears alone."

But recent events on this voyage didn't help diminish my apprehension. Much had gone wrong even before our last sighting of Scotland. Several had ship's fever and three had already died. Alain complained about the lack of leadership which wasn't helped by the mistrust between Captain Pennecuik and the other captains, especially the Drummond brothers. More importantly, between food rationing, boredom, and uncertainty, spirits were low while suspicions were high. Fever wasn't the only thing contagious.

The body of another passenger, the wife of Hugh Rose, was tossed overboard. Her name was like a song, Shona Rose.

Hugh was not a member of the Council. Therefore, he and his wife had few privileges. The freedom to walk on the open deck was limited, and much of each day was spent in the dark fetid space below. Their food rations were inadequate, a contrast to the table I sat at every night covered with linen, platters of food, and goblets filled with the best wine.

Shona and I had become friends. Given her living conditions she amazed me with her unbridled enthusiasm about the future colony. A few blond ringlets, that escaped her cap, seemed to quiver as she described her prospect with her new husband. I was fond of Hugh as well. Once I discovered he kept a journal of our voyage, he shared it with me. His entries included descriptions of shipboard life and our daily progression to our destination.

Whenever I saw the newlyweds, I'd rush over to greet them. Our meetings were a chance to share a few morsels I had confiscated the night before. We all knew that if caught, there was a price to pay, and it would be paid by Hugh and Shona. I shivered at the memory of a crew member caught stealing food. His punishment was to run the gauntlet. A double row of seamen lined the deck. Each held a cudgel, a switch, or a cat-o-tails. The accused, stripped to the waist, was beaten on his way between the two rows of men. His injuries would have been slight if he had been permitted to run. But his pace was restricted, forced to follow the slow cadence of an officer brandishing a sword. All were ordered to watch.

Three days ago, I found Hugh alone by the railing. We were nearing the island of Madeira, possibly two days out.

"Good evening, Hugh."

"Ah, Anna. My wife sends her regrets." His voice became a whisper. "Shona is feeling poorly and thought it best to remain hidden below."

Shona had complained of feeling disoriented and nauseous. She had looked paler. I had attributed her symptoms to seasickness. I was wrong.

"Would she like some company?"

He looked around to make sure no one was listening. "Shona doesn't want anyone to know she's ill. Now that three have died of fever, she's afraid the surgeon will force her to sickbay." His eyes searched the horizon while I noticed two pigeons circling the masts. Were they harbingers of land and good fortune?

"She's got the black vomit." Hugh hesitated and wiped his eyes. "I want to ask a favor. In case anything happens to me. I've always meant for my journal to get back to Scotland. Someday. I want it to go to the Directors of the company. Will you see to it?"

"Yes, of course. But…"

"Give it to Captain Drummond. I trust him. Ask him to take it back to Scotland."

We both knew why he preferred Robert Drummond, or even his brother Thomas, to Captain Pennecuik. The captain of the *St. Andrew* couldn't be trusted. If there were anything negative written about him, the journal would be tossed in the sea.

I left Hugh Rose where I found him - leaning against the railing. The birds were gone.

The next morning Shona was laid out on deck. Along with a cannonball, her body was sewn into her brown woolen cloak. Hugh, eyes swollen and red, stood by his wife's remains, daring any man to approach. He stiffened when he saw the board from the mess.

"Mr. Rose, I'm sorry for your loss, but don't force me to order my crew to restrain you," said Captain Pennecuik.

"Maybe she isn't dead yet. The body feels warm."

"Fever, Mr. Rose. That's what does it." While the captain spoke, he motioned to Duff and his crewmen. They took one step and paused, waiting to see how the widower would react. When he bowed his head and sobbed, they hefted the weighted body bag, placed it on the plank and lifted it to the railing.

"Crew, remove your hats," shouted Pennecuik. He waited until all heads were bare. "Lord, we commend Shona Rose to Your keeping. Watch over this good woman." He opened a small book to a marked page. "I am the resurrection and the life, saith the Lord: he that believeth in me, though he were dead, yet shall he live and whosoever liveth and believeth in me shall never die. Amen."

With a nod from the captain, Duff tilted the board, and Shona slid effortlessly into the deep. I couldn't tell if the splash was from the body hitting the water or the waves crashing against the ship. There was no mistaking Hugh's outburst. It accompanied his wife into the depths of the sea.

Shona was the fourth to die. As more went to sick bay, additional funerals were held. And yet, our spirits were buoyed by the idea that we might make sight of Madeira Island tomorrow. The pigeons had returned.

Many times, I would seek out Cook Innes in the galley. I enjoyed my visits because it didn't take much urging for him to describe his experiences on board ship. He had been sailing since the age of eleven after running away from home. His mother had died giving birth to her seventh child. Her distraught husband grieved by beating his only living child.

The *St. Andrew* was his fifth ship, Pennecuik was the sixth captain, but this was his first time as cook. He was surprised how much he enjoyed the assignment. No more suffering from the cold and never going hungry were two benefits, although the Captain, a 'stingy bugger' ordered every biscuit and drop of ale be accounted for.

On this day I found someone new in the galley. A young lad named Ben had been reassigned. I found Mr. Innes introducing the boy to his method of cookery.

Tall for his age, Ben stooped over a scarred wooden board with a chopping knife. Sniffling, he said, "I'm tryin', Mr. Innes. But I can't help cryin'. I'll try harder, sir."

"Keep breathin' deeply, I say, or the tears won't stop, and ye'll dry up like a wee old woman."

Mr. Innes saw me in the doorway. He winked and grinned impishly. Turning back to his apprentice, he said, "If ye want tae stop cryin' like a lassie, take deep breaths."

I peered around and saw Ben was chopping onions, and many more bulbs awaited execution. He tried his best to wield the knife while wiping his runny nose and eyes with his sleeve. Mr. Innes was enjoying the tearful initiation of his young helper.

Mr. Innes motioned for me to follow him to an open portal for some fresh air. Out of earshot, he bent over and laughed until his eyes matched Ben's. "Ha. How I love a virgin. Gullible, I tell ye. Thinks he kens everythin'. I had him blubberin' faster than he could wipe his arse."

I fanned fresh air into my face. "Won't he be furious once he finds out?"

"Nah. He's lovin' the galley and the leavin's he stuffs in his gullet when he thinks I'm not lookin'." Innes wiped his eyes and blew his nose. "So, Mrs. MacArthur, what can I do for ye taeday?"

"I don't know who else to ask. I was wondering about poor Mrs. Rose yesterday."

"Ah, you mean the burial. It's not often that we toss a woman overboard. It's a sad business." He paused for a moment of silence as if he hadn't finished paying his respects.

"Mr. Rose wanted to make sure before…Do you think she was…still alive?"

Mr. Innes put his little finger in one ear and turned it like a corkscrew. Then he bent his head and lightly boxed the same ear. "Ah, that's better. It itches." He wiped his finger on his stained apron. "It's hard to tell with the fever. The body takes longer to cool. But Mr. Duff did his job properly."

"What would Mr. Duff have to do with it?"

"He's the one who sewed up her cloak. The first stitch is always at the feet. The last is through the nose. If she were alive, we'd o' heard her. A few years back I served on a merchant ship. The captain, a real bastard, didn't wait for the person to look dead. No shroud, no cannonball, no nothin'. While they were still squirmin' the sick ones were tossed over the side. It didn't matter if they were young lads, like my bawler over there, or old salts like me."

"Did you report such barbarism to the authorities?"

"Not if I wanted tae sail on 'nother ship. No one wants a troublemaker. The Captain's the lord o' the vessel; his word is law. If you object ye may find yerself feedin' the sharks, keel hauled, or worse."

Innes stopped for a moment. The look on my face must have been one of disbelief.

"Sailin's serious business, Mrs. MacArthur. This is no pleasure boat. We are about makin' money for the owner and hopin' tae live long enough tae get tae the next port, have a few drinks, and find some female entertainment. The dyin' slow us down, and one way tae stop the disease is tae send it overboard."

"So, there was no possibility Mrs. Rose was alive?"

"Nay. I saw her body laid out on deck. She was dead alright. Stiff as the mess table they used tae heave her with."

"You were at the funeral? I didn't see you."

"Aye. I was makin' sure the Captain did right by her and said a few words tae keep Mrs. Rose's ghost from returnin'. I don't need her hauntin' me in the middle o' the night."

The next day we anchored off of Funchal, the capital city of Madeira Island under the sovereignty of Portugal. Just on shore there was a white castle nestled below cloud-covered mountains. We reunited with our fleet; some had arrived a few days ago. We anchored near a threatening fifty-gun man-o-war, flying a Genoese flag.

Mr. Innes had been to Madeira several times. He told me the climate was agreeable, the wine superior, and the island a pretty little thing. But he warned that the Portuguese were no better than thieves and the English merchants were spies for the Crown.

All on board were elated; our recent hardships were temporarily forgotten. The prospect of walking on solid earth had many backslapping. Some were prepared to sell their weapons or the clothes on their back to get something edible. I heard Mr. Duff announce that he and his lads were heading out in search of Madeira wine, food, and female companionship. The order didn't matter.

Shortly after we arrived, the Councilors met. Alain told me the order of business but only one item piqued my interest.

"What's this about a dinner on the Genoese ship?"

"The Governor of Madeira and the Captain of the ship have invited some of our Council members to dine tomorrow evening. Mr. Paterson, Captain Pennecuik, Robert Drummond. I was also invited. Two others, a bishop and a bride will be in attendance."

"No one else?"

"Lydia, of course. Mr. Paterson asked especially for her to attend. He thought it would be good for her."

"What? You didn't ask if I could join you." I longed to get off the ship.

Alain didn't respond right away until an impish smile turned his lips. "I told the Council you would be a lovely addition to the table and would show off Scotland at her finest. And…I wasn't going without you."

I rushed into his arms and smothered him with kisses, but just as quickly pulled back. "What will I wear? I can't go in this." I peered down at my skirt, examining the stains. "It's soiled and smells, and…so do I. I can wash, but what can I do with this dress? My other one is not much better."

Lifting the lid of the heavy trunk, I yanked the dress out. It was made of fine brown wool. I held the skirt against my body swishing it to and fro, wishing for a mirror. "Did I hear you right? Did you say there's a bride on board?"

"Aye. She was married by proxy. She'll be leaving shortly to meet her husband in Lisbon, bringing a handsome dowry – £15,000 Sterling."

"She must be a beauty to be worth that much."

"Aye. Or her father's trying to sell her off."

The orange brocade dress, with shades of gold and peach, fit perfectly. The underlining chemise had gold mesh lace that peeked out at the bodice and cascaded at the cuffs. The hem was embellished with embroidered trim. When I came out onto the deck, I sparkled like a diamond in the sunshine.

Alain was responsible for the dress. Earlier in the day he'd joined a group heading into Funchal seeking to trade for food. What they found was an island not as bountiful as they had hoped. The Madeirans had little to offer. Instead, Alain said he wandered through the alleys and found a seamstress who was desperate to part with the dress. It was made for a rich customer who had died of consumption before paying. Alain offered two pieces of silver. "She nearly knocked me over when she grabbed the coins and shoved the dress in my face." The chemise and fan came at no extra charge.

Once aboard the *Sancta Brigida,* we were ushered into a large dining room. In the center of the room was a table covered with dark red linen and gleaming silver trays overflowed with fresh fruit: bananas, apples, pears, and others I didn't recognize, In addition to the members of the Council and Lydia, Captain Ferrando sat at the head of the table and the Governor of the island at the other end. Still absent were the bishop and the bride.

"*Senhor* MacArthur. *Boa noite, Senhora.*" Ferrando bowed, kissed my hand, and turned to Alain. "Thank you for bringing your exquisite wife. She does us great honor by gracing our table with her beauty."

The clearing of someone's throat drew our attention to the doorway. There stood the bishop and the bride. He wore a black cassock with a large silver cross on his chest. His dress was much like Father Drummond's except it was made of finer material and had red piping that noted his elevated station in the church. The rings on his fingers announced his wealth.

The bride was dazzling in a gown of gold brocade. Every part of her skirt, the bodice and the paned sleeves were gathered to emphasize the yards of material needed to create such a dress. The seams were covered with embroidered ribbon sewn with metallic thread. From her dainty gold shoes to the mounds of her lovely breasts to her lustrous blond hair piled in curls on her head, she was a sight to behold.

Until you looked at her face. The bride was no beauty. Her features were similar to the animals on our farm. Her nostrils flared upward like a pig. Her chin was marked by a wattle that any rooster would have been proud of. Her only asset was her pearly teeth, but they were crooked and appeared too much for her mouth. All eyes followed as the Bishop escorted her to her seat, and I realized the only reason why men sought her attention was due to her father's wealth. I wondered if it would be enough for her husband.

"*Bem Vinda*. Welcome" said the captain. "Please, raise your glasses and let us toast our Scottish guests and the lovely ladies that grace this table. May you find good fortune wherever it takes you."

Crystal goblets clinked and were refilled by African slaves. More toasts were made to the Governor and the bride. His, for the hospitality shown thus far. Hers, for her future happiness. Only the bishop exaggerated the bride's beauty. I hid my reaction behind my fan. The bride would have been better served to have used hers.

"Captain Pennecuik," said the governor. "Where do you travel next?"

"We are heading down the west coast of Africa," lied the captain. "We have many goods to trade."

"I thought you were setting out to found a colony," said Captain Ferrando. "Rumors have been swirling about the intent of your country."

"Ah, they are just that. Rumors. Our mission is simple. Trade. My crew is anxious to go back to sea, make our owners rich, and return home."

Everyone around the table knew the truth. Women were necessary for colonization - to bring forth the next generation. Not trading.

After a rich broth, the main dishes were served: seasoned fish and meat rubbed with garlic, wrapped in bay leaves and grilled on sticks. After weeks of salted beef and hard rolls, the aroma was dizzying.

Alain and William Paterson queried the Governor about purchasing or trading for provisions. The answer was the same they had heard throughout the day. The island had few stores of bread and meat. This was hard to believe based on the bounty set before us. His Excellency made another offer. He was willing to part with barrels of fresh water and a bargain was made for Madeiran wine. The *Endeavor's* cargo would be exchanged for twenty-seven barrels of wine.

241

Our meal ended with delicate cakes, creamy puddings, and a fruit I had never seen before.

"This is passion fruit. *Granadilla*," said Captain Fererando. "It was first imported from Brazil. Madeira has the perfect climate for cultivation."

The fruit was small and round and gave slightly under my fingertips. Some were wrinkly but all were deep purple to almost black.

"Allow me." It was the bishop who spoke. Using a knife, he split the fruit in half. The yellow meat was filled with tiny, black seeds, and the juice dripped on the table. "This one is ripe. Scoop out the insides. The seeds are edible."

After tasting the fruit, I passed some to Alain.

Lydia, who hadn't said a word all evening, asked the Bishop why it was called Passion Fruit. For one who was shy, 'passion,' seemed a difficult word.

"It comes from the flower, *Passiflora edulis* which is most beautiful with its crimson petals," said the bishop. "When it was first discovered by missionaries, the flower reminded them of the last days of our Savior. The petals represent his crown; the red, his blood. The stigmas look like the nails that pierced Christ to the cross and the five anthers are his wounds. The missionaries sent the flower to our Holy Father in Rome who named it *passionem*."

"So, the name is a reminder of the last days of Christ?" asked Lydia.

"Yes, but let's not forget there's much more to the story."

"You mean a bunch of 'thou-shalt-nots' and everything that's pleasurable is a sin." said Robert Drummond. His third goblet of wine had loosened his tongue and reddened his nose to match his coat.

The prelate's smile disappeared and so did his lighthearted tone. "You forgot your catechism. He was sacrificed for your sins. After being deceived by the Devil Jews."

The bishop lowered his head and crossed himself. Others, including Alain, followed suit. I did – awkwardly. "Thank God for blessing us with our Holy Inquisition. The Hebrews are to be converted to the True Faith or they will be purified in ritual fire. There is no place they can hide. Like rats that scurry and disappear in dark places, we will snuff them out, even in our West Indian colonies." Then he turned to me. "Is something wrong my dear? You look pale."

"Yes. I do feel unwell. Perhaps, too much wine."

"We should head back to our ship. My wife needs to lie down."

As I rose, all of the men did the same. Their chairs simultaneously scraped across the deck. The governor came over and took my hand in his. "Perhaps it is the heat," he said. "Something Scots are not used to. I trust you will be well in the morning."

I nodded and Alain took my arm and led me up to the open deck. "I wanted to put my hands around that bishop's neck. The pompous—" He rubbed his head. For a moment he lost his balance and took a step back against the railing.

242

"Alain, what's wrong?"

He reached up to loosen his stock. Before he finished, he was down on his knees, and he turned his head toward the railing. Wiping his mouth with the back of his sleeve, he whispered, "Get me back to our ship."

THIRTY-TWO
Dead Reckoning
2005

Alec's doctor advised that he take two weeks off from work. Head trauma was not to be easily dismissed. Ira and the other professors covered Alec's classes and since he was well-liked and respected, everyone wanted to pitch-in and help. He reminded me of my dad in that way.

After a week of living together, we were convinced this arrangement should be permanent and that meant my becoming a legal resident of Scotland. But first, I had to resolve some issues in Philadelphia and Edinburgh.

I called Jess and asked if she would like to take over my apartment lease in Old Town Philly. She always liked the place, so I wasn't surprised when she jumped at the chance. But it all hinged on where her boyfriend found a position. Jess hoped it would be in Philadelphia, but if not, she had a coworker, the tuna fish lady, who might be interested.

Then, there was Grams. She appeared to be doing well at the senior facility. The progressive care would meet her needs from her independent living status until she warranted skilled nursing. Grams called it one-stop living.

Her old friend and neighbor, Mrs. Shasta, had died three months after moving in. I thought Grams would be devastated, but she took it in stride and moved onto other relationships. She kept herself busy and took advantage of the center's activities: mahjong, trivia night, bridge, and canasta. She joined the Silver Singers, participated in weekly line dancing, and exercised with Yuri the yoga-man.

"I'm heading to Atlantic City this weekend," she said. "About twenty residents are going."

"That sounds great. Will you play the slots or a little poker?"

"No, Bernie prefers to walk the boardwalk."

"Bernie?"

"Bernard Hirschbein. We became acquainted at an ice cream social a month ago." Like a schoolgirl, I could almost feel her long-distance blush.

"That's nice. Tell Bernie to take good care of my Grams. I hope to meet him some day."

"We're just friends," she repeated. "It's nice to have company. Next month we're heading to the art museum and when the weather gets nicer - New Hope. You know how I love the little shops."

I imagined Grams and her beau holding hands, laughing together, and having eyes only for each other. Perhaps I was way ahead of myself, but I hoped she was finding some happiness. I silently thanked Bernie for the joy I heard in her voice.

Before we hung up, Grams asked about Alec. When I mentioned that I was going to apply for permanent residence status, she said, "It's about time."

To become legal, I had to apply for a visa. My passport allowed me to stay for six months. I'd arrived in mid-June, and now it was almost December.

One afternoon, he sat sprawled on the sofa, and I, on the floor, leaned against Alec's leg. He read the regulations for permanent residence status aloud while I craned my neck to get a glimpse of the computer screen.

"Couldn't I just hide in your apartment?" I teased. "I'll eat very little and pay for my keep by ironing your shirts and making a home cooked meal every night." I chuckled when Alec raised one eyebrow. He kissed the top of my head. I loved these playful moments together.

"I don't need or want a housemaid. I want you legal, so Scotland Yard doesn't show up on my doorstep for harboring a fugitive, no matter how beautiful she is."

"Ha! So give me the executive summary. What's required?"

"Do you have good English language skills? Can you support yourself?"

"Absolutely, and as for my financial well-being, let's just say it's healthy. Besides, I know a young professor who will make sure I don't starve and will provide a warm bed at night."

"Hmm. Ye assume an awful lot, mistress."

He continued scanning the screen. "There are different tiers of visas. Some aren't applicable because they involve investing money in a business. Another is if an employer will sponsor you. The employer one might work. Ira could check with the university about a job. He has a lot of clout. Perhaps, you could be my secretary."

The playfulness returned. "Not a chance. Then we couldn't fraternize." I reached up and put my hand under his chin, drew him near, and kissed him.

Alec went back to reading. "Uh oh. The job angle won't work. It has to be one that no Scot can do. You can't take a job from a citizen." His brow furrowed as he continued reading. Then his eyes brightened. "You could get a student visa."

"Go back to school?"

"Why not? Work on your Masters, maybe a Ph.D. and apply for a teaching assistant position at the same time."

I wasn't looking to return to school this soon, but I needed an advanced degree to move forward in my field. "Maybe. I could concentrate on archaeology. Or maybe I'll get a Ph.D. in history and give you some competition."

"Doubtful. I'm Ira's favorite," he teased. "Besides, Ira only likes you because you're with me."

We both laughed. With a viable solution found, the visa instructions were forgotten. I gave the patient what he needed. A lot of tender loving care.

After assuring Alec I would find my way, I drove his car to Edinburgh to start my permanent living status.

Cleaning out my B&B was first. I stuffed my suitcase, and Alec lent me another for all the additional clothes I had purchased since coming to Scotland.

Next stop was the Royal Bank of Scotland to create a financial identity. Mr. Scott helped me open an account. All I needed was my passport, my Pennsylvania driver's license, which was good for twelve months, and a tenancy agreement. Since Ira was Alec's landlord, that was easy. With these documents, I procured a credit card and a cheque book. Mr. Scott congratulated me on my wise decision to make Scotland my home. Maggie, the bank hostess, was so excited she gave me a bear hug.

The next step, signing up with a local GP, would be done in St. Andrews.

By the end of the day, I returned to Alec's apartment, my new home. Another car was parked in Alec's spot. Many colleagues had been stopping by for a friendly chat. I grabbed both suitcases and lugged them down the concrete walkway to the entrance. I left one in the vestibule and dragged the other up the stairs. The door of the apartment opened as if I was expected.

Not looking, I said, "Thanks Alec. Can you hold the door for me so I can get—"

Iain filled the door frame. "Moving in?" He nodded toward the interior of the apartment. "You expected Sir Galahad to fetch your suitcases?"

"What are you doing here?" The cold November air rushed in through the gaps around the door frame, but that was not what chilled me to the bone.

Iain spoke in a harsh low voice. "I'm checking on my brother to see if he's being cared for properly. If not, I know someone who could do the job and then some." He looked at the suitcase I still held and the one at the bottom of the staircase. "Maybe you should turn around and go back from where you came."

"Hanna, is that you?" Alec's voice sounded distant.

Iain leaned closer. His breath hot and whisky saturated. "I promise, I will never allow a non-Catholic to marry into my family." He enunciated each word. Slowly.

I dropped the heavy suitcase on his toe and stared brazenly into his eyes. "I'm…not…going…anywhere. Get over your religious war and stop living in the seventeenth century. Or perhaps you're here to make sure I don't tell your brother that you came on to me in the hospital? If you really were concerned, it wouldn't have taken this long to check on Alec." I reached down and picked the suitcase off his foot. "Don't let me keep you from returning to the pub?"

His eyes reduced to slits. I envisioned clenched fists. I didn't care.

"Yes, Alec. It's me. I just have to get my suitcase by an obstacle."

"Do you need help?" Alec's voice seemed closer.

Iain pushed past and clunked down the stairs. He kicked the other suitcase out of the way and slammed the door.

Alec arrived just as his brother disappeared. His brow lowered, his lips thin, and nose flared.

"Did something happen with your brother?" I asked.

"Aye. Iain came over on the pretense of checking in on me. But it was about you. He said you came on to him at the hospital, and he had to push you away. He thought it was his obligation to warn me. I didn't believe him and told him to leave."

"Why that lying fucking bastard," I hissed. Both of Alec's eyebrows did a reversal and shot up.

I told Alec what really had occurred at the hospital.

He put his arm around me and drew me in. "Iain thinks he's on some mighty crusade." Then he looked down and smiled slightly. "He wants to save me from the infidel."

I couldn't help but think about Anna. I had never experienced religious bigotry before, but she had. It wasn't easy being a Jew in the seventeenth century. Religious acceptance wasn't simple in the twentieth-first century either.

September 9, 1698

We sailed from the Isle of Madeira seven days ago. The second sealed packet was opened. We were ordered to Crab Island in the West Indies & if none have possessed her, we are to raise the cross of St. Andrew. From there, we sail to the Bay of Darien & make settlement on the Golden Island & the Mainland.

247

Two or three die each day from fever & flux. Tossing the dead overboard has become routine. Today, Mr. Wilson's mate & the carpenter's apprentice died hours after they began coughing up the black vomit.

We are in calm waters & the crew whispers about the dreaded Doldrums. We could drift for days with less food & more dead.

"Alec? Are you awake?" I leaned over to get a better look.

One eye shot up. "Now I am."

During the last two weeks, we spent quiet evenings at home. But that routine was ending as Alec prepared to return to work tomorrow. We were in the living room and Alec was surrounded by stacks of books, white and yellow notecards, and piles of clipped papers. The floor, the lamp table, and his lap served as his office. I picked up the journal and sat on the floor next to him.

"Sorry. I hadn't realized you fell asleep. I hope your students find your lecture more stimulating than you do."

Alec chuckled. "I'd like to see you do better explaining seventeenth century navigation to eighteen-year-olds. Their brain cells are more interested in the cute lass on the front row."

"What about the female students?"

"They too, are preoccupied. Why else would the lass in the front row be so fetching?"

"Not to you, Dr. Grant?"

"Course not. I am wonderfully distracted elsewhere." Alec leaned over, put his hand in my hair and gently brought me forward to give him a kiss. This was interrupted by a shower of notecards cascading off his lap.

I helped retrieve his cards and piled them back into his lap.

"I was reading Anna's journal. She's now in the middle of the Atlantic." I talked about my ancestor as if three hundred years ago had happened yesterday. "The good news is she's left Madeira and the clutches of the Inquisition. I was afraid when the bishop broached the subject. Jews were still being punished in Madeira shortly before Anna arrived. The island was no haven for Jews."

"Ira once told me that if you wanted to understand world history, just follow the weave of anti-Semitism. Anna's story is a perfect example."

I pulled my fingers through the tangled mess on the top of my head. How I wished for a clip. Scanning the table tops and the lumpy sofa, I eyed one peeking out between the cushions. Once retrieved, the curls were tamed. "The bad news is the fever is unrelenting and they're now sailing toward an area where there is no wind."

"The Doldrums," said Alec. "Near the Equator. It's caused by low-pressure systems. A ship propelled only by sails could get trapped for days, perhaps weeks. Food and fresh water supplies dwindle or spoil, and disease can wipe out a crew."

"Couldn't they just avoid it? The ocean is large enough."

"The problem was no one realized they were in danger until too late. Navigation wasn't a precise science back then. They had tools like an astrolabe, the compass, and the sextant, and they used the stars and the moon to guide them. But almost every ship, sailing before the discovery of calculating longitude, was, at some point, lost at sea. It will be another seventy-five years until the technology is available."

"Technology?"

He tapped his watch. "It was as simple as this – an accurate timepiece. Well, it wasn't that easy. It had to be one that could withstand the ship's heaving in violent storms and the extremes of weather. But once discovered, sailing became less dangerous and more profitable."

"Okay, so how would a captain, like Pennecuik, get his ship from Scotland to Darien?"

"He would've used whatever charts were available at the time. The tools I mentioned would fix stars, but that only worked when clouds and fog didn't interfere. What was left was Dead Reckoning."

"Is this your lecture for tomorrow? No wonder you're gushing information. Okay, Professor, tell me about Dead Reckoning."

"The captain would use a point of land, a known location. Let's say it was St. Kilda, the last known sight of Scotland for the *St. Andrew*. Pennecuik would draw a line on his chart from St. Kilda to his next destination: Madeira. Based on the speed of the ship, he or his quartermaster would guess where the ship was every thirty minutes. But it was only a guess.

"By Anna's time, a long rope with knots, at measured intervals, was thrown off the front of the ship and unraveled as the ship moved forward. The number of knots was timed by an hourglass, and the speed of the ship was calculated."

"It doesn't sound like Dead Reckoning was the answer. It should have been called - blind sailing."

"It wasn't accurate at all. The errors became cumulative, and it was more likely to result in sunken ships and dead sailors."

While Alec talked, his hand played with the clip in my hair. His fiddling released the curls. They tumbled down my back and a few strayed in front of my eyes until I stuck out my lower lip and blew them away.

"Many a ship went down after crashing into unexpected rocky shores, especially at night. There are some sad tales of an entire fleet floundering. Or a captain making a wrong turn when the harbor he was looking for was within a day's sail. It became such an important issue, that in the eighteenth century, fat rewards were offered to anyone who could solve the riddle."

"You win. I wager your students stay awake and take lots of notes. You make it interesting. I'm also betting your students don't even notice the cute girl on the first row." I put my arms around his neck and drew him closer. "Or the handsome professor in the front of the class."

THIRTY-THREE
Grayness
September, 1698

After many days at sea, I had grown accustomed to the cadence of life on board. Routine was everything. The watch changed every four hours except for the two two-hour dog watches at the dinner hour. Wind and water continually eroded the ship thus making repairs to decking, sails, and rigging a daily chore. Fever created its own procedure. Decks were swabbed with vinegar, and the holds were smoked to reduce vermin.

The direction or velocity of the wind provided the only divergence from the endless blue. Gusts were a signal to unfurl sails. The intensity flapped the canvas taut, and the thick rope snapped, *pizzicato*-like, against masts and yardarms. The wind howled in and around the shrouds, whistling through tiny wooden gaps, the result of a carpenter's faulty plumb line. The pitch rose or deepened depending on the length and size of the crack. Whitecaps, rolling over and under the ship, thundered timpani-like, adding to the rising crescendo.

When the wind subsided, the melody became softer. For the past week, the music was at rest. We were entrenched in The Doldrums and were frozen in one of the hottest places on Earth. The deck planking was weathered and curled at the edges. It mirrored our parched throats and gray, leathery skin.

Except for an industrious few, who mended sails and repaired shrouds, most of the crew waited for the ill to take their leave. Captured in this grimness, there was no shortage of sickness and death. Today, the cook's helper, Ben, was laid out on the mess board. Nearby, Mr. Innes stood, his eyes lowered, cap in hand. I heard snatches of the Twenty-Third psalm whispered from his lips.

The funerary traditions observed at the beginning of our voyage had been abandoned. Sailcloth for shrouds couldn't be spared, and no nose piercing was done to ensure the dead were truly dead. Instead, a bag of rocks, tied around a bony ankle, dragged the skeleton to the depths below. Captain Pennecuik no longer demanded bowed heads or read comforting words from his Bible. With a quick nod, the board was up-ended.

I glanced over the rail and watched the body shatter the glassy sea. The boy's outstretched arms appeared to be flailing, trying to slow the inevitable descent to

Neptune's lair. His head was thrown back as if seeking the sun one last time before a watery darkness filled his eyes for eternity.

Alain wrapped his arm around me, and with one hand he turned my head. "No use watching, Anna. The boy is gone."

He was right, but I had hoped to find a faint spark of life in the boy's face.

With the disposal of the body over, Duff ordered the mess board returned to the galley. In a few hours, sailors would consume their scant meal and grog on the same board.

Each death heightened my sense of dread. After dinner on the *Sancta Brigida*, Alain had fallen alarmingly ill. Everything he'd eaten ended up in the sea. If it was the fever, *vomitus* usually resulted in death a few hours later. The next morning, Alain had roused from a fitful sleep. Thankfully, it was something he ate.

After another council meeting, Alain said, "This is a nasty business." He clenched his hands as he leaned over the railing. His brow furrowed. "The dead may be the lucky ones."

I felt someone come up from behind. It was Filib. We hadn't spoken much since Madeira when he'd helped me get Alain on board. Now in the heat of the day, Filib had removed his jacket. His dingy white shirt stuck to wet skin. He had taken on odd jobs around the ship that had been formerly done by deceased crewmen. This allowed him to come on deck, away from the fetid air and the sickness below.

Filib leaned on the rail and stared at the fixed horizon. "No one checks any more to see if the dead are really gone. As long as they look the part, off they go." Filib wrung his hands and fixed his cap. "Men aren't particular when their bellies are empty."

"It also means there are fewer crew to man the ship," Alain said.

With no breeze, the heavy, saturated air hung like a wet drape. I pulled the sleeves of my woolen dress to my elbows. "But we aren't going anywhere. We've been drifting for days. How will we ever find our way?"

"I asked the same of Duff," said Filib. "He told me that on the last sailing he served as navigator, He made the mistake of telling Pennecuik, in front of the crew, that they were heading in the wrong direction. The captain tossed him in the brig." The somber little Scot took out a gray cloth and wiped the sweat and grime off his neck. "Duff confided that ever since we left Madeira the captain doesn't know where we are."

Alain added a grisly story he had heard. "Captain Drummond told me about a tiny fleet of ships, like ours, was lost and floundered on the rocky shores of some island. Four of the five vessels broke up in minutes and only two crewmen made it to shore. One survivor was quickly bludgeoned to death by a sheepherder's wife when she saw a small bag of gold tied around her victim's waist."

It seemed there was no shortage of horrors to send shivers down my spine.

"I'm afraid that when we reach our destination our situation isn't going to get better." continued Alain. "The Council has approved a method of governance. Each Councilor will be president for seven days. Mr. Paterson, Robert Drummond, his brother and I objected. It's lunacy. How can one lead for a week? The new president will spend the first few days undoing the work of his predecessor and only have the rest of the week to get anything done. Then, the process will start all over again. When Mr. Paterson suggested a thirty-day term, we were the only ones who voted in favor. There's no trust—"

Alain gripped the railing, an unusual gesture because the ship wasn't moving. "I'm tired and a wee bit chilled. I need to lie down."

Filib and I looked at each other. Chilled? Both of us were sweating with barely any dry spots left on our clothes. Alain turned. His face was pale; his eyes were dull and dark. Grasping me tightly, he started to shiver. His legs buckled. Filib quickly grabbed Alain's arm and together we dragged him toward the ladder. I turned and scanned the deck. Duff appeared. Our eyes locked and then he vanished.

Filib removed Alain's boots and breaks. Wearing only his sark, we covered him with a woolen blanket. The shivering continued.

"Duff knows. He saw us. Will he tell?"

"I'll talk to the man. I doubt he'll tell Pennecuik. He steers clear of the man."

"Stay with Alain. I'm going to find Mr. Innes."

I didn't wait for Filib to reply before I shut the door between us. If anyone on the ship could help, it was the cook. At least that's what I hoped for.

I found Mr. Innes bent over a pot of soup stirring it with a wooden paddle while wiping his nose and eyes with the dirty gray neckerchief he always wore. With the loss of his apprentice, Innes had more room to work and less people to cook for.

He turned. His scowl brightened into a smile. "Ah. Mrs. MacArthur. Would ye like some soup? A biscuit?"

"Yes, I would, for my husband, please. He hurt his…foot on the stairs… he's resting in our cabin."

Innes reached for a wooden bowl and flicked something off the rim. "If your husband is feelin' poorly, perhaps he'd prefer a wee bit o' peppermint or chamomile tea. I've a special ingredient around here to make the tea work wonders. It'll take but a moment tae find it." He rummaged through some boxes in the back of the galley.

"Ah, here's what I was lookin' for." He held up a bottle of whisky. "I save this for special occasions…or medicinal purposes. I'll add a wee drop in the tea. It helps soothe the pain from a mangled ankle." Along with the tea, he offered a knowing smile while ladling a bowl of soup avoiding the chunks of meat." He leaned over and whispered. "It isn't fit for humans.

"Let me give ye some advice for that 'foot' o' his. It may take two weeks till he's feelin' a mite better. Don't let the surgeon touch him. That bugger thinks the cure is tae bring on the vomit. It will only make your husband weaker. Wash him down with cool water. His 'foot' will get a lot worse before it gets better."

"Thank you. I'm grateful for your advice."

"Just a bit more, if ye don't mind. The Captain's preparin' for a bit o' diversion, tae keep the men's minds off our situation. Tomorrow, he's goin' tae announce we're crossin' the Tropic o' Cancer. How he reckons where we are is a bit o' a fairy tale. They'll be a bit of celebratin' for first timers. It might be a good idea tae stay out o' the way. They'll be lots o' drinkin', and well, the rejoicin' could get a little out o' control. If ye know what I mean."

"Yes, I need to tend to my husband anyway."

Back in the cabin, I found Filib sitting on a low barrel. His back and head were leaning against the wall. Both men were asleep, and the room crackled with snoring. I shut the door and Filib awoke with a start almost tipping the barrel. The room went silent. No sound came from Alain. Filib rushed over. I followed, sloshing broth on my skirts before placing the bowl on the barrel.

"His chest is barely moving." I put my hand on his forehead and then around his wrist. "Oh my God. He's burning up. We need to cool him down."

Filib brought the basin of water over from the dresser and I tore two strips from my petticoat so we could work simultaneously. Filib lifted Alain, pulled up his sark. Angry, purplish spots covered his chest and shoulders. Filib turned Alain slightly. The purple storm continued on his back.

"Quickly, let's wash him down. Don't mind the rash. Mr. Innes said it would get a lot worse before there's any improvement. I hope this is the worst."

The next day, the sky was dismal and overcast. The door to our cabin creaked open. Filib held two mugs of tea. He put one cup into my hands and uncovered a biscuit from somewhere inside his shirt. The other mug was filled with a chamomile tea that would bring on a deeper sleep to help with Alain's healing.

I reached out to touch Alain. The fever and chills persisted. The rash was darker and appeared to cover more of his body – his buttocks, his arms, even his oxters. Once more, I bathed his face, neck and arms. When the tea had cooled, I held it to his lips hoping they'd part. No reaction. I maneuvered myself on the bed so I could hold his head in my lap, gently stroking his throat in the hope of awakening his swallowing reflex. Nothing.

Alain's rattled breathing was shallow. His chest barely rose. "Breathe, damn you. Breathe." I pushed on his chest. Harder. "Don't you dare leave me. It's your fault you're dying. This was your idea." Again, I pressed his chest. Then I started to pound.

Filib rushed over and grabbed my hand. "Lass, that won't help. He has to do this on his own, fight his way through." Filib pulled me away from the bed. "I'll sit with him now. You need fresh air."

I went on deck and was startled by the fresh air and a slight breeze. It was cool and refreshing. If only Alain could come up. It would bring his fever down.

On the other end of the ship I heard a commotion coming from the crew. The other vessels were close to the *St. Andrew*. The members of the Council were coming aboard while Pennecuik raised his pennant and fired his gun. The crew shouted hurrahs, sang songs, each held a mug in their hands sloshing the drink on each other and the deck. There was no rationing today. The celebration of crossing the Tropic of Cancer had begun and the smell of alcohol was everywhere.

I remembered Mr. Innes' warning to stay away, but it was too late. The crew, Duff, and the Captain noticed my presence. As the only woman, it was hard not to.

Mr. Innes sidled next to me, a gesture of protection. "Don't make eye contact with any o' them. They're drunk; they'll consider a look as good as an invitation tae do all sorts o' perversion. I'll stay by ye, but get your fresh air quickly, and then get ye tae your husband."

"Have we truly reached the Tropic of Cancer?"

"Pennecuik has no idea where we are."

I couldn't help but watch the festivities. "What is that man doing over there? An officer, wearing a disheveled uniform, balanced bottles of Madeira while he staggered around the deck."

"He's payin' his dues. If ye haven't crossed the Cancer ye need tae pay up. He must share with the crew three bottles o' Madeira or a bottle o' brandy. Those that can't pay the fee are tae be dunked three times. Most won't pay. They'll hide somewhere till the crew is so damn drunk they won't be able tae tell the difference between a tit and a teacup." He turned to me. "Excuse my language, Mrs. MacArthur, but initiation is part o' the life o' a seaman. It breaks the monotony o' sea life."

"Thank you, Mr. Innes. I must go back."

"Yere welcome Miss."

I turned to go, and Innes walked toward the crew.

"Mrs. MacArthur. Wait?"

It was Captain Pennecuik. Slowly I faced him. He was dressed in his finest uniform. Mr. Innes looked over his shoulder at the captain.

"That will be all Innes. Get your share of the grog. There will be no rationing tonight."

"Aye sir." He tipped his hat and went off but continued to look back.

"The Council is dining below. The only empty seat is Mr. MacArthur's. I trust he is feeling well?"

"Very well, sir. He had trouble sleeping last night. It's his ankle, you know. I gave him some tea to help him sleep."

"The word is that he was seen staggering off the deck. There are no secrets on this ship, and no one has seen your husband since. Not even the surgeon. I ask again, Madam. Is he well?"

"Yes sir. You are welcome to see for yourself."

"I just may do that." He hesitated and licked his dry lips, and then rubbed the back of his hand against them. "If not, he must go to sick bay. No exceptions, not even for members of the Council."

"I'll be sure to tell him. And now I'll leave you to your men. This is not a celebration where women are welcome."

He leaned in on the bulkhead putting one arm over my head. His gesture reminded me of Nathan. You shouldn't be away from your husband's protection especially on a ship full of drunken sailors who haven't had a woman in weeks."

"Thank you, Captain." I picked up my skirts and hurried down the stairs to the lower deck. Each step brought relief.

I was not quick enough.

"Mrs. MacArthur. Wait. I think I will speak to your husband about an important matter." He came down the ladder, offered his arm, and with his free hand he scratched his groin.

THIRTY-FOUR

The Master
September – October 3, 1698

Captain Pennecuik was the master of his ship. Nothing happened without his knowledge or permission, and in the end, he was expected to take ownership for the success or failure of any mission. His knowledge extended to every aspect of running a ship from the bilges to the topmast. He could dismiss anyone from their position, and he didn't need to give just cause. The final say in all matters was his right. His rank was more than a designation. At sea, he was God.

The captain had the authority to enter our cabin. I had to ensure that didn't happen. If he saw Alain in his present condition, he would be removed to sick bay which was a death sentence. Filib and I would be placed in the brig, or worse, for disobeying orders. My heart raced as I fumbled for a strategy.

"Captain, I appreciate your taking the time to look after my husband, but I can assure you his wretched ankle is healing."

He stopped not far from my cabin door. A mean smirk crossed his face. "Anna, your husband is of no importance to me. If he dies, he's just another who will feed the sharks. They need to eat, you know." His eyes, the color of coal, had no spark of humanity. "If I find what I believe is going on in your cabin, it will go badly for you. And your husband."

His words were frightening. The unwelcomed informality of using my first name was followed by his pressing me against the wall. Like a dog searching for a bone, his eyes lowered, searching for enticing gaps in my bodice. I turned my face to avoid his probing eyes and sour breath while trying to shrink from his hardened cock pressing against me.

At that moment, a plan came to mind.

I covered my mouth and emitted a deep guttural sound, as if I was about to vomit. Pennecuik gasped and took a step back. Even the lord of the ship wasn't immune to the fever. I pretended to recover by swallowing a couple of times and retrieved a handkerchief from my sleeve to mop my dry forehead.

"Forgive me. As you can see, I'm not feeling well." Feigning lightheadedness, I leaned against the bulkhead. "I'll inform…my husband that you've been most…attentive. He will be…grateful."

258

Pennecuik threw back his head and laughed heartily. One hand went to his eyes and wiped the wetness in the corners. "Madam, that was good. Are you sure you aren't an actress? Your act is entertaining. Please continue."

I pressed my hand against my waist. "You are heartless, sir. You have forced me to share something too personal." My tone sounded hurt and whiney. "No gentleman would force a woman to do so."

"Well, I'm no gentleman." He put his forefinger under my chin, raised my face so that our eyes met. "Which you probably know by now."

"When you saw me on deck, it wasn't to watch the celebration nor was I trying to tempt you or any of the crew. For a woman in my condition that was the last thing...." I lowered my eyelids and directed his attention to my hand pressed against my waist. "I felt nauseous and needed the fresh air."

His brows furrowed. I wasn't sure he believed my story, but I continued. "I didn't want to say anything...vomiting is a sign of the fever. But for a woman...for me...it signals something more fortuitous." For the first time I felt emboldened. "I wanted to be certain. I'm sure you can understand. I wanted to surprise my husband. We've been hoping for another child. We had to leave our daughter back in Scotland, and we miss her so much. I know Mr. Paterson will frown on our decision, but our son...our child will be the first true Caledonian." I dabbed my eyes with my handkerchief. "Don't take this joy away from my husband."

For a moment, Captain Pennecuik said nothing. I thought there was a glimmer of hope, and I had saved my husband's life.

"Do you think I care? You can still warm my bed. Besides, my dear, I believe you're lying through your teeth. If your husband is ill, and I do believe he is, you'll say anything to keep me away." He yanked me forward until we were within arm's reach of my cabin. And then, unexpectedly, he stopped.

"Unless." He pulled me around so that his face was inches from mine.

Playing the frightened, vulnerable woman wasn't working. I changed my tactic and stood on my toes to get eye-level with him and glared back. "Unless what?"

"You can stop the ruse, madam. I don't treat insubordination lightly. The crew wouldn't mind my cat o-nine tails kissing your lovely stripped torso. That and a full barrel of rum would be just as much a diversion as crossing the Cancer."

"You wouldn't dare." But I knew Captain Pennecuik meant every word. A picture of Mr. Innes's back haunted me, and my knees almost buckled.

"But you can avoid that and save your husband's life. Bide with me. If anyone should question your decision, you're to state it is of your own free will that you have chosen to leave your husband's bed." To emphasize the power he held over me, his calloused hand slowly moved down my thigh, lifted my dress and fondled my flesh.

I pushed against his chest. "Never. You bastard. Touch me again and I'll...."

"Oh, never mind, you're coming with me whether you like it or not." He grabbed my arm so hard I thought the bone would snap in two. He forced me in the opposite direction, and now his cabin loomed in front of us. I started to scream but with all of the celebration going on, no one heard.

The captain threw open the door and tossed me onto his bed. Jack, his cabin boy, jumped up from his mat on the floor. He barely had time to rub his eyes.

"Get out. I am not to be disturbed. Do you hear me?"

Before the boy could whimper a response, the door was slammed in his face. Pennecuik turned in my direction. An evil noise sputtered out of his throat as he removed his jacket, loosened his stock, and his strings.

I scuttled into the furthest corner of the bed. As he continued to disrobe, he snorted and told me how many other women he had delighted.

While he talked, I scanned the room for any kind of weapon. Nothing. I vowed that if I survived the day, I would never be unarmed again.

Just then, I heard a scuffle outside. I started to scream hoping to get anyone's attention. Captain Pennecuik pulled his arm back to strike, but before he brought it down, the door crashed open. There stood Filib. One fist was clenched, and the other held a dirk.

"Let go of the lass before I slice a bloody smile on your throat."

Unarmed and almost undressed, the captain was at a disadvantage. Before he could use me as a shield, I ran behind Filib. We walked backwards out of the cabin, turned, and then stepped around the trembling cabin boy.

We stopped at the door of my cabin. Filib took a deep breath. That's when I noticed his eyes were wet. I was coming to get you…saw you with the captain." He hung his head low. "Alain is dead. "

The fever had followed the usual course. Four hours after the first symptom Alain was gone. His body was stretched out on the bed, the blanket askew over and under him, and his hair unfurled like tentacles. The sark had stains of yellow and green, and dried food was glued to his chest and hair. I cradled Alain's head against my chest. He wasn't cold yet.

"The body needs time to learn it's dead."

I rocked Alain's head in my arms as if he was a newborn. "Who has declared him dead? You? The surgeon?"

Just then there was a knock, and the door opened before we could answer. Duff and another sailor entered. "The captain has ordered us tae take your husband tae sick bay." He stopped when he saw Alain.

"Get out," I hissed.

The boatswain looked at Filib for some direction. Filib nodded, and Duff backed out of the room and shut the door.

"It's no use, Lass. God Almighty Himself couldn't save Alain."

I pleaded with Filib to give me a little more time. I could see the anguish in his eyes. Although my heart was breaking, I knew Filib also suffered. He had recently lost Sally and now his best friend.

Silence wedged between us. Filib sat on the edge of the bed and buried his face in his hands. I continued to hold my love. I would do so as long as possible.

When the sun hovered just above the horizon, I laid Alain's head on the pillow, got out of bed, and touched Filib's shoulder. No words were needed. It was time.

Duff and his crewman carried Alain's body to the top deck. Filib and I followed. Through the blur of my tears I saw Mr. Innes, the Patersons, other passengers and the crew. They all had come to pay their respects. Even Captain Pennecuik was there with his Bible in hand. He hadn't said any verses for the dead recently. Was he prepared to do so now? Was this his way of asking forgiveness from God? From me?

In consideration of his rank as Councilor, a large piece of precious sailcloth was spread on the deck and the body was placed in the center. I collapsed next to Alain, embracing one last time, searching, until I found his dirk. Then I quickly stood and aimed the weapon at the captain.

"You hypocrite. How dare you speak God's holy words. Did you forget the ninth commandment? Thou shalt not covet your neighbor's wife." I spun around and looked in the eyes of all who were gathered. "Do you know what your good captain tried to do? While my husband lay dying, he made me an offer. He suggested he would keep Alain out of sick bay if I became his whore." I heard Lydia gasp as she grasped her husband's arm. "A captain should put his ship first, but not this one. He was willing to risk all of your lives to satisfy his lust." I turned back to Pennecuik and continued pointing the knife. "How dare you show your face at the funeral of the man you hoped would die, so you could take his wife. Not one word of consolation shall come from your lips."

Captain Pennecuik opened his mouth, but when he noticed the glares all around him, he turned away, and retreated below.

I dropped the knife and went back to the sailcloth. "Where is Mr. Wilson? I want to hear from his lips that my husband is dead."

Slowly from one side of the deck, the surgeon came forward. He tried not to stagger to retain as much dignity as possible.

261

"Mrs. MacArthur. I'm sorry. Your husband…was a fine—"

"You haven't examined him. How can you know he's dead?"

The surgeon came closer and spoke in a whisper. "If you'll permit me, madam."

I stepped aside. He pressed his ear on Alain's chest and then he raised each eyelid. The last test was to see if Alain was breathing. He picked up the knife and held it under Alain's nose. He quickly rose to his feet, shook his head, and returned to his place.

Duff approached with a ball of twine and a large needle.

"Before you stitch the shroud, please let me kiss my husband." Before anyone could answer I fell by his side, kissed his lips, stroked his cheek, and willed myself to remember this moment. I looked at Mr. Innes and then at Filib. "His body is still warm."

"Aye, that can happen in the tropics," said the cook. "The heat keeps the body from growin' cold."

I knew that also meant the body would deteriorate quickly. I stepped back and allowed Duff to begin his job. He placed a cannonball at Alain's feet, and then folded the sailcloth around him. He threaded the needle and began to sew large stitches. It was agonizing to watch Alain's body disappear with each poke of the sharp implement in the tough thick canvas. For the final stitch, there was only enough twine to make one more pass.

"Put the needle through his nose," I said.

Duff looked at me. His eyes wide. "No need. Mr. Wilson says he's gone."

"Do it. Or I will."

After having threatened the captain with a knife, Duff knew I was serious. He peered over at the cook. Mr. Innes nodded. "Get on with it, Mr. Duff. She has a right."

He placed the needle on one side of Alain's nose with one hand, and with the other, he pulled a small wooden block from his pocket to use as a mallet. He raised his hand and brought it down hard and swift.

At that moment, the most beautiful blood-curdling cry came from a dead man's lips.

September 29, 1698

Yesterday the lookouts sighted the island of Dezada, the Land of Desire on our larboard. Mr. Innes explained that Columbus had chosen the island's name. It was his first sighting of terra firma.

Crew & landsmen were joyous. We spent the day hanging over the rail to get a better view & stretched our arms as if that would bring the land closer. Everyone celebrated with an extra ration of ale.

A new illness has affected the crew & passengers alike - homesickness. We search each passing island for a familiar site: a small hillock, a grove of trees, or a recognizable coastline. Anything to remind us of home. But when our surgeon's mate, Walter Johnson, died from an overdose of laudanum in an attempt to treat his fever, we were reminded of our present condition.

It is cruel to be buried at sea. There is no marker for family to grieve. One spot in the ocean looks the same as another. I wish there were a way to bring the deceased to shore for a more pleasant resting place.

Now that we are days away from our destination, the Councilors have come aboard for another meeting. This was Alain's first since his miraculous recovery.

The last three weeks have been difficult as Filib & I nursed Alain round the clock. The surgeon allowed Alain to remain in our cabin. This was a small token of repentance. But Mr. Innes thought I was too generous. The surgeon was glad to have one less patient.

Mr. Innes prepared a special gruel for Alain. He claimed it had a secret ingredient, a generous helping of his reserved whisky. Once Alain started eating, his recovery began.

Hearing a commotion and the pounding of feet above, I put my quill down, but left the journal open so the ink would dry.

I came up on deck and found Filib and Alain leaning against the rail. I continually marveled at the sight of Alain. If hearts skipped a beat, mine missed several. I joined the men and wrapped my arm through Alain's. A welcome breeze picked up my skirts and whipped my hair around my face. After a week in the Doldrums, the wind felt glorious.

"What's going on? Are we being attacked?"

"We wouldn't be standing here if we were." Alain chuckled. "The fleet is about to separate. The *Unicorn* and the *Dolphin* are heading to the Danish island of St. Thomas with Mr. Paterson. He knows the people there and will find a pilot to take us to Darien Bay and Caledonia. Meanwhile, we are off to Crab Island." He nodded toward the cannon, "We are firing a farewell salute."

The gun crew took their assigned places alongside the smaller black cannon used for ceremonial purposes. One sailor pushed the powder through the bore; a wad of hay followed. When the captain gave the order, Duff ignited the charge through the vent. The gun exploded and recoiled.

Within moments, our salute was answered by each ship. Then slowly the two heading for St. Thomas veered off. It didn't take long before they became specks on the horizon.

I leaned my head on Alain's arm and wondered if the five ships would ever be together again.

A few days later, on October 3, we sighted Crab Island. We spent the entire day circumnavigating the island to be sure it was uninhabited. The land was lush and except for the shoreline it was covered with grass and clumps of trees. Close to the water's edge, palm trees nestled in the sand. Crawling along the beach were huge crabs.

After we were assured the island was deserted, the captain called for the sails to be furled, the anchor lowered, and a scouting party climbed down the ladder to the longboat. The honored crewmen, the first to plant the Saltire of Scotland in the West Indies, would claim the land for their country.

Loud cheers arose from crew and passenger alike when the flag was thrust into the sand. Casks of ale were opened. The first part of our assignment completed; Scotland became the newest colonial power.

Our festive mood continued when the scouts returned, and each was congratulated as if they had just discovered a whole new world. Drinks were put in their hands and toasts made. The deck was bathed from sloshed drinks, and, once again, the air was filled with the smell of alcohol, worn-out bodies, and the sea.

Unexpectedly, a sailor yelled, "Ship to starboard." Our collective gaze turned to the same place – where the sea met the sky.

Coming closer, at a fast clip, was a three-masted ship. As it grew larger, whispers traveled up and down the deck. Everyone wondered what flag she flew. If it was Spanish, we were doomed. The Spaniards had already claimed the island to our west, six miles away. They wouldn't want intruders in their empire. If it were the English, they would barricade our path and force us to Jamaica. The English wanted no trouble from the Spaniards. Either way, it meant that Scotland's dream of colonization was over.

As the mysterious ship neared, only one word swirled from bow to stern.

Pirates.

THIRTY-FIVE
Stupid Amateur
2005

Charles Smith had set up a meeting with a DNA expert who was an old college roommate. Since they intended to meet up in St. Andrews, finding a convenient time wasn't difficult. Ira and Alec planned to join us. Charles' spacious office in the new science building could accommodate everyone.

Everyone called Dr. Jonathan Johnson - Dr. J. I wondered if it had anything to do with the Philadelphia basketball superstar, Julius Erving. My father had idolized the gifted hoopster and often talked about the winning Sixers when the 'Doctor' was in the house.

Dr. J had a friendly smile that immediately drew me in despite his anemic handshake. His frizzy white hair and a bushy white moustache gave him an Einstein-look, and I wondered how he ate spaghetti or drank coffee without staining his snowy whiskers. His height and lean body reminded me of the basketball connection.

"Have you ever heard of Julius Erving? The Sixers?"

"Of course." A smile peeked out from under his moustache. "I worshipped the player and watching him encouraged me to join a pick-up game in Glasgow back in the late 70's. I tried to imitate Erving's slam dunks but didn't come close to his genius. I wasn't bad. At least that's what one pretty co-ed told me."

When Charles chuckled and patted his friend on the back, I surmised that co-ed became Mrs. J.

"I didn't realize basketball existed in Scotland. I thought Scots were only interested in soccer or rugby."

"Basketball has grown in popularity. There's a team in Glasgow, and young boys are joining the local leagues. There's nothing more exhilarating than experiencing taking a ball downtown. Not that I did it often." He held out his hands and slowly moved his fingers. "Unfortunately, MS has prevented me from picking up a ball. Memories will have to suffice."

While we talked and got to know each other better, Charles fumbled in a closet uncovering five mugs. In the corner of the office was a make-shift galley with an apartment-sized microwave, mini-frig, and an electric coffee pot. The little glass dome on top of the pot gurgled; the fresh coffee smelled heavenly.

When all were seated with their mugs, Charles thanked our guest for coming, reiterated the meeting's purpose, and informed us he had taken the liberty to share with Dr. J what he knew about the lock of hair.

"The request for DNA information from a hair sample is not unusual, because it's a common item to inherit," said Dr. J. "Our ancestors often gave hair as a token of love or a keepsake. It might have been a gift that an engaged couple shared. Or taken before a family member was buried. People preserved their loved-one's hair in lockets or pressed between the pages of the family Bible."

"That's what happened to the woman in my journal. Anna and her husband left their only child to found a new colony. She left a lock of her hair with the child, to remember her by."

Dr. J nodded and added another sugar cube to his mug. "I understand you'd like to establish your relationship with this woman. But I'm afraid I have good news… and bad." After another sip, he added three more cubes. Satisfied with the sweet result, he reached for a napkin to dab his lips and brushed his mustache with his fingertips. "And I'm afraid, the bad will outweigh the little good I have to offer.

"Let's begin with how we gene detectives earn a paycheck. There are two kinds of hair samples. The first is with the root still attached. That's the whitish nub on the tip of a strand. The expression of pulling your hair out by the roots is exactly that. The other sample is hair cut with a knife or scissors which I understand is what you have from your ancestor. That's the bad news. It's basically a bunch of dead cells minus the nuclei…and the DNA."

I brought the mug up to my lips to hide my disappointment.

"I'm afraid that even if you had Anna's rooted hair, it wouldn't have helped any way. Each additional generation weakens the probability for a definitive answer. Twelve generations are too much of a gap. Also, hair deteriorates over time; the DNA mutates. And mitochondrial DNA lab work, the only test that might work if we had your grandmother's rooted hair, is extremely expensive."

I felt we had hit a roadblock, until he said, "We need another way to solve this." He took a sip of coffee and made a face. Without asking, Charles took the mug, poured out the cold contents, and filled it with fresh brew. Dr. J added four lumps of sugar and placed the mug on the nearby coaster. "I have another idea, a cheaper one with quicker results."

"I like the sound of that."

"Why don't you do your own DNA sampling? All that's needed is a wee bit of spit. That would tell us if your ancestors spent any time in the UK."

"My grandmother claimed we had some Scots' blood. Perhaps some Spanish or Jewish too."

"And Some Viking thrown in for good measure," Alec chimed in.

And who knows what else?

Alec and I walked back to his apartment. I was awed by the late afternoon sunset, clouds of various shades of pink and purple. A brisk northwesterly breeze buffeted my scarf and whipped my hair around my face.

We walked by Martyr's Monument. Even in frigid temperatures, I got a warm feeling about the place as I was reminded of my first visit. What had now become routine, Alec pulled me against the cold stone and kissed me hard. His lips lingered. I playfully bit his lower lip.

"Are you hungry, mistress?"

"For food. Or for you?"

Alec raised one eyebrow and the edge of his lips started to curl. "For me, of course. What's food compared to the nourishment of the flesh?"

He drew me closer and reached inside my jacket. His warm hands pressed against me, massaging my back. I wondered how Alec could create so much warmth when I could barely feel my fingers or toes. And my nipples were as hard as rocks. I blamed that on Alec rather than the temperature.

On cue, random snowflakes began to fall. Quickly, they thickened and played in the overhead lights that had just turned on.

He grabbed my hand. "Come on. Let's go."

When we arrived at Alec's apartment we were greeted with flashing lights and several uniformed officers. Alec approached one wearing a bright yellow visibility jacket; his eyes were downcast, focused on a notepad in his hands.

"Officer, what's going on? I live in this building."

"There's been a fire and a burglary. Can I see your ID?"

Alec whipped out his wallet from his jean's pocket and offered his university identification.

"And you, miss?"

I fumbled in my bag for my passport and felt the impatient stare of the official. After removing the protective case, I flipped it open to my picture.

He glanced at our documents. "I'll be back. Wait here."

As he walked away, I noticed other officers going in and out of the apartment building. The entrance door splayed open, creating long shadows from the hallway light. Bright yellow police tape cordoned off the front entrance while neighbors huddled nearby.

The officer returned and asked Alec to follow him. I grabbed his hand.

"Miss, you should stand with the others. We need to ask Mr. Grant a few questions."

Alec nodded, but it didn't erase the concern on his face. I watched him disappear into the building.

"My apartment's been broken into."

"What? Anything taken? How?"

Alec pulled me away from the crowd of onlookers. "Someone started a fire in the back. The police think the thief meant to draw attention away from his real purpose."

"To break into your apartment?" I asked. "What did he want?"

"Whoever did this, wanted nothing from me. The burglar wanted something from you."

"My clothes? My shoes? I have nothing of value."

"Miss Duncan." The same officer returned. "Will you and Mr. Grant come with me?"

My mind raced. What did I have that someone would want? I stopped. "It's Anna. Is that it?"

"Yes. The thief knew what to go for."

"Please, Miss Duncan. The lead investigator needs to clear up some details just as soon as the photographer finishes, and we dust for fingerprints. It should be a few minutes. This way."

As we entered the apartment, a young man with a bulky briefcase and another with a camera around his neck were on their way out. The first spoke to the officer. "All done here. The boss is waiting for you in the bedroom. He's not in a good mood. Said something about his wife being on his case - missing their anniversary. Good luck. Night."

The door to Alec's apartment was propped open, and every light turned on. A large man who just fit through the bedroom door frame said in a gravelly voice, "Mr. Grant, Miss Duncan. I'm Lead Detective MacKenzie. It looks like the burglar tried to divert our attention with the fire." He mumbled, "Stupid amateur." MacKenzie gestured for us to follow him. "Be careful where you walk. Your stuff is everywhere."

Dresser drawers hung open and empty; contents lay helter-skelter. The bedcover was pulled back. The mattress lay crooked on the box spring. Shelves in the closet had been rifled through and boots, tops, shoes, and jeans were knee-deep on the floor. The bare hangers hung haphazardly. Only one item remained untouched: Alec's kilt.

Detective MacKenzie turned his attention toward me. "Mr. Grant tells me you have some items of value. Tell me about them."

"I already told you when we met a few minutes ago," said Alec.

"I want to hear from Miss Duncan."

On the floor was a pile of overturned shoes boxes. I picked up a blue and white one. It was empty. "I had a lock of hair and a ring."

Mackenzie scribbled on his notepad. "What kind of ring?"

"Gold. With an amethyst stone. It looked like a thistle. I don't know the value of it, but it was important to me. A family heirloom."

After a minute of adding to his notes, the investigator sighed impatiently. "Anything else, Miss Duncan?"

"Hanna, what about the candlesticks?" asked Alec.

"I hid them in a safe place."

Alec looked at me quizzically.

"After I spoke to my grandmother the other day, and told her that we were living together, she suggested I find a place to hide them. They're quite valuable." paused. "Not to hide them from you, Alec. But to keep them safe from...this."

The investigator glanced up from his notetaking and glowered at us. couldn't tell if his disapproving look was for my naiveté or our living arrangement.

Alec asked, "Where did you put them?"

"In the kitchen."

Both men followed me. When I opened the cabinet doors underneath the sink a musty, damp odor escaped. I got down on my knees and reached behind cleaning supplies and plumbing. I retrieved a canvas grocery sack, reached inside, and pulled out the blue velvet bag.

Alec sighed with relief. The detective scratched his head and bit the end of his pen.

"Might I make a suggestion?" grumbled Mackenzie. Keep your valuables in safe deposit box."

"Holy crap! The journal. I left it on your desk last night after I finished reading."

"Journal?" The word was jotted down in the notebook.

I ran back into the bedroom and plowed through the books and papers strewn all over the floor. As Alec stacked his books on the desk, the rug reappeared. The journal was nowhere.

"I know the journal was here. Last night. Why would someone steal it? It only means something to me."

270

"Not if you're a collector, miss. Something that old. There are a lot of unscrupulous collectors who would pay big money."

"I can't believe I was so stupid leaving it out in the open."

"Hanna!" Alec bent down by the edge of the bed, put his hand under the box spring and pulled out the journal. He turned it over before handing it to me. Some of the pages were creased, but nothing torn or ripped out.

"You're very lucky, miss. Seems like the thief never realized what he was doing when he threw everything off the desk. Stupid amateur."

When the report on the missing ring was completed, MacKenzie and his team departed. Alec and I spent the rest of the evening clearing the mess. We ordered in pizza and pretended we could move on.

Later that night we crawled into bed, exhausted. It wasn't only a physical tiredness but an emotional one.

"I feel like I've been violated. Some bastard has gone through my things...intimate things. He knows what toothpaste I use and what my underwear feels like. For all I know he may have laid down in our bed and spit on our pillows. We'll always wonder if he's watching us or when he may come back again. We'll be too afraid to leave, but even more afraid to stay. I don't know how I...we can live here."

"We'll get through this together. It will take time. But if you want, we'll look for a new place. That might be a good idea anyway. We should start fresh, and you should have a say where we live."

I melted into his arms and let him hold me tight. "I hope you don't mind but I'm so tired. I know we had every intention of...could I take a raincheck?"

A soft chuckle gurgled from his throat. His arms wrapped around me, providing his protection.

"Alec? Don't you think it's weird? Twice now, I've been involved with a burglary and the police since I opened the safe deposit box? It's like King Tut's curse."

Nothing.

"Alec? Are you awake?"

Silence.

"I love you."

In the morning as soon as enough light peeked through the shades, I grabbed the journal from the end table, plumped up the pillows, and pulled the covers up under my arms.

Alec stirred but didn't awaken.

Deliciously quiet, I opened the journal to where I had left off. The pages were crumpled. Carefully, I flattened them while remembering this book had been through so much more than an incompetent burglar.

I snuggled down to find a comfortable position.

October 3, 1698

What we thought was a pirate ship turned out to be Danish. They are not pleased with our presence on Crab Island. When our men planted the Saltire & erected a tent, the Danes did the same. Now both claimants, on opposite ends of the island, refuse to give in. There could have been bloodshed, but now we are negotiating to trade.

The Danes scoffed at the goods we brought. Woolen stockings, plaids, & heavy wigs are not wanted in the tropics. We offered practical goods too, like nails, needles, & horn-spoons. But our asking price forced the Danes to walk away without purchasing or trading a single item. Mr. Paterson argued with the Council that it was better to trade at a loss, than sell nothing. The council ignored his advice & our provisions remain low.

October 7, 1698

Before our tiny fleet sailed away from Crab Island, the water barrels were refilled. Three men were left behind. Michael Pearson, frightened of what was to come, fled into the woods, never to be seen again. The other two were heaved overboard. They died of the flux.

Disease is still rampant on all the ships, & hundreds are gone. Whether its sex, wealth, or status, the fever does not discriminate. The ocean is littered with a trail of bodies from St. Kilda to the West Indies.

October 27, 1698

Sailing toward the isthmus has been perilous. High winds & strong currents carried us in the wrong direction. Then it takes days to make a correction, while decimating our provisions.

Lightning lights the sky, tempting us with momentary glimpses of mountains, forests, & a fort. The unrelenting heat continues & so does the death toll. Five more perished including the wife of Lieutenant Hay. As her body dropped overboard, a sudden gust whipped a topsail from the yardarm. The sailors, a superstitious lot, consider it an ominous sign.

October 28, 1698

Today, we dropped anchor. Not even the captain is sure if this is our destination - Darien Bay or the Golden Island. We are low on water & desperate. What was collected at Crab Island turned foul. A crew went ashore to search for more, but they came back with nothing.

Word has reached us from the other ships that seven more have died including the respected & well-liked Reverend James. Guns were fired in his honor.

As if Alec had heard the shots, he turned over. Eyes open.

I closed the book and laid it on my stomach. "I think you should call your mother."

"My mother?"

"Yes. I've been thinking who would have wanted to get into your apartment, and then zero in on my things. The thief knew what he wanted."

"Wait, you think my mother had something to do with this?"

"No, of course not. But how many people know we're living together, and that I have valuable Scottish artifacts? I can count the number on one hand: Ira, Esther, Dr. J, Charles, and his wife. None of them had reason to do this."

"Don't forget Mr. Scott. You told me you gave him my address when you opened the checking account."

"Mr. Scott is too strait-laced, plays by the rules."

"I still don't understand what my mother has to do with this. Believe me, she's done plenty wrong, and I'm usually the last to defend her. But why her?"

"Your brother."

THIRTY-SIX
One-Hundred-Ten Days
October - November 2, 1698

"*He* wants you to do what?" I couldn't believe my ears.

Cook Innes stood at his cutting board, glanced up, and smiled. He was telling one of his colorful stories, and this one was humorously gruesome. He repositioned his knife to attack the last bits of meat after scraping off the moldy parts, and then tossed the offending flesh into the stew pot unleashing a sour smell.

"Ye heard me. Duff and I are under strict orders tae follow the Captain's final wishes in case he breathes his last aboard ship."

I waved my hand in front of my face. "Is that what this barrel of rum is for?"

"Aye. It bears the captain's name." He thumped the cask to prove his point. "It's off limits tae the crew even if they are dyin' o' thirst. I've been told m'life won't be worth shite if one drop is missin'."

Except for Pennecuik's name stamped on the lid, the barrel was like all the others I'd seen in the bilges. They contained provisions, trade goods, water, alcohol, and tools. While the barrels remained full, they provided the necessary ballast. But this barrel of rum, stored in the galley, was the captain's coffin.

"Innes, did you ever see anyone buried in a barrel?"

"Aye. Many years ago. I was on a different ship with another captain. A nasty bastard without a forgivin' bone in his whole body." Innes leaned away from his cutting board and spit into a bucket. "We were out tae sea durin' a verra bad storm. The sky lit up with bolts o' lightnin' and waterfalls o' rain fell till everythin' was soaked. The captain had just finished chewin' out his first mate, when a monster wave, as tall as the main-yard, smashed the side o' the ship. The ole man slipped on the deck and cracked his head like an egg. It's a sound I'll never forget."

"It must have been awful."

"Nah. The crew rejoiced and had every right for celebratin'. They hated the man. That is...till." He paused and looked up. Waiting for my response.

"Until?"

Innes smiled. "Until they realized their grog was goin' tae pickle the captain."

"Ugh! I don't want to hear any more." I hesitated and swallowed. "Then, what happened?"

274

Like most Scots, Innes had a knack for storytelling. A delicious sinister smile emerged. "I and the first mate knew the captain did not want tae be buried at sea. He was scared o' sharks and squid. And he couldn't swim."

"But…"

"I know, Lassie. What does it matter if yere dead? But the captain gave us strict orders tae be buried back home. He wanted his loved ones tae pay their respects. Although I don't think there were any who cared. His wife was dead, lucky woman, and his son had run away when he was a laddie."

Innes lifted the lid and sniffed the stew. The offending odor was gone, replaced by burnt root vegetables. He dipped a large spoon in the mixture, stirred and tasted some. He nodded in silent approval.

"Mr. Innes, go on with your story."

"Ye have tae remember, in the tropics, ye canna keep a body laid out verra long, and we still had two months before we'd be back in Scotland. So, before his body putrefied, I stuffed the captain in a barrel and filled it with rum." Innes licked his lips. I imagined him picturing the wasted drink. "Funny. The captain wasn't difficult when he was dead."

"What do you mean?"

"He was short. He easily fit in the barrel." Innes chuckled, covered his mouth knowing he'd succeeded in piquing my interest again.

"You didn't keep the barrel in the galley, did you?"

"I wasn't the cook then. But no. The crew lashed the barrel tae the main mast, but it almost came loose durin' a storm. It would've been amusin' if the captain went overboard tae his watery grave after all.

"Many weeks later, we were almost home, when one o' the crew who had the night watch, reported poppin' and fizzin' sounds coming from the cask. He thought the captain's ghost was tryin' tae escape. O' the old man was fartin' in his eternal sleep. But I'll tell ye, many a crew member became religious after that. They muttered prayers to the Almighty whenever they walked by the coffin."

"Did the captain make it back to Scotland?"

"Aye. The coroner opened the barrel when we returned tae Leith. It's a sight I never hope tae see again. The face was hideous; the skin fell off when the coroner touched it. You'll not be surprised tae hear that the burial happened right away. The captain wasn't fit for a public viewin'."

"Does Captain Pennecuik know about this?"

"Aye. He was the first mate."

275

Voices grew louder as I came to the main deck. While most spoke words of wonder and surprise, others sprinkled theirs with an undertone of fear. The crew and passengers leaned over the rail, fingers pointing in the direction of land. And something else.

I noticed Alain and Filib in the midst of onlookers. Alain ran over and pulled me to his vacated spot. He stood behind and wrapped his arms across my waist. His chin rested on the top of my head. "Anna, look."

I put one hand above my eyes to shield them from bursts of light that played on the ripples of turquoise water.

"There." I followed his forefinger to the shoreline and a row of emerald-green trees set behind a strand of pearl-white sand. Mr. Alliston, our pilot, proclaimed this the Golden Island. That meant Darien Bay and our colony Caledonia, were a short distance away. It seemed unbelievable that we had found our destination so easily.

But it wasn't the land that Alain pointed to. Two small boats, filled with smiling, dark-skinned natives were rowing toward our ship.

Filib gripped his sword, narrowed his eyes, and looked around at the Captain and crew. "No one is prepared to defend the ship. Mumph." In his usual manner, the little Scot said only what was necessary.

"The Indians' lances are lowered," Alain said, "we outnumber them. They'd be foolish to take us on."

"Aye. But weapons can be raised. Knives can be hidden."

"The Council discussed this with Mr. Paterson and our pilot. They've been here before and said there's no danger. We need to get the natives talking to get the information we need. The risk of not knowing is too great."

"And how will you do that? Get them talking, I mean," I asked.

"Whisky."

"Speaking of Mr. Paterson, I haven't seen Lydia about lately."

"She's doing poorly and staying in her cabin."

"Maybe I should visit her."

"Anna, I'd rather you didn't. Her husband fears for her life. There's enough fever all around us, without our seeking it out. I don't know what I'd do if I lost you." He drew me closer kissing the top of my head. "Mr. Paterson's clerk is caring for her."

"Thomas…Mr. Fenner? Lydia would probably prefer a woman."

"He's an old friend of the family and apparently has knowledge of herbs and healing practices. The Patersons trust him."

Our conversation was cut short by an eruption of guffaws and gasps. A dozen, half-naked Indian males stood before us. Each had a string tied around their waist which held a small loin cloth. It did a poor job of covering their genitalia. Their short black hair was unadorned, but their skin was not. Intricate designs covered faces and upper bodies with a black dye.

We had no idea which tribe they represented. Many inhabited this area of the Indies, but Mr. Paterson said it was either the Embera or Wounnan. Perhaps the tattoos on their skin or the bone fragments and teeth hanging from their necks held the answer. To me, they looked like a fascinating new race of man.

The Indians neither mingled nor spoke. But their shyness changed when Innes opened a cask of grog and the smell of ale filled the air. Smiles erupted when the Indians were given full mugs, and as Alain predicted, they started talking.

One, who was taller than the rest and more regal in his bearing, stood in the front. He appeared to be the leader. He surprised us with a few English words but was more fluent in Spanish.

"Find Mr. Spense," ordered Captain Pennecuik. "We need to know what this bugger is blathering about."

A short man with a ruddy complexion and bowed legs hobbled his way through the crew. Benjamin Spense, the Spanish interpreter, was one of four hired by the Scots.

"Aye s-s-sir. D-d-did ye call?" A few snickers greeted the man. I wasn't sure if his stuttering resulted from fear of the captain or something he was born with.

"What are these heathens saying? Be quick about it before they empty the barrel."

Spense jabbered back and forth with the Indian leader. Every so often I heard a familiar word similar to English: *Inglés, españoles. capitán,* and *isla.* When the interpreter finished, he lifted his cap, and scratched the top of his head. "Well, Captain, s-s-seems that these chaps thought we were English. Your red p-p-pennant on the fore-p-p-peak," his eyes gazing upward, "was mistaken for an English s-s-standard."

"Tell them we're bloody Scots."

Mr. Spense turned to the chief. Words and gestures flew back and forth ending with the Indian shrugging his shoulders.

"S-S-Sir, It's meaningless to them. They've only dealt with the English and the Spanish."

"Never mind. Damn it. Did you find out if this land is already claimed?"

"I'm afraid s-s-so. Th-Th-They—"

"Speak up." Pennecuik stepped closer. "Come on man. Spit it out."

Mr. Spense removed a dirty cloth from his shirt and wiped the perspiration off his forehead and around his neck. "The Spanish, C-C-Captain. This land is p-p-part of their West Indies Empire. The Indians are at war with them. They were hoping we were English because they promised to return and help the Indians in their fight. Th-th-that was two years ago."

I looked at the crew and passengers. The joy of ending our voyage had vanished. Duff turned away in disgust. Filib muttered something in Gaelic which caught Alain's attention. One of the officer's wives starting sobbing, placing her head on her husband's chest.

Tears welled up in my eyes. We'd left our child behind for a fool's errand.

Only the Indians seemed unaffected once another barrel of grog was opened.

"S-S-Sir. If I might add." All eyes turned on Spense.

"Yes, yes, Mr. Spense. More good news from our drunken friends?"

"The Indians have told me th-th-they don't think we've come to the right place. Th-th-they s-s-say this is not the Golden Island or Darien B-B-Bay. The land we are s-s-seeking is three to four leagues to the west."

The captain glared at Spense, and then in a slow, even voice he said to Duff, "Find Mr. Alliston. Bring his arse here."

Pennecuik turned to the Indians. "Mr. Innes, fill our guests' cups again and why don't you bring out your stew. Mr. Spense, tell our friends they are welcome to sleep on board tonight." Then he said to Duff, "Sleeping in the scuppers will do. They'll be too drunk to find land any way."

The next day the Indians went home loaded with gifts: mirrors, felt hats, and knives. As they snaked their way back to shore, their rowing was slowed by the mirrors. Their reflections fascinated them.

On October 31, at dawn, the pilot announced we had arrived at the Golden Island. No one put much stock in his navigational skills, but we were willing to accept our location based on the more reliable information we'd gotten from our new friends.

All gathered to witness the end of the journey. Disturbed by our presence, thousands of seabirds took flight simultaneously, scattering in many directions. The sound of their discordant birdsong was music to my ears. The haze felt thick, and the saturated air spit a fine mist coating everything and dripped from the furled sails. Tiny, crystal-like droplets adhered to Alain's hair and cascaded down his back pasting his shirt to his skin.

The obscuration resulted in the island being ill-defined to the naked eye even though we were anchored less than a half mile out. But by mid-morning the sun broke through, burning away the low-lying clouds. The unrelenting heat returned.

We acknowledged this occasion the way we did all others with another burial at sea.

"Mr. MacArthur." Mr. Paterson raised his voice to be heard above the birds and the waves lapping against the hull. His face was haggard; his eyes narrowed and dull. His wife's illness was to blame even though Thomas Fenner continued to care for Lydia. He brought her food and water and carried away her soiled things. Perhaps because of Thomas's care, Lydia would last longer than most.

"Yes, Mr. Paterson."

"The captain is sure there's no harbor on the island large enough to protect our ships. From here, he sees only an inlet of sand. So, he's taking a few men to inspect the mainland, and when he returns, he'll make a full report. The captain asked if a member of the Council would join him. I can't leave my wife, and now Thomas is not feeling well. I suggested your name, sir."

Alain's face turned dark; his hand clenched into a fist. "I prefer not to be in the captain's company."

Mr. Paterson paused.

"It's personal Mr. Paterson. No offense."

"No offense taken. I'll see if I can find another. But I believe I'll get no volunteers. The captain is a difficult man, and none calls him friend. It's a dirty business being master of the ship."

Alain bit his lip to hold his tongue. But if he was thinking the same as I, the captain created his own problems.

Our attention was diverted when Duff nominated four crewmen for the scouting party. None looked happy about the new assignment, and one muttered under his breath. Duff grabbed the offender by his collar and pushed him against the rail. The man's back bent so far that he fell overboard.

Duff cupped his mouth and leaned over the rail. "Now ye'll right the boat when it's lowered, or we'll sail away without ye."

The sailor thrashed his way to the rope ladder. He didn't know how to swim. The other three unleashed the lightweight pinnace, and with a system of ropes and pulleys lowered it over the side. Then they and Mr. Spense climbed hand-over-hand down the rope ladder. They set the oars in the locks and pulled their soaked comrade into the tender. When all was ready, Captain Pennecuik climbed down and took his seat behind the rowers.

"Is he afraid one of the men will hit him over the head?" I asked.

"I wouldn't blame them if they did. But I wished I was the one to put an end to his miserable life."

Hours later the scouts returned with the trophies of their hunt: a limp wild turkey, two hens, and a cock. They raised the birds over their heads in victory.

"Twenty Indians greeted us. They were friendly and offered these gifts," said Pennecuik. "The chief promised to pay us a visit."

"What is the land like? Will it suit our needs?" Mr. Paterson was impatient for the important details.

"It's a wonder. There's a wide harbor for our ships and the land is formed in such a way it can provide adequate defense from storms and enemy alike. To enter the harbor, a ship must sail alongside a narrow peninsula. There are cliffs on both sides and once we build a fort, nothing can threaten our settlement."

"What about fresh water?"

The mention of water reminded me we had so little. I watched others lick their lips, and my hand went to my throat.

"There's plenty of sweet water. The land will take some clearing, but we saw no swamps."

The news was too good to believe. After 110 days we had finally reached our destination. A feeling of unbridled optimism allowed me to accept that our days of rationing, sickness, and death were over. My fears were replaced by hope and momentary joy.

No one noticed the surgeon approach and whisper in Mr. Paterson's ear. His faced paled. He turned and shuffled away.

News spread quickly. It wasn't Lydia, as I had feared. Mr. Paterson's clerk and friend, Thomas Fenner, was dead.

Three days after we arrived, the Indian known as Captain Andreas boarded the ship. His appearance left no mistaking this was an important man. He was dressed in a red jacket much too large for his small frame and left it unbuttoned so he could proudly reveal a heavily painted chest. In particular, he showed off what he had between his legs—a decorated silver cone covering his male organ. A wide-brimmed hat completed the look.

Accompanied by twelve naked bodyguards, he paraded unsmilingly around the deck and stopped in front of Captain Pennecuik and Mr. Paterson. The captain wore his scarlet coat with shiny gold buttons and a monstrous plumed hat that made him appear taller. Mr. Paterson donned his blue jacket and gray wig with hundreds of tight curls cascading to his shoulders. Alain wore his kilt and jacket. His hand rested on the hilt of his broadsword slung low on his hip.

Benjamin Spense's services were called for again.

"Captain. The Indians w-w-want to ken why we're here."

"Tell them we are to settle and to trade." Mr. Paterson answered in place of the captain. "We will be happy to offer any goods to Andreas, his family, and his men. To prove our friendship is sincere, we will offer these commodities at a fair price."

The captain glowered and mumbled under his breath. He didn't like to be outmaneuvered.

"Better prices than the Spanish could offer," added Mr. Paterson. "Tell him that."

Mr. Spense conversed with Andreas and said the Indian wanted to know if we were friends of the Spanish.

"Tell them this, Mr. Spense," said the captain before Mr. Paterson could speak. "We are not, but we aren't at war with them either. We'll resist any who threaten us."

Mr. Spense continued a long back and forth dialogue which tried the patience of the captain.

"Well, what are they jabbering about now?"

"Andreas has told me about the b-b-buccaneers and the friendship he had with them when th-th-they raided S-S-Santa Maria many years ago."

"What's this Santa Maria?" the captain asked Mr. Paterson.

"Thirteen years ago, it was a Spanish stronghold on the isthmus of Darien. It was said to contain a large amount of gold dust. Before the raid by the buccaneers and their Indian allies, the gold was removed to Panama. A battle ensued, and the Spanish lost three ships. The gold was never recovered."

"Spense," said the captain. "He thinks he can scare us with his alliance with a bunch of thieves. You tell this bugger's arse that we are not dirty pirates but traders. No need for Andreas to get the wrong idea."

The interpreter looked fearfully at the captain.

"You heard me. Translate my words exactly." If this were a game of chess, Pennecuik had just saved his king.

Spense did as he was told. Andreas scowled. He turned to his guards. They mumbled and shook their heads. But their anger was short-lived. As soon as they were presented with gifts, a Scottish flag and a new beaver hat for Andreas, they returned to their boats in good humor.

The next day we weighed anchor and four ships, not five, sailed into the harbor. The *Endeavor* smashed its hull on a large rock. Although it didn't sink, its sailing days were over.

Men from each ship went ashore to start the building of New Edinburgh. Their first order of business was to clear the land, cut down the virgin forests, and build shelters for the sick. They also set about digging a cemetery.

The first to be buried in Caledonia was Lydia Paterson.

THIRTY-SEVEN
On the Edge of a Precipice
November - December 24, 1698

Alain burst into our cabin. "The rain is coming down in buckets and no sign of it stopping." He took off his drenched jacket and shirt and threw them in the corner of the room. The skin on his chest and back glistened. Puddles formed around mud-caked boots. "Sometimes I think we're living in the time of Genesis, and this is Noah's ark. How many days has it rained?"

"At least seven. This is the rainy season. Mr. Innes said the rest of the year is unbearably hot and dry."

"You mean it's not hot now?" He grabbed a cloth and dried his hair.

"All we're missing are the animals. *Two by two they came to Noah to the ark, male and female, as God had commanded Noah.*"

Alain put his arms around me. "God had it right, you know. It's the male and female part of the story I'm in favor of. I don't care if it rains forty days as long as I have you for forty nights."

"You know that God brought the floods to punish the sinners."

"Aye." He stepped back, untied my laces until my clothes slithered to my knees. "I'm feeling terribly sinful right now. I need punishing."

He removed his breeks and gently pushed me down onto the bed. My legs spread as he lowered himself, and my arms wrapped around his neck. I pulled him closer, breathing in his damp and earthy musk. He was hard, aching, and anxious, but held off to arouse my pleasure.

His hands were everywhere, stroking the inside of my thighs, cradling my head, and fondling my breasts. His hot breath came fast and uneven as he nuzzled my neck and nibbled my ears. My hand pressed against his chest; the springy matt of auburn hair had dried. His nipples were as hard as mine.

"Anna, I cannot wait much longer. It's been too long."

I responded instinctively by raising my hips, inviting him, guiding him. He thrust and gasped and thrust several more times until he collapsed on top. "We need to do that more often."

284

Alain and I continued to lie in each other's arms. I watched his chest rise and fall. Every so often he sighed deeply. "No matter how bad it is on board," he said, "it's worse on land. At least we have a dry bed and a roof over our heads."

Alain knew of what he spoke. During the day he supervised the building of the new fort. In the evening he returned to the ship. It was a courtesy afforded because of his status.

"Why can't the landsmen sleep on board? Even a hammock on the gun deck is better than lying in the mud." The word landsmen was an insult created by Captain Pennecuik, meant to differentiate us from his valued seamen.

"Pennecuik refuses. He says they'll bring disease with them. But their condition is untenable. Many are skin and bones; their clothes barely covering them. There's not enough food to give them the strength to raise a settlement. During the day, there's the unrelenting heat and rain. At night, they shiver in their make-shift shelters from the wind and rain."

"The crew isn't well off either," I said. "They're bored. All they want is to set sail. They spend their days gambling and drinking. Disagreements start over a look or a word that is misconstrued as an insult."

"Aye, but the sailors eat better and don't do the hard labor."

"If the landsmen are weak, it's because of the captain. Mr. Innes has been ordered to send ashore only the food barrels that are bug infested and rotted."

Alain readjusted his arm, held me tighter, and pressed his lips to the top of my head. "Today, I met a man lying in a muddy ditch…too weak to get up. His clothes were threadbare, he was almost naked, and his skin was covered with sores from the wee beasties who have made a feast of him. When I inquired what he needed…do you know what he asked for? Not food… or a dry bed. He wanted ale."

His voice trembled. He brought his arm around as he turned onto his back. "Yesterday, I saw young Robbie MacGregor sitting in a ditch. His father worked for mine for many years. He was so drunk I had to throttle him hard to get him to open his eyes. I asked when he'd eaten last. He said he gambled his food away for drink. Alcohol did a better job of filling his empty stomach.

"Others have said they won't work unless they get more drink, and for the first time, I have heard rumblings of abandoning the colony."

Alain's stories frightened me. It was only his councilman status that saved him from being the man in the ditch. If the landsmen continued to die at the present alarming rate, what would keep Alain from being conscripted to fill someone's place?

One look at my husband and I was reminded that his illness had taken its toll. Like everyone he was thinner, but having survived ship's fever, haggard was a better description. His face looked drawn. The creases around his eyes and on his forehead were deeper. His scar was more pronounced. When he removed his shirt, the glory of his once well-developed torso was now a bony framework.

The pace of illness and death did not slow. Since our arrival, we'd lost eight, and I was sure that number would double before December. With no more burials at sea, the dead were delivered to the graveyard; the bodies stacked like logs waiting for the gravediggers. But the men assigned to inter the dead were either too weak or too drunk. Or refused to work.

"How is Filib? Is he getting the food?" Every day, we saved a portion of our ration, and Alain would deliver it.

"He's faring better than most. I've been able to find him less strenuous work. I don't know how long that will last. His healthier appearance is a double-edged sword. Others wonder why he's not assigned to more arduous tasks. It's been suggested that Filib dig the graves."

Occasionally there were days when we could forget the misery ashore. We had another visit by Andreas. This time he brought his wife and another woman whom we believed was his sister. Dressed in white linen, the women's arms and necks were covered in colorful beads, and gold rings hung from their nostrils.

Through our interpreter we learned Andreas had four wives and boasted that he could have as many as he wanted. That brought on a sneer from a nearby sailor to his mate.

"Ach. Four, he says. One wife is tae many, if ye ask me."

"I could handle more than one. That last night in Madeira? My hands were full o'—"

"Shut yere hole," said Duff. "Find yereselves a sail tae mend."

The two skulked away giving Duff angry looks.

Mr. Spense explained that the shorter woman was Andreas's traveling wife. It was clear she knew her place and deferred to her husband by walking or standing slightly behind him and remaining silent. But that didn't stop her from staring at me.

Slowly Andreas's revealed the purpose of his visit. He was convinced that trade was not our only mission. He based his conclusion on his experience with the English. Two years ago, they had kidnapped some of his tribe. Andreas gestured angrily when speaking to Mr. Spense. He narrowed his eyes as they flitted from man to man returning to the captain and Mr. Paterson. Then the four, including Spense, huddled in conversation. We all waited, expecting bad news.

"Our friend, Captain Andreas has graciously extended an invitation to visit his village," said Mr. Paterson. 'We have agreed that several representatives from the

Council will leave tomorrow morning with a guide. I'll take volunteers first for this honor. Please step forward if you wish to represent your country."

No one moved.

Mr. Paterson scanned the deck and motioned to each council member. Two accepted reluctantly. My eyes dared Mr. Paterson's to look elsewhere, but he stopped at Alain.

"Mr. MacArthur, will you join this great prospect? Andreas has specifically extended an invitation to you."

"Me, Sir? What the devil for?"

"He believes Anna won't come without you."

We were a party of ten: Mr. Paterson, Mr. Spense, four armed soldiers, and two other members of the Council: James Montgomery and Robert Scott. Our boat was tied to a log on shore, and one of our guards stayed behind to protect it.

We ventured into the dense forest following our guide, a surly fellow, not prone to chatter. The gold ring in his nostril and the wide metal blade he carried made him appear threatening. With no warning, the guide slashed at something in front of him. Alain and others in our party gripped their swords or unsheathed their knives. I froze, until I realized the guide was cutting down leaves blocking our way. I wondered how often this had to be done. Andreas had just visited us yesterday. Had the vegetation grown back so quickly?

We crossed several rivulets, and at times we could hear a splash of water. When Mr. Paterson whispered, "Crocodile," I didn't turn around to look.

Everything was damp. Water dripped from the leaves around us and overhead. My skirt became drenched, and my hair was plastered against my neck and face. Our shoes sank into the soft spongy earth creating sucking sounds with every step. If there were animals nearby, they had plenty of warning to make their escape.

The smell of exotic flowers and rotting vegetation was everywhere. The forest was thick with trees, and little sunlight penetrated the canopy. The darkness was frightening, made worse by the unusual cries of blue, yellow, and green macaws and jaguars on the hunt. Howler monkeys, perched above our heads, screamed their objection at our invading their territory. Huge leafy vines, in a hundred shades of green, curled around huge tree limbs.

Our guide stopped abruptly. He pointed to some trees and yelled, *"Palma negra."*

Before Mr. Spense could interpret, Mr. Montgomery screamed and grabbed his chest.

287

Off to the side, close to the path, was a large palm. Its bark, covered with long, sharp needles, had pierced his skin. Circles of blood appeared. "Damn it." He lifted his shirt. Puncture holes oozed. Some needles stuck out of his skin, while others had broken off leaving long black splinters.

The guide spoke to Spense. His voice urgent.

"The Indian s-s-says we have to get Montgomery to his village qu-qu-quickly. The thorns are deadly. Covered with some kind of p-p-poison. He needs to get help before he starts to sw-sw-swell."

We increased our pace as best we could with the injured man. His whimpering hushed the sounds of the animals. I made a wide berth around the tree noticing the broken spines. The remaining ones were covered with bird droppings.

As soon as we arrived in the village, Mr. Montgomery was rushed to the hut of the medicine man. The rest of the men were ushered toward a large structure in the center.

I was greeted by another of Andreas's wives. Her name was Inez. She surprised me by knowing a few English words. She must have learned when the British visited two years ago.

A dozen thatched huts made up the village. They were all built on stilts and were at least ten feet off the ground. Through the process of gestures and the few words we shared, Inez provided a simple explanation for the architecture. "Jaguars, fire ants, and flood."

Inez led me to one of the huts. A notched log was set before the elevated entrance. Barefoot, Inez climbed quickly and easily. With my long skirts and shoes, I needed help from above and behind. My arrival was greeted by muffled titters which sounded like tiny birds.

The hut was a large square space with a fire pit in one corner. Two of the sides had no walls, and when a slight breeze lifted my skirts, I understood the reason for the openness.

After I entered, one woman reached down to turn the notched side of the log-ladder over.

"No man," said Inez. With one hand, she gestured welcome. "Woman house."

Slowly, I noticed the other women seated on the floor. They shared the same black hair, brown skin, and dark eyes. Some were old grannies, others young girls just blossoming into puberty and many had a babe in their arms. A few were regal in their bearing while others appeared to be servants. Each wore a plain cloth around the waist. Their chests were bare except for many strands of colorful beaded necklaces. In the case of Inez, hers crisscrossed, covering each breast. Their skin was covered with black painted tattoos, but the designs on their faces were tinged in red. I wondered what it meant, and if it had anything to do with status.

"Women's house?" I asked.

"Women. Moon. No men."

288

I understood. When a woman bled, she had to leave her home. She was considered untouchable or dirty, and an abomination to have sexual relations. In my religion, women bathed before returning to their husbands. On the surface we were so different, but as women we were much alike.

Inez took my hand and pulled me forward to meet a middle-aged woman. She was tall, straight-backed, and queenly looking with long hair streaked with gray. She was surrounded by others, plainer in dress, who served her.

"Wife of Ambrosio. Big chief." She spread out her hands to show how big, but I wasn't sure if she meant he was important or overweight.

"Fat?"

"No." Inez chuckled. "Andreas." She spread her hands to her sides. "Ambrosio." Inez spread her hands wider.

I nodded toward another woman. "Is she married to Ambrosio?"

"No. Daughter Ambrosio. Pedro wife"

"Pedro?"

Inez made an even larger gesture suggesting Pedro's importance.

"Pedro is the captain of all your people?"

Inez's eyes lit up' She displayed small white teeth when she smiled.

"So, Pedro is married to Ambrosio's daughter."

"Yes. Number one wife." She held up one finger to make sure I understood the woman's importance.

Then Inez gestured toward a much younger woman who resembled Pedro's wife, except she had the saddest eyes. Her long black hair fell like a waterfall over her breasts, and her hands were covered with silver bracelets.

"Beatrice. Daughter. Wife. Pedro."

"He's married to his daughter?" I hadn't met Pedro, but already I disliked him.

"Yes. Married. Beatrice. No babies."

Maybe that explained her sadness. "She can't have babies?"

Inez pointed at the young woman. "Babies burned."

"Burned? Babies?" I wondered if I misunderstood.

Through a difficult conversation, hampered by the lack of words but aided with a lot of gesturing, I learned that the older women seated next to Beatrice was her mother and her mother-in-law. As long as Pedro's first wife lived, any babies Beatrice brought into the world were burned alive.

A serving woman offered me a small wooden cup filled with hot liquid. I buried my face in the steam to hide my disgust. The fermented contents were bitter, and after the first sip I pretended to drink.

How casually these women accepted the fate of Beatrice's babies. I said nothing while they chattered around me. Some reached out, fingering the fabric of my skirt, nodding in approval. I kept starring at Beatrice, wondering how she could

289

accept this. It was only then that I noticed her hand caressing the small round bump that protruded from her skirt.

Alain stood outside the women's hut calling my name. I hurried to the entrance hoping he would rescue me from this awful place.

"We got what we came for. A treaty."

"Can we leave now? Please." I found the confines of the ship preferable to this.

"Not yet." Alain helped me down the log-ladder. In a matter of minutes, we met up with the other men in our group. "If we left now, we would have to walk back in darkness. We will return in the morning."

"Can I stay with you?"

"No, Anna. You're must remain with the women. The men have been invited to spend the night in the Chief's great house."

There was no mistaking which house belonged to the leader of the village. It's peaked thatched roof made it look like a church. At the entrance, a smiling Chief Ambrosio waited to greet us. Or was it Pedro? Dressed in a white fringed cloak, he was surrounded by many of his men holding feathered lances. Next to him was an old lady.

"Who's she?"

"It's Ambrosio's grandmother. He claims she's 120 years old."

"She's so young looking."

"I didn't believe it either until he ordered six generations from her body to stand before us."

"This is a strange place," I said. "I'll be glad when we are gone. How is Montgomery?"

"His body is starting to swell. It's not a good sign. He may not be able to leave tomorrow. Their medicine man is looking after him."

"Are you sure it's safe to leave him?"

"Do you think he would fare better under the care of Mr. Wilson?"

I didn't answer. My mind returned to Beatrice and the new, doomed life she was carrying. What I wanted more than anything right now was to hold Alexandra in my arms.

The next day, November 23, we returned to the ship. Paterson and Pennecuik were pleased with the proposed treaty and the gifts of fresh killed partridges. Our visit was considered a success. What occurred in our absence was not.

A great argument had arisen in Council between Captain Pennecuik and Mr. Paterson. The land chosen by Pennecuik for the fort and the town was unsuitable. But the captain bullied the other members until they acquiesced in his favor.

The English ship, the *Rupert,* had come and gone while we were away. We lost the opportunity to send dispatches back home. No one knew when the ship would return or if another would arrive.

Councilor Major James Cunningham announced his intention to quit the colony and leave on the next ship. This created a dilemma for the Council. Some considered Cunningham a traitor and wanted him placed in irons. Others disagreed. No decision was made, and Cunningham continued complaining lowering the morale among the landsmen.

The next day an Indian arrived with two messages. Andreas and Ambrosio planned to come to ratify the treaty. The other news - Mr. Montgomery had died.

Two weeks later, alarming information reached us from a French lieutenant. His ship, the *Maurepas* had dropped anchor in the harbor, and it didn't take long for him to board the *Saint Andrew*. He claimed a Spanish fleet of seven ships from Cartagena was on its way to root out all European privateers from their sphere of influence. The Spaniards were enraged over our settlement. Rumors from our Indian neighbors supported the Frenchman, and they added the prospect of a land attack by 600 Spanish soldiers.

The relocation of a new battery became a priority. Proposals included a pentagon-shaped fort to hold forty cannon and house up to 1,000 men. Alain supervised the trenching for a moat using the earth to fill in between stakes for a palisade. *Chevaux de fries,* were to be installed to provide further protection.

The Spanish threat encouraged even the weakest, and it became a race against time to complete the fort. But then, all work stopped when *The Rupert* returned and joined the *Maurepas* in the harbor. The English ship re-ignited the promise of sending messages to loved ones resulting in men putting down their shovels to pick up quills. A flurry of letter-writing paralyzed the landsmen, and the completion of the fort was delayed.

"I've finished several letters for Alexandra," I said.

"You know she can't read yet."

"Of course. But someday…until then, Davina can read them to her." I folded the paper, sealed them, and pressed them to my lips. "I wish I were these letters."

Alain looked up from his own writing.

"Alexandra will place her little fingers on these pages. She will see my words. Perhaps she will place her lips...." Words caught in my throat.

On December 24, the *Maurepas* floundered.

Her captain tried to sail out of the harbor during a storm, and the crew, drunk from celebrating the night before, hit a submerged rock. There was only minor damage to the hull. The captain tried again, but the winds turned the ship around smashing it onto the rock. This time half of the crew, and all but two officers were lost.

Four days later the *Rupert* sailed to Jamaica with our precious letters and three representatives, including Major Cunningham. His orders were to make a full report to the Directors of the Scots Company. He was told to say that the settlement was progressing, and Caledonia was a Garden of Eden. I doubted the lies would fool the Directors because Cunningham was to stress the desperate need for provisions, and he carried Hugh Rose's journal.

Alain and I went ashore to watch the ship depart. We climbed the narrow steep path that led to the top of a cliff and the unfinished fort. The wind rose up from the sea carrying a fine mist that covered my hair and dress. The skies darkened and drops of rain stung my face as I stared at the ship and watched her crew race to turn her about.

We remained silent in each other's arms, standing on the edge of a precipice. Below I watched the waves rock *The Rupert;* her saturated red oak hull appeared as dark as ebony. When the storm clouds burst open, the rain hid the vessel behind a veil of gray. I forced my eyes to search until I could only imagine its path toward the horizon.

THIRTY-EIGHT

Answers
December 2005

"*It* wasn't Iain. He didn't break into the apartment."

"Did you talk to your mother?"

"Aye. She said he's out of the country."

Alec bunched both pillows under his neck, and then pulled the quilt level to his chest. I laid my head in the crook of his shoulder.

"Where'd he go?"

"Paris. With some friends and plans to stay through New Year's."

"That's good news, but now we're back where we started."

"Not exactly. I heard from Officer Mackenzie."

Alec paused before continuing. My impatience gnawed at my stomach.

"Okay. What did he say? I feel like we're playing twenty questions."

"Hmm. You've only asked three so far."

I rolled over, prepared to playfully punch him in the arm, but he caught my fist before I made contact. In retaliation, I tugged sharply on the quilt, uncovering his bare legs and smooth buttocks.

"Hey. It's wintertime in Scotland." He grabbed the other end of the covers and tugged back as much as he could, but I held taut until he reached to tickle my waist. I surrendered in a burst of giggles until he pulled me closer. "I need some warmth."

"Not until you answer my question."

Alec rolled on his back and tucked the quilt under his legs. His voice turned serious. "MacKenzie told me there's a university security camera on the street. He's dropping by later this morning because he wants to know if I can identify the woman."

"A woman? Any ideas?"

"Hmm. Not sure. But—"

"Who? Come on, or I'll pull the quilt off again."

I felt Alec's leg muscles tighten before he rolled over, pinned my wrists, and got on top. "No more questions."

Shortly before noon we were seated with Officer Mackenzie. He placed some grainy, eight-by-ten, black and white photos on the kitchen table.

"These are enlarged stills from the video."

Alec picked up the half dozen photos, shuffled them like a poker hand, and kept returning to one.

"Take your time. No pressure, but you're our last hope. None of your neighbors could help."

"May I?" I asked.

Alec handed over one photo of a young woman with dark hair in a ponytail. A ball cap covered her forehead and hid her eyes. The lower part of her face was concealed by a cowl.

Officer Mackenzie fidgeted in his chair.

"I'm not sure. She looks like someone I was involved with. I couldn't swear to it, but if it's who I'm thinking of, why would she go after Hanna's belongings?"

"Jealousy is a strong incentive. One of the seven deadly sins."

"Yeah, but that was a couple years ago. The break-up was mutual. No hard feelings. At least I thought so."

"A spurned woman has a long memory. I see it all the time. Give me her name, and I'll take it from there."

"But I wouldn't want to accuse her when I'm not positive."

"I promise. We'll be discreet. She won't even know we're sniffing around unless we get enough evidence." MacKenzie gathered up the pictures and stuffed them in a plastic binder. He took out his notebook, handed it and a pen to Alec, and asked him to write down the name of the person he suspected. In a matter of minutes, Mackenzie walked out the door shouting, "I'll get back to you."

When we were left alone, I asked, "Who do you know in the picture?"

"Kate."

I remembered Kate was a beautiful girl. I hoped the suspect was someone else. I wasn't crazy about any kind of reunion — no matter the circumstances.

The next day Alec went to work. I envied the structure and professional satisfaction his job offered. For the first time since graduation I longed for the same. The lack of resolution in my life created a gap which I now craved to fill.

There were legal issues regarding my residence in Scotland. I applied for a student visa, but it all hinged on my acceptance into a doctoral program. The

University of Aberdeen, a two-hour drive away, was the only college in the country that offered a Ph.D. in archaeology.

Thoughts about my future in Scotland led me to think about Grams. I felt guilty when I forgot to call or when the post arrived with her letters. Most times we talked on the phone, but every so often she would write. Grams loved the feel of a pen in her hand, expressing herself on flowery stationary. Her last letter was several pages. It started with the usual. How was Alec? What was the latest on Anna? She told me about the activities she participated in and the gossipy female 'inmates;' her word to describe the other women at Paradise Gardens.

She saved her favorite topic for last: Bernie. She described their close friendship, every meal they ate together, and how they loved a lot of the same things: classical music, dining out, and the theater.

Grams said the 'inmates' were resentful. Unattached men were scarce in senior facilities. The women suggested she and Bernie were having an affair and were probably sneaking into each other's rooms at night. I chuckled at the thought of Bernie, in striped pajamas, tiptoeing into Gram's room. Recently, I had read an article how seniors were having more sex than most realized. Knowing my grandmother, nothing surprised me. She was a nineteen-year old girl trapped in an aging body.

I froze when I read the last page.

Bernie and I went shopping at the coat outlet. I needed something new rather than the outdated brown rag I've owned for years. When I took out my wallet, Bernie stopped me. He said he wanted to buy it, and if I agreed, he wanted to pay for everything I needed for the rest of our lives. Then he got down on one knee, right in front of the cashier and the customers waiting in line. Bernie asked me to marry him, and I said yes. I had to help him get to his feet, his knees aren't so good. But when he did, we kissed. Everyone applauded and congratulated us. Someone made an announcement on the store's intercom.

It wasn't the ideal proposal that some men plan with meticulous care. There were no rose petals scattered on a bed at the Plaza, nor was a skywriter hired to inscribe the question in the clouds. But no matter how the offer was pitched, it was romantic.

I was happy for them — a final chance at love. But I was saddened too. Although they only had a brief time remaining to enjoy each other, it was better than a life of loneliness

The letter was dated a week ago. Grams had probably grown tired of waiting for my call. I glanced at the clock. It was the middle of the night back in the States. My call would have to wait. I didn't want to disturb them.

Instead, I picked up the journal from the end table and read.

December 26, 1699

Hogmanay approaches. Our food situation is dire. What remains is spoiled. The maggots will feast instead. We are surrounded by fresh fish. But the Directors did not provide tools to harvest the sea.

The natives will not trade their food. They complain our prices are steep & we have already consumed much of their yucca, platano, & bananas.

Many are fearful & question our reason for coming. Return to Scotland is whispered.

To set an example, Mr. Paterson has moved ashore. But damp conditions have brought on a catarrh imperiling his health. Alain wishes to follow Mr. Paterson, but I am the reason he has not done so. I am glad of it.

Tonight, starts the Sabbath. I feel a desperate need to light a candle & pray to the Almighty to spare Alain & Filib from danger.

I found Alec in his office. He had company. Ira was settled in the only available chair. He immediately got up to offer his seat while balancing a mug in one hand and checking his head with the other.

Behind Alec was a padded folded chair meant for unexpected guests. He carried it around to the front of his desk and proffered it to Ira.

Once the three of us were seated, Ira said, "Charles got your DNA results. He will be joining us any moment."

I was glad that the biology professor had not arrived yet. I wanted to talk about the disturbing journal entry.

"Conditions aren't good in Caledonia. The odds are not in their favor that either will make it. How can Anna survive without a man's protection?"

"The historical facts are - the colony failed miserably. The surviving Scots high-tailed it back to Scotland and were greeted like scoundrels, or worse, cowards," said Alec. "But I think we can assume that Anna survives since there's more written in her journal. If you're really wondering, why don't you jump ahead?"

"That's like reading the last page of a book before you've read the first."

"I agree, but I'm curious about something," said Ira. "If the Sabbath candlesticks are the same you brought to my home, why does she only mention one?"

"Well, I didn't find them together, so somewhere along the way they were separated."

"Maybe, Anna returned to Scotland. Or perhaps the answer to the puzzle hasn't been born yet," said Alec. His raised eyebrow suggested the mystery was clear in his mind.

Our conversation was disrupted by a racket in the hallway. The door to Alec's office had been left open, and Charles entered the room out of breath. From one arm dangled a battered briefcase, from the other, a folded chair.

"Sorry, I'm late. At the last minute I remembered the need for another seat." His eyes surveyed the room. "We should've met in Ira's office. It's a suite compared to this. But then again, seniority, you know."

Once seated, Charles placed the briefcase on his lap and clicked the dual locks that opened the lid. His eyes lit up when he found what he was looking for in the lid pocket. He handed a manila envelope to me. "Jonathan sends his apologies. He wanted to be here, but like the conscientious good researcher he is, he's presenting at the International Conference on Genetic Genealogy in Prague. Must be nice to spend the holidays in a beautiful city like that – all expenses paid. He gave me some general information so I can handle the explanation of your DNA and try to answer your questions."

I broke the seal and pulled out several sheets filled with pie charts, a colorful world map with percentages, and an explanation. The easiest to read was the map.

"Looks like I'm mostly European. My ancestors came from northern, western, and southern Europe. There's another section labeled Unassigned, whatever that means."

"May I?" asked Charles.

He took out a small spiral notebook from his briefcase and stroked his chin while flipping through the paperwork. "The results show that the largest percentage of your DNA comes from northwestern Europe. Britain, Ireland, Scandinavia, France, Germany, and Iceland."

"Wait. Not Scotland?"

"It's not labeled that way. Scotland is not a separate subset. It comes under Britain and Ireland because the people intermingled so much. There's not enough data yet to differentiate an Irishman from a Scot. Perhaps in the future, as more take this test, that will be possible."

"That makes sense," said Alec. "The Irish and the Scots have had a connection since the Irish invaded in the fifth century. From the beginning they shared a religion, a language, music, and even the wearing of the kilt."

"Your second largest grouping is southern Europe," said Charles. "Mostly Iberia."

"Can the test be more specific?" Alec asked. "Narrow the results down to one country or the other?"

298

"I'm afraid not. Just like the Scots, the people from this area mixed with other Europeans and North Africans. Iberia is as close as you're going to get."

"Is there any such thing as Jewish DNA?" Alec asked.

"Jews from Eastern Europe have a distinct genetic marker." Charles turned to me, stroked his chin again. "You told me your ancestor came from Spain. She wouldn't have had the Ashkenazi marker, and based on your test, neither do you."

"Okay. So, from the results, Is Anna my ancestor?"

"Could be. With the southern European marker and no Askenazi gene, she could be your many-times great-grandmother. But your strong northwestern European markers could also be attributed to your many times great-grandfather. A Scot, I hear?"

"Yes, a Highlander."

"That would account for it. But don't forget about your mother's side of the story."

"Her family came from France and Germany, so more markers from northern Europe." I pointed to a section on the paper labeled, 'Unassigned.'

"That's the part of your DNA that's either shared with too many population groups, or it doesn't match any of the reference populations."

"It could be your cavewoman heritage," said Alec. "We all carry a bit of primitive man with us."

"Some more than others," I glared at Alec, and he chuckled.

"True." said Charles. "Unless your ancestors lived in sub-Saharan Africa. I guess there's no worry about that."

With the explanation concluded I folded the papers and returned them to the envelope.

"My turn," said Ira.

All eyes turned to the little professor who had sat quietly up until now.

"Hanna's search piqued my interest. I thought I'd give it a try" Ira tore open his envelope, read silently, and nodded his head. "Nothing I didn't already know. My DNA is predictable, southern and northern Europe, like yours, plus Ashkenazi from my mother's German family."

"I thought you said your family came from France at one time."

"Yes. My father's side. When I came to England in 1940 at the age of five, the name pinned on my coat was Ira St. Martin. My adoptive parents, the Masons, gave me their name. I'm forever grateful to them."

"St. Martin's not very Jewish sounding," said Charles.

"I'm sure it was chosen for that reason by my ancestors. But it didn't save us from the Nazis.

"St. Martin? I read that name in Anna's journal. Maurice St. Martin. He was betrothed to Anna, and the candlesticks were a gift."

"Was he a Frenchman?" asked Alec.

"She doesn't say where he was from."

"Well, St. Martin was a common French surname. Whatever family history was told to me is gone. I was too young."

Ira had tossed out some titillating details about his life. But for some reason he seemed uncomfortable and changed the subject.

"Hanna, what about school and your visa?"

"The University of Aberdeen has the program I want. It's three years if I attend full-time. I'm going to apply and hopefully get my tier-4 student visa."

"Once Hanna's in school we'll move to a flat halfway between Aberdeen and St. Andrews," said Alec. "After the break-in, we want a new place. A fresh start."

"Have you found out who's responsible? The thief, I mean," asked Ira.

"Not yet, but the police are getting closer."

The conversation veered toward more mundane talk regarding the next semester, the need to hire another professor—hopefully one who specialized in the Italian Renaissance—and the inadequacies of next year's history department budget.

I was relieved when my phone started buzzing. I looked down at the screen and saw it was Grams. After excusing myself, I left the office and found a seat on the second step of a nearby staircase.

"Hey Grams. Sorry I didn't call earlier today, but I was afraid I'd wake you."

"Did you get my letter?"

"Yes. Yes. I'm so happy for you. Bernie seems like a special guy."

"He'd like to speak to you. He's right here."

There was a moment of silence as I pictured Grams handing the phone to her beau. Muffled words turned into a loud male voice shouting into the phone. "Hello. Hello, Hanna."

"Yes. It's Hanna. It's nice to talk to you."

"Your grandmother has honored me by agreeing to be my bride. We'll spend the rest of our lives together."

"I'm happy for both of you." To match Bernie's decibel level, I too shouted into the phone.

"I promise to take good care of her and will love her always."

I began to choke up at his pronouncement and was relieved when I heard a sniffle or two on his end.

"Y-y-your grandmother and I are hoping you'll come for the wedding. I'd like you to meet my family. I have three children and five grands."

"I wouldn't miss it for the world."

"Wonderful. That'll please your grandmother."

"Bernie? Thank you. Thank you for making Grams so happy"

"Okay. Sure. Here let me give the phone back to her. She's anxious to speak to you."

I heard more muffled words, but clearly heard Bernie say, "Sweetheart."

"Hanna? Isn't he wonderful?"

"He sounds like a dream, Grams."

"And you won't be alone anymore. Bernie has a large family. I want that for you. After I'm gone…we are planning to get married on New Years' Eve. We don't want to wait. I'm so happy you're coming. I can't wait to see you and meet your young man. I want you to be my maid of honor. Of course, if anything changes, you could be my matron of honor."

"No chance of that happening any time soon."

We ended our call with promises to talk again — soon. I returned to Alec's office. Ira and Charles were walking out the door at the same time. Alec grabbed his backpack, shoved a few papers and a book inside, and reached for his jacket on the hook.

We headed for the door when his phone rang. He looked at the screen. "It's Officer MacKenzie."

The conversation was brief. The investigation hit a dead-end. It wasn't Kate.

"How do they know?"

"She has an air-tight alibi."

Alec sighed heavily. Perhaps he was relieved. I know I was.

As we exited the building, Alec put his hands in his pockets. The air was cold and the smell of wood burning in someone's fireplace conjured an image of a cozy evening. I put my arm through Alec's drawing closer to share in his warmth.

The trees were bare, but the wind played with the thinnest branches, swinging them back and forth causing a racket. The air had a dampness that suggested snow in the forecast.

"There's a Scottish word to describe this weather. *Dreich*. It means when the sky is gloomy, and it's drizzly, cold, and miserable."

"I would never expect *dreich* to mean a bright sunny day at the beach." I pulled my neck warmer over my nose and around my ears. "If we were in Philadelphia, I would say it feels like snow. Speaking of Philadelphia…." I told Alec about my conversation with Grams and Bernie and my promise to attend their wedding. "You'll come? I know Grams wants to meet you."

He stopped; his eyes downcast as I unwrapped myself from his arm. He took my hands in his. Something was bothering him.

"I knew something like this would happen. I'm afraid I can't go with you. When I called my mother, she reminded me about coming home for the holidays."

"Christmas? Grams and Bernie aren't getting married until New Year's Eve."

"Not Christmas. Hogmanay. It's an important tradition, and my mother wanted to be sure I'll be home." As if it would improve the situation Alec mentioned that his mother invited me too.

"That's nice of her, but, you understand, I have to go home."

He put one hand under my chin. "Yes. Of course. But this isn't the way I envisioned spending our first New Years together. I was hoping—"

"I'll return as soon as the wedding's over. Besides, knowing those two lovebirds, they're planning a honeymoon somewhere even if it's a hotel in Hoboken. I hope your mother won't be offended."

"She'll understand the special circumstances. Besides, there's always next year, and the year after that." Alec's eyes had a dreamy far-away look. It was lovely to know I was included in his future.

As we approached the apartment walkway my phone buzzed. The display started with the numbers - six-zero-nine, the area code for New Jersey.

"That's funny. Grams and I just talked."

I pressed the button. "Hello. Grams?"

"Is this Hanna Duncan?"

"Yes. It is." My heart sank to the pit of my stomach and stayed there.

"I'm the duty nurse at the Paradise Gardens. I'm calling about your grandmother. I'm afraid…."

My hands trembled. I willed my ears to turn deaf and my brain to cease comprehension.

I turned into Alec, leaned against his strength, and buried my face in his jacket.

"Hanna, what is it?" Alec asked.

Words left me. Tears did not.

THIRTY-NINE
Mr. Innes
March – June 22, 1699

Every day Alain shared his disappointment with the lack of progress in the colony. Shelters weren't being built fast enough, no crop was planted, and no trade route was carved out to the Pacific coast. Foul weather impeded the completion of the fort. Ale and sickness did not help, nor did the lack of relief ships loaded with provisions. With four hundred souls lying in the graveyard, it was evident God ignored us.

Alain tried to keep the worst to himself, but his eyes didn't lie. A forced smile couldn't conceal the truth. "Mr. Paterson's health has deteriorated. His coughing spells bring on such heaving that I'm afraid his chest will rip open." Alain spoke while sitting on the edge of our bed to take off his boots. The hardened mud broke off and scattered about.

"He should never have gone ashore," I looked around at our sparse accommodations. "At least we still have this."

"I'm afraid that's coming to an end. Pennecuik has ordered me off the ship. We're to be permanent residents of New Edinburgh."

I lifted Alain's feet, placed them on the mattress and tucked him in with a thin gray blanket. "What about your position on the Council?"

"Our meetings will now be at Mr. Paterson's hut."

"I feared this would happen. Mr. Paterson wanted to prove he was no better than any landsman but look what it's done to him. Even if he had food and his health, the conditions are abominable. The hut he is living in—"

Alain's loud snoring suggested I was talking to the wind. I kissed his brow and quietly shut the door behind me.

On May 3, the Council sent the second mate of the *Unicorn* on a mission with as much coin as the colony could muster. He was given a boat and ordered to stop any passing ship, purchase food, and return as quickly as possible. For two weeks, all eyes strained toward the harbor's entrance. At times, a boat was thought to be sighted, but the mirage led to great heartbreak. By mid-May, the Council tried again. First-mate Henry Paton sailed away. He returned a week later with news no one expected.

Mr. Paton came aboard the *St. Andrew* and handed a rolled document to the captain. The crew watched anxiously as Pennecuik and Paton disappeared below.

When Duff reminded the sailors there was work to do, they ignored his order. The anticipation of the secret document was too great. Several sailors offered to pay Mr. Innes to use his legendary prowess to solve the mystery. I shared the crew's excitement when my friend took on the challenge.

An hour later, the cook rose like a phoenix from the deck below. A huge grin was plastered on his face and he strutted about as if he were Caesar returning from the Gaelic Wars. Close to where I was standing, he motioned for the crew to come closer. Before he began, he winked at me. The entertainment was about to begin.

Like a cunning master, who knew how to play with his audience, every second of delay built up the tension.

"Mr. Innes, how'd ye get in the captain's quarters?" asked one impatient crew member.

"Thinkin' that Mr. Paton might be parched after his long journey, I asked Mr. Pennecuik if I could brin' refreshment."

"Did ye overhear what was said?" asked the same sailor.

"What'd ye take me for? An eavesdropper?" Mr. Innes's serious face hovered for a moment and then collapsed into a smirk. "O' course. But the captain made it easy. He asked me tae stay and keep the mugs from goin' dry." The cook smacked his lips and rubbed his hands together as if he was about to partake in a mug of the finest brew.

Mr. Innes cupped his hand over his mouth and leaned in my direction. Although he lowered his voice, he made sure his mates heard every word. "Watch me, Lassie. I'm about tae become a rich man."

"So? What's the word? I'm bettin' you don't ken," said a second sailor. A few nodded in agreement.

"Shut yer yaps," said Duff. "Let's hear what Innes has tae say."

All eyes turned to the cook.

"The paper ain't good news." He held back, revealing just a little so that each man would beg for more. "Pennecuik blew up when he read the words and said the king's nothin' but a wart on his arse and a lot o' other terrible words which I won't repeat with a lady nearby. Then Pennecuik did a most surprisin' thin'."

"What?" several men asked in unison.

"He picked up a half-full decanter of whisky and tossed it out the porthole."

One wide-eyed sailor wiped his drool with his sleeve. "Ye mean, Captain Pennecuik threw out perfectly good drink."

"Aye. Ye heard me. It was that special whisky o' his, too."

From where I stood it looked as if the sailor was going to faint.

Mr. Innes continued. "Then Mr. Paton turned to our captain and said—"

Duff, chewing on some tobacco, stepped forward, and spit across the rail near where I was standing. "Cook. Tell us already. The…bad…news. Stop playin' with our heads."

Mr. Innes' lips curled slightly. To continue the ruse, he rubbed his chin whiskers and removed his cap to scratch his head. "O' course. Well, here it is lads — King William doesn't like us." Innes looked downcast and shook his head. "He has declared an embargo on this colony. There's tae be no ships bringin' provisions. The embargo covers everythin' and everybody. King Wullie doesn't want tae anger his royal cousin, the king of Spain."

Several sailors called out in angry voices.

"This land isn't owned by anyone. I'm bettin' he wants it for hisself."

"We're starvin' and that fuckin' walloper only cares about how fat his purse is."

"English bastard."

"That's how it is, my lads," said Innes. So much for the bad. Now for the good." With the suggestion of something fortuitous, all became quiet. Mr. Innes opened the palm of his hand. "Time to lighten your pockets and fill mine."

All of the members of the Council, except for the ships' captains, relocated ashore. Since we were a married couple, Alain and I were given living quarters of our own. It was the smallest hut, but the privacy was an extravagance that no other enjoyed except for Mr. Paterson.

Twenty-one hovels lined either side of a trench that served as a main street. It ran the length of what had been christened New Edinburgh. Wooden planks were thrown haphazardly across, and all were warned to stay on the walkway as no one was sure of the exact depth of the ditch. The muddy estuary reminded me of Cheery Close.

Mr. Paterson was confined to his hut. With the death of his wife, and the surgeon attending others, I offered to care for him. Since most Council meetings were held in his hut, it gave me the opportunity to see Alain more often.

I found my patient lying in a cot that was much too small. Wearing only his shirt and stockings, his middle was covered with a threadbare blanket. His feet dangled over the edge. The tip of his filthy hose was marked with tiny holes, and his toes, covered in muck, were slightly exposed. I wondered if small animals had been nibbling.

Flies and mosquitos were thick, especially with the constant dampness. The insects preferred easy targets like Mr. Paterson's legs and arms. The Botflies were particularly troublesome when the females deposited their eggs under the skin. The removal of a maggot was painful. No one had ever seen a Botfly implant their larvae, but the nesting area became inflamed shortly after the arrival of mosquitos. Somehow the Botflies and the mosquitos worked symbiotically

Mr. Paterson's illness had one fortunate side effect. Oatmeal was set aside for the infirm and every morning I cooked the gruel for my patient. But with no cream, honey, or butter, the watery gruel was tasteless. Even so, I tried to force him to take the nourishment.

"Anna, I have no appetite today. The itching is driving me mad."

He pulled aside the blanket so that I could see the offending soft-white flesh of his inner thigh. A volcanic-like mound, with a hole in the center, oozed yellowish lava and dripped down his leg. He lifted his head as far as he could, until his weakened condition forced him to drop to his pillow. "Do you see what's causing the inflammation?"

"Yes. Let me find the surgeon."

One look at the sick man's leg, and Mr. Wilson diagnosed the Botfly larva. According to the natives, the maggots had to be smothered so they would surface to breathe. He tied a cloth over the eruption and said he would return.

The next day, the bandage was removed. Mr. Wilson opened a folded cloth that held his surgical tools in tiny pockets. A pincer was chosen, and after wiping it on his shirt, he bent low over Mr. Paterson's leg.

"This'll hurt, I'm afraid."

"I don't care. Dammit. Get the wee beastie out."

"Mrs. MacArthur, hold down his leg. At the knee. It will go easier and faster if he canna move." He paused. "Yere not squeamish, are ye?"

"I won't watch." But the minute the patient screamed, I looked at the surgeon's handiwork. In the grip of his pincer, a wiggling, cream-colored worm resisted removal from its warm environment. A blood-curdling cry accompanied each time the surgeon tugged. After several pulls, Mr. Wilson was victorious, and the patient quieted to a whimper. The intruder was tossed on the ground and then squashed with the heel of a boot.

"You'll be fine now. Keep covered as much as ye can, and if ye don't want another bugger makin' a home in yereself, I suggest ye smoke some tobacco." Mr. Wilson wiped the pincer on his shirt again, placed it back into the fold, and was out the door.

I cleaned Mr. Paterson's leg and offered some oatmeal. He chose to sleep. I left him to get some fresh air and immediately brought up my last meal.

A few hours later, the Council arrived for its daily meeting. They now called themselves a Parliament and against Captain Pennecuik's objection, they added three new members.

Respecting the Council's privacy, I stepped outside, however, the gaps in the walls of the palm-frond hut allowed for no secrecy. Others gathered to eavesdrop. Every word, argument, and decision became public knowledge before the Council adjourned.

Shortly after they started, the smell of tobacco filled the air. At first the aroma was rich, but as the fumes thickened, white smoke poured above the fronds and singed the back of my throat. Whether it was the smoke or the smell, the flies and the mosquitos disappeared.

First to be discussed was food. Or lack of it.

"There should be a full accounting of what we have left," said Mr. Paterson. "And that means what's on your ship as well, Captain Pennecuik. A committee, chosen by this Council, will go aboard and tally the remaining provisions."

"No damn committee will board my ship. I told ye there was barely one month's supply left. I won't have anyone spreadin' illness to my crew."

"That's not what I heard," said Robert Drummond. The two captains were still bitter foes and each did what they could to discredit the other. "Did ye not invite some o' your friends and allies to a feast in your cabin recently? Or was there somethin' more sinister goin' on? I hear you ate and drank verra well."

Captain Pennecuik placed his hand on the hilt of his sword. "Take care o' your words, sir."

Captain Drummond gestured the same. "I hear talk that you and the master o' the *Unicorn* are preparing a quick get-away to abandon the colony. You've been fillin' your casks wi' fresh water for ballast."

"And what proof do ye have?"

"Sailors gossip when they're bored. Yere own crew is braggin' yere leavin' to make a fortune in piracy."

"Are ye callin' me a traitor?" This was followed by grunts, shouts of warnings, and the clinking of metal. The audience outside moved closer. Calmer voices called for order, and another, Mr. Paterson's, shamed the two captains to behave like gentlemen. "If any ship attempts to leave, I'll order the landsmen to fire the cannon at the harbor entrance and destroy the vessel. Do I make myself understood, gentlemen?" Mr. Paterson's threat ended with a heavy cough and an interval of respectful silence.

"There is another urgent matter — the king's proclamation of embargo," said Mr. Paterson.

"Mr. Paton found a French trading ship outside our harbor," said Captain Pennecuik. "When he entreated the captain to anchor and bide with us, the Frenchie refused and gave Mr. Paton this proclamation. All of the territory from Canada to the Caribbean, every governor and captain has been issued the same order."

"William means to destroy us." said one of the new members.

"The blasted Sassenach. English parasite," said another.

"Aye," said Pennecuik. "The king claims our colonizing goes against some damn treaty."

"What treaty?" asked another.

"An agreement that says this land belongs to the Spanish and we are interlopers," said Mr. Paterson.

"That's hypocrisy," said Alain. "The king wanted to take this land for himself. Just two years ago the English Board of Trade advised William to seize Darien and set up lucrative trade routes. And do it before the Scots." There were angry shouts from inside, and several on the outside shook their fists. "I'm afraid all is lost, gentlemen. Without food, we are too weak. If the Spaniards come, we're no match. With King William's decree we can't trade. We have too many dying from fever. Every day we dig more graves. Our only recourse is to abandon Caledonia, and do it quickly. Or there will be no one left to dig ours."

The Council members shouted in agreement. Outside, many nodded.

"No. I will not leave. This land is our country's future. I will die here if I have to," said Mr. Paterson.

"Then you can stay and rot," said Pennecuik.

"Captain, how do you think we will be received back home?" asked Mr. Paterson. "Will we be welcomed as heroes? Women strewing flowers and our countrymen singing our praises as we parade down The Mile? No sir. We will be scorned and mocked because we have brought shame upon our homeland and our name."

"Better to be scorned on Earth than welcomed like a hero in hell."

Preparations were made for an orderly evacuation. But it turned into chaos. Fear of abandonment consumed the colony. Many hoarded what goods they could find, trusted no one, and watched every movement of the ships' crews. If the landsmen suspected a ship was leaving, they would rush to the water and fling themselves into any available boat.

The sick had few options. They either lay shrieking in their huts or stumbled to the beach begging for assistance. Most were left to fend for themselves.

I continued to care for Mr. Paterson, but his condition didn't improve. His fever-induced hallucinations wracked his body. Whenever documents arrived from the Council, I watched the messenger force a pen into Mr. Paterson's hand to scribble his signature. On this day, Alain brought the order for the colony's abandonment. He held Mr. Paterson's right hand until it was signed.

"Anna, gather your things. Bring only what's necessary. We're leaving now. Some men are coming to carry Mr. Paterson to a ship."

"I won't leave him. He's been our friend."

"They are right behind me. We must hurry."

"No. I'll wait until I'm sure he's safe."

"Captain Drummond will only wait so long."

"Drummond? Not the *St. Andrew?*"

"We're going on the *Caledonia.* It's our only chance to get away from Pennecuik. Besides, I don't want to be on his ship if the rumors of his turning to piracy are true."

"Does Filib know we won't be on the *St. Andrew?*"

"I told one of his mates to pass the word along."

At that moment two men barreled into the hut. Each took an end of Mr. Paterson's cot. As if it weighed nothing, they carried him away.

We ran outside, Alain grabbed my hand, and pulled me in the opposite direction. I turned to look at my patient one more time. "Godspeed, Mr. Paterson."

Colonists ran in and out of their huts clutching their dearest possessions. Some fought over a ragged shirt, shredding it until it was useless. Another held a knife to a friend's throat to steal his boots. The outstretched arms of the sick were ignored. Like frightened animals, we hurried to the beach. Escape was everything.

Alain and I had to fight our way, against the tide, to get to our hut. We quickly chose what we needed and stuffed it in two satchels. I wrapped the candlestick in my other dress. Alain held out his hand to stop me.

"Leave it behind. It's too heavy."

"No. I'll carry it."

"If anyone sees it, they'll kill you for it. These men are desperate."

"I won't go without it." I hugged the heavy satchel to my chest. When he saw I was resolute, he gave in.

We headed toward the shore and joined the hordes waiting for rescue. The beach was strewn with discarded possessions: ragged stockings, tangled wigs, and a sole-less shoe. Manners were forgotten, and there was no deference toward sex. We

310

waited and prayed that the ships wouldn't leave without us. When a boat arrived everyone ran at once.

"Mrs. MacArthur. Here. Over here."

I followed the familiar voice. It was Mr. Innes. He was hanging over a small boat, his body bobbing every time a wave hit the side.

I shouted over the voices of others. "We aren't going on the *St. Andrew*. We're on a different ship."

"Aye. The *Caledonia*. That's where I'm headin'. Captain Drummond made me an offer. No more Pennecuik for me. Come! Quickly, before some bugger tips the boat."

Mr. Innes held out a strong bronzed arm and pulled me in. Alain followed. I hugged my satchel and sat next to two cannons. "Drummond doesn't want the Spaniards to get these." He patted the iron hulks. "So, if ye don't mind a little company."

"Thank you, Mr. Innes. But why are you—"

I never heard his reply. The next thing I felt was an overpowering urge to lean over the side of the boat. I retched until I thought my heart would burst.

FORTY
Tides
June – August 1699

Captain Drummond ordered his crew to weigh anchor and unfurl the sails. They instantly filled and snapped taut. The helmsman spun the massive wheel to turn the vessel toward the harbor entrance and the open sea.

From the deck of the *Caledonia* I watched six men crawl along the water's edge. They appeared like ragged splotches against the white sand. We were leaving six behind. One of the splotches pulled himself to his knees and held out his arms. Was he praying, waving us on, or asking for help? Giving up, he collapsed.

Alarmed at what I saw, I pulled on Alain's arm. "It's Filib. The one nearest the water."

Alain shielded his eyes and followed my finger. He ran over to the captain who was standing by the ship's wheel. The Master shook his head. Alain's voice became louder and angrier, his gestures threatening. The captain turned his back, but Alain grabbed his shoulder and forced him around.

Captain Drummond's face hardened. "I will forgive you for that. This time. But I will not miss the tide."

"How can you leave men to die?"

"They will die anyway from the fever. If you want to rescue your friend, you have my permission. But we won't come back for you. You'll have to wait for the relief ships. If they ever come." Drummond nodded in my direction. "Talk to your wife. She may not agree with your decision."

Alain rushed back to the rail. He examined the water, the beach, and the distant splotch of his friend.

I placed my hand on his arm. "We thought him safe on another ship."

"I have to go back. I can't leave him. Filib would never—"

I tightened my grip. "Please don't go. If not for me, then for the child."

"Alexandra." He whispered her name as if to remind himself he had a daughter.

"Yes. For Alexandra…and for another."

At that moment, the world seemed to stop spinning. The crashing waves made no sound. The sun was obscured, and the crew disappeared. There was only the two of us.

"I'm going to have a child."

He pulled away from my grasp. His eyes resolute; he stared straight into mine. "I don't want to leave you. But I must. I must go back." We pulled ourselves apart. Alain turned to the captain. "Will you give me a boat, sir?"

"Aye, but I won't wait. I'm determined to leave this damned place. With the tide."

Several men helped Alain begin the process of lowering a long boat over the side.

"I'm going with you."

He grabbed my arms tightly, pressed them against my body, and walked me away from the rail. "No. You can't risk your life and the child's." After a frantic kiss, he hurried back to the rail, and when he had flung one leg over to catch the rope ladder, he looked at me one last time. "I will come back to you. Do you hear me, Anna? I will come back."

I reached out and held on to Alain before he would disappear over the side. Just then my eye caught some movement on the shore.

"Wait. Look." I pointed.

From the edge of the jungle, a group of Indians emerged. They went to each of the castaways. When they came to Filib, he tried to crawl away like a crab. Perhaps he thought the native was about to kill him. Filib reached for his dirk, and instead of using it to defend himself, he raised his hand, and forced it into himself. His body went limp.

As the ship sailed out with the tide toward the sea, we watched the Indian move onto the next sick man. He was alive. The native knelt, lifted the man as if he were a babe, and carried him off. Together they disappeared in the thick foliage.

The next day, the coastline hid behind the clouds. Mourning his loss, Alain stayed in our cabin, a luxury afforded to us once again because I was the only woman on board. But I chose to spend my time on deck. The breeze and the horizon helped to alleviate my nausea.

A familiar voice came from behind.

"They'll probably be proclaimed heroes, ye ken."

It was Mr. Innes. He placed his elbows on the rail. For one who had access to more food than most, his frame was gaunt.

"Heroes, Mr. Innes?"

"The six left behind. They'll be the champions of Scotland. Poets will sing their praises — the six who'd rather die than return as cowards."

"And we're the cowards?"

"Aye. Do ye think your countrymen will be glad tae see any o' these ships return? Filled with unsold goods, manned by walkin' corpses with tales o' disaster. Ye'll be a reminder that the colony is lost which a bankrupt Scotland can ill afford."

"But it's the Directors who miscalculated. They didn't provide adequate provisions and burdened us with goods that were impossible to trade. Where were the promised relief ships that should have arrived months ago?"

"It doesn't matter. Not tae those in power. Ye'll be the sacrificial lamb for desertin' the colony. The dead will be heralded as the victors o' the cause. "

"So, the men left behind, their families would prefer their death rather than be shamed?"

"Aye. That's the way o' it."

I remembered what my father predicted when he turned down Laird MacArthur's request for financial backing. He said the scheme was doomed to collapse, and for a Jewish investor, if the colony failed, he would be the scapegoat. We survivors were like the Jews.

"What will you do once we return to Scotland?" I asked Mr. Innes. "Will you find another ship?"

"Not sure if it's my bailiwick anymore. Perhaps it's time I looked into somethin' else. Somethin' a wee bit healthier. Maybe I'll be a farmer. A landsman." He spit into the ocean as if 'landsman' was a distasteful word. "Find myself a lass, get married, and have a bunch o' bairns."

The vision of Mr. Innes sitting in front of a fireplace with a child on each knee made me smile.

"Ye dinna believe I could be domesticated?"

"I think it's a lovely idea. You will make a wonderful father. You're a great storyteller, and children love stories." I wiped a tear from my face.

"Is the image o' my bein' a father bringin' tears tae your eyes?"

"These are tears of a different sort, Mr. Innes." I patted my growing belly. "There's another on the way."

"Aye, its good tae have new life amidst so much...." He hesitated. Perhaps, he didn't want to remind me about the coupling of birthing and death. "Dinna ye worry none. In less than a fortnight we'll be in Port Royal. We'll get food for you and the wee one, make repairs, restore ourselves, and be on our way. Perhaps, we'll get lucky and trade our worthless goods so we can return home with a chest full o' gold."

I didn't tell Mr. Innes that real contentment would come when my family was reunited.

Ten days later we arrived in Port Royal. The port, founded by the Spanish, was now in English control. I heard the crew describe how the land had changed since they'd last visited. Seven years earlier, an earthquake, followed by a tidal wave, devastated the town. Rebuilding was everywhere, but according to the sailors, Port Royal would never recapture its former glory.

"Anna," said Alain. "Captain Drummond has asked me to go ashore with him. We are seeking permission from the Governor-General to trade and procure provisions. The captain would like you to accompany us."

"Why me?" The thought of going ashore sounded wonderful, but I was curious.

"The captain believes that a woman would lend a sense of civility to our cause and soften the heart of the English. The governor might find it easy to turn the captain down, but decency wouldn't permit a woman to starve."

It didn't take long before we reached Sir William Beeston's manse, a large two-story home set on top of a hill over-looking the harbor. Two large chimneys rose like masts on either side of the house and the white slats on the exterior were blinding in the sun. Its elevated location was perfect. Sir Beeston knew about our ship's arrival before we knocked on his front door.

A young barefoot African slave met us at the entrance. He was dressed in breeches with a loose-fitting shirt that hung almost to his knees. He led us to the front parlor, a small room off the foyer, where we waited for our host. The wide-open windows encouraged the ocean breeze to funnel the scent of the jasmine that lined the walkway.

I'd chosen to wear my blue woolen dress. The hem was frayed, and the sleeves were stained, but at least it didn't smell of vomit and blood and death.

How long had it been since I was in a room such as this. The fireplace, although unlit, was swept and clean. The flooring, made of rich mahogany planks, was covered with plush Turkey carpets. The furniture, also of mahogany, resisted the termites that lived in huge hives that clung to the trees on the hillside. On the sideboard, that stretched across the wall on the far side of the room, sat crystal decanters filled with various shades of amber and dark red. The slave returned with a tray of small cakes. He placed them on the sideboard and left. The scent from the buttered delicacies sprinkled with sugar and cinnamon unleashed a river of saliva.

Thoughts of food were interrupted by the arrival of Sir Beeston, the Crown's representative in the West Indies. He looked to be in his early sixties, but he was fit, with no paunch, and used no cane. Only his graying hair, which fell over his shoulders and the lines on his face, gave his years away.

After polite introductions were made, Drummond's eyes drifted to the wine and food. Scottish hospitality demanded refreshment for guests. But Sir Beeston was English. He ignored Captain Drummond's eyes and forgot his manners.

"What can I do for you gentleman? And lady?"

"Your Excellency. We have just arrived from our colonial post in the land between the Americas, what the Directors of the Company of Scotland call Caledonia."

"I'm well aware of your country's movements in this hemisphere. Nothing escapes the Home Office."

"Then our being here should be of no surprise," said Captain Drummond.

"Well I am puzzled about one thing. Why are you here? And not there?" He pointed out the window as if our colony was just down the hill.

Our clothes and malnourished bodies told our tale. Asking for an explanation was a cruel game.

"Sir Beeston." The governor appeared startled by a female voice. "We are in Port Royal because it's time for the first colonial expedition to return to Scotland. Relief ships, loaded with fresh colonists and provisions, are expected at any moment to continue what we started."

"Why didn't you wait in place until relief arrived?"

"There is a small contingent of settlers still in Caledonia at this very moment, waiting to greet them."

"Madam. Your defense of the colony is charming. But the civilized world knows about the failure of your colony, and the Crown has ordered that none is to offer assistance. To put it plainly, I can give you no shelter, nor can I trade or sell any provisions. Furthermore, it's my duty to demand that you return to your ship and depart on the next tide."

Alain glared at the cakes. Sir Beeston followed his gaze. "I cannot even offer you a morsel of food. I'm ever the King's loyal subject."

"Not even for my wife?" asked Alain. "It's common decency. Or is that something your King has forgotten? What kind of man are you?"

"One who follows the law, sir." He raised his voice. "Isaiah?"

A door on the other side of the room opened. The black slave returned.

"Remove the cakes. Leave the wine."

The boy did as he was told. But on his way out, Sir Beeston snatched one of the delicacies and popped it into his mouth. Crumbs became snarled in his moustache. He walked over to the sideboard and lifted the decanter with one hand and a goblet with the other.

"Good day gentleman. Lady. I trust you know the way out."

As I looked at Sir William one last time, he sucked each sugary finger and lifted his half-filled glass and gulped the wine. I hoped he choked on it.

The next day, preparations were made to leave Port Royal, but only after the rigging and a splintered mast were repaired. With such a grim prospect, we didn't recognize that our chances were about to improve. It began with the unexpected arrival of the *St Andrew*.

As the ship neared the harbor entrance, something seemed different. Captain Pennecuik's pennant was missing.

"He must be dead," said Alain. "That's the only way his ship would sail without it."

His prediction caught my breath, and although I had no fondness for the man, it was still shocking. "Perhaps the crew mutinied, and he's in chains."

"Either way, good riddance."

The ship entered the port. The crew scurried on deck making ready to dock at the pier. At the same time, a government longboat, filled with six rowers, another at the rudder, and someone seated in the stern headed out to greet the *St Andrew*. When the two vessels were within earshot, the man in the stern stood and shouted to a representative on the larger ship.

"What do you think they're saying?" I asked.

"I think that's the governor's man, and he's refusing permission for the ship to dock. Sir Beeston doesn't want another Scottish vessel filled with starving men." Alain was proven correct when we saw the anchor splash into the water.

The longboat turned once the official took his seat after placing a cloth to his face. That's when I smelled the stench. It was from the *St. Andrew* and drifted across the harbor mingling with our own. When the longboat returned to the pier, the man jumped out, and walked quickly to our ship. He asked to speak to Captain Drummond in private.

After a short discussion, the captain called for Alain. "A word, please. In my quarters. And bring your wife."

Captain Drummond got right to the point. "Governor Beeston wants us gone immediately. To encourage our haste, he is offering casks of fresh water and food — enough to last us for a couple of weeks."

"Is that enough to get us home?" asked Alain.

"No, especially if we are delayed by bad weather. Our only option is to leave, make landfall in New England, and hopefully trade for more food. Or steal it if we have to."

"New England! I thought we were headed for Scotland."

"Yes. Madam, but now there's a new problem. In the middle of the night, twenty-two of our crew and landsmen jumped ship."

"You mean they aren't coming back?" I asked.

"They are aware of the penalty if they are found. My guess is they've either joined another trading ship with better prospects, or they have sold themselves as bondsmen."

I realized I hadn't seen my friend this morning. "Was one of them Mr. Innes?" I asked.

"I'm afraid so. His desertion is most troubling. Of all the men on board, he had it the best. No cook suffers even when there's a shortage of food."

I remembered how Innes told me of his future plans. Perhaps he decided to start them sooner than he thought.

"Any word about the *St. Andrew?*" asked Alain.

"Her new captain is Colin Campbell. Pennecuik died of the fever."

The captain turned and fumbled through some papers on his desk. He searched for his spectacles, found them in his pocket, and perched them on his nose. He said nothing more than a grunt or two while reading.

I caught a glimpse from Alain. His eyes said it was time to go. But I couldn't leave without knowing.

"Captain Drummond?"

He peered over the half-moons of his spectacles.

"What happened to Captain Pennecuik's body?"

"He was dumped over the side like the lowest deckhand, with little fanfare or ceremony."

"Thank you, sir."

"Mrs. MacArthur. Don't believe everything Cook Innes tells you. He's a wonder with his far-fetched imagination." For a moment, his lips turned upward, but then he quickly resumed his attention to the paper in his hand.

Alain reached for the door and as we turned to go, there was a thunderous pounding on the deck above us. It was like the stomping of hooves or men fighting.

"What in God's name is that?" asked the captain.

When we reached the main deck, there stood Mr. Innes with a rope in his hand. The other end was tied around a goat's neck. The jittery animal's hooves plodded on the wooden planks, her full udders swinging beneath. The crew laughed as Mr. Innes struggled to control the goat.

"Mr. Innes," called the captain. "What's going on here? I should have you clapped in irons for desertion."

"Me, sir? I dinna abandon the ship. I'd never do such a filthy thin'."

"Then, where were you?"

"I went tae get a goat. A nanny goat with teats so full they're beggin' tae be squeezed."

"I can see it's a goat."

More laughter flitted among the crew.

"With my eyeglass, I spotted this here goat wanderin' the hillside. Just mindin' her business eatin' grass as nicely as she pleased. I got to thinkin'. Fresh milk would improve our porridge, and I dinna see anyone tendin' the dear beast. She looked lonely, like she needed a home."

More laughter and a few guffaws. Again, he held the audience in his hand.

"Did you ask permission to leave the ship?"

"Why no. For that I'm guilty and will take what punishment is comin', but I couldna wait because the goat might have gone off to another hill. It's as if she was beggin' me to come and milk her. So, I obliged."

The goat seemed to agree. She turned her head, looked longingly at Mr. Innes, and bleated.

"Get that animal down in the hold. Your punishment is to clean her stall daily. If I see one bit of shite...."

Considering the captain could have hung Mr. Innes for desertion, he got off easy. The cook pulled the animal toward the stairs and her new home. Several of the crew came forward to help.

"Mr. Innes," I said. "I'm glad you've returned. For a while, I thought—"

He turned to look at me. "I did it so the babe would have decent nourishment. Tis no place for a woman in your condition." Then he offered an impish grin and a wink. "Besides, this is the beginnin' of my learnin' farmin' ways." His eyes drifted toward the grassy hill. "And the goat-herder was a very generous woman."

The next day, on the outgoing tide, our ship and the *St. Andrew* set sail. Port Royal quickly became a blur. For the first time in many weeks, our ballast consisted of barrels filled with flour and meat. And, thanks to Mr. Innes, oatmeal tasted much better.

We headed north along the eastern shore of the English colonies. Being that it was mid-July, the air was hot and sultry, but a gentle waft whispered across the ship making the journey bearable. On August 4, 1699, we entered the harbor of New York and docked on the East River.

Once under Dutch rule, New Netherlands had been conquered thirty years ago by the English and renamed in honor of the Duke of York. The Dutch influence was still evident. The streets were lined with rows of tall, narrow red-roofed houses built in bricks of many colors. But the English were slowly rebuilding the city. Where there had once been a canal, the Heere Grach, was now filled with rubble and a wide boulevard took its place.

Our situation had deteriorated again. To make it to Scotland, we needed additional stores.

Captain Drummond immediately set out to meet the King's representative, Richard Coote, the Earl of Bellomont. He was the governor of New York, Massachusetts and New Hampshire. Once again Alain and I accompanied him. I was becoming great with child, and the captain thought my condition would encourage the Governor's sympathy. But the Governor was away negotiating a treaty with the Iroquois. Instead, we met with his Lieutenant-Governor, John Nantan.

"I'm sorry. The Earl will not be back for another fortnight, and I'm afraid he'll have little patience to hear your concern. There's the proclamation, you know, and one of your compatriots, William Kidd, has caused quite a stir trying to bribe the Governor's wife, the Lady Bellomont. Mr. Kidd has made it worse by declaring he hoped to join his fellow Scots in Caledonia."

"I assure you we had no knowledge of Mr. Kidd's intentions," said Drummond. "We're on our way home and all we ask is to purchase or trade for provisions. Once we've concluded our business, we will sail with the next high tide."

"I will send your message to the Governor. I cannot rule without his permission."

"Thank you, sir," I said. Playing my part, I placed my hand on the back of the chair, pushing my protruding belly forward. With Alain's assistance I righted myself. For a moment, I thought I saw Mr. Nantan step forward – a momentary suggestion of kindness. "I know you'll do all you can to help us. We're only asking for what we need to get home." I placed my hand on my belly and looked down as if holding the new babe. "I'm anxious to be home for my lying-in."

"Yes, Madam. I'll see what I can do. Um. Perhaps, we have some provisions that we could send over immediately, to tide you over, that is, on credit, of course."

"Of course. That's most kind of you. I will remember your name in my prayers."

"And Captain. Until I hear from the Governor, your crew is not to leave the ship. Only you and the MacArthurs, if you wish, may obtain lodgings until your ship is ready to sail."

"Thank you, Mr. Nantan. I cannot leave my crew, but I'm sure Mrs. MacArthur would appreciate the hospitality of an inn even if it's for a short stay."

I smiled and nodded my thanks again to the Lieutenant-Governor. We got much more than we expected.

It didn't take long for Alain and me to gather our belongings. Before leaving, I went to the galley and found Mr. Innes stowing the new provisions.

"I came to tell you that I'll be off the ship for a couple of days. Until we're ready to sail."

"Let me get you some goat's milk tae take with ye."

"No, that won't be necessary. I'll get some at the inn."

"Aye." He hesitated. "I need tae tell ye somethin', but ye must swear tae tell no one."

320

"Of course."

"I wilna be here when ye return. I've decided to find my way in these colonies. I and a couple o' the others are plannin' to leave tonight. There's plenty o' opportunity for someone like myself."

"Maybe you'll find that farm you've been dreaming of. And a wife."

He smiled and turned away for a moment.

"Mr. Innes. If you will allow me." I leaned into him and kissed his scratchy, wet cheek. "God speed, sir. I will always remember you."

Tears blinded my way. I only remember hearing the swish of my skirts as I rushed to the stairs and out in the sunshine.

From the inn I could see the masts of the *Caledonia*. I dreaded returning to the ship, but I knew I must if I wanted to see Alexandra.

"Anna, I need to talk to you." Alain took my hand and brought it to his lips. "We must stay here in New York. To go back on that ship is to die. Every day, more desert. Fever still exists. The ship needs repairs again. It creaks and strains when we are at full sail. I fear the main mast will spring. If I were alone, I would chance it, but I cannot do that with you. Not in your condition."

"How will we get back to Scotland? What about Alexandra."

"After the child is born, we'll take the first ship back. I promise."

"We gave our word that these would be temporary lodgings."

"No one would expect a man to keep his oath when it would harm his wife and bairn."

"Harm?"

"Yes. You'll say you're in great pain. Scream a bit. To make it more believable, I'll cut myself and stain the bed. Make it look like you're bleeding. I'll call for a mid-wife. She'll say you cannot be moved, or you and the child will perish."

As soon as we received word that the ship was to leave on the next high tide, we proceeded with Alain's plan and word reached Mr. Nantan. He ordered that we stay in New York until I gave birth and offered the services of the Governor's doctor.

The next morning, I rose before the sun. I sat alone by the window and watched the first rays of light flicker over the water and stretch across the sleepy town that was beginning another day. I opened the window and breathed in the sea and the sunshine. The awakening wharves were restless and noisy. Two young aproned men pushed loaded carts toward the direction of the market. A vendor had just opened his shop and buffed his sign with the sleeve of his shirt. Nearby, an industrious matron scrubbed her stoop.

Without turning I felt Alain's warmth. I stood and leaned into him. He wrapped his arms around me, stretching to encompass my belly. I turned and kissed the warrior's old scar that crossed his cheek.

My gaze returned to the scene outside the window and followed the gray cobblestone street to the dock. The familiar grove of masts was gone. The tide had turned and rushed out to sea carrying the *Caledonia* to the Atlantic and home.

FORTY-ONE
Family Ties
December 30, 2005 - January 1, 2006

In a semi-darkened hospital room on the fifth floor of the ICU wing, I sat by Grams' bed. Various life-saving machines assaulted the quiet. The digital numbers, keeping track of blood pressure, heart rate, and respiration, cast an eerie, greenish glow. A cardiac monitor pulsed tracing along the bottom of a screen accompanied by regular beeps bookended by silent intervals.

Tubes and wires laced around Grams' withered body. Like a highway, they crisscrossed her bed, each taking an off-ramp to an unknown location under her hospital gown. Clipped to her earlobe was an oximeter to check oxygen levels, and next to her right hand was a call monitor in case she needed help or wanted to turn on the overhead television. Grams was doing neither. She had been mostly unconscious since Bernie found her sprawled on her bedroom floor three days ago.

I cradled my grandmother's fragile left hand, the only part free of needles and tubes. Her long slender fingers, with the telltale indentation of a missing wedding ring ended with neatly filed nails polished in Summer Rose. Never a fashionista, Grams gave in to her one indulgence — a weekly manicure. As I moved my thumb over her age-spotted hand, her paper-thin skin wrinkled easily into tiny furrows.

"Miss Duncan."

The overnight shift nurse arrived. A young woman, about my age, breezed in, and went right to work. She was just friendly enough so as not to get emotionally involved with her short-term guests. Dressed in a loose-fitting, dark-blue uniform, sneakers, and a cardigan, she dashed about the room, her blond ponytail swaying.

"Hi. I'm Kelly. I'll be taking care of your grandmother."

In case I forgot, she erased the previous nurse's name and scribbled hers on the whiteboard that hung on the wall opposite Grams' bed. I was grateful for the reminder. So many hospital workers passed through. It was difficult to keep them straight.

"Please, call me Hanna."

"Sure. I heard you just got here. From Scotland, was it?"

"Yes. I live there now. As soon as I heard about Grams, I caught a flight to Newark."

"I'm sure your grandmother's happy you're here. But not the way you wanted to spend New Year's Eve."

I glanced at Grams — looking so small and defenseless in her bed. She had no clue I was present.

"I'm getting your grandmother ready for a test. Her doctor has ordered a CT scan."

"What's that?"

"X-rays. Of her brain. It will give us detailed pictures of the area that was damaged by the stroke."

"Is that necessary? Does the doctor think it will help?"

"Don't worry. It's fast and painless and non-invasive. Just one more piece of information."

"Oh. I thought nothing more could be done."

The young nurse grabbed a pen from her pocket, picked up Gram's chart, and began to flip some pages. "Yes, it was severe, but the test will help decide our next course of action."

She used the word 'our' as if we were all in this together. Actually, it was Grams who would be traveling down this road alone. I would be there to support her, but there was only so far I could go.

"It won't take long," said Kelly. "No need for you to come. There's a family room down the hall with a couch and some vending machines. If the couch is unoccupied, get some sleep. Or if you prefer, I just brewed some fresh coffee. It's at the nurses' station near the Christmas tree. The aide can get some for you."

For a moment, I thought I caught a whiff of the nutty aroma, like residue clinging to Kelly's clothes. It was intoxicating. That is, until it collided with the scent of the institutional disinfectant that was on everything, and the urine that dripped from the catheter to the bag hanging from Gram's hospital bed.

"Thanks, Kelly. Let me know the minute she's back. I'll check on Bernie."

As I walked out of the room, I could hear Kelly talking to Grams as if they were having a friendly chat, and then the rude interruption of the clanging metal bedrails being locked in place. It wouldn't take long to get Grams ready to be wheeled away for a procedure that I thought was a waste of time. But I wasn't the doctor, and my father always said, *Where there's life, there's hope.*

It was a short walk down the hallway to the family room. Hospitals used words like 'family room' in a desperate attempt to create a homey feeling. The space was small and simple with drab off-white walls, a few pieces of uncomfortable-looking furniture, and a flat-screened TV. Above the television hung a 'Happy New Year' decoration. The room was stark and impersonal. It was where loved ones waited for the inevitable.

I found Bernie there. Grateful he was asleep; I was in no mood to talk. He was a nice man — attentive and devoted to Grams. I could see why she enjoyed his company. But I wondered if they were truly in love or if their impending marriage was an effort to drive away the loneliness of widowhood. I felt sorry for Bernie.

We'd met when I arrived at the hospital last night. We'd agreed to meet in the lobby; he was easy to find. The waiting area was mostly empty, and he was the only one with gray hair.

Seated alone, in a corner of the room, his eyes were downcast. I would've guessed he was asleep except for the constant handwringing. When I stopped in front of him, he looked up, and adjusted his glasses.

"Hanna? Is that you?"

His voice sound far-off, tired, not the jovial one I remembered from our phone conversation.

"Bernie? Nice to meet you. Finally." I extended my hand to shake his, but instead he opened his arms and gathered me in for a hug. We were almost family.

"I wish it was under better circumstances, but I'm glad you're here. Your grandmother will be too. How was your flight? Is the hotel nearby?" He hesitated as if he forgot something. "Forgive my questions. You must be exhausted. I know you want to see your grandmother, but her room is being cleaned, and I was asked not to return for a few minutes. Besides, this will give us a chance to talk."

He sat down and I pulled over a plastic chair.

"The nurse gave your grandmother something to calm her down. She was agitated. I was told that is normal in stroke victims, but then she mumbled something that sounded like a man's name."

"Was it yours? My grandfather's?"

"No. Someone I never heard of before. Will or Phil. My hearing's not so good anymore."

"Phil. She didn't tell you about my father? His name was Philip." I hadn't thought about my dad's first name in a long time. To me he was 'Dad.' I used to tease him about his old-fashioned name. *Who names their child Philip anymore?*

Dad would remind me that, someday, if I had a son, I should continue the family tradition. "Don't forget. It's Philip with one L, the Scottish spelling. It's an old family name passed down. I don't know why or how it came to be…."

And suddenly, I knew. Filib. Here was another connection to Anna. I might have missed it completely if it hadn't been for Bernie.

"Of course, I knew about your father," Bernie continued. "And what happened. But I don't remember her ever mentioning his name. Well, now it makes sense. But she asked where he was, and why he wasn't visiting her. That's when I knew her brain was severely damaged."

326

He stopped and put his hand on mine. "Hanna, are you okay? Do you need to rest? Something to eat?"

"No. Sorry. I was just thinking about my dad. You reminded me of…. Please, go on."

"I know he was killed on 9/11, but the way she asked for him it sounded like she expected him to walk into her room at any moment."

"Did my grandmother tell you how Dad died?"

"In the twin towers."

"Yes…but after saving his best friend's life." A sob caught in my throat. It was still difficult. "Dad's friend, from his college days, worked in an office on the same floor. The man was handicapped and in a wheelchair. My father carried him down twenty flights until he met a firefighter who carried the friend the rest of the way. Then, my father went back up."

"Why?"

"He went for Carly. His assistant. When the planes hit, she was too frightened to move. He returned to save her."

"Didn't anyone try to talk him out of it?"

"Yeah. Those going down tried to restrain him, but in the end they all wanted to get out of there. My dad always talked about doing the right thing, sort of a code of honor. He wasn't going to leave Carly there, to die alone."

"Is that when the building collapsed?"

"No. My father died before that. The smoke or the fire must have been too intense, trapping him. There was only one way out of the North Tower."

"Oh my God. He was a jumper?"

"Yes. No. That would imply he had a choice and chose to commit suicide. There were no good options that day."

"Sorry, I meant no disrespect."

"None taken. But you'll notice, no one, neither the newspapers, nor speakers at memorial programs, talk about those who felt compelled to make that horrific decision. It's as if they were…invisible. But I know the truth. My dad was a hero. My hero."

I took Kelly's advice and got a cup of coffee. My fingers hugged the cup; its warmth reassuring. I walked the hall for a bit, and when I returned to the family room, Bernie was still out cold. His soft snoring was like the purr of a kitten. The couch was now occupied by a family of three. They were all asleep, one head leaning against the other like a staircase. The muted TV flashed scenes from some reality show which seemed surreal in a hospital where there was too much reality.

I curled up in the chair closest to Bernie. The quiet offered me the opportunity to retrieve a letter from my bag. It was from Alec. He had secretly stowed it in my carry-on luggage and didn't tell me about it until I called to let him know the plane had landed safely. He made me promise not to open it until tonight. New Year's Eve.

At first, I thought the letter was unusual because we could talk any time on the phone, but I remembered he had a penchant for old-fashioned things, like letter writing. In that, he was like Grams.

I checked my watch. The old year was running out of time. I carefully removed the folded pages from its envelope and held it to my nose hoping to detect Alec's scent and savor what he had touched not long ago.

His greeting, *Mistress Hanna,* made me smile. I remembered how I hadn't cared for it at first.

I so wanted us to be together at this time – a new year – a new beginning for you and me. But I know your grandmother needs you. Your close relationship with her and what you have learned from Anna are reminders of how precious family is.

I hope you can forgive me. I should have come with you. My excuse is I have always been my family's First Foot for Hogmanay. My family takes this custom seriously; they are depending on me. I know it sounds crazy, but Hogmanay is a festival inherited from our Viking ancestors to celebrate the winter solstice and the New Year. When Scots weren't permitted to recognise Christmas for centuries, Hogmanay became even more important. As First Foot, I'm the first one to step over the threshold of my home in the New Year. Superstition? Yes. But it's a small request my parents make of me.

You may ask, why couldn't my brother do it? He can't; he's a redhead. Redheads - and especially blonds - are forbidden. They are a reminder of the invading Norsemen. Instead, the First Foot must be tall and dark-haired. I meet the requirements.

"Hanna. Your grandmother is back in her room. You can see her now. The doctor will be in shortly."

I folded the letter and inserted it into my pocket. Bernie awakened. The sleeping family never moved.

I put my hand on Bernie's. "Why don't you get something to eat? I'll sit with Grams. When you return, I'll go to the cafeteria. This way she won't be alone."

He nodded and left quickly. If this was the end, I wanted to be alone with Grams.

When I returned to the room, the doctor was writing instructions on a chart. Kelly readjusted Gram's pillow, tucked in her blanket, and installed a new bag on the intravenous drip.

"Miss Duncan. You are Ann Duncan's granddaughter?"

328

"Yes."

"I'm Dr. Jacobson. You know your grandmother suffered a massive stroke. The test results aren't encouraging. She may have a moment of lucidity, but much of it will seem like trying to struggle through a dense fog. Eventually, she won't be able to keep up the fight. I'm telling you this, so you know what to expect. If there's a moment when she recognizes you, say what needs to be said."

It was hard to focus on his words. I didn't want to hear them. "I understand. Thank you."

He placed a caring hand on my shoulder. "It's better for someone in her condition to go quickly. I'm sorry."

I nodded, and he left. Kelly followed, pulling the privacy curtain behind her. I moved the chair close to the bed and held Grams' hand in mine while listening to her rattled breathing keeping rhythm with the machines. My other hand felt Alec's letter in my pocket. It would have to wait.

I was startled as Grams' breathy voice broke the silence. "Hanna?" Her cloudy blue eyes were half opened.

"Yes, Grams, I'm here. I'm not going anywhere."

"I...am."

"Grams, I love you. I always will."

I put my hand on her lined forehead to comfort her. Her eyes closed. The death rattle resumed.

Kelly returned to adjust the meds. "It's to make her comfortable."

"My grandmother just spoke to me. Maybe...."

"Looks like she's sleeping peacefully now. Her forehead is not as furrowed. The pain meds are doing their job." Before Kelly left, she touched my back. I interpreted the comforting gesture; it wouldn't be long now.

A half hour later, Grams remained asleep. Bernie hadn't returned. Perhaps it was too painful for him. Losing someone again.

I reached in my pocket and pulled out Alec's letter.

Minutes before the end of the old year, I will step outside my house. It will be pitch black; no moonlight to block the brilliance of the Milky Way. I'll be thinking of you 3,000 miles away, wondering if you will see the same beautiful sight.

At midnight, my family will congratulate each other and sing 'Auld Lang Syne.' When they finish and all is silent, I'll follow the ancient custom. I'll knock on the door. My father and mother will welcome me as I step over the threshold. I'll offer the traditional gifts: a piece of coal, bread, salt, and whisky, symbols meant to ensure warmth and a bountiful table for the coming year.

Tiny gasps emanated from Grams' throat. Breathing had become irregular. I pushed the letter back in my pocket and pressed her frail hand against my wet cheek. I stared at the numbers on the blood pressure monitor. They were lower.

I leaned in close to Grams, and in a whispered voice, I said, "When you see Dad, tell him about Alec and me. Tell him about Anna." The lump in my throat would not go away. "Tell Dad I miss him."

The labored breathing halted momentarily. Like a sympathetic response I held my breath until she resumed hers.

I must have dozed because when I awoke, I found a cup of lukewarm coffee alongside a cherry Danish on the table next to me. The monitor told me Grams was still alive. I pulled out the crumpled letter, smoothed it and found my place.

You have come full circle. You've just learned that Anna made it safely to the colonies, after the tragic death of a close friend. Now you're there – near where Anna came ashore, and you are about to lose someone dear.

I know this is probably not the way you dreamed it would happen. Maybe I should've waited until you returned. But the events of the last few days, has made me realise that we shouldn't waste another moment apart. Mistress Hanna, I am on bended knee, asking for your hand in marriage. I want to spend the rest of my days by your side. Allow me to be your lover, your friend, and your husband.

I squeezed my eyes shut, willing the tears not to flow. Several found their way onto the letter. I wiped my face with the back of my sleeve. I reread the last paragraph aloud to Grams. Then I crushed the pages against my chest.

"After Gramps died, you told me to find the love of my life, marry him sooner rather than later, and have lots of babies. I was listening. Alec is my soulmate. I only wish you could've known him."

Kelly's footsteps squeaked into the room.

I bent over, about to kiss Grams' smooth forehead, when I noticed something was not right. Something was missing. I muffled a gasp.

The nurse checked for signs of life. She shook her head. My beloved grandmother was gone.

Bernie came to her bedside. I stepped back and allowed him a last precious moment with Grams. He whispered something, kissed her softly on the cheek, and sobbed silently. After a few moments, he walked out.

We were alone together again. I continued to hold her hand until it was no longer warm. I kissed her for the last time and placed Alec's letter on Gram's stilled chest. Tears clouded my vision as I walked out. Tears of joy. Tears of sadness. It was all the same.

Notes:

This book is historical fiction, but it is based on a real event – the creation of the Scottish colony in Darien, Central America, in 1698. As much as possible, I have kept to the facts, but at times, imaginative details were added, stretched and kneaded to advance the story. The following are some of those fabrications.

The main crux of the story centers around a Jewess caught up in the creation of the failed Scottish colony in Darien. As far as records show, there were no Jews living in Scotland in the 17th century. But that does not mean that perhaps a few escaped the history books and migrated from Spain and Portugal traveling north of England. Without actual proof of a Sephardim existence, I took artistic license and created the Isaac family.

There are about 80 closes and wynds that connect to the Royal Mile in Edinburgh. There is a Lady Stairs Close, a Fleshmarket, Skinner, and Bailie Fife. Cheery Close does not exist.

The Royal Bank of Scotland should not be confused with the Bank of Scotland. The first was created in 1727; the latter, 1695. Neither bank offered safe deposit boxes until the second half of the 19th century when the first modern boxes arrived in the UK. At the time of this story, goldsmiths provided banking services and would offer to safeguard valuable items in their vaults. Therefore, RBS did not have twelve original safe deposit boxes that could only be opened with a special thistle key identified by a block of beeswax.

Although there were others who wrote about the expedition, I chose to include the historic figure Hugh Rose, who served as the official Clerk for the Colony. In addition to his famous journal which included descriptions of the Indians, the weather, and the behavior of the crew, Rose also attended Councilor meetings where he acted as recording secretary. If he was married, there was no mention of a wife named Shona Rose or by any other name.

Benjamin Spense was one of six interpreters hired by the Directors. There is no evidence that he stuttered. He was eventually caught by the Spanish and jailed.

Preserving a body in a barrel, as described by Cook Innes, was based on the preservation of Admiral Horatio Nelson's body in a barrel of rum or brandy after he was killed in the Battle of Trafalgar, in 1805. In this way, the hero could be returned to England rather than buried at sea. Since then, many tales, true or not, have been told of animals and people preserved in this manner. The story usually includes some imbibers who unknowingly satisfied their thirst by drinking from the unsuspected tombs.

William Paterson and his wife sailed on the *Unicorn*, not the *St. Andrew*. There is scant information about his wife. One historian has suggested her name was Hannah. For obvious reasons, I had to change her name. It is true Mrs. Paterson was buried in Darien, and some believe a child of the Patersons' died as well. There is no evidence that Mrs. Paterson was pregnant while sailing to Darien. William Paterson returned to Scotland and died in 1719.

Botflies exist in Central America, and the method of extraction, as described in the book, is authentic; however, there is no record of Paterson suffering from Botfly infestation.

It is true that when the Scots abandoned Darien, six were left behind. The Indians provided shelter for them. There is no record that any of the six committed suicide. Scotland declared the six as heroes for not leaving the colony.

Readers might wonder why I chose to write about Darien. My curiosity about the history of Scotland manifested itself after reading a historical novel series. That piqued my interest to learn more about Scottish history. I started with *A History of Scotland* by Neil Oliver and *How the Scots Invented the Modern World* by Arthur Herman. It was in Oliver's book that I learned that the Scots hoped to create a colony like the English, French, Spanish and the Dutch. Herman's book began with the arrest, trial, and condemnation of Thomas Aikenhead - the last known person to be executed for blasphemy in Scotland. I found it interesting enough to include in my book. Further investigation about Darien brought me to John Prebble's *Darien* and John McKendrick's *Darien: A Journey in Search of Empire*.

After the first colonial attempt failed, the Scots sent a second expedition consisting of four ships. They arrived in Darien on November 30, 1699 just 9 days after the *Caledonia* limped down the River Clyde. The new expedition was no match for the Spanish forces who were unwilling to accept intruders. After a desperate attempt to fight it out, the Scots surrendered and were forced to leave on April 12, 1700. The Spaniards took possession of Darien. Of the four Scottish ships in the second expedition, one was surrendered, another went down near Cuba, and the last two were destroyed in a hurricane off the North Carolina coast.

There are some ironic twists to the story. One colonist on the second expedition was Rev. Archibald Stobo. His ship made it to the Carolinas where he got off, never to return to Scotland. One of his descendants was Theodore Roosevelt. Two hundred years later, President Roosevelt would oversee the building of the Panama Canal - establishing a trade route across the isthmus - something his ancestor failed to do.

As a result of the two unsuccessful expeditions, Scotland could not meet its financial obligations and went further into debt. (Isn't this what Anna's father predicted?) The Scots blamed England for their situation, and the English refused to allow the Scots to reignite their colonial dream. Instead, they made a different offer. On January 16, 1707, the Scottish Parliament voted to accept the Act of Union with England. On May 1, the Scottish Parliament dissolved, and the United Kingdom was born. The Act included the English paying off Scottish debt which meant shareholders, widows, sailors, merchants, shipbuilders, and bakers could be repaid.

Even William Paterson received remuneration to help fortify his meager income as a math tutor. With the Act, came trade for the Scots but only with British colonies.

But that's not the end of the story. The Union left a bitter taste in the mouths of many Scots. Their hope of an independent Scotland was gone but not forgotten. Several uprisings to remove English rule and restore a Scottish king would be fought – the last of which was on the moor of Culloden in 1746. In less than an hour, the English were victorious, and punishment almost decimated Scottish culture. The hoped-for Scottish independence is still argued and debated until this day.

Acknowledgements:

My goal for writing historical fiction is so my readers can learn something new. Everyone I questioned, including history teachers and avid readers of historical fiction, were unfamiliar with the Darien story. I saw it as a golden opportunity to educate.

Although writing is mostly a solo activity, there are many people who share in the creation of this book. First, I must thank my two devoted readers, authors in their own right, who have been with me from the start: John Matthews and Kyra Robinov. Their reviews and insights carried me all the way to the end, and then some. They were willing to read the manuscript multiple times to ensure correctness, clarity, and consistency. If a character got out of harm's way too easily, I was reminded to make them pay. As a result, they helped make me a better storyteller.

Others who deserve my gratitude are my husband Arne. He was always on-call for any computer glitch which was always solved quickly much to my amazement. My daughter, Jessica Scott, a talented photographer, is responsible for the photo on the back cover. Artist Ellen Gewen created the thistle found throughout. Judy Bullard of www.customebookcovers.com was the creative genius behind the book cover. Anna Bazhaw-Hyscher offered her expertise and understanding of 17th century dress. Others who rendered their advice early-on were members of various writing groups: Manheim Township Library, and two online groups: The Literary Forum and The Next Big Writer.

Being married to a writer can be a lonely prospect. My husband has spent many evenings, during the last four years, on his own. He always offered encouragement and support at those points when I wasn't sure which way the story would go. Without him, I might not have reached this point, or it may have taken a whole lot longer. For his love, I am forever grateful.

Sherry V. Ostroff

If you have enjoyed *Caledonia*, please consider leaving a review on Amazon or Goodreads. Reviews help to spread the word about the book.

Sherry V. Ostroff is available to meet with book clubs and provides programs for *Caledonia* and *The Lucky One.* The author can be contacted at svostroff528@gmail.com. Her website is at sherryvostroff.com.

A sequel, *Mannahatta,* is presently in the works. The first chapter follows.

The Sequel

One
Punto Escocés
2008

"*Alec*, Anna was right. Max and I found it."

"Huh?" Alec rubbed his eyes and mumbled, "Max? Wait! What?"

My noisy declaration jolted Alec into a sitting position, almost toppling him out of the hammock that dangled two feet off the soft black earth. He grabbed the center tent pole to check his balance. The fragile shelter wobbled, sending wiggly rivulets of rainwater down the nylon roof cascading into puddles of mud.

This tent and three more made up our campsite near the beach. The largest served as an all-purpose room for dining, instruction, and meetings. Two were designated as sleeping quarters for the ten members of our archaeological team. The smallest tent held the tools of our trade: boxes for artifacts, camera equipment, chemicals, logbooks, and buckets filled with mattocks, trowels, and shovels. Each shelter had walls made of a fine mesh allowing the cool ocean breeze to enter and stymied, but did not entirely deter, mosquitos, no-see-ums, and other Dracula-like insects.

"Oh, sorry to wake you. I'll come back later. Go back to sleep."

Dr. Alec Grant, history professor and my fiancé, had every right to be tired. He had traveled from Scotland to join me on a dig in Darien National Park not far from the Panamanian and Colombian border. The first leg of his journey, a sixteen-hour flight to Panama City, was the easy part. What should have been a short trek across the isthmus to our campsite was not. The contrariness of the Kuna tribe and the remoteness of *Punto Escocés,* once called Caledonia by Scottish colonists, made the trip unpredictable, chaotic, and dreadful.

The next part of Alec's journey included a stop in Muluputu, a tiny island off the eastern coast of Panama. Although Muluputu was a mere one-hour boat ride away from Caledonia, a guide with a motorized *cayuco* had to be hired. But first, clever negotiation skills along with sufficient cash to grease the palm of the local chieftain were necessary. Until a traveler showed proper obeisance, Caledonia could've been a continent away.

Alec's case was postponed until late in the day, and then the tribal chief decided to hold off on his decision until the next morning. Instead of heading for Caledonia, Alec had to shell out more cash than was necessary for a plate of fried fish, rice, and a can of beer, along with a dirty cot in the back room of a noisy makeshift cantina.

"No. Stay. It's fine. It's time I was up." He slapped his bare arm and then his neck. "I thought I left the midges at home."

I tossed a small bottle of insect spray into his lap. "Use this liberally, button up, and roll your sleeves down. The chiggers are worse in the morning and at sunset. And keep your shoes on. You don't want bullet ants to find your toes."

Alec looked up with his usual raised eyebrow and a slight uplift in the corners of his mouth. How I adored that characteristic look of his, a mixture of surprise, playful disapproval, and flirtation. It reminded me how much I'd missed Alec since we parted weeks ago, and how much I loved him.

"Bullet ants? Sounds delightful."

Catching my breath, "Yes…I hope you never meet up with the nasty critters."

"Aye." Alec swung himself out of the hammock; his head almost grazed the roof of the tent. He buttoned his shirt to the neck, and then the cuffs. "So what's all the excitement about?"

"I told you there were two other digs here, one in the seventies and the other in 2003. The BBC did a documentary on the last one. I watched it many times, to see where Anna had lived. When I suggested doing another dig, Max…er…Dr. Jones wasn't so keen about the idea. He said there was nothing left to find in Caledonia. He changed his mind when I showed him Anna's journal, and he learned about the knife. And now, I think we may have found it."

"You mean—"

"Yes. Filib's knife."

Anna Rachel Isaacs MacArthur was my many-times great-grandmother. When I tell anyone how I learned of her existence, they are shocked to hear that I found her when my father was killed at the World Trade Center on 9/11. Their response always had the same puzzled look and a question: *How could 9/11 have a connection with an ancient ancestor living on another continent?*

The answer was simple. I inherited a three-hundred-year-old key that opened a safe deposit box in Edinburgh. That's where I found artifacts that uncovered Anna's story: two silver candlesticks, a ring, a lock of hair, and, most importantly, her journal.

"So, the real reason for the dig wasn't to search for the remains of the Scottish colonists?"

"That was for public consumption, an emotional pretext to open checkbooks."

339

"But you know, returning with even one bone would make headlines. *The Scotsman* would crown you a national heroine."

"Yeah, true. I'd be famous like, um…Carter discovering King Tut's tomb." I chuckled as I remembered as a kid reading every book at the local library on the famous 1922 find. By the time I was fourteen, I dreamt of becoming an archaeologist. My friends scoffed at the notion. Grams worried I'd get lost in the Egyptian desert and never come home again. But not Dad. He took my passion seriously and took me to an exhibition on the boy-king in Washington, DC.

"With only a few days left, I've started to give up hope. Max has insisted on our working from dawn to dusk."

Alec's forehead furrowed and his eyes turned away as if he had something else on his mind. His usual reaction whenever I mentioned Max: my professor and mentor. Then, as if to reclaim what Max could never have, he encircled me with his arms and brought me tight against his damp shirt, kissing me long and hard. I hardly flinched at the sheen of moisture on his scruffy beard that left its wetness on my cheeks and throat. Although we were alone at the campsite, for the moment, I wished more than anything for the privacy of a real tent.

Alec stepped away from our damp embrace, but I pulled him back. "I'm glad you're safe. I worried when you didn't arrive on schedule. I feared the Chief had other plans for you." I playfully pushed him away and straightened my shirt. "A trussed up professor for dinner."

His chuckle ended when he forced the conversation to what stood between us. "Your Dr. Jones, or Max, sounds like a slave-driver."

"He's not 'my' Dr. Jones." I edged closer and stared into his eyes. "But you are 'my' Dr. Grant. And don't forget it. Besides, there's not much else to do in this no-man's land. Work keeps our minds occupied living in such unbearable conditions. I've never experienced such suffocating humidity. I promise never to complain about mid-summer in Philadelphia."

Alec was right about one thing. I did talk a lot about Dr. Maximillian Jones. He was the first instructor I met at the University of Aberdeen. Like Alec, he was a gifted professor, and I signed up to do several independent studies with him. When he received the grant for a dig in Caledonia, I jumped at the chance to join in. I hoped to take a leadership role since I was close to earning my Ph.D.

Dr. Jones hinted at the possibility of my teaching at Aberdeen. That didn't thrill Alec. But going back to college had been his idea, and with a job offer, I was assured of remaining in Scotland and becoming a citizen. Dr. Hanna Duncan. I liked the sound of that. Wouldn't Dad and even Grams be proud?

"You know, we should have married in Philadelphia when we went to your friend Jess's wedding. I'm a hungry man, Mistress Hanna." He said my pet name with a raised eyebrow. "There's only so long I can wait. You promised to marry me three years ago."

340

"I know, but I have to finish my degree first. You do remember how much work is involved. Dr. Jones says — I mean. I promise, as soon as I'm done."

Talk of marriage reminded me of Alec's unusual proposal set in a letter. It was New Year's Eve, and I was sitting by my dying grandmother in a Philadelphia hospital. Alec was 3,000 miles away, celebrating Hogmanay with his family. I'd read Alec's words many times. They are seared into my memory.

I know this is probably not the way you dreamed it would happen. Maybe I should've waited until you returned. But the events of the last few days, has made me realise that we shouldn't waste another moment apart. Mistress Hanna, I am on bended knee, asking for your hand in marriage. I want to spend the rest of my days by your side. Allow me to be your lover, your friend, and your husband.

As I read it aloud during the last gasps of the old year, my grandmother passed away.

A year later, when my college roommate, Jess, was planning her wedding at a vineyard in Brandywine, she begged me to have a double ceremony. We could've shared the costs, and her father offered to walk me down the aisle.

But life got in the way.

I remembered saying to Alec, "Maybe we should wait until after we find a new flat." Our old place, Alec's rental, was a five-minute walk from the St. Andrew campus. But it had been broken into. The thief had stolen Anna's ring. I didn't feel comfortable living there after that.

And then there was my doctoral work.

"Let me get through my first year and get used to a school routine again."

The third excuse came from Alec.

His father had Fibrodysplasia, the clinical term for Stoneman's Disease. His muscles were calcifying, and the illness was progressing at a much faster pace than the doctors expected. As Alec's future wife I was included in the family get-togethers, but I was hardly welcome. The issue was my religion, or lack of one, and now it seemed my ancient ancestor, Anna, was Jewish.

Alec's mother, Mora, was polite, said the right words, but was distant. Iain, his brother, a fierce Nationalist, wanted nothing more than Scotland's independence and a return to the old ways which didn't include me. We had a few run-ins, like when he came onto me while Alec was hospitalized after an accident. He groused at Alec including me in discussing family business. Iain once said I would never be accepted into the family. His actions were true to his word. The fact that Kate, Alec's ex, always seemed to show up when I was there, made it crystal clear.

341

Three weeks ago, my schoolmates and I flew on a prop-plane from Panama City. When the pilot realized we were an archaeological team headed for Caledonia, he announced we would fly over *Punta Escosés*. From the air, the point looked like a giant's left thumb jutting into the Caribbean. As a defensive position, it was a perfect location for the Scots to set up their first and only colony in the New World in 1699. A crude fort was built on a promontory to protect the fledgling settlement meant to control the trade between the two oceans. Had the scheme worked, Scotland would be independent today. But it failed, and the only way out of massive debt was for Scotland to unite with England in 1707.

Dr. Jones reminded us that the Scots had been unwelcome by the Spanish, the English, and the Natives. Add into the mix the constant rain, extreme temperatures, poor soil, lack of food, yellow-fever, malaria, and inept governance; the colony was doomed. In six months, the first expedition limped back to Scotland with one-fourth of those who began the adventure.

The flight attendant, a young woman, offered an impromptu tour. We peered out the small windows straining to hear her words over the twin engines.

"The Pan-American Highway runs right through the jungle below. It's part of a 19,000-mile-long road that connects the two Americas from Alaska to Chile."

"You mean I could drive from LA to Darien?" asked one member of our team – a pretty blonde who looked like she belonged in high school.

"Unfortunately, no. Fifty-five miles in the Darien Gap are still unpaved. The jungle, the hilly terrain, the gangs, the weather, and the indigenous tribes prevent the job from getting done. But that doesn't stop the flow of paramilitary groups, drug smugglers, and human traffickers swindling immigrants on their way north. Many a foolish tourist has been kidnapped or lost their life here.

The flight attendant's comments were discomforting, and that was in addition to the pictures of gigantic spiders and poisonous frogs I had seen in an old *National Geographic*. I must have looked frightened because the next thing I knew, Max reached over the aisle and squeezed my hand. I looked over and smiled politely.

Now, two weeks later, Alec had arrived. Last minute paperwork and final grades delayed his travel and the start of a six-month sabbatical. During his time-off, he planned to write a book about Caledonia from a woman's viewpoint. Anna's journal would serve as the centerpiece. Although his announced purpose for coming was for research, I suspected there was another. Alec wanted to ensure I didn't get kidnapped either by the notorious gangs that plied the dense jungle or by Dr. Maximillian Jones.